A HOLIDAY OF WITCHES

WICKED WITCHES OF THE MIDWEST SHORTS 6-10

AMANDA M. LEE

WINCHESTERSHAW PUBLICATIONS

Created with Vellum

BEWITCHED

A WICKED WITCHES OF THE MIDWEST SHORT

2/2/2016

ONE

SEVERAL MONTHS AGO

"This town is full of crazy people."

I sipped my coffee and regarded Brian Kelly with weary eyes. He was a pain. There was no getting around it. His ego was bigger than his room-temperature IQ, and he thought far too highly of himself. When you're the new guy in town, though, you can't afford to be choosy.

That's me, Sam Cornell. I'm the new guy in a town the size of a pinprick on a roadmap. Fitting in isn't easy when everyone already knows absolutely everything about one another, so I'm muddling along the best I can. Sometimes I think it's going well. Other times I think I made the biggest mistake of my life when I purchased a business in a witchy tourist town, intent on turning it into a haunted attraction. I guess the jury is still out ... or perhaps the verdict is in, and I'm simply too blind to see it.

"I think you're exaggerating," I said, glancing around the small diner and watching Hemlock Cove's denizens chat with one another with one breath and cater to their tourist base with the next. I'd been in town only a few weeks, but it was obvious the people here knew what they were doing when it came to their magical-branded business endeavor.

"Oh, I'm right," Brian said, wrinkling his nose derisively as he forced a smile for one of the young women sitting at a nearby table. She wore striped stockings, a black dress with jewel adornments, and a purple witch's hat. "This whole town is off its rocker."

"I don't think it's wise to say things like that when you rely on half of these crazy people to put food on your table," I pointed out. Brian inherited Hemlock Cove's lone weekly newspaper – The Whistler – upon his grandfather's death. Since Hemlock Cove boasted almost weekly festivals, many of the businesses ran ads for special events. Brian needed these "crazy people" to keep the newspaper running at a profit. "Besides, I think when you're talking about this many people in a small space you're probably safer going with the word 'eccentric,' at least if you don't want them to spit in your coffee when you're not looking."

"They wouldn't do that," Brian scoffed, although the look he shot the waitress was dubious. "They wouldn't do that, would they?"

I didn't have the heart to tell Brian that if I were waiting on him I would not only spit in his coffee but lick his silverware for good measure. "Of course they wouldn't do that," I lied. "I was just messing with you."

Brian's smile was wide, but I couldn't stop myself from internally chuckling as he studied his coffee before taking another sip. "So, how are things out at the Dandridge?"

I bought the Dandridge on a whim two weeks ago. Technically, I bought the building; the state still owns the land. Thanks to a deal I worked out with the historical commission, though, as long as I promise to keep the original structure and have updates approved by the commission, I have a lifetime lease for the property. It's a win-win situation.

When I first came to Hemlock Cove it was because I was interested in witches. No, you read that right. I've always been fascinated by the occult. I've read so many books on pagan traditions I've lost count. My mother was a solitary practitioner, mostly directing her modest talents toward kitchen recipes and herbal remedies. My father looked the other way. He didn't particularly care what my mother believed or practiced. As long as she didn't broadcast her witchy ways to the neighbors, he was fine with whatever made her happy.

When I was a teenager, I realized I could see ghosts. In hindsight, I probably saw ghosts when I was younger but couldn't understand what I saw. My first encounter was minor. I was walking home from high school, thoughts of asking Missy Brennan to the homecoming dance working their way through my crush-infused mind, when a figure appeared on the sidewalk in front of me.

My reflexes kicked in and I tilted to the side to avoid the figure, but instead of a smooth escape I tripped over my own feet and fell through a woman. I hit the pavement hard enough to knock the breath out of me, and when I swiveled to make sure she was okay I realized I could see through her.

It was a sobering experience, and after helping the woman realize that the house she was looking for burned down years before – that's how she died and she was caught in an endless loop of confusion as she searched for her home – she disappeared. I couldn't wait to tell my mother what happened. She wasn't as thrilled with my new ability, explaining that her grandmother had the same gift and it drove her insane. She warned me to be careful, and then sent me on my merry way.

I learned to keep my ghostly visions to myself relatively quickly. While I thought it was cool, I earned a reputation as a weirdo when I told my best friend – and he used the information to steal Missy Brennan's affection. It was a hard lesson, but I learned it well.

After college I kept to my reading habits, infusing pagan lore with Michigan history and stumbled across an interesting legend in the northwestern part of the Lower Peninsula. Supposedly a family of witches lived in a small town named Hemlock Cove, previously known as Walkerville. Their last name was Winchester – and I was immediately smitten with the idea of learning from real, practicing witches.

I asked my mother about the Winchesters, and when she said she'd heard of them I was intrigued. She said the family was known for being powerful – and weird – so I arranged my schedule so I could visit Hemlock Cove, selling my business services to Brian in an effort to increase circulation at The Whistler.

That's where I met Bay Winchester. I knew she was gifted the moment I saw her, despite the fact that she was nervous and suspicious. I spent days watching her, enjoying the way she interacted with her cousins Thistle and Clove. Before I realized what was happening, I started following them. I was determined to catch them in the act – talking to ghosts, casting spells, anything really – but each time they saw me they became more suspicious (and in Thistle's case belligerent and mean). I guess I don't blame them.

In an effort to alleviate the tension – and the dirty looks Bay's great-aunt Tillie kept scorching me with – I admitted I knew they were witches. Bay turned white … and then red … and then kicked me out of the Winchesters' inn.

Even after that blew up in my face, I didn't want to leave Hemlock Cove. Despite the tension, it felt like home. That's when my love of history and business degree came together, and I purchased the Dandridge.

It was working out well – except for the endless hours of actual work. That's why I was too tired to put up with Brian's whining. I had whining of my own and only one option for a semi-sympathetic ear.

"It's a lot of work," I said. "I have a contractor working on the inside of the building, and it should be ready for drywall and paint in about a week."

"How are you living out there?" Brian asked.

"I'm living on the main floor while they're working upstairs," I replied. "Then I'll switch when they're working on the main floor. I'll probably have to find another place to sleep for three nights or so, but otherwise it should work out fine. It's not like there's a shortage of inns around this area."

"You could go back out to The Overlook," Brian suggested. "I'm sure the Winchesters wouldn't put up a fight if you needed to stay there for a few days."

I was the last person the Winchesters wanted to see. I'd kept that little tidbit from Brian because I didn't want his suspicions about the

Winchesters to jump to me. "I don't think I'm their favorite person," I said, choosing my words carefully. "Aunt Tillie thinks I'm evil."

Brian snorted. "Aunt Tillie thinks everyone is evil," he said. "I ran into her in the hallway the other day – she was wearing a combat helmet, if you can believe that – and she told me she was hunting for squirrels."

"In the hallway?" That sounded odd, even for an elderly curmudgeon who had more in common with a rattlesnake than a cuddly kitten.

"She had a pellet gun and she was whistling," Brian explained. "She told me to watch my nuts … and then she laughed and said she didn't mean that in a perverted way but was worried because squirrels like to hoard small things."

I bit my lip to keep from laughing, the mental picture almost too much to bear.

"Then she told me I should probably invest in an athletic cup because she was pretty sure she was going to come down with Restless Leg Syndrome and start kicking people willy-nilly whenever the mood struck," Brian continued. "She's crazy."

"I think when you're as old as Aunt Tillie it's called 'eccentric,'" I clarified. "Plus, if you slip and call her crazy, you're going to see what a rabid squirrel looks like, because she's going to be the one going after your … um … nuts."

Brian shifted uncomfortably. "Let's not talk about that," he said, unconsciously shielding his groin. "Aunt Tillie … worries me."

"I think you mean she terrifies you," I corrected.

"She's a little old lady," Brian scoffed. "She's harmless."

I arched a challenging eyebrow. "This town is rich on rumors," I supplied. "One woman – the one who owns that porcelain unicorn store – told me that Tillie Winchester sacrifices goats and can read minds.

"One of those freaky red-haired twins – the ones who look like real-life Chucky dolls – told me that Aunt Tillie told him she would curse his tongue to fall out if he ever called her a witch again," I continued. "And that woman who sells caramel apples at the fairs?

Yeah, she told me that all the Winchesters dance naked under every full moon and cast spells to make sure the town stays prosperous."

"I'm not sure what all that means," Brian said.

"It means that whatever she is, Aunt Tillie is not harmless," I said. "She's … ."

"Crazy," Brian finished.

"I was going to say formidable," I corrected. "You can make fun all you want, but you couldn't pay me to take that woman on. She is … beyond messing with."

Brian was unperturbed. "I think she's crazy, and that entire family lets her get away with murder because they're too sweet to put her in a home," he said. "That's where she belongs. She should be strapped down and medicated."

The young woman in the witch hat tapped Brian on the arm, drawing his attention. "Are you talking about Ms. Tillie?" she asked.

Brian nodded. "She's crazy."

"You know that she can hear when people talk badly about her, right?" the woman pressed. "Annabelle Dickinson told Madison Wilson that Ms. Tillie had fake teeth, and the next day Annabelle's pants wouldn't fit."

"I'm not sure what that means," Brian said, exchanging a curious look with me. "Do you know what that means?"

"I think it means that Aunt Tillie cursed Annabelle Dickinson and made her fat," I filled in.

"That's the most ridiculous thing I've ever heard," Brian sputtered.

"Callie Mulligan once said that Ms. Tillie looked like an angry garden gnome and was just as smart – this was after Ms. Tillie refused to give her a bottle of her special wine because she was underage – and the next day Callie couldn't do anything but bark like a dog."

"Did you ever consider she was faking it?" Brian challenged.

"Actual dogs could understand what she was saying," the woman countered. "She held conversations with them. I swear to God it's true."

"Uh-huh." Brian shot me an "I told you so" look. "How do you know the dogs understood her?"

"You could see it on their faces," the woman answered. "If I were you, I would beg Ms. Tillie for forgiveness. If you don't, you'll probably wake up tomorrow to find something horrible has gone wrong."

"Like?" Brian obviously wasn't convinced of Aunt Tillie's evil prowess. I, on the other hand, thought she was probably capable of much more than most people gave her credit for. She'd earned her reputation for a reason.

"I heard that she made Dan Millikan's thing shrink so small that he thought it was a pimple while he was dreaming and tried to pop it," the woman replied, not missing a beat. "He left town to become a priest because he was so depressed."

"Well ... okay," Brian said, squaring his shoulders as he turned back to me. "Do you still think the people in this town aren't crazy?"

"I think they're ... colorful," I said.

"Yes, that's a great way to look at it," Brian deadpanned. "They're colorful ... not certifiable at all."

I shifted my eyes to the edge of the table, where the woman in the witch hat was back for more. She looked as if she was on her way out – which was probably a good thing.

"You might not believe me about Ms. Tillie, but you will," the woman warned. "Dan Millikan spent two weeks being tortured by all the guys in town for the pimple incident. They put Stridex pads on his locker ... and left Clearasil on his desk. I hear he runs screaming whenever he sees a Proactive commercial now. Think about that before you take on Ms. Tillie."

The woman flounced off, leaving Brian to scowl and me to laugh.

"How can you encourage stuff like that?" Brian asked, incredulous.

"I find it funny," I said. "Come on. You have to admire a woman who has convinced an entire town that arguing with her will cause them great bodily harm."

"She's crazy," Brian said, digging into his wallet and drawing out a few bills to leave on the table as a tip. "There's no getting around it. I don't know how she's snowed this entire town, but I'm not afraid of her. She's all talk."

For some reason I couldn't wait until Aunt Tillie proved Brian's assertion wrong. "I guess we'll just have to agree to disagree," I said. "Are you going back to the newspaper office?"

"Yeah, I have to talk to Bay about a new idea I have for advertorial business pieces," Brian said. "I have a feeling she's going to put up a fight when I tell her what I want to do to boost revenue."

"Have you ever considered letting Bay run the editorial division and sticking to the advertising?" I asked. "She seems to know what she's doing."

"I'm the boss," Brian said. "It's my job to lead her to the stories. It will be fine."

I had my doubts. Bay was persnickety on a good day – and downright mouthy on a bad one. "Well, have fun," I said, tossing a few more dollars on the table for good measure. The last thing I wanted to do was tick off the diner's waitstaff. If they banned me I would have absolutely nowhere to eat.

I ran through my mental to-do list as I walked toward the front of the restaurant, so lost in thought I didn't notice the door opening and a figure walking through it until I rammed into a tiny woman, knocking her to the ground and listing to the side as I struggled to retain my footing.

I opened my mouth to apologize and froze when I realized who it was.

"Hello, Clove," I said, internally sighing. "I am so sorry."

TWO

"I... oh... I am so sorry."

My cheeks burned as I leaned over to help Clove to her feet. Her face was flushed, and she looked at my outstretched hand as if it was covered in pus and boils before finally taking it and letting me help her to a standing position.

"I didn't see you," I said, brushing off the arm of her coat. It was spring, but it wasn't yet warm enough to go without layers unless it was sunny. "I... are you okay?"

Clove's dark eyes flashed as she jerked her arm away. "I'm fine," she said, shooting me a hostile look. "I... you should watch where you're going. You could've killed me."

Despite my embarrassment, I couldn't help but smile at the admonishment. "I could've killed you?"

"I might have accidentally hit my head when I fell," Clove sniffed, crossing her arms over her chest. "That's a thing. I saw it on television. I could've gotten a closed head injury that went unnoticed for days and filled my head with blood until it exploded. That would've sucked."

I pressed my lips together to keep from laughing. "Did you hit your head?"

Clove reluctantly shook her head, her long dark hair brushing her shoulders. She was tiny – even for a woman. If I had to guess, she didn't clear five feet. Her nose was pert and upturned, a smattering of light freckles on her cheeks. Her eyes were the same color as a chocolate bar, and while her cousins often wore hostile expressions, she smiled more than the rest of her family combined. I liked that about her. I especially liked that her smile was never malevolent or indicative of mayhem. That was something I couldn't say about the rest of the Winchester family.

"I really am sorry for running into you," I offered. "I was thinking about everything I had to do out at the lighthouse today, and I was … overwhelmed. That doesn't excuse almost killing you, but I really am sorry."

"I'm fine," Clove said, waving off my apology. "I shouldn't have been mean to you. It's not fair."

If that was her version of mean – especially given those she shares genes with – she had a vastly different definition of the word than I did. "You weren't mean," I said. "You were … worried about the head wound."

Despite herself, Clove laughed. It was a cute sound. Everything about her was cute. She was the least flashy of the Winchesters in her age group, and for some reason that made me gravitate toward her. Of course, Thistle and Bay once threatened to set me on fire, so I wasn't particularly fond of them.

"How are things going out at the Dandridge?" Clove asked, changing the subject. "That has to be a big job."

Clove was familiar with the Dandridge thanks to her father's former girlfriend, a woman who used the facility to aid a human trafficking operation that stowed a large container ship in the nearby cove. She worked with her cousins – and Aunt Tillie – and saved several children, releasing a female ghost at the same time. I was still unclear how Aunt Tillie helped, but I was too much of a gentleman to ask. Actually, that's not true. I'm terrified of Aunt Tillie. I'm manly enough to admit my faults.

"It's a lot of work, but I'm enjoying it," I said. "There's constant construction going on, which is a pain. I've seen some computer renderings of what the inside is going to look like when everything is finished, and it's going to be beautiful. That's keeping me going right now."

"How much living space do you have?" Clove asked. "The building looks big because of the tower, but I can't imagine there's a lot of room to wander around."

"The main floor is actually more than two thousand square feet," I replied. "There's also a landing area on the second floor and another room on the top floor. I'm turning the top floor into my bedroom and closing it off so visitors can't go inside. The landing on the second floor is going to be transformed into a library. I'm ordering a bunch of antique books."

"That sounds cool," Clove said, her smile genuine. For some reason my heart hopped at the expression. I had no idea why. "Aren't you worried about Bigfoot, though?"

I frowned. "I ... what?"

"Bigfoot," Clove repeated. "Thistle and Bay said it hangs out in the woods by the lighthouse."

"And you believe that?" She was cute, but I was starting to worry Brian was right about the "crazy" factor overtaking Hemlock Cove.

"No," Clove replied hurriedly. "I know they were only trying to scare me."

"Are you sure?"

"Fine," Clove said, resigned. "Now that they've told me Bigfoot lives out there that's all I can think about. I have to think Bigfoot is mean and nasty."

"I'm guessing if Bigfoot is real – and I'm pretty sure he's not – that he's probably pretty easygoing," I said. "He would have to be ... congenial ... to live under the radar like he does. If he was mean someone would see him and he'd be arrested ... or at least forced into anger management classes."

Clove chuckled at my lame joke. "That's a good point," she said. "I'm still convinced he's going to hunt me down and eat me."

"Bay and Thistle mess with you a lot, don't they?"

"I'm their favorite target," Clove confirmed. "It's okay. I'm used to it."

"That doesn't sound fair to me," I said. "You should tell them where to stick it when they tell you things about … Bigfoot."

Clove shrugged. "I'm not really worried about it," she said. "They're my best friends. I mess with them, too."

"You mess with Thistle?" I was doubtful.

"Only when I'm hungry for dirt," Clove answered, causing me to knit my eyebrows. I had no idea what that meant.

"Well, if you ever want to see inside the lighthouse – and I promise a Bigfoot-free experience – don't hesitate to stop by," I offered. "You'll probably like it, and because you own your own business in town, I would welcome any insight you have for when I open the Dandridge."

"I'm not sure that's a good idea," Clove hedged, shifting from one foot to the other. "We probably shouldn't hang out."

"You don't like me because of Bay, right?"

"I don't dislike you," Clove argued. "I just … Bay doesn't trust you."

"Do you agree with her?"

"I don't know," Clove said. "I … you seem nice to me. Thistle and Bay see it another way."

"Bay is convinced I'm up to something nefarious, and Thistle likes to hate everyone," I supplied. "I get it."

"Thistle doesn't hate everyone," Clove argued.

"Other than Marcus and the other members of your family, who does she like?"

"She's fond of the UPS delivery guy," Clove said. "He always hits on her and thinks she's bohemian and chic. She likes him."

"Well, that's something," I said, tamping down my irritation. In truth, I couldn't blame Bay for being suspicious. I lied and infiltrated her place of business, and then followed her around town trying to get proof regarding my witchy suspicions. That was all before I ambushed her with the truth and put her on the defensive. Thistle was another story. She was just … unpleasant. "I hope you know that I don't mean your family any harm."

"I would like to believe that," Clove said, her face unreadable.

"You don't, though, do you?"

"I would like to," Clove said. "It really doesn't matter. Thistle and Bay don't believe you, and I have faith in them. They're my family … and my friends. I'm loyal to them."

That pretty much summed it up. I forced a tight smile for Clove's benefit, hoping she wouldn't think I was upset about her admission. "Well, if you change your mind, stop out whenever you want," I said. "I think you'll like it … whether Bigfoot pays a visit for tea or not."

I SPENT the bulk of my afternoon in the front of the building, the overgrown garden giving me fits as I tried to clean up the area. I had no idea what was a weed or a legitimate plant. I knew the garden was gorgeous at one time, but it was so out of control now that the life was being choked out of it.

The sound of a vehicle door closing caught my attention, and when I glanced over my shoulder I recognized the figure moving up the gravel walkway. Terry Davenport was Hemlock Cove's top cop. He was beloved by the residents and tight with the Winchesters. This couldn't be good.

For a brief moment I wondered whether Clove accused me of trying to kill her – she appeared serious about that head wound thing – but I dismissed the notion. She was too kind to do anything of the sort.

I pushed myself to a standing position, brushing my hands off on my jeans as I waited for Chief Terry to close the distance between us. I pasted what I hoped resembled a pleasant smile on my face. "Welcome to my ongoing nightmare," I said.

"Is something wrong?" Chief Terry asked, furrowing his brow. "Are you having trouble?"

"I am having trouble," I confirmed. "It's not your kind of trouble, though. Unless … do you know the difference between weeds and legitimate plants?"

Chief Terry arched an eyebrow and shifted so he could look around me. "That's creeping thistle," he said. "It's a weed, and it hurts if you step on it. You need to dig under it to get it out … and I recommend wearing gloves if you don't want to shred your hands."

"Thistle, huh?" Why didn't that surprise me? It seemed thistle was out to get me … in more ways than one. "That's just … perfect."

Chief Terry chuckled, taking me by surprise. "I take it you're still fighting with the Winchesters," he said. "I would tread carefully around them if I were you."

"I'm well aware of your special relationship with the family," I said. "I sat through a few meals with you, if you remember correctly."

"I remember," Chief Terry said. "You're less popular than your buddy Brian Kelly. That's a neat feat, because they pretty much despise him."

"And you're very popular with the middle-aged women in the Winchester family," I shot back. "That's a neat feat, too. I love how they fall all over you."

"I love it, too," Chief Terry said dryly. "Do you want to tell me how you managed to tick them off?"

"I think you already know," I said. "Don't they tell you everything?"

"They don't tell anyone everything," Chief Terry said. "I know you upset Bay. Whatever you did, I'm on her side. Keep that in mind. And don't tick them off again."

"Is that an official warning?"

"Take it however you want," Chief Terry said. "I'm not here about that, though. I have official business; but before we get to that I want to compliment you on the building. It's looking good. I want to give you props for that. I never liked how the state let this place fall apart. I'm glad you're refurbishing it."

"Thanks, I guess," I said, my internal danger alarm sounding. Why would Hemlock Cove's police chief visit me on official business? "What's going on?"

"Well, we've had reports of local teenagers raising a ruckus out here," Chief Terry said. "I want you to be on the lookout in case they try to break into the lighthouse or vandalize any of the construction."

"I've been living out here," I pointed out. "I think I would've heard something like that."

"We've gotten four different reports from neighbors," Chief Terry supplied. "I think the kids are partying out here from the sounds of it, but Lionel Strong claims that they're out here sacrificing chickens, so I have to exert due diligence."

Despite its size, there's never a dull moment in Hemlock Cove. "Sacrificing chickens?"

"Listen, I don't think that's what's going on," Chief Terry said. "The teenagers around here pick different spots in the woods to party. A lot of them go out to Hollow Creek, but when they're feeling adventurous they branch out."

"I guess I'm not sure why it's a problem," I said. "They're teenagers. Isn't partying in the woods pretty much what teenagers do?"

"I'm a police officer."

"I noticed."

"I look the other way a lot of the time when it comes to the partying," Chief Terry said. "If I catch them, most of the time I call their parents and let them off with a warning. This is a small town, and I don't see the need to bust kids for doing what comes naturally.

"That being said, if they're doing something else ... like sacrificing chickens ... I really can't ignore it," he continued.

"Just out of curiosity, why would teenagers sacrifice chickens?" I had to ask. It was going to bug me if I didn't.

"Lionel Strong is eighty years old and has cataracts," Chief Terry replied. "He swears up and down he heard chickens screaming. Personally, I didn't know chickens screamed.

"The thing to remember is that Lionel also came into the station last month and told me that witches were haunting the woods in this area," he continued. "He was convinced they were out here casting spells and calling dead souls to eat the living."

"Technically Bay, Thistle and Clove Winchester were running around these woods last month," I said. "Some people claim they're witches. Lionel wasn't far off."

"I hadn't considered that," Chief Terry said, rubbing the back of his neck. "Still, I'm pretty sure no one is sacrificing chickens."

"How can you be sure?"

"Because people report stolen chickens faster than they do stolen cars in this town," Chief Terry replied. "I think it's more likely Lionel heard cackling of an amorous nature."

It took me a moment to grasp what he was insinuating. "Oh. You think the kids were partying ... and maybe fornicating ... and Lionel misunderstood what he heard. That's what you're saying, right?"

"I'm not thrilled with the word 'fornicating,' but that's exactly what I'm saying," Chief Terry said. "Just ... be on the lookout. I don't think anyone is plotting world domination or doing anything worse than drinking and carousing, but you should keep your eyes open.

"If I've learned anything doing this job, it's that kids will be kids," he continued. "I've also learned that sometimes kids don't think things through before they do something stupid. Be careful, and report any vandalism. In fact, report anything out of the ordinary, just to be on the safe side."

It seemed like overkill to me, but the last thing I wanted was to be on Chief Terry's bad side. "No problem," I said. "I haven't heard anything so far, but if that changes, you're the first one I'll call."

THREE

I woke in the middle of the night, something jarring me out of my sleep. I'd been enjoying a particularly nice dream, although I could only remember fragments about a dark-haired woman and the magical sound of her laughter when I wrenched my eyes open.

It took me a moment to get my bearings, and when I remembered I was sleeping on the main floor of the Dandridge, I rolled so I could scan the fields outside the nearby window. It was dark outside, the blackness momentarily reminding me just how isolated I was in respect to the rest of the town. That's when I heard a distinctive noise again. It was the unmistakable sound of laughter.

I knit my eyebrows together, briefly wondering whether what I heard was representative of the giggling I heard in my dream. The day's events rushed back, and I knew without a doubt what was happening.

I grabbed a sweatshirt and tugged it over my head, slipping into my shoes before pushing open the front door and trudging outside. If Chief Terry hadn't gone out of his way to stop by with his warning, I would've ignored the noise. Confronting partying teenagers isn't my idea of a thrilling midnight excursion.

I followed the sound of the voices, stopping twice to adjust my trajectory, and when I found the source about two hundred feet into the densely wooded area I wasn't surprised to see a bonfire, several cases of beer and about ten rowdy kids. It brought back fond memories – which I quickly tamped down because I'm a responsible adult now.

"Hey, guys." I greeted the kids with a sheepish smile and upturned palms. "Um … it's kind of late."

Multiple heads snapped in my direction, although no one made a move to hide what they were doing. The pungent odor of marijuana wafted by, and I briefly pressed my eyes shut before addressing them again.

"This is private property," I said. "You're not supposed to be out here. I don't suppose you can … I don't know … move your party about a half mile in that direction, could you?" I pointed to the east, hoping my smile came off as congenial instead of creepy.

"Are you saying this is your property?" One of the boys, a swarthy kid with broad shoulders, dishwater blond hair and too much swagger for his age, narrowed his eyes as he looked me up and down. "I think you're probably lost."

"Don't cause trouble, Andy," one of the girls warned.

Andy didn't look happy with the admonishment. "Thank you, Tess. I don't believe I asked your opinion."

Tess had the grace to look abashed, shifting her gaze between faces before lowering her eyes. "I just meant … ."

"Shut up," Andy snapped. "No one is talking to you. You're lucky to have been invited at all. I'll handle this."

I never boasted aspirations to act as a member of the Neighborhood Watch, but the way Andy verbally abused Tess was beyond the limits of my patience. "Don't talk to her like that," I chided. "There's no reason to be rude."

"I think there is a reason to be rude," Andy countered, squaring his shoulders and taking a step toward me. It didn't escape my attention that he was a good six inches taller than me, and a lot more muscular. I didn't back down despite the irrational fear tap dancing in the pit of my stomach. "Why don't you go back to whatever you were doing and leave us to our business? How does that sound?"

I ran my tongue over my teeth as I considered my options. "That sounds like a great idea," I said finally, taking a moment to study each face in turn and then swiveling back toward the Dandridge. "Just so you know, I'll be contacting Chief Terry. He asked me to call if I heard any kids partying in the woods. I'm sure he'll be thrilled to drive out here and bust you guys."

Someone mime-coughed the word "narc," and I couldn't help but wonder when I became the type of adult who threatened to call the cops.

"Wait … ." Andy called to my back. "I … there's no need to do that."

I tried to keep my expression from crossing over into smug territory … and failed. "I think that's exactly what I need to do," I replied. "Don't worry, though. You can keep doing your … business … to your heart's content."

I CONSIDERED GOING into town for breakfast the next morning, instead settling for Raisin Bran and an apple before returning to my garden project. If I was going to be an adult, I figured being a responsible one was probably my best course of action.

I tracked down a pair of gloves in the shed out back and was on my way to the front garden when I changed my trajectory and headed to the previous evening's party spot.

It took me a few minutes, but when I arrived I wasn't surprised to find garbage and empty beer cans strewn about, discarded in haste when the teenagers made a run for it after my threat. For the record, I didn't follow through on it. Now I was reconsidering my decision.

I made a disgusted sound in the back of my throat and briefly considered leaving the mess – or calling Chief Terry to find out who Andy was so I could call his parents – before returning to the lighthouse to retrieve a garbage bag.

When I got back to the small clearing I was surprised to find a visitor. I recognized the dark hair and short stature before Clove turned around.

"Holy crud! You scared me," Clove said, hopping when she caught sight of me and pressing a hand to the spot over her heart.

"I'm sorry," I said, holding my hands up, the garbage bag dangling in the wind. "I promise I wasn't trying to scare you."

"That's okay," Clove said, her face flushed. "I ... um ... ."

Before I realized what was happening she lashed out and slapped my arm. "What was that for?" I asked, taking an involuntary step back and fixing Clove with an incredulous look.

"You scared me," Clove said. "You had it coming."

"You can't just walk around slapping people," I said. "That's mean. I didn't mean to frighten you."

"Well ... then you should announce your presence when you walk into someone's ... spot in the woods," Clove said, her cheeks reddening. "I'm sorry I hit you. That wasn't nice."

"Did you think I was Bigfoot?"

Clove narrowed her eyes, screwing her face up into what I'm sure she considered a diabolical look. Unfortunately, it was too adorable to be considered anything other than entertaining. "I hope Bigfoot eats you for his next snack."

In her mind she probably thought that was a terrible thing to say. I waited a moment to see if the guilt would catch up to her. I wasn't disappointed.

"That was a really horrible thing to say," Clove said. "I'm sorry."

"I accept your apology."

Clove covered her upper lip with her lower as she stared at the ground.

"You don't have to worry about my feelings being hurt," I offered. "I didn't really think you wanted Bigfoot to eat me."

"Still, it wasn't a nice thing to say," Clove said, shifting from one foot to the other. "I think Bay and Thistle are a bad influence on me sometimes. I was in a good mood until ... ."

"You saw me?" I prodded.

"Actually, I was going to say I was in a good mood until you scared the life out of me," Clove replied. "If you must know, seeing you doesn't dampen my mood."

For some reason, the statement warmed me. "I see."

"Don't let that go to your head," Clove warned, extending a finger. "I didn't say seeing you made me happy."

"Duly noted," I said, fighting the urge to laugh. "Not that I'm not happy to see you, but what are you doing out here?"

"Oh, well … ." Clove looked caught, and I was pretty sure I knew why.

"Did you come out to see the Dandridge?"

"Maybe," Clove hedged.

Realization washed over me. "I'm guessing you're interested in seeing the Dandridge but you don't want to see me."

"That's not exactly it," Clove said.

"Clove, I had a really long night," I said, tugging on my limited patience. "If you don't want to tell me why you're here, then … you can help me clean up." I handed her the garbage bag. "Hold that open."

Clove wordlessly took the bag and watched as I picked my way around the clearing and gathered the trash. Her face was hard to read, and finally I couldn't take the silence one second longer.

"What are you thinking?" I asked.

"I'm thinking that you're a little old to be partying in the woods," Clove replied, not missing a beat. "I'm not judging you, but once you hit twenty-five you're officially too old to be drinking Milwaukee's Best around a bonfire … especially when you have a perfectly good lighthouse to drink in."

I barked out a laugh. "Do you really think I drink Milwaukee's Best?"

Clove shrugged. "For all I know you could be drinking on a budget."

"Honey, I would rather give up drinking than imbibe this swill," I said, dropping the final can into the bag. "You don't have to worry about me being so poor I have to drink Milwaukee's Best. I'm not rich, but I'm not destitute either."

Clove didn't look convinced. "Then why were you partying in the woods?"

"I wasn't partying in the woods," I protested. "There was a group of kids partying out here last night. I interrupted them and told them I was going to call the police. They left before cleaning up their mess."

"That's disappointing."

"Teenagers," I said. "They do what they do. I don't know how disappointing it is. It was rude. Disappointing, though? Meh."

"I was talking about you," Clove said, closing the bag and handing it to me. "Don't throw those cans away. Michigan has a returnable law. You need to take the cans back to the store."

"I've lived in Michigan my entire life," I shot back. "I know about the returnable law."

"I was just checking. I don't want you to inadvertently break the law."

"Yes, the hard time I would be sentenced to for throwing away a beer can would haunt me for a very long time," I deadpanned. "What did you mean when you said you were disappointed in me?"

"It's nothing bad," Clove replied. "I just never pictured you as a snitch."

"I'll have you know that Chief Terry stopped out here yesterday to warn me about kids partying in the woods," I explained. "Some guy named Lionel has been complaining. He thinks they're sacrificing chickens."

Clove giggled. "I love Lionel," she said. "Last year he thought clowns were invading because someone's tablecloth blew off their clothesline in the middle of a storm and he thought the clown from *It* was spying on him. He kept ordering people to lay siege to the sewage plant – even though we don't have one."

"I came out here to see what they were doing," I said. "One of the kids got mouthy, so I told him I was going to call Chief Terry. For the record, I didn't. The threat was enough to make the kids scatter, though."

"Without picking up their mess," Clove surmised. "I get it. I'm sorry for thinking you were partying in the woods. That's probably worse than hitting you, huh?"

"Probably," I agreed, rolling my eyes.

"Well, um, I guess I should be going," Clove said, shifting her feet as she glanced around. "I'm sorry I hit you."

I considered letting her go, but a niggling voice inside wouldn't let me. "Clove, do you want to see the Dandridge?"

Clove's face split with a wide grin. "Yes, please."

"Come on," I said, heading back in the direction of the lighthouse. "By the way, do you like gardening?"

"I love gardening. Why?"

"I have a way you can pay me back for hitting me," I said. "I think you're going to really enjoy it."

"I CAN'T BELIEVE you're making me do this," Clove huffed an hour later, her hands covered by the gardening gloves as she yanked on the thistle plant. "Do you have any idea how much these prickly things hurt?"

"Why do you think I gave up yanking it out yesterday?"

"You're a putz," Clove muttered, giving the weed another tug and flying backward when the root system finally gave way. She landed with a grunt, causing me to chuckle.

"Have you ever considered that you're not great at insulting people?" I asked, opening the lawn and leaf bag so Clove could shove the huge thistle stalk inside.

"I'll have you know that I'm great at insulting people," Clove countered. "I'm a Winchester. The ability to insult people comes with the genes."

"I've noticed how good your family is at it," I conceded. "I don't think you're good at it, though. I think you want to be good at it because you think you should be able to equal Thistle and Bay when they get in a mood, but you're too sweet."

"I'm not sweet," Clove scoffed. "I'm ... mean."

"Yes, you're terrifying."

"No one needs the sarcasm," Clove said. "Fine. You're probably right. I am terrible at insulting people. That doesn't mean I'm sweet."

"It wasn't an insult, Clove," I pointed out. "Being sweet isn't a bad thing."

"It is in my family."

I tilted my head to the side as I looked her up and down. She sat on the ground, carefully folding the stalk so it fit in the bag. She had a smudge of dirt on her nose and she seemed intent on her task. It probably wasn't the time for a deep conversation. I didn't want to lose my chance to question her about her family, though.

"What's the deal with you guys?" I asked finally.

"What do you mean?"

That was a loaded question. "You fight like cats and dogs, people in town swear up and down Aunt Tillie once shrank some guy's … um … family jewels and then he accidentally popped it like a zit, and you all seem to turn on each other when the mood strikes."

"I think you're only seeing what you want to see," Clove argued. "You don't want to like us because you're upset about Bay kicking you out of the inn. She had a good reason for that, by the way. You know that. You just don't want to admit it.

"We do fight, though," she continued. "I think most families fight. They might not be as loud as we are, but we always know where we stand with one another. Despite the fights, my family is loyal. No matter how angry Bay and Thistle get with me, I know they'll always be there for me. That's what a true family is all about."

"That was almost poetic," I said, offering her a rueful smile. "I would be lying if I said your family didn't fascinate me. And, for the record, I do understand why Bay is upset. I should've told her the truth from the beginning. That's on me."

"Why didn't you tell her the truth?" Clove's expression was so earnest she momentarily resembled a child.

"I guess it was fear," I explained. "I've always wanted to find someone else who shared my gift. I never considered how I would feel if someone was spying on me. I just … wanted to see what she could do."

"I understand the curiosity," Clove said. "You went about this the wrong way, though."

"Do you think your family will ever forgive me?"

"I have no idea," Clove said. "I guess we'll both have to wait to find out."

"Does that mean you're leaving?"

"I can't leave," Clove said, shooting me a small smile. "If I don't stay, this thistle will destroy your entire garden. I know a thing or two about controlling … thistle."

"Very cute," I said, taking the lawn and leaf bag from her. "Thank you."

"You're welcome."

"Now, tell me about the kid who popped a pimple and became a priest," I instructed. "That sounds like a great story."

FOUR

"So, wait … are you saying that Aunt Tillie curses you whenever she feels you're being disrespectful?"

Three hours later Clove and I remained in the garden, work was mostly forgotten. We sat on the small patio's pavers, drinking from water bottles as she regaled me with a series of hilarious family stories that boggled the mind.

"Aunt Tillie has cursed me so many times I've lost count," Clove confirmed.

"I need examples," I said. "I can't picture this. Are you saying she did it when you were little, too?"

"Oh, she did it regularly when we were little," Clove said. "She once cursed Bay so she could only make right turns. It took her forever to get where she was going for an entire week."

I laughed. I couldn't help myself. "And how did Bay react?"

"She was furious."

"I can imagine." I tried to picture the scene, but it was practically impossible. The Bay I knew was not someone I could envision walking in an endless series of circles to get to the newspaper office. "What's the deal with Bay?"

"What do you mean?" Clove asked, knitting her eyebrows together.

"She's my cousin. She's a reporter. She's dating an FBI agent. What else do you want to know?"

"She seems ... angry."

"Bay isn't angry," Clove replied, shaking her head. "She's ... cautious."

"You don't have to worry about hurting my feelings," I said. "I know Bay doesn't like me. I understand why she doesn't like me. I've probably earned it. You have to understand, when I came to town I was excited because I thought I was finally going to meet some actual witches."

I could tell my blunt explanation made Clove uncomfortable because she averted her gaze and focused on a nearby bush.

"I know you guys are militant about keeping your secret," I offered. "I get it. People react negatively to what they don't understand. I understand, though. I'm different. You don't have to hide from me."

"I'm not saying we're witches," Clove said, choosing her words carefully. "If we were, though, why would we hide it? Hemlock Cove is supposed to be full of witches and warlocks. We're supposed to tell tourists that ghosts are running around ... and maybe even some werewolves. Why would we hide what we are?"

"If you're really witches, right?" I was teasing, but she didn't look amused, so I wiped the smirk off my face. "I think it's one thing to pretend to be witches in a magically-branded town and even regale people with tales about Aunt Tillie's notorious curses. I think it's quite another thing to actually be witches in a magic town.

"I think you guys are real witches pretending to be fake witches," I continued. "It's very ... theatrical. It's also completely unnecessary. Everyone in town knows what you are."

"Everyone in town thinks they know what we are," Clove clarified. "Personally, I like to believe that I defy categorization."

She was definitely cute. There was no getting around that. She was also a member of the one family in town that hated me. Still, I was attracted to her. She felt the same way. I could tell by the way she kept tugging her hair behind her ear and casting quick looks in my direction out of the corner of her eye.

Her family would never sit back and let us date, though. I inherently knew that without asking the question. It was like *Romeo and Juliet* ... and we all know how that ended. "You're a mystery," I said, smiling despite myself. "Why did you admit Aunt Tillie cursed you five minutes ago and now you're denying you're a witch?"

Clove's cheeks colored. "I ... didn't think of that."

"It's okay to admit you're a witch," I prodded. "Would it help if I told you my mother was a witch, too?"

"Maybe a little," Clove conceded. "What type of witch is she?"

That was an odd question. "Um ... the regular type."

Clove's forehead wrinkled as she pondered my answer. "I don't think you understand the question," she said finally. "There are many different types of witches."

"What type are you?"

"I'm an earth witch." Clove's response was simple and matter-of-fact. I couldn't help but be surprised by her honesty.

"What does that mean?"

"It means I draw my power from natural elements," Clove replied. "Our entire line consists of earth witches, although Aunt Tillie defies categorization, too, and Thistle is convinced she is part devil witch."

"Is that a real thing?"

"No."

I chuckled as I considered what she was suggesting. "Are you saying you have actual powers other than seeing ghosts?"

Clove stilled. "I don't see ghosts."

Her answer was a dodge. I recognized that right away. "So Bay is the only one who can see ghosts," I mused. "Why do you think that is?"

"Aunt Tillie can see ghosts, too," Clove responded. "She doesn't like them, though, and she rarely acknowledges their existence. She says they're needy ... like a high school chick trying to date the quarterback even though she knows he's really gay."

"I'm starting to think Brian might be right about her being crazy."

"Don't ever say that unless you want Aunt Tillie to curse you," Clove said, her tone serious. "If you thought that story about her turning that kid into a priest was a joke, it wasn't."

"What about the pimple part?"

Clove held her hands palms up and shrugged. "I have no firsthand knowledge of that situation."

"That's probably a good thing," I said. "So, what has Aunt Tillie cursed you with?"

"Zits, ill-fitting pants ... flatulence."

I pressed my lips together to keep from laughing.

"I can see you're struggling to hold it together," Clove said. "That's such a guy thing to do, by the way. I was eight years old and Thistle decided to steal Aunt Tillie's bra because she wanted to stuff it and pretend she had boobs.

"She made me help her and we got caught," she continued. "The next day we found that we made farting sounds whenever we walked. It was the worst day of my life – and I've almost died several times over the past year."

"You're really cute." The words were out of my mouth before I had a chance to think about the intelligence associated with saying them. Clove's smile was worth my embarrassment. "I ... ." I didn't get a chance to apologize ... or make things worse ... because the sound of a vehicle door closing in the parking lot drew my attention.

"It's Chief Terry," Clove said, leaning forward. "I wonder what he's doing here."

"You're not missing, right?" I asked, winking to let her know I was joking. "I would hate to get on Aunt Tillie's bad side if she thinks I kidnapped you. I don't want to make farting sounds for the rest of my life. That might seriously cut down on my business."

"Oh, if Aunt Tillie thought you kidnapped me, there'd be no need to worry about farting," Clove said. "Dead people don't fart."

"You sure know how to ruin a nice afternoon," I said, pushing myself to a standing position so I could greet Chief Terry.

"Hey," Chief Terry said, furrowing his brow when he caught sight of Clove. "What are you doing here, Clove?"

"I'm helping Sam garden," Clove explained. "He doesn't know how to yank out thistle without hurting himself."

"Uh-huh."

"What?" Clove sounded defensive. "I'm not doing anything."

Chief Terry glanced over his shoulder and studied the parking lot. "Where is your car?"

"I parked downtown and walked out here," Clove replied.

"Why?"

"Why do you care?" I asked, my gaze bouncing between Clove and Chief Terry as I tried to figure out why Hemlock Cove's top cop appeared to have his nose out of joint regarding a grown woman's afternoon gardening activities.

"I've known Clove her entire life," Chief Terry replied, not missing a beat. "She's not my daughter, but I'm extremely fond of her. I happen to know that her family isn't keen on you, although no one will tell me the extended version of why they don't like you. I keep getting an abbreviated version. I'm curious about how Clove ended up out here."

"I ran into Sam at the diner yesterday, and he invited me to come out and see the Dandridge renovations," Clove replied. "I decided to take a walk because Thistle was being ... well, Thistle ... and I stumbled across him in the woods. I helped him pick up after the kids and then we got to talking and I decided to help him with his thistle problem. I've handled a lot of thistle problems over the years."

"Ha, ha," Chief Terry intoned. "Does your family know you're out here?"

"I'm an adult." Clove crossed her arms over her chest. "Just because you see me as a five-year-old doesn't mean I need someone to babysit me."

"Don't have a meltdown," Chief Terry warned. "I was asking out of concern. I'm not big on gossip. I don't think Bay would like it if she knew you were out here."

"I guess I must've been absent from the family the day Bay was put in charge of my life," Clove deadpanned. "That was probably the worst family meeting to miss, huh?"

Chief Terry scowled. "No one needs the sarcasm."

"I'm sorry." Clove's tone said otherwise.

"While I'm loving this ... angry father act, I'm kind of curious why you're out here," I interjected, shifting the onus of the conversation away from Clove. "Is something going on?"

"Yes," Chief Terry said, dragging his eyes away from Clove and fixing them on me. "Clove said she ran across you in the woods when you were picking up after a party. Is there anything you want to tell me?"

I sighed, resigned. "I was going to call you," I offered. "I kind of forgot when I ran into Clove and we started talking. There was a group of kids out here last night. They woke me.

"I went out there to ask them to quiet down, and some kid named Andy gave me lip," I continued. "He was a big kid, so I decided to walk away. I told them I was going to call you and they scattered pretty quickly."

"What were they doing?" Chief Terry asked. "If they had a chicken, I'm going to arrest you for concealing evidence. You've been warned."

"There was no chicken," I replied. "There were ten kids – I counted them. It was seven boys and three girls. They had a couple cases of Milwaukee's Best, and I'm pretty sure I smelled pot, although I didn't see anyone smoking a joint."

Chief Terry arched a challenging eyebrow. "That's it?"

"That's it," I confirmed. "The Andy kid was rude and obnoxious. I didn't want to get into a slap fight with a teenager. I threatened them and they left. I definitely didn't see a chicken."

"You said there were three girls?" Chief Terry prodded.

I nodded.

"Was one of them a cute little brunette with curly hair and green eyes?"

"I wasn't close enough to see her eyes, but there was a short girl with curly dark hair," I answered. "She tried to get the big kid to calm down, and he was rude to her. She didn't say anything after that."

"What's going on?" Clove asked.

"Tess Britton didn't make it home last night," Chief Terry replied. "Her mother called the station in a panic this morning. She was convinced an intruder snuck into the house and kidnapped her daughter. When I explained that probably wasn't what happened, she threatened to have my badge revoked. I explained I was elected, which she didn't take well, and then I decided to check out here on a whim."

"They all left after I threatened to call you," I supplied. "I listened, but it was quiet as soon as I got back to the Dandridge."

"Do you mind if I have a look around?"

"No."

"Wait a second," Clove interrupted. "You don't think Sam did something to Tess, do you?"

"I don't think Sam is going after teenage girls," Chief Terry clarified. "I want to be able to tell her mother that I checked, though. I also need to look at where they were partying."

"She's not out there," I said. "We spent twenty minutes cleaning up and didn't see anyone."

"I still need to look."

"Okay," I said, seeing no reason to stop him from searching. "Go nuts."

"**I TAKE** it Chief Terry didn't find anything."

Clove was gardening when I returned to the Dandridge. I was both pleased and surprised.

"I thought you left."

"Why would I leave?" Clove asked. "I promised to help you with your gardening project. You have no idea what you're doing. You haven't even gotten to the pokeweed yet."

"Okay, I'll bite," I said, kneeling next to her. "What is pokeweed?"

Clove pointed at a tall plant. Until she told me it was a weed, I assumed it was a mutant bush. "That's pretty big," I said. "How are we going to get that out of there?"

"Well, we could dig it up, but that will probably take all day," Clove said. "If you want to do it quickly, though, I have an idea."

"And what is that?"

"We could tie one end of a rope to it and tie the other to your car and pull it out."

That sounded both fun and simple. "I like that idea," I said. "I'll find a rope."

"I'll keep working on the thistle."

By the time I got back with the rope Clove had managed to clear most of the front garden. She was efficient. I had to give her that.

"I feel like I should pay you for all this work you're doing," I said. "I spent hours working on this yesterday and barely got one corner done. How do you know about all of this?"

"My mother loves gardening," Clove replied. "Aunt Tillie does, too, although she won't pull weeds. When we got in trouble as kids, our mothers used to punish us by making us weed their gardens."

"So you're saying today has been like a childhood punishment?" I teased.

"I wouldn't say that," Clove said. "It's been ... fun."

I made up my mind on the spot. It was probably a mistake, but I couldn't stop myself from asking the question if there was a chance she would agree to my suggestion. "Do you want to have dinner with me?"

Clove's mouth dropped open, surprise washing over her features. "I ... ."

"I promise I'm not out to get your family and I won't do anything embarrassing in public," I prodded. "It's just dinner. I enjoy spending time with you, and I think you've earned a nice meal after volunteering so much of your time helping me despite how much your family hates me."

"Okay," Clove said, grinning. "If you try to do anything hinky, though, I'm going to tell Aunt Tillie."

"And what will she do?"

"I have no idea," Clove answered. "She knows how to hide a body, though, so you should keep that in mind."

"Consider me sufficiently warned," I said, smirking.

It was probably a terrible idea and yet I couldn't tamp down my enthusiasm. For the first time since moving to Hemlock Cove, I genuinely looked forward to something.

It was definitely a start.

FIVE

In my head I knew only girls spent hours getting ready for dates. The last time I gave myself more than a cursory glance in a mirror to make sure I was presentable when leaving the house was right before my senior prom. Of course, I hoped to get lucky that night.

Because the mirror at the Dandridge was old and dusty, it was easy to tell myself I kept staring at my reflection … and changing my shirt … and fiddling with my hair … and practicing conversational topics that would make me seem smart and charming … because the image staring back at me was distorted. In truth, I think I was merely nervous. I couldn't help myself.

I headed downtown a full half hour before I was supposed to meet Clove in front of the diner. I envisioned taking her to a nice restaurant outside of Hemlock Cove, but I realized that might put too much pressure on me to deliver the perfect date. I also worried that picking a local spot where everyone knew us would put too much pressure on both of us. It would be like conducting a date in the middle of a zoo exhibit. Still, when it came down to it, I wanted Clove to be comfortable. That's why I picked the diner. I figured we could have a light dinner and then take a walk, maybe even stop in at whatever hokey festival Hemlock Cove played host to this week.

I was lost in thought, excitement and nervous energy distracting me enough to tune out the bulk of the bustling street activity, when the distinctive sound of familiar laughter caught my attention from across the street. I shifted, narrowing my eyes when Bay Winchester hopped into view. Her honey blond hair bounced as she jumped between sidewalk sections, almost as if playing a game. She wasn't alone. Her FBI boyfriend, Landon Michaels, trailed behind her, encouraging whatever she was doing with enthusiastic comments and hearty guffaws.

I watched them for a moment, conflicted. When I first came to town the idea of bonding with Bay because of our shared gift seemed the first order of business. Instead of welcoming me with open arms as I wanted – which I admit in hindsight was a ridiculous expectation – she turned cold and distant. I didn't blame her, yet I was irked.

Landon was another story. While Bay at least pretended to be polite – especially in front of others – he couldn't be bothered to muster anything other than disdain while in my presence. I don't know whether he dislikes me because he thinks I'm after his girlfriend, or perhaps because he sees me as a threat to her secret, but it's obvious he would rather punch me in the throat than play nice.

Bay continued to hop between concrete sections, casting the occasional glance over her shoulder to say something to Landon. He amiably chatted back, jerking forward at one point and grabbing her around the waist to scoop her off her feet and swing her around. Their laughter was loud, their happiness palpable.

I realized they'd stopped their cavorting about three seconds too late. Unfortunately I was their new point of interest.

"Hey," I offered, internally cringing at the lame greeting. "How are you guys?"

"We're good," Bay replied, briefly glancing at Landon as he lowered her back to the sidewalk. "How are you?"

"I'm good," I said, crossing the road with heavy feet. I refused to back down no matter how annoyed they were with my move to

Hemlock Cove. Eventually they would have to get over it … or find a place to bury my body. “Looks like you were having a good time. Don’t let me stop you from doing … whatever it was you were doing.”

“We were playing the crack game,” Bay said.

“I don’t know what that is.”

“You know, I was avoiding the cracks so I wouldn’t break my mother’s back.” Bay’s cheeks colored. She was clearly embarrassed to be caught acting like a child. “It’s stupid.”

“I’m familiar with the game,” I offered, forcing a smile. “I honestly didn’t mean to interrupt you guys.”

“Then why were you staring?” Landon challenged, knitting his eyebrows together. He’s a tall guy, well built and muscular. He has shoulder-length hair, which I’m sure women find attractive, but doesn’t scream “FBI agent.” His suspicious eyes more than make up for it, though.

“I didn’t mean to stare,” I said. “I couldn’t figure out what you were doing and then … .” I didn’t have anywhere to go with that statement, so I left it hanging.

“It’s fine,” Bay said, squeezing Landon’s wrist. It was either a silent warning or plea to not make a scene. I couldn’t be sure which. Their relationship was … odd. On paper they made absolutely no sense. Bay was a witch hiding supernatural abilities, and Landon was a law enforcement officer sworn to tell the truth. Despite that, they seemed to genuinely care about one another.

“How are things going out at the Dandridge?” Bay asked, seemingly at a loss for something to curb Landon’s bad mood.

“It’s an ongoing process,” I answered. “There’s a lot of work that needs to be done, and the weeds are out of control.”

“I heard Chief Terry stopped by today,” Landon interjected, earning a surprised look from Bay. “He says the lighthouse is looking good. He also said a teenage girl disappeared near your property last night.”

“Landon,” Bay cautioned, her voice low. “Maybe … .”

“It’s fine,” I said, waving off her concern. “I’m well aware of what Landon thinks of me. For the record, I did not kidnap Tess Britton.”

"Chief Terry says you talked with her," Landon pressed. "He made it sound as if there was some … tension."

"I had words with some kid named Andy," I explained. "He was rude and full of himself, a typical alpha male. I'm sure you can relate to that."

I have no idea why I feel the need to mouth off whenever Landon is around. There's something about him that just … makes me want to cut his hair and reveal him as an ugly guy masquerading as Hemlock Cove's resident stud muffin. It could happen. Haircuts have brought down entire television shows. Just ask that chick from *Felicity*.

I'm good looking. I know that. Women don't fall at my feet like they do for Landon, but I'm fine with that. Okay, I'm jealous. I can't help it. He seems to have the world at his fingertips, while I struggle to yank weeds and argue with teenagers. Sometimes life isn't fair.

"You're a funny guy," Landon said.

"Thank you."

"It's not going to be so funny if that girl doesn't show up," Landon pointed out.

"Probably not," I conceded.

"We don't know anything happened to Tess," Bay said, inching forward to put her body in front of Landon's. I was curious to see whether he would push her out of the way. Instead he rested his hand on her hip and tugged her closer. He was clearly in a romantic mood. "She's a teenager. She probably just … wandered off."

"Are you insinuating there's a missing teenager lost in the woods?" Landon asked.

"I'm insinuating that she probably got drunk, missed her curfew and then spent today trying to figure a way to get out of trouble," Bay countered. "That's what teenagers do. They're not known for rationality."

"You sound as if you're speaking from experience, sweetie," Landon said. "How many times did you get drunk and miss your curfew when you were a teenager?"

"I was a good girl," Bay said primly. "I never missed curfew."

Landon didn't look convinced. "You know I'm going to ask your mother whether that's true over breakfast tomorrow, right?"

"My mother has memory problems," Bay replied.

"Uh-huh." Landon was unruffled when he turned back to me. "I guess it's probably good you don't seem like a demented pervert out to kidnap teenage girls," he said. "If that girl remains missing, though, you should probably expect a search team to show up on your property."

"I look forward to it," I said dryly, fighting the urge to roll my eyes. "Will there be anything else?"

"You came over to us," Bay reminded me, slipping her hand into Landon's and tugging on his arm, prompting him to put some distance between us. "Let's go to the fair. I want an elephant ear."

"We're going," Landon said, casting one more derisive glance in my direction. "I can't believe I'm saying this, because I feel exactly the opposite, but you probably don't want to leave town until Tess turns up."

"I have no intention of leaving town," I said. "In fact ... I had a really good day. I expect to have a lot more good days in Hemlock Cove. I guess you'll have to get used to me."

"Or we'll leave Aunt Tillie in charge of hiding your body," Landon shot back, smoothly sidestepping Bay's elbow when she tried to jab it into his stomach. "Hah! You're not as fast as you thought, are you?" Apparently my part of the conversation was done, because Landon and Bay returned to their walk, heading in the direction of the festival.

"You're an FBI agent," Bay chided. "You're not supposed to threaten people with imminent death."

"I didn't threaten him with death," Landon argued. "I merely told him that Aunt Tillie might kill him. That's not the same thing."

"Since when?"

"Don't worry your pretty little head about it," Landon said. "I have everything under control. Now, come on. I hear there's a haunted funhouse. I want to take you inside so you get frightened and grab me in public."

"You're really sick," Bay muttered.

I watched them go, unease rolling through me. Landon always pushed my buttons, but usually I could work up some sympathy for Bay. She appeared to be a woman caught between two worlds. The problem was it wasn't dislike for Landon fueling me. It was ... yearning. I wanted what they had.

As if on cue, Clove picked that moment to move out from beneath the awning of the nearby bakery. "Hi." Her smile was shy as she smoothed the front of her peasant top. She looked unbelievably cute and casual. I couldn't help but wonder whether she changed her clothes ten times before our date, too.

"Hi," I said, offering her a genuine grin. "You look nice."

"Thank you," Clove said. "Um ... you look nice, too."

"Thanks."

We lapsed into uncomfortable silence, all those conversational points of interest I rehearsed before leaving the Dandridge completely disappearing from my brain. Thankfully Clove wasn't acting as spastic as I felt.

"Did I just see Bay and Landon?" she asked.

"Yeah," I replied. "They're going to the festival. They were playing the 'step on a crack' game and then Landon and I insulted each other for a few minutes."

Clove wrinkled her nose. "When we used to play 'step on a crack' as kids, Thistle would purposely jump on the cracks and say that it was for Aunt Tillie. She was convinced she could finally get the better of her if Aunt Tillie had a broken back."

I snickered. "That doesn't surprise me."

"Did Landon mention whether they found Tess Britton?"

"Not yet," I said. "Landon warned me not to leave town in case he wants to get all manly and beat me up."

"He didn't say that," Clove scoffed.

"He wanted to say it."

"You should give Landon a break," Clove said. "He has a tough job, and he's still struggling with all of this ... witch ... stuff."

"Do you like him?" I asked.

"I like him a lot," Clove answered. "He's brave … and he makes Bay laugh. They're very cute together."

"I saw that."

"I know you don't like him because he's mean to you, but you should understand that he's not doing that to be a jerk," Clove said. "Landon will do whatever it takes to keep Bay safe. He's … loyal.

"Now, I'm not saying everything he does is right," she continued. "I am saying that Bay deserves to be happy, and I've never seen her this happy."

"Don't you worry that their relationship is doomed?" I asked.

"Doomed?"

"He's an FBI agent," I said. "He's supposed to tell the truth, and the longer they're together the more he's going to have to lie. It's not as though he can tell his boss he's getting magical help from a witch who talks to ghosts."

"I don't think that matters," Clove countered. "It's not as if covering for Bay is a big lie, and I think he's already weighed that. You probably don't know this – and I'm not sure it's my place to tell you, but I don't like you speaking badly about Landon when it's unnecessary – but Landon left after Bay admitted we were witches."

I stilled, surprised. "I didn't know that. He obviously came back."

"Because he decided that he wanted to be with her," Clove supplied. "He had a chance to walk away with a clean break. Instead, he searched his heart and came to the conclusion that Bay was worth keeping in his life no matter how many lies he had to tell to protect her. He's not the type of guy who is going to walk away a second time."

"You think Bay and Landon are going to get married, don't you?"

Clove shrugged, her smile mischievous. "I think some things are meant to be," she said. "I think that certain difficulties are worth going through to get a happy ending. Bay and Thistle make fun of me because they think I'm … naïve. I'm not naïve. I just see things differently than they do."

"I definitely don't think you're naïve," I said, my heart warming at her earnest expression. "In fact, I think you're kind of refreshing. I like the way you see things."

"Thank you."

Something occurred to me. "Were you hiding so they didn't see you?"

"Why would you ask that?"

It wasn't a denial. "You're not ready for them to know I asked you out yet, are you?"

"I want to go on this date," Clove clarified. "I want to make sure we actually like each other before I … upset … the delicate balance of the Winchester household. I hope you understand that I'm not ashamed to go on a date with you or anything. It's just … my family is difficult."

"I understand that, and I agree with your reasoning," I said, surprised to find that the excitement of doing something under the Winchester witches' noses held a strange appeal. "We don't even know if we'll want to go on a second date yet. That's a very pragmatic decision."

Clove giggled. "I wasn't trying to be pragmatic," she said. "I'm only trying to make sure that you still have man parts if we ever get to a place where you might want to use them."

"I … don't understand."

"I told you the story about the priest isn't a lie," Clove said. "If Aunt Tillie hears about this before I have a chance to soften her up, um, you might find yourself considering a job change, too."

"Well, in that case, I definitely agree with you," I said, shifting my hips to protect my groin area. "You know I'm going to have nightmares, right?"

Clove smirked. "Come on. I'm starving. Let's start our date."

"That's the best offer I've had all day."

SIX

"I think you should put a garden in that spot by your back patio," Clove said the next morning, her face bright when I opened the door.

"Good morning to you, too," I muttered, instinctively running a hand through my tousled hair. I'd almost ignored the insistent knocking on the front door when it first jarred me out of a really happy dream – this time I recognized the brunette and her delightful laugh – but I figured if Landon was outside ready to conduct a search, ignoring his knock would make me sink even lower in his estimation ... if that was possible.

"Were you asleep?" Clove asked, frowning. "I ... oh, you were. I'm so sorry. I didn't even think before I came out here."

"It's fine," I said, ushering her inside. "Do you want some coffee?"

"You know it's almost nine, right?"

"Actually I didn't know that," I said, trudging toward the kitchen. "I thought it was the middle of the night." I know I shouldn't be irritated by having my really happy dream interrupted by the real thing, but if she could've held off five minutes ... .

"I take it you're not a morning person," Clove said, her energy level off the charts for someone who was out late the previous evening.

Our date was magical, for lack of a better word. I know that sounds cheesy, but I can't remember having a better time on a first date. We chatted about everything, including favorite childhood memories, Hemlock Cove lore and the Winchester family tree. I was genuinely thrilled to see her, although it would've been nicer after I showered and cleaned the morning crusties from my eyes.

"We didn't finish our date until ... what ... two in the morning?" I reminded Clove.

"I had a good time."

"I had a good time, too," I said. "I also had only six hours of sleep. How can you be so ... cute and happy on six hours of sleep?"

Clove blushed. "You think I'm cute?"

"I think that goes without saying," I said, smirking as I filled the coffee machine's water basin. "How long have you been up?"

"If we want breakfast at the inn we have to be there when they're feeding the guests," Clove explained. "There's a special tour group staying at The Overlook this week. They had to leave early because they were getting on a bus for Traverse City. If I wanted something other than an egg that's been in our refrigerator for at least six months, I had to get up early."

"You're saying your mother won't let you slide on breakfast even after you've had the date of your dreams?"

"Are you fishing for a compliment?" Clove asked, narrowing her eyes.

"Maybe."

"Meal times at The Overlook are etched in stone," Clove said. "Thistle, Bay and I can't cook. Sometimes laziness is the easiest way to go, and sometimes it comes back to bite you. This morning was an example of biting."

I laughed. I couldn't help myself. She was adorable ... even if she did ruin my dream before I hit the good part. "Not that I'm unhappy to see you – I really am happy to see you – but what are you doing out here? I thought I was going to call you after lunch."

After a nice dinner, we decided to take a walk and forgo the festival. A crowded town square risked too many prying eyes invading our get-to-know-you session, and we already knew Landon and Bay were running around stuffing themselves on elephant ears and groping each other in the funhouse. We returned to the Dandridge and sat by the lake, building a bonfire in the fire pit, and talking long into the night. Neither one of us wanted the date to end, but we finally were left with only two options: saying goodnight or going to bed together. It was too soon for the latter, so we were forced into the former. I was mildly disappointed.

"Oh, well … ." Clove looked caught. "Because the tour group is going to be out of town today, and Thistle is being a pain, I thought I could help you finish your gardening project."

"I see."

"If you're doing something else, though, I totally understand," Clove added hurriedly. "I … wow. I should've called before I stopped out here. I didn't think. I must seem really pathetic, huh?"

She was definitely cute … and maybe a little insecure. We would have to work on that. "For the record, you can stop in whenever you feel like it," I said. "I encourage you to do it, in fact. I'm sorry I was grumpy. You just took me by surprise.

"I think gardening sounds like a great way to spend the day," I continued. "I still have a lot of work to do, and I'm never going to turn down free help."

"Okay, good," Clove said, exhaling heavily. "I … um … have ideas for punching up the patio on the other side of the lighthouse, by the way."

"I'll happily listen to your ideas once I take a shower," I offered. "Can you give me twenty minutes?"

"Oh, sure. I can wait outside until you're ready."

"How about you just wait down here?" I said, tickled by her nervous energy. "I'll go shower, and then we can get dirty together in the garden."

Clove pressed her lips together to keep from laughing.

"That came out wrong," I said.

"I got the gist of it," Clove said. "Take your time in the shower. I'll make sure to call before I stop in next time."

"That's completely unnecessary," I replied, moving toward the stairwell. "By the way, Clove, next time you want to hang out with me it's not necessary to make up a story about wanting to garden." I winked to let her know I was teasing, but that didn't stop the blush from climbing her cheeks. "I'll be right back."

"**SO,** how did Landon and Bay enjoy the festival last night?" I asked several hours later, leaning back in one of my lawn chairs and watching Clove sip from her glass of iced tea.

After three hours of work, gossip and laughter, we were both relaxed. We decided to take a break in the shade. Even though it was spring and the weather wasn't overly warm, the sun was strong enough to cause me to shed my jacket and Clove's cheeks to pink up over the course of our morning chores.

"They had a good time," Clove replied. "Bay said Landon got fresh in the funhouse, and Landon said Bay ate enough junk food to make an entire kindergarten class throw up."

"Sounds like fun," I said. "Are you sorry we didn't go?"

"Not particularly," Clove answered, not missing a beat. "I'm glad we had a chance to hang out by ourselves. Are you sorry we didn't go?"

"Not really," I said. "Don't get me wrong, I'm a big fan of a good festival. You were more fun than ten festivals last night. We made the right decision. I'm sure there will be plenty of other festivals to attend."

"You're charming when you want to be," Clove said.

"Thank you."

"Why are you only charming with me?"

That was an odd – and difficult – question. "What makes you think that I'm charming only with you?"

"When you answer a question with a question, that means you're uncomfortable," Clove said. "Bay taught me that."

"Who taught her that?" I asked. "It was Landon, wasn't it?"

"No," Clove said, shaking her head. "Bay came up with that one on her own. I think she learned it from interviewing people for the newspaper."

"Do the people of Hemlock Cove often answer questions with questions?"

"You did it again."

I sighed, exasperated. "I try to be charming with everyone," I explained. "You get an extra dose because you're so cute."

"That's still not an answer," Clove pressed. "It was a very enjoyable attempt at flirting, though."

"I assume we're back to talking about my problems with Bay and Landon," I said, tamping down my frustration. "I tried to be charming with Bay, and that backfired. I don't know what you want me to say."

"You didn't try charming Bay," Clove argued. "You lied to her about why you were in Hemlock Cove, annoyed her by siding with Brian Kelly about stupid ways to increase The Whistler's circulation, and then ambushed her when she was especially vulnerable."

"How was she especially vulnerable?" I asked, genuinely curious. "I waited until you guys found those kids on the ship. She should've been happy that day. You were heroes, and everyone in town was talking about you."

"We didn't save all of the kids," Clove clarified. "There was a dead girl on that ship. We were too late to save her."

"I ... never thought about that," I admitted, embarrassed at missing a big clue that would've at least partly explained Bay's behavior. "Did Bay see her ghost?"

"Bay did see her ghost," Clove confirmed. "Bay also saw another ghost named Erika. She was from a different ship a long time ago. She died a horrible death, too. Bay was upset by what happened, and Landon was angry at the time because we almost died doing something stupid. She was not in a good place the day you went after her."

"Bay and Landon seemed to have made up."

"They never really fought, although Bay worried that he would walk away again," Clove said. "You shouldn't have approached Bay they way you did."

"How should I have approached her? Should I have written her a note?"

"Don't get pouty," Clove warned, wagging a finger. "I know you're on the defensive, and I get that, but you ambushed Bay because you wanted to catch her off guard. You wanted to shock her into an admission. There's no sense in lying. I know that's why you handled things the way you did."

"Fine," I said, holding up my hands in mock surrender. "I hoped she would admit the truth before she had a chance to change her mind. I … really wanted to talk to her about the ghost thing. She's the only other person I know who can see them."

"Bay doesn't consider talking to ghosts cool and hip," Clove explained. "Bay spent her childhood haunted by things she didn't want to see and taunted because people misunderstood and thought she was talking to herself. Do you know how hard that was on her?"

"I never really considered it," I said, rubbing the back of my neck. "I didn't see my first ghost until I was a teenager. Well, that's not exactly true. I probably saw my first ghost before that but had no idea what I saw."

"Bay didn't have that luxury," Clove said. "People thought she was weird … and that stupid Lila Stevens even suggested she was crazy. I hate her."

"Who is Lila Stevens?"

"This girl we went to school with," Clove answered, making a face. "She was mean to Bay."

"Bay doesn't strike me as the type of person to sit back and take abuse."

"Bay has more confidence now than she did as a kid," Clove said. "She's a different person. I know you're desperate for someone to be like you, but Bay really isn't. She's in a class all by herself. It's harder for her."

"I guess I'm starting to see that," I said. "I always thought seeing ghosts was a game … fun even … but I guess from Bay's perspective it's the opposite. How many ghosts has she seen?"

"I have no idea," Clove replied. "She doesn't like to talk about it."

"Even with Landon?"

"What is your obsession with Bay and Landon?" Clove asked, her eyes narrowing. "Are you interested in Bay?"

"No," I sputtered, stunned by the question. "If I was interested in Bay, why would I ask you out?"

Clove shrugged. "Maybe you want to get close to Bay and you're using me to do it."

"No," I said, shaking my head. "No offense to Bay, and I think she has some ... interesting ... qualities, but I'm not interested in her. I would love to talk to her about ghosts one day, but I see now that my approach has been completely wrong and that will probably never happen."

Clove wordlessly pressed her lips together.

"I'm not interested in Bay," I repeated. "I'm only interested in you."

"Okay," Clove said, although she still looked dubious.

"Clove, I had a great time last night, and I want to keep having great times ... with you," I said. "I'm sorry if I've put you in an awkward position with your family. I've tried apologizing to Bay. She's not interested in hearing anything I have to say."

"She'll get over it," Clove said. "If you want to help, though, you need to stop fighting with Landon and show that charm of yours to everyone. That's the only way this will work."

"Well, I want it to work, so I guess I don't have much of a choice," I said. "Now, come on and finish your iced tea. You have a lot of work to do if you want me to buy you pizza for dinner."

"You want me to stay for dinner?" Clove looked please with the invitation. "See, that was charming the way you did that."

"You have to earn your supper first," I said. "I'll supervise to make sure you do it right. Maybe I can find a pad of paper so I can make a list."

Clove's smile slipped. "That charm thing comes and goes, doesn't it?"

DESPITE OUR SERIOUS CONVERSATION, Clove and I spent the rest of the day gardening and enjoying each other's company. She was a witty conversationalist, and I got the feeling that she didn't get a chance to shine very often because she was often relegated to hiding in Thistle and Bay's rather large shadows. She left shortly before ten, even though I tried to think of an excuse for her to stay – I wasn't above using a possible Bigfoot sighting – but ultimately I walked her to the parking lot and watched her drive off.

I was exhausted. Clove's early morning arrival jarred me from a dream I hoped to find my way back into. I climbed into bed, closed my eyes, and passed out minutes after my head hit the pillow.

I woke shortly after midnight, bolting to a sitting position and scanning the dark lighthouse. I was still becoming accustomed to the expansive space, so it took me a few seconds to get my bearings. I didn't so much hear something as feel something.

I walked to the front window and scanned the open expanse outside. I pushed the window open so I could ascertain if my friendly neighborhood teenagers were back with their Milwaukee's Best to ruin my night. There was nothing but rustling leaves and a slight breeze on the other side of the screen.

Something woke me. I was sure of it. But what?

I scanned the yard again, hoping for a glimpse of movement. After a few fruitless minutes I gave up and returned to bed. If someone was outside, they were gone now. I could only hope it wasn't Bigfoot, because if he was I would never convince Clove to spend the night.

SEVEN

The next morning, I was still bothered by my late night wakeup call. I was even more bothered when I remembered Clove wasn't going to stop by and surprise me again. She apologized profusely before leaving the night before, but Thistle needed to make a run to Traverse City for candle supplies, so that meant Clove had to run the magic shop they co-owned.

I knew it was ridiculous to let a little thing like Clove's business serve as a source of disappointment, but after two days of sharing her company I already missed her. That was a little pathetic … and needy … and sad. I recognized the symptoms and found I didn't care. I liked being with her, although I was definitely going to have to work on her self-esteem.

Without realizing what I was doing, I headed into the woods. I was convinced something woke me from my heavy sleep the night before, and on a whim I decided to check the small clearing to see whether my underage friends had returned. If they had left another pile of garbage behind, I was definitely calling the police … or maybe Clove. She would tell me to call the police when I asked what to do, but at least I would be able to talk to her without looking like a fool.

The clearing was free of debris, but I recognized Bay's familiar blond head from behind when I moved into the space to her left. She jumped when she heard me, her hand moving to the spot above her heart, and she exhaled heavily when she recognized me.

"I'm sorry," I said, holding up my hands in a placating manner. "I didn't mean to frighten you."

"It's okay," Bay said, tugging a hand through her hair and squaring her shoulders. She didn't like appearing weak – especially in front of me – and she seemed determined to show me she was in charge of this situation. "I ... what are you doing out here?"

"This is my property," I reminded her. "Technically, you're trespassing. That means you're the one in the wrong ... for a change."

Bay furrowed her brow and scowled. "Listen ... ."

"I'm sorry," I said, shaking my head as Clove's words from the previous evening echoed through my mind. "That was a genuinely stupid thing to say. I don't mean to be obnoxious. I was surprised to see you. You're welcome here whenever you want to visit."

"Really?"

"Really," I confirmed.

"Why?" Bay asked.

"What do you mean why?"

"You shouldn't answer a question with a question," Bay chided. "People will think you're hiding something."

"Yes, I've heard that," I deadpanned. "Listen, I'm actually glad I ran into you – although I'm still confused about why you're out here in the first place – but I need to apologize for the way I ambushed you about being able to see ghosts."

Bay narrowed her eyes. "I don't know why you think I can see ghosts, but I can't."

"Okay, I'm sorry for accusing you of being able to see ghosts when you can't," I said, changing tactics. I wasn't supposed to know for a fact that she could see ghosts. I didn't want to risk Clove's standing within her family to make amends with Bay. "I can see ghosts, and I was under the mistaken impression you could see them, too. I'm sorry for upsetting you."

"Why are you all of a sudden sorry?" Bay asked.

"I've been sorry since it happened," I replied. "I didn't think you'd react the way you did. Sometimes I speak before I think. That's what happened that day at the inn. I am truly sorry."

"Why do you admit being able to see ghosts?"

I wasn't surprised by her bluntness as much as the curiosity shining through her eyes. "Why not?"

"I don't know," Bay hedged. "Some people might think that admitting you can see ghosts is a sign of insanity."

"Are you one of those people?"

"I haven't decided."

I tugged on my limited patience and tamped down my sigh. "I guess I'm not big on hiding who I am."

"That's funny, because you hid who you were and why you really came to town for weeks," Bay argued. "That seems to fly in the face of your honesty policy."

She obviously wasn't going to let that go. "I was trying to feel you out," I admitted, Clove's pleas for patience where Bay was concerned pushing to the forefront of my mind. "I was excited to meet you and your family. I did things in the worst possible way. I'm ... sorry."

Bay bit her lip and shifted from one foot to the other. "Okay," she said finally. "I don't want this to keep being a thing. You're staying in town. This is my home and I'm not leaving. I don't see a reason to fight."

"Thank you," I said. "Now what are you doing out here?"

"Oh, right, I should probably announce my presence next time I trespass," Bay replied. "I'm looking for Tess Britton."

I tilted my head to the side, surprised. "Wait ... she's not home yet?"

Bay shook her head. "She's been missing for more than forty-eight hours now. I think I might've been wrong about her hiding from her parents."

"So what are you doing here?"

"I ... ." Bay broke off, her face conflicted. That's when I realized what she was doing on my property. "You're looking to see if you can find Tess Britton's ghost, aren't you?"

"How many times do I have to tell you that I don't see ghosts?" Bay's voice bordered on shrill.

I opened my mouth to answer, snapping it shut when another figure moved into the clearing from my right. It was Landon. I shouldn't have been surprised, but his presence was enough to set my teeth on edge.

Landon was lost in his own little world, not even glancing in my direction as he approached Bay. "I can't see anything around this area," he said. "I don't see signs of a struggle. I don't see discarded clothing. There's no sign of blood."

"That's good, right?" Bay asked, her gaze locked with mine.

"I don't know," Landon answered. "We need clues. A teenage girl doesn't just vanish this close to town. Something had to happen to her. Without anything to go on, though … ."

"You'll find something," Bay said. "You always do."

"What about you?" Landon asked. He still hadn't bothered looking at me. "Have you found anything?"

"No."

I cleared my throat in an attempt to announce my presence and Landon jolted at the sound, instinctively stepping in front of Bay to shield her. "Good morning, Landon."

Landon relaxed when he recognized me. "What are you doing here?"

"I live here."

"Big whoop," Landon muttered. "Why are you specifically in this area?"

"Why are you trespassing?" I challenged, immediately regretting the words. This conversation wasn't going to elevate me in Clove's estimation when she found out about it.

"I'm searching for a missing teenager," Landon shot back. "What are you doing?"

"I came to see whether anyone was partying out her last night," I answered, fighting the urge to roll my eyes. I had no idea why he irritated me so much. "Something woke me in the middle of the night, and I wanted to make sure those kids didn't leave a mess out here again."

"What woke you?" Bay asked.

"I'm not sure," I responded. "I was sound asleep … I mean dead to the world … and something jerked me awake."

"Did you go outside and look around?" Landon asked, his implacable "cop face" in place.

"No."

"Why not?"

"Because I looked out the window and didn't see anything," I replied. "I opened the window to see whether I could hear anything, but it was quiet. My first instinct when I woke was that another party was going on out here."

"I don't think anyone was out here last night," Bay said.

"No," I agreed. "Last time they were out here they left a huge mess for me and … my lack of sleep … to clean up." I'd almost slipped and mentioned Clove's visits. We were going to have to take on her family eventually. I wanted to postpone that for as long as possible … or at least until Bay didn't make a face that looked as though she smelled rotten pickles whenever I spoke with her.

"You don't have the stuff they left out here the other night, by any chance, do you?" Landon asked.

"It's in a garbage bag in the shed," I replied. "The contractor is bringing one of those industrial waste bins out here next week. I was going to hold onto it until then."

"Can I see it?"

I shrugged. "I don't see why not. Come on."

I led Landon and Bay to the shed, internally smirking when I saw Bay's eyes widen after she caught a glimpse of all of the lawn and leaf bags Clove and I filled over the course of the past few days. They were stacked close to the shed, and the pile was mountainous. "It's in here."

I grabbed the bag in question and handed it to Landon.

He unceremoniously dumped the contents on my lawn, causing me to frown.

"Was that really necessary?" I asked.

"I'm conducting an investigation," Landon replied, not missing a beat. "Everything I do is necessary."

Bay made a face and flicked his ear. "Be nice."

"You be nice," Landon shot back, although his expression softened when he took in her serious face. "Fine. I'll pick it up when I'm done. Are you happy?"

"I'm happier," Bay clarified. "You can buy me lunch at the diner to make me really happy."

"I'm going to do something else later to make us both really happy," Landon muttered, turning to his task. "Oh, gross. Who drinks Milwaukee's Best?"

"Teenagers on a tight budget," Bay replied, lifting her eyes to the Dandridge's white walls. "Did you have this place pressure washed? It looks cleaner."

"We tried that," I replied. "It didn't work. I ended up repainting."

"They did a good job," Bay said, trailing her fingers over the bags of yard refuse as she wandered closer to the building. "Do you have to follow historical rules for the refurbishment?"

I nodded. "Some of them are a pain – like I can't have cement poured in the patio area, but I can buy new stones for it – but most of them aren't too bad." I was happy to engage in mundane conversation if it meant Bay softened her stance and began trusting me.

"It's going to be pretty when you're done," Bay said. "Your proximity to the water is nice, too. What are you going to do with the gardens?"

"I haven't decided yet," I lied. "I want to put some hardy bushes in, and maybe a few flowers to brighten the walkway. I'm not keen on things that need a lot of work, though, so I'm going to have to do some research." In truth, I was happy to let Clove plant whatever her heart desired as long as it meant she came back to care for it.

"There's not much in here," Landon said, his frustration evident. "It's basically beer cans, an empty pizza box and some other random garbage."

"I could've told you that, and I'm not even a professional investigator," I said.

Landon ignored the dig. "Tell me about your run-in with the kids," he instructed. "Chief Terry said it got contentious."

"I don't know that 'contentious' is the right word, but when I heard the kids partying I walked out there and found them," I said. "The one kid – Tess called him Andy – got belligerent and told me to go away."

"What did you do?" Landon asked.

"I told him I was going back to the lighthouse to call Chief Terry," I answered, embarrassed by the admission. "I felt like a narc. One of the kids even fake coughed that into his hand. I wouldn't have made the threat if Chief Terry hadn't stopped by and warned me about what was going on earlier that day."

"I get kids partying in the woods," Landon said. "I think that's been going on as long as there have been teenagers and beer. I don't understand why they would do it so close to the lighthouse. They had to know you were inside."

"Maybe they thought he would ignore the noise," Bay suggested.

"Maybe," Landon said, shoving the garbage back in the bag. "This whole thing is weird. You said this Andy was belligerent. Do you think he would've fought with you if you hadn't left?"

"I have no idea," I said. "He seemed to be the one in control of everything. That Tess girl tried to calm him down, but he told her to shut her mouth. He said something about her being lucky to be invited."

Landon shifted his contemplative eyes to Bay. "Do you know anything about Andy?"

"His name is Andy Hodgins," Bay replied. "He's … a tool."

Landon chuckled. "I believe that's how you referred to me when we first met."

"You were a tool, too," Bay said, unruffled.

"I was an undercover tool. I was supposed to be putting on an act."

"You did a good job," Bay said. "I was convinced you really were a tool."

"You're lucky you're cute," Landon grumbled.

"Andy is … fairly normal," Bay said, poking Landon's side to get him to relax. "I've never heard of him getting in real trouble. He's on a few of the Hemlock Cove sports teams. As far as I know he's not a terrible kid."

"What about girlfriends?" Landon asked. "Is Tess Britton his girlfriend? Does he have a girlfriend?"

"I know this might come as a total shock, but I'm not really up on the teenage dating scene," Bay said. "If you want an answer to that question, you'll have to ask a teenager."

"I think I'm going to have to ask Andy," Landon said.

"Hasn't Chief Terry already questioned him?" I asked.

"He has," Landon confirmed. "Andy claims that Tess took off after you threatened to call Chief Terry. He says he has no idea where she went or what happened to her."

"Do you believe him?"

"I haven't talked to him yet," Landon answered. "The longer this goes on, though, the more worried I am about Tess Britton. We can't find a reason for her to run away. She seemed to have a good relationship with her parents, although people describe them as 'strict.' I just ... don't know."

"I don't know whether it matters, but someone was smoking pot that night," I offered. "I never saw an actual joint, but I could smell it when I first came up on them."

"Pot doesn't generally make people violent," Bay pointed out.

"No, but it does make them paranoid and stupid," Landon said, handing the garbage bag back to me. "Thanks for letting me look through that."

It was the nicest thing he'd ever said to me ... which was a little sad. "No problem."

"It's against the law to throw returnables away in Michigan," Landon added. "You might want to separate those cans out so I don't have to arrest you."

I made an exasperated sound in the back of my throat. Apparently his pleasant attitude had the same shelf life as my charm. "I'll get right on that."

EIGHT

"I heard Bay and Landon were out here earlier," Clove said after dinner, settling on the couch and fixing me with a curious look. "How did that go?"

"Are you asking whether I told them we'd been hanging out?"

"No," Clove replied. "I'm asking whether you fought with Bay and Landon."

"What did they say?"

"You're doing that answering-a-question-with-a-question thing again," Clove scolded. "I don't like it."

"Bay didn't like it either."

Clove's sigh was low and exasperated. "Okay, we don't have to talk about it," she said. "I'm sorry I asked."

"No, I'm sorry," I said, instantly regretting my attitude. A full day of working in the garden without her left me grumpy. "I didn't sleep well last night, and I'm taking it out on you. That's not fair."

"Why didn't you sleep well?"

"I fell asleep right away," I replied. "Something woke me a few hours later. I have no idea what it was. I looked out the window and didn't see anything. When I got up this morning I decided to check the clearing in case the partiers came back, but it was clean and empty."

"Is that where you ran into Bay and Landon?"

"That's where I ran into Bay," I clarified. "She was alone and looking around. We ... talked."

"About Tess Britton?"

"We talked about Tess, but we also talked about the way I ambushed her about seeing ghosts," I replied. "I apologized for how it happened. She denied being able to see ghosts again ... twice ... and then said she didn't want to fight and we should put it behind us."

"Hmm." Clove wrinkled her nose.

"What does that mean?"

"Bay didn't mention making up with you," Clove said. "I would have thought she'd volunteer that after everything that's happened."

"I don't know that I would consider it 'making up,'" I said. "She said she didn't want to fight. She didn't say she wanted to be best friends and invite me over for a slumber party."

Clove snorted. "We never had slumber parties, so that doesn't surprise me."

"Don't all girls have slumber parties?"

"We only hung around with each other, and we already lived together, so I guess you could say we had nonstop slumber parties," Clove explained. "Because we hated each other a lot of the time, I can honestly say they weren't fun."

"Did you freeze each other's bras?"

"You need to stop watching eighties movies," Clove said. "We definitely didn't do that to one another."

"You've ruined my fantasies," I teased, smiling.

"I'm sorry to crush you so unfairly," Clove shot back. "Tell me more about what happened with Bay and Landon. I'm hoping things will be less tense now that you've talked things out."

"I don't know about that," I said. "Basically Landon asked me questions about the kids, then he searched through that bag of garbage we collected, and then he warned me that he would arrest me if I threw the returnables out with the trash."

Clove giggled, the sound warming me. "I told you."

"You're both beautiful and wise."

Clove's cheeks reddened. "That was charming."

"I'm working on being charming twenty-four hours a day," I said. "You bring it out quite easily. Landon is another story."

"Landon is a good guy," Clove said. "Don't talk badly about him. He saved my life … several times."

"Well, then I guess I have to like him," I said.

We lapsed into amiable silence, Clove's eyes darting to the clock on the table. Because the living room doubled as my bedroom these days, nothing was organized. She was debating leaving, something I absolutely didn't want to happen. I decided to head her off before she voiced the suggestion.

"Do you know what we should do?"

Clove's eyes widened. "Um … ."

It took me a moment to realize where her mind headed when I asked the question. "Not that," I said, trying to hide my smirk and failing miserably. "I'll try to be smoother when I suggest that."

"I didn't … I wasn't … I … ." Clove was mortified, which only made her more adorable.

"I was going to suggest we go for a walk," I said, rescuing her from embarrassment. "It's a nice night. We don't have to go far, but … I don't want you to leave yet."

"You're being charming again."

"It's a constant struggle," I said. "I'm working on it."

"YOU SHOULD PUT some lanterns out here," Clove said as we walked past the patio twenty minutes later.

"I have to change out the paver stones first," I said. "If I don't, we'll be pulling weeds once a month."

"Would that be so bad?"

The moon was full, offering a bright halo of light to illuminate Clove's pleasing features. She was beyond cute. "I'll come up with other tasks if you're such a slave to gardening," I said. "Tell me your idea about the lanterns."

"I've seen these hooks you can plant into the ground and hang lanterns from," Clove explained. "It would be romantic if you put a bistro table out here so we – I mean you and whoever you choose – could enjoy dinner during the summer."

It was too dark to see the blush creeping up her cheeks, but I knew it was there. "I think we should definitely do that," I said. "I stress the word 'we.'"

"Do you want to know what else you should do?" Clove asked.

I knew exactly what I wanted to do – something that I kept getting really close to doing and then chickening out before achieving my goal. I shuffled closer to her, intent on finally giving her the kiss I'd been dreaming about for three nights, but she took a step away from me and pointed toward the woods. "I think you should put a bonfire pit in the clearing."

I knit my eyebrows. Did she do that on purpose? She fixated on a task until she completed it, which was both cute and efficient. She was great at picking up on some social cues only to completely miss others. I edged closer to test my theory, but she didn't even glance in my direction. She was too busy staring at the thick expanse of trees.

"I have a bonfire pit by the lake," I reminded her. "Why do I need one in the woods, too?"

"Because if you develop that clearing into a fake cemetery and hold bonfires there you could have big events and draw more people to the lighthouse," Clove said, swiveling her shoulders. "I … ." She broke off, jolting when she realized how close I was.

"I like the fake cemetery idea," I said, locking gazes and extending my chin so it crossed over into her personal space. "People can tell ghost stories and … scare each other."

"You can add a Bigfoot tour, too," Clove said, swallowing hard. "I … what are you doing?"

"I haven't decided yet," I admitted. "I'm thinking really hard about kissing you, though."

"Most people don't announce that before they do it."

"I'm not most people."

"I know," Clove said. "Why now? Why didn't you do it after our first date?"

"I got nervous."

"Why not when you walked me to my car last night?" Clove pressed.

"We were both nervous then," I replied. "You kept gripping your fingers together and jumping every time I got too close."

"You can't kiss me now," Clove said, her pragmatic side taking over. "We've talked about it too long, and no matter what, it will feel anticlimactic now."

I tilted my head to the side, considering. Was she saying that because she was nervous? Would I look wimpy if I didn't take advantage of the situation – and the extremely favorable lighting?

Clove took another step back, a small smile playing at the corners of her mouth. "You can't kiss me now, and we both know it."

"I haven't decided whether I know anything yet," I clarified. "It does seem as if we're building up unnecessary stress regarding this, so maybe we should get it out of the way."

"You don't get a first kiss out of the way," Clove chided. "You make it special, so you never forget it."

"Well, now you've really ruined the mood," I said. "Go back to your bonfire idea. How could I market that?" If I can't kiss her, I might as well plot business moves. I need something to take my mind off her lips – even though she keeps licking them and driving me crazy.

"You can do weekend lighthouse tours," Clove suggested. "You can price for different packages. You know what else you could do?" She was excited, really getting into planning instead of being relieved I wasn't trying to kiss her.

"What?"

"You should see if you can buy an old ship," Clove said. "I don't know what your money situation is, and I have no idea how much a big boat costs, but you don't need a boat to sail. You just need one to anchor next to the dock."

I realized what she was getting at, and I liked it. "You think I should do a haunted boat attraction, too, don't you?"

"Think about it," Clove said. "You can decorate different compartments of the boat. You can even turn one into a gift shop. There are tons of cool model ships. Thistle is really good with a paintbrush. I mean … scary good. She would jump at the chance to take some of those old ship models and turn them into haunted ships. You guys could split the profits."

"I really like this idea," I said, my mind shifting from kissing to the possibility of making money. I didn't completely give up on the kissing idea, but I did push it away for now. Next time I won't give her a chance to talk me out of it. I would just do it. "I wonder where I could buy an old boat. You're right about not having to sail it. I'll bet I could get a great deal on a ship without a working engine."

"I'm so excited," Clove said, hopping up and down. "Can I help you decorate?"

"I wouldn't consider doing it without you," I said. "Come on." I held out my hand.

"Where are we going?" Clove asked, slipping her hand into mine. She didn't even think before she did it, which made me happy. We were the type of people who liked to think before we did things. We had that in common, but I was ready to become a doer.

"Let's go look at the clearing," I suggested. "I have a flashlight on the shelf in the storage shed. I want to see your ideas for the fake cemetery."

Clove's enthusiasm slipped. "But … it's dark."

"That's what the flashlight is for."

"But … what if Bigfoot is out there?"

I couldn't help but smile. "I'll protect you from Bigfoot. Don't worry about that."

"Okay," Clove said, giving in after only a few seconds of cursory worry. "I'll be sad if Bigfoot eats you, but I'll make sure everyone in town knows you were a hero."

"That's all I ask."

I grabbed the flashlight and led Clove into the woods, making sure to pick a slow pace so she wouldn't trip over something as she tried to keep up. I was familiar with the path between the lighthouse and the clearing by now, and we were almost to the location when a low murmur grabbed my attention and caused me to instinctively click the flashlight off.

"What are you doing?" Clove hissed. "How are we going to see?"

"Shh."

"Don't shush me," Clove said. "I . . . ."

I clamped my hand over her mouth, straining until the sound of voices filtered through the dense trees. Clove heard it, too. I could tell by the way her shoulders shifted. I dropped my hand and glanced down at her face. It was too dark to tell whether she was frightened or curious.

"Is that the clearing?" Clove asked, her voice barely audible.

"No," I replied. "That's out farther. Keep hold of my hand. I want to see who it is."

"It's probably just kids partying again." I didn't have to be psychic to know that the last thing Clove wanted to do was spy on teenagers. I couldn't really blame her.

"Tess Britton is still missing," I reminded her. "I want to know whether she's out here."

"And if she is?"

"We'll call Chief Terry."

"Fine," Clove grumbled. "If I die out here, though, I'll never forgive you."

"Duly noted," I whispered, guiding Clove through the trees.

It took a few minutes to find the source of the voices, and when I did I pushed Clove to a kneeling position behind a tree and joined her. I leaned forward, peering around the trunk so I could observe the small gathering.

It was another bonfire – which didn't surprise me – but this time only three kids were present. I recognized Andy right away, my heart jumping at the possibility of seeing Tess. Both of the other teenagers were boys, though, and I couldn't help but feel mildly disappointed.

"We're going to end up in a lot of trouble if we're not careful,

Andy," one of the boys said. "The cops have been asking questions. That FBI agent even showed up at school today."

"We're not going to get in trouble as long as you keep your mouth shut, Jack," Andy shot back. "The cops don't have anything on us."

"They obviously think they know something," Jack argued. "Why did we come back out here, by the way? This is just asking for trouble. We should've gone to Hollow Creek."

"I don't want to hang out with the losers at Hollow Creek," Andy said. "There are too many people out there these days."

"That doesn't mean we had to come here," Jack said. "That lighthouse guy could hear us and call Chief Terry."

"I'm not worried about Chief Terry," Andy spit. "And I'm especially not worried about that douche at the lighthouse. He's a wimp."

I frowned. I would argue with the "wimp" assertion, but I was crouching behind a tree and hiding from kids who didn't look old enough to shave.

"What about Tess?" Jack prodded.

"What about Tess?" Andy shot back. "She's not our problem. She's obviously not talking."

"What's going to stop her from talking when she gets back?"

"Who says she's coming back?" Andy asked. "I'm guessing wherever Tess disappeared to, she's gone for good. That's good for us. Everything is going to get better from here on out."

NINE

"Thanks for coming on short notice," I said, leaning against the lighthouse and forcing a smile as Landon exited his vehicle. Bay was with him, her hair pulled back in a simple ponytail and her face devoid of makeup. They were clearly caught off guard by Chief Terry's call.

After discovering the teenagers – and hearing what they had to say regarding Tess – I was in a pickle. It wasn't something that could wait until morning, and I had to call the police.

Clove left so she wouldn't have to explain her presence to Landon, and I already missed her. I couldn't help but wonder when I became so pathetic.

"What's going on?" Landon asked, ushering Bay ahead of him as they trudged up the sidewalk. "Chief Terry called and told me to come out here. He's having dinner with an aunt and can't get out of it."

"And we were ready for bed," Bay grumbled.

"Don't worry, sweetie," Landon said. "I'll wow you when we get home. I'm up for the challenge."

Bay made a face that would've been comical under different circumstances. "I was looking forward to reading the new book I bought today, for your information."

"It had better be a dirty book, otherwise we're going to have problems," Landon said, unruffled. "What's going on? Chief Terry said you sounded strange on the phone."

"The teenagers are back in the woods," I explained. "There are only three of them this time, but they're definitely out there."

"Are they in the same clearing?" Landon's demeanor switched from agitated to serious. "Is Tess with them?"

"Tess is not with them," I replied. "It's three boys, including Andy. They mentioned Tess, although they're not in the same spot as that first night."

"You eavesdropped on them?" Bay asked, wrinkling her nose. "That seems … ."

"If you say wimpy I'll kick you off my property right now," I warned.

"I was going to say sneaky," Bay retorted, elbowing Landon when he snickered. "It's not funny. Why do you always think it's funny when I stick my foot in my mouth?"

"I find everything you do funny," Landon said before turning back to me. "What did they say?"

"Just that they were worried about the cops sniffing around, and one of the other kids – I think his name is Jack – was worried Tess would show up and rat them out for something."

"It must be Jack Dunham," Bay supplied. "He hangs around with Andy Hodgins."

"What do you know about him?" Landon asked.

"Not much. His mother owns the scone place on Main Street. She seems nice."

"Are they still out there?" Landon asked.

"They were when I called," I responded. "I thought it was better to wait for you here. When I called Chief Terry, he said he was going to send you, although he didn't say why. I didn't mean to ruin a family gathering."

"You did the right thing," Landon said, narrowing his eyes as he glanced around. "Can you tell me why you were wandering around in the woods this late at night?"

"It's not even ten," Bay reminded him.

"I know that, Bay," Landon said, his temper obviously wearing thin. "I have to ask the question."

"Don't get snippy with me," Bay warned. "I'm never going to read that dirty book to you if you insist on being snippy."

"I'm not being snippy," Landon countered. "I knew that book was dirty, too. I saw you and Thistle whispering while you looked at it before dinner. I'm an excellent investigator."

"Whatever," Bay grumbled, crossing her arms over her chest.

"You two should have your own reality show," I said dryly. "Can we focus on the teenagers in the woods instead of your love life?"

"Stop being a … what's that word you used to describe Clove the other day?" Landon asked. I realized he was trying to cajole Bay out of her mood, but I didn't want to hear anything negative about Clove, especially when I couldn't stand up for her without tipping my hand.

"Kvetch," Bay supplied. "Aunt Tillie began calling her that when she was five."

"Why?" I asked, hoping my voice didn't sound as angry as I felt.

"Because she always demanded that we focus on her when we got distracted by other things," Bay explained, narrowing her eyes. "Why do you care what we used to call Clove?"

"Why do you care that I care?" Whoops. I'd just answered another question with a question. That wasn't going to ease her suspicious nature.

"I don't know what's going on between the two of you, but we need to focus on the teenagers," Landon interjected. "And before you say anything, Bay, I'm not being a kvetch. I'm just … really anxious to take a look at that book. Even Thistle blushed when she looked at it."

"It's a good thing you're handsome," Bay said. "Otherwise you would have absolutely nothing going for you."

"Except my wit and charm," Landon countered. "Take me to where the kids are. I'll question them and hopefully get to the bottom of all of this."

"Great," I said, moving toward the trees. "Bay, do you want to stay here?"

"Why would I want to stay here?" Bay was already at Landon's side, their fingers linked.

"I don't know," I said. "I thought maybe you were afraid of Bigfoot, too."

Bay frowned. "Clove is afraid of Bigfoot," she said. "I'm not afraid of Bigfoot. Why ... ?" She trailed off, her mind clearly working overtime.

I'm terrible at subterfuge. Every time I try to fool someone I fail miserably. "Clove stopped by to see the work on the lighthouse the other day," I offered. "She was interested in the construction and potential tours. She mentioned that you and Thistle told her Bigfoot hung around here. I had to reassure her that he doesn't." I hoped that sounded plausible.

"We did do that," Bay said, snickering.

"You guys are mean to her," Landon said, falling into step next to me and pulling Bay closer to his side. "You know she's sensitive. Why would you terrorize her with Bigfoot?"

Bay shrugged. "It was Thistle's idea."

"You have a mean streak when you team up with Thistle," Landon said. "I think you should give Clove a break."

"I agree," I said.

This time Landon shot me an odd look. "Why do you care about Clove?"

"Because she was really upset about Bigfoot," I lied. "I don't think scaring someone to the point where they're legitimately afraid of a mythical dogman attacking them is fun, no matter how you look at it."

"Fine," Bay said. "I'll apologize first thing when we get home."

"That can wait until morning," Landon said. "I want to see that book."

"What is it with you two?" I asked, frustrated. I couldn't even work up the courage to kiss my almost-girlfriend and these two were practically fornicating in front of me.

"Hey, I'm out here because of you," Landon reminded me. "You're the reason I don't know what's in that book."

"Ugh. I feel like I'm in high school again and the popular kids are speaking a language I don't understand."

"Well, if that's the way you feel, don't make me give you a wedgie for being a kvetch. Get moving," Landon prodded. "I have a book waiting and a girlfriend to ... cuddle."

"Nice save," Bay intoned.

"Thank you," Landon said.

I led the duo back toward the small bonfire. Everyone lapsed into silence once we crossed into the woods. I watched Landon from the corner of my eye. His weapon remained holstered on his hip, but he was alert. He kept one hand on Bay's back as he maneuvered her in front of him. He instinctively protected her. It was fairly impressive, especially because I'd forced Clove to hide behind a tree with me an hour earlier.

Once the bonfire popped into view, Landon pressed his finger to his lips and shifted Bay so she was between the two of us. For some reason I felt better knowing that he considered me a viable protection alternative for Bay should things go south.

The teenagers continued chattering, but the conversation had turned to mundane topics like their soccer season and a litany of complaints regarding the lack of cheerleaders for spring sports.

"I'm just saying that I think the soccer team should get cheerleaders, too," Andy said. "I need something to look at between halfs."

"That sounds like a fabulous idea," Landon said, stepping into the clearing and offering the assembled boys a flat smile. "I think that all women should wear cheerleading uniforms every chance they get. Write that down, Bay."

"I think I'll remember it without a physical reminder," Bay said, rolling her eyes as she moved to Landon's side.

Landon's fortitude took me by surprise as I loitered in the shadows behind him. It took me a moment to realize that Bay also was braver than me, which didn't feel very good. I reluctantly moved to Landon's other side and pressed my lips together.

"Oh, man, I should've known," Andy said. "It's the lighthouse douche."

"Hey! I am not a douche," I argued. "I am … a concerned property owner. Show some respect."

"That's probably why he thinks you're a douche," Landon offered.

"You're a concerned property owner?" Bay asked, arching a dubious eyebrow. "That's definitely a douche way to explain something."

"Oh, really? Why don't you tell them about your dirty book?"

"Let's go back to talking about cheerleaders," Landon suggested. "I love talking about cheerleaders."

"You're sleeping alone tonight," Bay threatened.

"Not when you have a dirty book, I'm not," Landon shot back.

"I want to hear more about this dirty book," Andy said. "What kind of book are we talking about? Does it have photos?"

"Don't worry about the book," Bay said. "I'm going to burn the book."

"Yes, let's move on from the book," Landon agreed. "Well, wait … does the book have photos?"

"I can't believe you're actually an FBI agent," I said. "Just how do you solve cases if this is the way you approach them?"

"You're definitely a kvetch," Landon supplied.

"I agree," Bay said.

"I have no idea what a kvetch is, but if it's something like a douche I agree with the cop and the hot chick," Andy offered.

Landon decided to shift gears. "I'm not a cop, but I am working in an official capacity," he said. "What are you guys doing out here?"

"We're lost," Andy replied, not missing a beat. "We were taking a hike and lost our bearings."

"And decided to start a fire?" Landon asked.

"We needed it for warmth."

Andy was a gifted liar. I had to give him that. He didn't seem nervous in the face of Landon's questions, although his two friends were another story. They couldn't distance themselves from Andy fast enough. Landon noticed their furtive movements, too.

"If you two take off running in the woods, I'll be really ticked off,"

Landon warned. "Not only will I arrest you once I track you down, I'll also throw your parents in jail for good measure."

"You can't do that," Andy argued.

"I can do whatever I want," Landon said. "I work for the federal government."

"That was really impressive," Bay deadpanned.

"I know," Landon said, smirking.

"You don't even know who we are," Andy challenged. "You're an outsider."

"You're Andy Hodgins," Bay supplied. "That's Jack Dunham. The third boy hiding by that tree is ... can you look at me?"

The boy shook his head.

"Look at her or I'll shoot you in the foot," Landon threatened.

The boy reluctantly lifted his head.

"Oh, that's Matt Barnes," Bay said. "His mother works at the diner."

"Thank you, Ms. Winchester," Landon said. "You've proven to be an invaluable asset this evening ... and we haven't even read the book yet."

"I'm really close to throwing up," I said.

"No one cares," Landon said, his eyes locked on Andy's defiant gaze. "What are you doing out here?"

"I told you that we were lost," Andy said. "Why don't you believe me?"

"Because I have trouble believing anyone could get lost twice in the same week," Landon replied. "In the same woods, no less. That would mean you're some kind of idiot. Are you an idiot, Andy?"

"I don't have to answer your questions," Andy charged. "I'm a minor, and you can't question me without a parent or lawyer present. I know my rights."

"That's pretty good," Landon said, his face unreadable. "There are exceptions to that rule, like when I catch you breaking the law, for example."

"And what law am I breaking?"

"Trespassing, for one."

"I got lost," Andy said, holding his hands palms up and pasting an

"I'm innocent and you can't possibly suspect me of doing anything nefarious" look on his face.

"Where is Tess Britton?" Landon asked, unmoved by Andy's act.

"How should I know?" Andy asked.

"Because you were out here with her the night she disappeared," Landon supplied.

"You can't prove that," Andy argued.

"He saw you out here with Tess Britton," Landon said, pointing at me for emphasis. "What else have you got?"

"I told you he was a narc," Jack said, causing me to scowl.

"I am not a narc!"

"Shh, you're starting to sound like a woman," Landon said.

"Hey!" Bay shot Landon a dark look.

"Not a woman like you," Landon clarified. "More like a … whiny woman. You're not whiny."

"Nice one, man," Andy offered. "You should teach lessons on how to get hot chicks."

"I'll take it under consideration," Landon said. "Now, where is Tess Britton?"

"I have no idea where Tess is," Andy replied. "I haven't seen her since the last bonfire."

"I thought you were lost?" Landon challenged.

"I … ." Andy was flummoxed.

"That's what I thought," Landon said, glancing at Bay. "Okay, here's what's going to happen: The three of you are going to put out that fire and walk back to the lighthouse with me. Then I'm going to take you to the police station, where you can call your parents. Then we're going to get some answers."

"And what if I don't want to go with you?" Andy asked.

"Then I'll arrest you, and we'll do things the hard way."

It was a pretty impressive threat. I could tell Jack and Matt were immediately swayed. Andy took longer, but he finally came to the same realization as his friends.

"Fine," Andy said. "When my father shows up, though, you'll regret messing with me."

"Because you're making me miss a night with my girl and her dirty book, your father will be full of regret," Landon said. "Now … get moving."

TEN

"You look terrible."

Clove found me sitting on one of the patio lawn chairs the next morning, a mug of coffee clutched in my hand as I debated the merits of working in the garden versus going to bed for the rest of the day.

"Thank you, Clove," I said, forcing a smile for her benefit. "You look … pretty." She did. She was dressed in simple cargo pants and a T-shirt, but she always looked beautiful. It was effortless for her. That was one of the things I liked best about her.

"Did you get any sleep?" Clove asked, shuffling to my side. "You look … ."

"Terrible," I interjected. "You've already told me."

"You look handsome," Clove clarified. "Only you look like a handsome man who could use some sleep."

"I got about three hours of sleep after the state police cleared out," I supplied. "I wanted to sleep longer, but my internal clock kind of fought it. They had dogs and a search team out here for hours, but they didn't find a thing."

"Bay and Landon looked tired this morning, too," Clove said.

"They got up for breakfast and then immediately climbed back in bed. They didn't say a lot about what happened last night."

"What did they say?"

"They said that Andy Hodgins is in custody for theft and pot possession, but that they didn't find Tess," Clove replied. "I think they're worried that she's dead."

"I'm worried that she's dead, too," I admitted. "If she is dead, we may never find her. This area is huge, and we have no way of knowing where they dumped her body. They had dogs out here, but it rained two nights ago, and they didn't find anything."

"Do you really think Andy is a murderer?" Clove asked, sitting in the second chair and fixing me with a sympathetic look. "It sounds like he's up to something, but I have trouble believing he could kill Tess."

"I don't know what to think," I said, rubbing my forehead. "My brain doesn't seem to be firing on all cylinders this morning. Andy is a real pain in the ass, but I'm not sure he's a murderer. He doesn't act like a murderer."

"What does Landon think?"

"Landon can't stand him," I replied. "He called his father, and when Andrew Senior showed up at the station he got into a screaming match with Landon that almost came to blows. I give Landon credit, though; he didn't back down."

"He never does," Clove said. "All Bay would say is that Andy is acting as if he's hiding something. I don't think she wants to believe Tess is dead, so she keeps trying to think of a different scenario that allows Tess to be alive."

"Can you think of a scenario that allows Tess to be alive?"

"I have no idea what Andy is doing in the woods, but I do have one idea about where Tess could be hiding," Clove offered.

"I'm officially intrigued."

"Where did human traffickers hide an entire boat without anyone being able to see it?" Clove asked. "Where is the one place in this area that we know things go missing?"

"The cove."

Clove nodded. "The cove."

"Give me twenty minutes to take a shower," I said. "Let's check out that cove."

"I HAVE a theory about what's going on," Clove offered a half hour later as we navigated the dense underbrush and pushed closer to the water. I'd only been to the cove once before, and I wasn't sure I could find it again. I was impressed that Clove seemed to know exactly where she was going.

"What's your theory?"

"I think Andy, Jack and Matt were doing something illegal, but probably not what we think they were doing," Clove answered. "You said you smelled pot that first night. Have we considered they were dealing it and that's what they're trying to cover up?"

"I guess that's possible," I conceded. "What does that have to do with Tess?"

"Her mother works on Andy's father's farm," Clove supplied. "People have been gossiping about Andrew Hodgins for years. They say that he's not just growing corn out there."

"If people are gossiping about it, why wouldn't the police arrest him?"

"This whole town is inundated with gossip – some of it true and some absurd," Clove said. "People think Aunt Tillie has her own pot field, too. In fact, if the rumors are to be believed, at least five people have pot fields."

"Why would this area have so many pot growers?"

"It's open and the police presence is minimal," Clove answered. "Pot isn't a big deal these days when you have meth and cocaine to worry about. Aunt Tillie claims her field is medicinal."

I stilled. Did she just admit her great-aunt illegally grew pot? "Um … ."

"I mean, if she did have a field she would claim it was medicinal," Clove offered hurriedly. "I … oh, crap. There's a reason Bay and Thistle keep secrets from me. I do have a big mouth."

"I don't care about Aunt Tillie's pot field," I said. "I'm just … stunned. She's a tiny old woman."

"Her field isn't very big," Clove clarified. "And, trust me, you don't want to ever call her an 'old woman' when she's in hearing distance. In fact, you might want to erase that phrase from your memory."

"I heard rumors that she grows pot, but … I didn't think they were true," I said. "Brian was convinced they were, but … wow."

"Don't tell anyone," Clove pleaded. "I … please don't tell anyone."

"I won't tell anyone," I said, holding up my hands. "I promise. Go back to Andy's father, though. Even if he was growing pot, what would Tess have to do with that? According to Andy, they weren't dating. How did she get involved?"

"That's a very good question," Clove said, screwing her face up in concentration. "What if Tess was visiting her mother and stumbled on the pot field?"

"So what?"

"You said that Andy was mean to Tess that first night out at the Dandridge," Clove said. "Tess never struck me as one of the popular kids."

"And Andy is one of the popular kids," I surmised. "You think Tess blackmailed Andy into including her in group outings by threatening to tell the police about the pot field. That's an interesting thought, but …."

"It was his father's field," Clove finished, already seeing the hole in her logic. "We don't even know that Andrew Hodgins had a pot field. I'm just assuming he did because I have pot on the brain because of Aunt Tillie. That's probably a mistake. I would make a terrible cop."

"I think you're probably good at whatever you do," I countered, tilting my head when I caught a hint of movement in the cove. I narrowed my eyes and smiled when I realized what I saw. "In fact, I think you're so good you just found a missing girl."

Clove followed my gaze, focusing on the disheveled figure leaning against a tree. "It's Tess. What should we do?"

"We're going back to the Dandridge and calling Chief Terry," I said.

"We're not police officers and we don't want to risk her running. Come on."

"You know I'm going to have to leave again, right?" Clove asked, scampering behind me as I strode toward the lighthouse. "I'm not ready to admit we're dating yet. I need time to prepare for that."

"I know."

"I ... do you want to tell people we're dating?"

"Not today," I answered. "Soon, though. Come on, Clove. Let's solve the case of the missing teenager and then talk about our relationship."

"Can I call you my boyfriend yet?"

I smirked. "You can in a few hours. One thing at a time."

BY THE TIME darkness descended I was officially exhausted. Clove made her escape moments before Landon and Chief Terry arrived to collect Tess. They found her in the cove, and she was a sobbing mess when they reappeared with her shaking frame corralled between them.

It seems Clove's pot theory was way off. I accompanied Landon and Chief Terry to the police station. I wanted to see the things through so I could put the past where it belonged and look toward the future.

Andy's bravado slipped when Tess walked into the station, and then it became a finger-pointing extravaganza. I couldn't wait to catch Clove up, which was why I hurried toward the parking lot when I heard a car door slam.

Clove jumped when I appeared in front of her, gasping as she caught her breath. "You frightened me!"

"I'm sorry," I said, offering a small smile. "It feels like I've been waiting for you forever." I realized the words could have a double meaning, but I was okay with that.

"Dinner took longer than I expected," Clove said. "We waited for Bay and Landon as long as we could, but finally we ate without them.

Landon is going to be upset when he realizes he missed pot roast and chocolate cake. I was hoping to hear what happened from them."

"Why did you want to hear the story from Bay and Landon instead of me?" I hoped I didn't sound too whiny.

"Because now I'll have to listen to them tell the story a second time and act like I haven't heard it a first time," Clove replied. "This whole 'hiding our relationship thing' is starting to get difficult."

"I agree," I said. "I want to talk about that in a second, but I thought we would talk about what really happened with Tess first."

"Okay," Clove said, although her eyes briefly clouded with worry. "What happened to Tess?"

"You were kind of right with your theory, and kind of wrong, too," I supplied. "Tess did stumble across something at the Hodgins farm, and she was using it to blackmail Andy. It wasn't pot, though."

"What was it?"

"They were running an illegal cockfighting ring on their property," I explained.

"The chickens," Clove said, things shifting into place. "Lionel said he heard chickens in the woods, and no one believed him."

"It seems Andy, Jack and Matt transported the birds, and they brought some into the woods in crates one night to run a side business and make money off some of their schoolmates," I said. "Tess not only knew about Andrew Hodgins' operation, she found out about Andy's attempt to rip off his father. They're both in a lot of trouble, by the way."

"I should hope so," Clove said, making a face. "I can't believe anyone would purposely hurt animals like that. It makes me sick."

"Landon called in federal help and they confiscated twenty birds," I said. "Andy rolled over on his father pretty quickly. It doesn't seem like there's a very good relationship there."

"I still don't understand why Tess was hiding in the woods," Clove pressed. "If she was blackmailing Andy, why would she take off?"

"According to Tess, she got in over her head," I said. "She thought that hanging out with the popular kids was going to be fun and make her popular by extension. Instead Andy treated her like a slave and talked down to her.

"She got scared when I went to the bonfire that night, and believed I was going to call Chief Terry," I continued. "She thought she was going to be arrested for knowing about the cockfighting ring and not saying anything."

"So … she ran because she thought everyone was going to be arrested," Clove surmised. "Why would she stay out in the woods for … what … four days? That's just … ridiculous."

"She was afraid," I said. "She thought the police were looking for her, and she didn't think she would do well in prison. She was really worked up about the idea of being locked up. She said she had no idea what she was going to do. She was hungry and upset, and she is in trouble for keeping quiet about the cockfighting."

"I think she's paid enough," Clove said.

"I don't think she's going to get in big trouble," I clarified. "Chief Terry wants to send a message, though. He was really angry."

"He loves animals, too," Clove supplied. "He got us a puppy for Christmas one year. We had that dog for a long time before he died. Chief Terry would come out and play with the puppy – and us by extension – all the time when we were little."

"He sounds like a good guy."

"He is," Clove said. "Why did Andy think Tess wasn't going to show up again?"

"He thought she ran away for good," I answered. "He was convinced she was going to start a new life … like he sees people do on crime shows. He's not very bright."

"He's also in big trouble, which makes me happy," Clove said. "I hope he gets locked up for a long time."

"His father definitely will be," I said. "I think Andy will probably get a slap on the wrist because of his age."

"That's a bummer."

"That's definitely a bummer," I said, studying Clove's profile for a moment. I made up my mind on the spot. It was time. I grabbed her chin and shifted her face so I had a clear shot, and pressed my mouth against hers, taking us both by surprise.

Instead of pulling away, Clove sank into the kiss. I pulled her closer, enjoying the way her body melted against mine. When we finally came up for air, Clove widened her eyes and fixed me with a dark look.

"I thought you were going to announce it before you kissed me. I wasn't ready for that."

"I decided to switch things up," I said. "I like you. I think you like me, too. I don't want to wait for things to happen where you're concerned. I want to make things happen."

"That was a very nice speech," Clove said. "We still have a problem, though."

"Your family hates me."

"My family hates you, and they're not going to understand us dating," Clove conceded.

"Does that mean you don't want to date me?"

"No. That means we need to put our heads together and figure out how we're going to tell them that we're dating."

"Do we have to do that tonight?" I asked.

Clove shook her head.

"Do we have to do that this week?"

"No," Clove said, giggling. "We are going to have to do it eventually, though."

"I like the idea of being able to spend time with you before we have to tell them," I said. "I'm not asking you to lie, but … can we spare a little time before we become part of The Overlook's nightly dinner theater?"

"I think that sounds like a great idea," Clove enthused. "That will give me time to fix your gardens."

"I … thought it would give us time to get to know one another better," I said, unable to hide my smile. "If we do that while working on the garden, I have absolutely no complaints."

"Can I help you pick out paint for the inside of the lighthouse, too?"

"You're really a renovation junkie, aren't you?"

"I like to think of myself as a taskmaster," Clove clarified. "I never get to be the boss on stuff like this. I'm really looking forward to it."

I narrowed my eyes. "Who says you get to be the boss?"

"I do," Clove answered, grinning. "Don't worry. I think you'll like it when I'm in charge." She slipped her hand in mine. "We can start now."

"Oh, yeah? What do you want to be in charge of tonight?"

"Kissing."

I could live with that. The rest would come when it was time. For tonight, kissing sounds like the perfect way to move forward.

"It's a hard job, but I think I'm up to it."

"I think we both are," Clove said.

A SOLSTICE CELEBRATION

A WICKED WITCHES OF THE MIDWEST SHORT 4/5/2016

ONE

SUMMER 2005

"Girls, I need you to go out to the clearing to help me clean up."

I cocked my head to the side, listening hard for the telltale sign of footsteps on the upstairs floor. I didn't hear it.

"Girls!"

"Stop your screeching!" Aunt Tillie wandered into the room, her face screwed up into a petulant frown, and fixed me with a dark look. "Has anyone ever told you that your voice has a lot in common with screeching cats … or dying mice … or really horny dogs?"

I narrowed my eyes. I love my aunt – I would never say otherwise – but there are times I want to … well, I can't even think it because she'll know and curse me. I have enough on my plate without that.

I pressed my lips together and regarded the Winchester family matriarch with what I hoped would pass as a friendly expression. "Hello, Aunt Tillie," I said. "Have you seen the girls?"

"I think they're wilding about in the front of the house," Aunt Tillie replied, grabbing a cookie from the cooling rack. "There was some bold talk about boys and which girl could get which boy without flashing her boobs. I can't remember what they said. It's all noise to me – just like when you were their age."

"Yes, well … that was possibly very flattering." Or probably insulting, I silently added. My aunt likes to get in digs whenever possible. "Do you think you could get them for me?"

"Do I look like your servant?" Aunt Tillie challenged, reaching for another cookie.

I slapped her hand away and earned a scorching glare for my efforts. "Those are for later," I informed her. "You don't need that many cookies anyway. Dinner is in a few hours. You can have another one after that."

"Has anyone ever told you that you're a kvetch?" Aunt Tillie asked, grabbing a cookie anyway and practically daring me to rebuke her. "All you do is whine. All any of you do is whine.

"Now, Marnie, a third of the time you're one of my three favorite nieces," she continued. "This is not one of those times. You're beginning to wear on me."

What else was new? I was used to wearing on my aunt. I'd been doing it since I was a teenager when she took us in after our mother's death. She raised us, she truly loved us, but that didn't mean she wasn't a pill. In fact, she was a horse pill, the ones that were impossible to swallow.

"Aunt Tillie, I have a lot on my plate," I said, choosing my words carefully. "Between the girls and their upkeep … and Twila and whatever she's doing at random times of the day … and the upcoming solstice celebration, the one thing I need right now is help. Can you please help me?"

"No," Aunt Tillie said, filching a third cookie. "If you ask me, what those girls need is a good swift kick in the behind. All they do is giggle and prance around now. It's … unseemly."

"They aren't doing anything wrong," I argued. "They're acting like normal teenage girls."

"That's what I'm talking about," Aunt Tillie said. "I think they might be in heat. Have you seen the way they look at the construction workers when we pass them on the street? It's like being in a porn movie … and not a good one!"

"Whatever," I muttered. "I guess I'll get the girls. Can I trust you with the cookies?"

Aunt Tillie had the audacity to look incensed. "What is that supposed to mean?"

"It means that you've eaten three already, and I promised the girls cookies for dessert," I answered. "It means you can't eat all of them."

"I won't eat all of them," Aunt Tillie scoffed. "I'm watching my figure."

I didn't have the heart to tell her that the only thing she was watching her figure do was expand. It didn't really matter because she'd taken to wearing combat pants and boots. She was at war with the neighbors across the road – she's always at war with someone, just for the record – and she said she had to dress the part if she wanted to win. At least, I think that's what she said. I tune her out as much as she tunes out the girls.

"Just … don't eat all of them," I said, tamping down my irritation and keeping my forced smile in place. "I don't have time to make more, and the girls will screech if there aren't cookies for dessert. Do you want to hear them screech?"

Aunt Tillie shrugged, noncommittal. "If they screech I'll just tie their tongues with a curse," she said. "I don't really care. That might be the better option, because that way they won't be able to swap spit and touch tongues with those three ruffians who keep hiding in the bushes when they think no one is around."

"Who are you talking about?" I asked, irritated as I removed my apron.

"Those three dark-haired boys," Aunt Tillie said. "I think the one's last name is Simpson."

I racked my brain and finally realized who she meant after a few moments. "Do you mean Eric Simpson and his friends Dylan Johnson and Chad Martin?"

"I like to think of them as Frick, Frack and Dumb-as-a-tack."

"Whatever," I said, rolling my eyes. "Don't eat all of the cookies. I'm taking the girls to the clearing for a quick cleanup. If Winnie calls, tell her everything is under control and not to worry."

"So you want me to lie?" Aunt Tillie asked dryly, not bothering to blink as she reached for another cookie. "If you want me to lie to my favorite niece, it's going to cost you."

"How can Winnie be your favorite niece?" I challenged. "She's been gone for days."

"That's why she's my favorite niece," Aunt Tillie replied, unruffled. "Out of sight equals tons of love."

"You drive me crazy," I muttered. "Just … hold down the fort. I'll be back in time to handle dinner."

"Yes, ma'am." Aunt Tillie clicked her heels together and offered me a saucy salute.

"I'm pretty sure you're worse than all of the girls combined," I said, striding out of the kitchen and moving through the bed and breakfast. It would be full of guests – all witches – very soon. For now it was empty, though, and I couldn't be happier, because that meant one less issue to deal with.

My name is Marnie Winchester, and I'm a really cranky witch right now. My older sister Winnie is out of town at a conference because we plan to turn our bed and breakfast into a full inn to take advantage of the area's tourist trade in the next few years. In addition to that, my daughter and her cousins are running roughshod over the male population of Walkerville, and my aunt is trying to give me an ulcer. That's on top of my younger sister, Twila, who has it in her head that she's going to become a singer in her off time and keeps belting out Broadway tunes to prove how tone deaf she isn't. For the record, it's not working. She doesn't hear that, though.

Honestly, the only thing I've got going for me right now is an empty inn. I would be completely overwhelmed otherwise. Don't tell Winnie. I'll never live it down. She didn't think leaving me in charge was a good idea because I "don't do well with structure." Those were her words, mind you. I do great with structure. I just find it boring most of the time.

She didn't have a lot of options when it came to designating a Winchester boss for the week she would be gone, though. Ceding the throne was more difficult than forcing Aunt Tillie to be nice to the mailman, who she is convinced is trying to get a peek under her combat pants whenever he stops by. She thinks he's a pervert, and he very well may be, but he's certainly not interested in looking inside her pants. She doesn't have the right parts, if you know what I mean.

Anyway, Winnie likes to be in control … of everything. She's wound tighter than Nellie Oleson's curls and is only half as pleasant when disappointed. That's why leaving me in charge is such a big deal. She expects me to fail, and the only reason she left is because the conference is important for our plans – making contacts and meeting suppliers, you know the drill – so that meant she had to flee town before one of our biggest annual parties. Because Twila walks around with her head in the clouds, and Aunt Tillie would rather start fires than put them out, that left me. Trust me. No one is happy about it.

I found my daughter, Clove, standing on the front lawn with her cousins Bay and Thistle when I stepped onto the front porch. They didn't see me right away, so I took the opportunity to eavesdrop. The older they get, the more secrets they keep. It's beyond annoying … and no, I'm not a busybody. I don't care what the rest of the family says.

"He likes me best," Thistle said, running a hand over her short-cropped hair. It was naturally blond but she'd taken to dying it funky colors whenever the mood strikes. Today it's black with white highlights.

"He doesn't like you best," Bay argued, hopping on one foot as she jumped from paver stone to paver stone. We were having the driveway redone and it was kind of a mess. "He likes me better. Didn't you see the way he smiled at me when we were in town the other day?"

"He had gas," Thistle said, waving off Bay's statement. "That's always the way he looks before he farts."

"Oh, gross," Clove said, her dark hair pulled back in a ponytail. She's the cutest of the three, with her upturned nose and tiny stature. What? I'm not biased at all. "I have a better shot than both of you. I have bigger boobs."

It was true. Clove inherited my figure, which means she's essentially short and stacked. Like … really stacked. Like she's going to have to rest them on the table when she hits forty, otherwise she'll have back problems stacked.

"Boys like big boobs," Clove said.

"Not all boys like big boobs," Bay argued, glancing down at her flatter chest. She didn't have a lot going on in that department, although she was much better off than Thistle. "Besides, I'm the witty one. Boys like funny girls."

Thistle snorted. "Who told you that?"

"Mom."

"Of course your mother would say that," Thistle said. "She thinks she's the funny one. By the way, she's not."

Good one, Thistle, I internally cheered her on. She's usually a petulant little puss, but she's hilarious when she wants to be.

"My mom is the funny one," Thistle continued. "Unfortunately, it's not always on purpose. Okay, it's rarely on purpose."

"My mom is funny," Clove protested, causing me to puff out my chest.

"Your mom isn't funny," Thistle scoffed. "She tells all those jokes, but none of them make sense. People only laugh because they feel sorry for her. They think she's slow."

Well, I'd had about enough. I cleared my throat, causing all three teens to swivel, their faces whitening. I pasted a chilly smile on my face as I regarded them. "Girls, I need your help cleaning the clearing and making sure there's no brush or anything around the ritual site."

Oh, you're probably wondering what the ritual site is. I wasn't lying when I said I was a witch. We're all witches. We've owned our parcel of land for more than a century, each family member passing it down to the next. There's a clearing about a quarter of a mile into the trees, and that's where we hold all of our solstice and equinox parties. The summer solstice is a big one for us, and we usually travel around to celebrate with other area witches. This year we're the hosts, and I have no intention of falling down on the job. It's a big deal.

"Do we have to?" Thistle whined, making a face.

"I would love to help," Clove said, skipping in my direction. I love her, but she's a total suck up sometimes. "What can I do?"

"Make your cousins come with us right now, because we don't have a lot of time," I informed her. "I still have to cook dinner."

"I don't want to clean up the stupid clearing," Bay said, although she clomped her exceedingly heavy feet in my direction. "Can't Clove do it?"

"It will go faster if we all do it," I said, snapping my fingers for emphasis and moving down the porch steps and leading the girls around the side of the bed and breakfast. "If we all go out there now we can be done in half an hour."

"That sounds like a great way to spend a summer day," Thistle drawled, sarcasm practically dripping from her tongue.

"Well, what can I say? I'm a laugh a minute," I said, locking gazes with Thistle.

Unlike her cousins, Thistle is less prone to embarrassment. She knew I heard what she said, but she didn't care. "I'm not laughing now," Thistle said. "I feel like crying."

"Me, too," Bay said, sighing. "If my mom was here she would do it. She says the only way things get done the right way is if she does them herself."

I bit the inside of my cheek to cut off a nasty retort. It only half worked. "That's because Winnie is a martyr," I supplied. "She says she's tired of doing all the work herself, but that's not true. She couldn't complain about doing all the work herself if anyone helped."

"Are you mad at us?" Clove asked, her voice small as she fell into step with me for the walk to the clearing. "Did you hear what Thistle said?"

"I heard."

"I think you're very funny," Clove said. "You make me laugh all the time."

"Hey, Clove? Your nose is turning brown," Thistle snapped.

I didn't want to encourage Thistle, but I couldn't help but chuckle. Despite their quirks and idiosyncrasies, the three of them get along as if they are sisters. In fact, they get along almost exactly as I did with my two sisters. Wow! That's a sobering thought.

"Do we have to fight?" I asked, hoping to steer the conversation to something more entertaining. "I don't think there's a reason to fight."

"There's always a reason to fight," Bay intoned. "That's what Aunt Tillie says."

"Do you always listen to Aunt Tillie?" I challenged.

Bay shrugged. "Sometimes she's smart."

"Sometimes she is," I conceded.

"Sometimes she's mean," Clove added.

"Sometimes she is," I said, nodding.

"She's always evil and up to something," Thistle said, her eyes dark when I locked gazes with her. Of all the younger girls, Thistle fought the most with Aunt Tillie. I think it's because they are the most alike – which is enough to kill them both, so don't tell them.

"She's not evil," I clarified. "She's ... mischievous."

"Close enough," Thistle said, exhaling heavily as we approached the clearing. "Are you making us do this because you want to prove Aunt Winnie wrong and throw a better solstice celebration than she could?"

Thistle knows how to needle someone. It's not a pleasant trait. "Of course not."

"I don't believe you," Thistle said.

"Me either," Bay said. "I ... ." She broke off, her blue eyes trained on a spot at the far side of the clearing.

"What were you saying, Bay?" I asked, bending over to pick up a fallen branch. We can use the debris for our bonfire after the ritual.

When Bay didn't immediately answer, I lifted my eyes and found her moving away from the clearing and toward something only she could see. Uh-oh. This couldn't be good. All Winchester witches have particular gifts. Unfortunately for Bay, her gift is one of the worst.

"What do you see, Bay?" I asked, almost dreading the answer.

"There's a ghost here," Bay announced.

Of course there is. Can my day get any worse?

TWO

"Holy crapsticks, Bay! Are you sure?"

Deep down I knew she was certain. She's no alarmist and she never embellishes ghost stories. She is uncomfortable with her gift. She doesn't want to see ghosts. Sometimes when she converses with them, other people see her and assume she's talking to herself. She'd been labeled "weird" in the process, something that galls her even though she won't admit it. There's no way she was making up this sighting. I held onto hope all the same.

Bay pressed her lips together and nodded. "She's right there." Bay inclined her head in the direction of a small opening amongst four trees on the far side of the clearing.

"Do you recognize her?" Thistle asked, intrigued. She loves the idea of ghosts and openly wishes she'd been blessed with Bay's gift. Given her temperament, though, I can't help but feel Bay is the right girl to get the gift – if any of them had to get it, that is. Aunt Tillie can see ghosts, too, so it was a foregone conclusion that someone in the family would inherit the ability.

Bay shook her head. "I don't think so."

"Does she look normal?" Clove timidly asked. Unlike Thistle, she's terrified by the idea of ghosts. "She doesn't look mangled or anything, right?"

"She looks normal," Bay said, rolling her eyes. She is used to everyone asking questions. That doesn't mean she likes answering the same questions repeatedly.

"That's too bad," Thistle said. "It would be cooler if she was dripping with blood and missing an eye."

"You are a morbid little thing sometimes," I grumbled, flicking her ear as I moved past her and joined Bay. "Will she talk to you?"

Bay shrugged. She didn't look thrilled with the prospect of approaching the lost soul. "She's just staring at me right now."

I licked my lips as I decided how to proceed. Winnie was used to dealing with situations like this. Not only was Bay her daughter, Winnie was also the most pragmatic of all of us. She always keeps a cool head. Don't ever tell her I said that. I'll never hear the end of it.

"Try talking to her," I prodded.

Bay nodded, resigned, and then took a step toward a woman only she could see. "Hi. Do you need help?"

I watched Bay interact with air, my heart going out to her as she struggled to communicate with someone who had likely been snuffed out of existence far too early.

"I can help you if you talk to me," Bay said. "I … don't know who you are or anything, but if you tell me we'll probably be able to figure out why you're hanging around."

"Good job, Bay," I encouraged.

"Is she saying anything?" Clove asked.

Bay mutely shook her head.

"Is that because her jaw has been ripped off her face by a monster and she can't talk?" Clove pressed.

I made a disgusted sound in the back of my throat and glared at Clove. "What have you been watching?"

"Nothing," Clove protested, holding up her hands. I can tell when she's lying, and she's definitely lying. "I haven't done anything I wasn't supposed to do."

I shifted my eyes to Thistle. "What have you guys been watching?

And before you answer, just know I'll let Aunt Tillie decide punishments if you lie."

"We may have watched the horror movie festival on AMC the other night," Thistle hedged. "No one made her watch it, so if you're going to freak out . . . ."

"You know she can't watch movies like that, Thistle," I chided. "She'll have nightmares."

"I know," Thistle replied. "She's been trying to make Bay and me sleep with her because she's so freaked out. We told her she was a big girl and had to work things out on her own. That's why she's been sleeping in the closet."

"I'm going to make you pay later," I threatened, extending my index finger and frowning. When did I inherit my mother's accusatory finger? I swore I would never be one of "those" parents. Now, here I am, threatening Thistle with a finger. And not even the fun finger to boot. She probably thinks it's as ridiculous as I did when I was her age.

"She won't talk," Bay said. "She looks afraid. She's hiding behind a tree and watching us."

"What do you suggest?" I asked. "We can't leave her out here with the solstice celebration coming up. She'll upset the balance of the ritual."

Bay shrugged. "How should I know what to do? I'm seventeen. Why are you asking me?"

"Because you're the one who can see ghosts," Thistle answered. "Duh."

"That's enough of that," I said, tugging on Thistle's hair to keep her in line while I decided what to do. "We'll go back to the house and ask Aunt Tillie what to do. She'll help us."

Thistle snorted, the sound causing my stomach to turn. "Did you just meet her? That old lady is crazy, and she likes making other people crazy. She's won't help us."

"Yes, she will," I argued, although my stomach twisted at the thought of asking her for help. "She knows how important this weekend is. She'll help." I shifted my eyes to Bay, hoping she would agree with me.

"She's going to laugh at you and tell you to solve it yourself," Bay volunteered. "We all know it. Either way, I don't want to stay out here any longer. We have to go back and feed Pepper. It's his dinner time."

Pepper, the girls' dog, is an odd-looking mutt who protects the girls with every breath. That's the only reason I tolerate him. I'm not fond of dogs. They slobber and get hair all over the place. What? Not everyone can be an animal person.

"Fine," I said. "Mark my words, though, Aunt Tillie will surprise you. She'll be happy to help."

"I'M NOT HELPING," Aunt Tillie declared twenty minutes later, making a face that would've been comical under different circumstances. "I don't want to help, so I'm not going to help."

"I told you," Bay said, grabbing a cookie from the rack.

I considered ordering her to put it back, but it seemed pointless now. Half the batch was already gone. "Aunt Tillie, we have to figure out who the ghost is and get rid of her," I said.

"Don't you mean help her move on from her tortured existence?" Thistle interjected.

"Don't make me slap you, Thistle," I warned.

"I'll do it," Aunt Tillie said, cuffing the back of Thistle's head and earning a murderous look in response. "Don't even think about saying anything, Mouth. My fingers are itching to curse someone right now and you look mighty appealing."

"I thought Mom said you couldn't curse anyone while she was gone?" Bay said, her mouth full of cookie.

"Don't talk with your mouth full," I ordered.

"Nobody tells me what I can and can't do," Aunt Tillie snapped. "I can do whatever I want. I'm not afraid of Winnie."

That's mostly true. Aunt Tillie isn't afraid of anyone. That doesn't mean Winnie won't go after her given the right set of circumstances. Winnie isn't here to deal with the current problem, though, and for that I silently cursed her.

"We can't conduct our solstice ritual with a lost soul out there," I said. "The other witches will pitch a fit if they find out. Penelope Jansen is coming. You know how she is."

"You're right," Aunt Tillie said, nodding. "I do know how she is. That's why I'm going to curse her, too."

"You'll do nothing of the sort," I spat. "I'm in charge! I'm the boss! You're going to find out who that ghost is and get rid of her!"

Aunt Tillie's face shifted from eager to disinterested. "Make me."

"I just ... why do you have to be like this?" I asked, my stomach churning as I considered what would happen should Aunt Tillie refuse to solve this dilemma. "We're the strongest witches in the bunch. We're supposed to set an example, especially during a solstice ritual. What kind of example will we be setting if we allow a ghost at the celebration?"

Aunt Tillie shrugged. "You're talking to me as if I care what these other witches think," she said. "I don't. I never have. I never will. I don't like them any more than I like those old biddies in town. I wouldn't help them either. Why would I help these people?"

I tugged on my limited patience, which was waning fast, and opted for the final weapon in my arsenal – begging. "Please?"

"No," Aunt Tillie said, not missing a beat. "It's not only that I don't like the other witches and want them to have a rotten time – although that is a major concern for me. I don't like talking to ghosts. They're always whiny. It's all, 'Why me? Why?'" Aunt Tillie clutched the front of her shirt as she performed her imitation, even screeching out some of the words. "I'll tell you why it's them; it's because they're whiny. You never meet a cool ghost."

Bay nodded in agreement. "Word."

"Don't encourage her," I said, poking Bay's side. She seemed to have rebounded from seeing the ghost and was now enjoying Aunt Tillie's performance. I was torn: I didn't want her upset, but I certainly didn't want Aunt Tillie playing to an audience.

"What's going on?" Twila asked, popping her head into the kitchen. She seems to have a sixth sense for the exact worst time to appear.

"There's a ghost in the ritual clearing and Aunt Tillie won't help us get her out," I explained.

"Oh, that's so sad," Twila said, bopping her red head as she pressed her lips together. "We should definitely help her."

"Why don't you go outside and sing to her?" Aunt Tillie suggested, her eyes flashing. "That won't help, but it will definitely scare her away. And that's what you're going to have to do, because I'm not going to help!"

The sound of someone clearing his throat near the kitchen door caught my attention, and I shifted my gaze to find Terry Davenport, Walkerville's newest police chief, standing in the doorway. Uh-oh. How much did he hear?

"Am I interrupting?" Terry asked, shifting uncomfortably.

"Of course not," I said hurriedly. "We were only eating cookies and … chatting."

Aunt Tillie blew a raspberry at the lie and reached for another cookie. I was almost positive Terry knew every witchy secret we tried to keep. He had selective amnesia, though. He knew Aunt Tillie could control the weather and curse whoever crossed her path, yet he didn't mention it. He knew Bay could talk to ghosts, and he protected her with his life. He still didn't like talking about our witchy shenanigans.

"Is something wrong?" I asked, gesturing toward the cookies. "Help yourself."

"Actually, something is wrong," Terry confirmed. "I received a report of a missing woman. I was wondering if you might have seen her during your daily travels."

Thistle made a derisive sound in the back of her throat. "And just in time for dinner, too. How convenient is that?"

"Shut up," I warned. "You know what? You and Clove need to go back to the clearing and finish cleaning it for our … picnic." I probably didn't want to mention a ritual in front of law enforcement. That would have his mind jumping to animal sacrifices and naked dancing. Only one of those things would really happen. "Clean everything up and stack all the tree branches for our bonfire."

"But … what about Bay?" Thistle's expression was murderous. She doesn't mind manual labor, but she hates the idea of Bay getting out of chores. The need to win is large in Thistle's world.

"I need Bay to stick close for a little while so we can … strategize … about this weekend's guests," I lied.

"Whatever," Thistle muttered. "Come on, Clove. We'll go row beneath the ship for our slave master while Bay eats cookies with our oppressors."

"I don't want to row," Clove complained, hopping off her stool and following Thistle. "I don't want to clean either. I'll give you five bucks if you do it yourself."

"You don't have five bucks," Thistle shot back.

"I do, too," Clove said. "It's in my secret hiding spot."

"You mean in your shoe? Yeah. I found that two days ago and spent it. You snooze, you lose."

"I'm going to kill you, Thistle!" Clove shrieked, chasing her cackling cousin out the rear door.

Once it was just the five of us, I graced Terry with my best "come hither" smile. With Winnie gone, I had a clear shot at him tonight. I hoped to make it count. "Would you like to stay for dinner?"

"Oh, what are you having?" Terry asked, oblivious to my mood. He is always oblivious. I was starting to think it's on purpose.

"Roasted chicken, redskin potatoes, corn, cookies and fresh bread," I answered.

"I'm making the bread," Twila said, leaning in closer and winking at Terry.

"Do you have something in your eye?" I asked.

"Just floating hearts," Twila said, grinning.

"Right," Terry said, moving from one foot to the other. "About the missing woman, um, it's Constance Warren, by the way. It seems she was seen going into her house yesterday afternoon for lunch. No one has seen her since. I stopped at the house. Everything looks ordinary, but it's locked up tight and I have no reason to enter."

"If you're looking to get around that, I could break you in," Aunt Tillie offered. "It will only cost you fifty bucks. I'm running a special this month."

"Aunt Tillie!" I was mortified.

Aunt Tillie ignored me. "I could make one of the girls do it if you're really uncomfortable going in yourself," she said. "That will cost more, though. Clove is out because she's terrified of finding dead bodies, but I can make Bay and Thistle do it."

"I'm not doing it," Bay protested. "That's illegal."

"And that's why you're my good girl," Terry said, smiling at Bay. He has a soft spot a mile wide for her. It bugs me, and not because I don't love Bay. It bothers me because Clove is cuter … and sweeter … and far less trouble. What? I'm not jealous. It's the truth.

"Remind me who Constance Warren is," Aunt Tillie said. "Isn't she that old biddy who cheats at euchre at the senior center every Wednesday morning? She has purple hair, right?"

"I believe her hair is gray," Terry clarified. "She does go to the senior center several times a week. I have no idea whether she plays euchre. Her daughter Delia called. She's out of town on a business trip and says her mother has been having problems lately, you know, getting confused and forgetting. After twelve hours of calling and no answer, Delia got concerned."

I exchanged a look with Bay. We had the same thought regarding the new ghost.

"Um … do you have a photo of her?" Bay asked.

Terry nodded and pulled a ragged print from his pocket, holding it up for Bay. "Do you recognize her?"

"I'm not sure," Bay said, shaking her head. She waited until Terry's back was turned to fervently nod in my direction.

Crapsticks! Constance Warren was floating around as a ghost behind our house. That probably meant her body was somewhere close. "Bay, why don't you go to the clearing and supervise your cousins?" I suggested. "Twila and I will make dinner while Terry relaxes."

Terry balked. "That doesn't seem right," he said. "I can help."

"Don't be ridiculous," Twila said, batting her eyelashes as she rested her head against Terry's shoulder. "We wouldn't dream of putting you to work after a hard day keeping the residents of Walkerville safe."

I grabbed Twila's arm and yanked her away, ignoring her dramatic yelp. "You should definitely put your feet up and watch the news in the other room," I said. "We'll handle dinner. Afterward, um, maybe we'll come up with a solution for finding Constance. I'm sure Aunt Tillie would love to help."

"No, I wouldn't," Aunt Tillie said, reaching for another cookie. "Time is money. No money, no time."

This time I slapped her hand hard. "You've had more than enough cookies."

"Well, I'm definitely not helping now," Aunt Tillie sniffed.

"You don't have to help," I said. "In fact, why don't you go to the clearing with Bay and not help the girls? You can supervise while not helping to do everything else."

"That's not going to be any help," Bay said dryly.

"Oh, now I'm definitely coming, wiseass," Aunt Tillie said, jumping down from her stool and shuffling toward Bay. "I'm in charge now. Live in fear!"

Sadly, we all lived in fear. We didn't admit it because it gave Aunt Tillie power. She was frightening enough without our voiced terror backing it up.

THREE

"Can I get you anything else, Terry? More pot roast?" I shot Terry the flirtiest smile in my arsenal. "You should make sure you're full. You put in a hard day's work."

"I have more bread here, and it's still warm," Twila said, shoving the breadbasket in Terry's face. "Warm bread is better than pot roast."

She was trying to goad me. There's no way I would let that happen. "There're more potatoes, too," I said. "I cooked those."

"But the bread is the best," Twila said. "Just think of that warm butter dripping over it."

"I'm ... um ... good, ladies," Terry said, shifting in his chair. "I'm really good, in fact."

Thistle snorted, earning a warning look from Twila. My sister rarely disciplines her daughter, but when she does, Thistle usually – okay, sometimes – listens.

"So, girls, tell me what you're doing over your summer break," Terry urged, trying to focus the conversation on anything but himself.

"They're in a competition to see who can catch the most boys," Aunt Tillie supplied. "It's gross."

"We are not," Bay argued. "We're just ... hanging around."

Terry narrowed his eyes. Because Bay is his favorite, he looks after her above all else. "What boys?"

"No boys," Bay said, shaking her head. "Boys are icky."

"Except for you, of course," Clove said, flashing an impish smile.

"You're going to be some man's worst nightmare someday," Terry said, shaking his head at Clove. "You act all innocent, but you've got manipulation down pat."

That sounded like an insult. Was that an insult?

"What about me?" Thistle asked. She hated being left out.

"You're going to make some man lose all of his hair one day," Terry said, not missing a beat. "You'll probably be attracted to him because he has long hair or something, but he'll be bald before he hits twenty-five if you have anything to say about it."

"I can live with that," Thistle said. "I like bald men."

"You would," Bay muttered.

"What about Bay?" Clove asked.

Terry pursed his lips. "Bay is going to be a good girl," he said after a moment. "She'll wait until she finds the perfect man. You and Thistle will run roughshod over a lot of boys. I can tell already. Bay is going to be choosy."

"Does that mean I'm not going to be choosy?" Clove asked, offended.

"You'll be choosy in the end," Terry answered. "I think you're going to be boy crazy first. You've got that look about you. The good news is that you're smarter than all the boys combined, so they won't be able to put one over on you."

Clove preened under the compliment. "Will Thistle be choosy? I bet she marries a bum."

Terry made a face. "Thistle won't marry a bum," he said, chuckling. "She'll find the perfect man, but he's going to have to catch her. That's the only way it will work."

Clove giggled. "But he'll be bald, right?"

"Right," Terry said.

"I want a guy with long hair," Bay announced. "I think guys with long hair are hot."

"Oh, no, missy," Terry said, wagging a finger for emphasis. "Men with long hair are bad news. Stay away from them."

"Why?"

"Men with long hair are rabble rousers," Terry explained. "You don't want a rabble rouser, do you?"

Bay shrugged. "I have no idea what that means."

"Trust me. You don't want one."

"Speaking of rabble rousers, girls, why don't you go occupy yourselves somewhere else?" I suggested, "preferably upstairs or on the back patio. It's nice out. You should get some fresh air."

"We spent half the day outside," Clove complained.

"She wants us out of the house so she can flirt with Chief Terry, dingbat," Thistle said, cuffing Clove. "Pay attention."

"You're so mean," Clove hissed. "You're just like Aunt Tillie."

"Take that as a compliment," Aunt Tillie said, pushing herself up from the table. "As for me, I will take my leave, too."

That was far too easy. I hadn't even figured out a way to get rid of Aunt Tillie yet. She never volunteered to leave – unless she was up to something. "Where are you going?"

"What's it to you?"

"I just … ." How was I supposed to answer that without risking a curse? "I'm concerned for your welfare," I said finally. "You should rest after a big meal."

"I always thought you were supposed to take a walk after a big meal," Twila said, knitting her eyebrows. "I read somewhere that it helps with digestion."

She really needs a good smack. "Aunt Tillie defies modern science," I said.

"You've got that right," Aunt Tillie said.

AFTER SHUFFLING the girls off to find mischief elsewhere – and I was certain that's what they were doing, given that the last time I saw Thistle and Bay they had their heads bent together as they whispered – I relocated Terry to the living room for a mug of coffee and a talk.

My actions weren't purely selfish – I promise – but I had to feel him out before I dropped Bay's ghost bomb. I just wasn't sure how to do it.

"What do you think happened to Constance?" I asked, going for the easy question first.

"I think she's off with a man having a good time," Twila said, taking on a dreamy expression.

"I was talking to Terry," I snapped. "Don't you have something to do – I don't know – in another room or something?"

Twila shook her head. "And leave Terry? Never."

Terry smiled. I could tell he was uncomfortable, but he was also amused. "How have the girls been handling the news that you plan to turn this place into a full-blown inn?" He completely blew off the Constance question, which was frustrating.

"They seem fine with it," I replied. "It's still years down the road. We have a plan and we know what we want, but we have to save up the money first."

"Aunt Tillie wants us to join in her wine business," Twila said. "She thinks we'll make more than enough money in six months if we become her runners."

Terry scowled. "You know that her wine business is illegal, right?"

The meaning behind the question flew right over Twila's head, as so many things often did. "Oh, I know," Twila said. "She doesn't care, though."

"I think what Terry is saying is that he cares," I pointed out.

"Oh, right," Twila said, her cheeks coloring. "I didn't think of that."

"Of course you didn't," I muttered. "We're going to save up the old-fashioned way. We think an inn could be a real moneymaker. We should have enough money in a few years. We can wait."

"It's good that you're patient," Terry said. "What about the girls and school, though? Don't they want to go to college?"

That was a sticky question. "Bay does," I answered. "She wants to be a writer."

"A journalist," Twila corrected.

She was obviously trying to bug me. "What's the difference?"

"She doesn't want to write novels or poetry," Twila answered. "She wants to cover news stories. I think she wants to move to the city so she can cover big crimes and court trials. I heard her talking with Winnie."

"What does Winnie think of that?" Terry asked, leaning forward.

"She doesn't want Bay to move," Twila replied. "Bay isn't happy here, though. She needs to see the world before she can find her place in it."

"Walkerville is Bay's home," Terry argued. "We have a newspaper here. William Kelly loves Bay. I'm sure he would give her a job."

"Bay needs to roam first," I said. "People here look at her as if she's odd and strange. She doesn't like it. She loves Walkerville as a home, but as long as people think she's weird she'll never be happy. She wants to move to a place where no one knows her."

"But … ."

"Don't worry," Twila said, patting Terry's arm. "Bay will come home when she's ready. Eventually she'll realize it's okay to be weird. I mean … look at me."

Frankly, I was tired of looking at her. "About Constance … ."

Terry wasn't about to be dissuaded from the conversation about Bay. "She shouldn't have to leave home because of what other people think," he said. "She's a good girl. She belongs here."

"I think you're saying that because you love her," Twila said. "Bay loves you, too. Children are supposed to leave the nest, though. Bay will leave on her own terms, and come back on her own terms. I have faith."

"What about Clove and Thistle?" Terry asked. "Will they leave, too?"

I shrugged. "Clove is a homebody at heart," I said. "I don't expect her to leave. In fact, I think she'll probably focus her attention here. Everyone in town thinks we're weird, but Clove has skirted most of the derision because she's so cute. She'll probably open her own store or something."

"And Thistle?"

"Thistle is an artist," Twila replied. "I expect she'll create her own place in this town. She won't leave either. Unlike Clove and Bay, she feeds off people thinking she's weird. She embraces it. Heck, she revels in it."

"But … ." Terry didn't get a chance to finish because Aunt Tillie picked that moment to storm into the living room. "What's going on?" No one could miss the fire in her eyes. She was obviously on the warpath.

"Where are the girls?" Aunt Tillie asked, her chest heaving. Whatever Bay, Clove and Thistle were up to, Aunt Tillie was up to something worse. I could feel it.

"I think they're upstairs," I hedged.

"No, they're not," Aunt Tillie shot back. "I looked. They're not up there."

"Did you check the back patio?" Twila asked. "We told them to get some fresh air. That's probably where they went."

"Do I look like an idiot?" Aunt Tillie seethed. "That was the first place I checked. They can't hide in the house and do … what I know they're doing." She was angry, but she didn't want to reveal what she was angry about. This couldn't be good.

"What do you think they're doing?" Terry asked, tilting his head to the side. "Are they in trouble?"

"You have no idea what kind of trouble I'm going to rain down on those little … great-nieces of mine," Aunt Tillie gritted out. "It's going to be legendary."

"Slow down," I said, raising my hand. "Where have you been?"

"In the basement."

I exhaled heavily, annoyed. "Were you making wine?"

Aunt Tillie risked a glance at Terry. "Of course not! That's illegal."

Terry was dubious. "Okay, so you were making wine and something happened to tick you off," he said. "What was it?"

"I … can't tell you," Aunt Tillie said.

"Why not?" Terry has infinite patience. He's also terrified of Aunt Tillie. When he needs to press her for answers, though, he puts his fear aside. It's one of the things I like best about him. It doesn't hurt that Twila and Winnie both have crushes on him, too. That's another thing I like about him. I want to win, darn it! I want to crush them and squash them and … huh, what were we talking about again?

"Do you have a search warrant?" Aunt Tillie challenged, causing me to internally cringe.

"No," Terry said. "Do I need one?"

"Just tell us what's going on," Twila prodded. "Terry isn't going to arrest you … unless, well, maybe I shouldn't say that. He might arrest you."

Twila is always good in a crisis. Holy crapsticks is she annoying sometimes. "Tell us what's going on right now," I ordered. "If the girls are in trouble … ."

"I'm going to kill them," Aunt Tillie said. "That's how much trouble they're in."

"Tell me what they did," Terry instructed. "I will help you find them if you tell me."

"They stole my wine!" Aunt Tillie barked out, her hands on her hips. "Those little gluttons stole my wine."

I blew out a frustrated sigh. "How much did they take?"

"Three bottles."

Aunt Tillie's home brew is strong. One bottle is enough to knock them on their rotten behinds. Three would pretty much incapacitate them. "I'm sure I know where they are," I said, moving toward the back door.

"Where?" Terry asked.

"They're in the clearing," I said. "They cleaned it today and probably figured a way to hide the wine. I think they stole it this afternoon. The clearing is done now until the … picnic … so they probably thought they could get away with it."

"The only thing they're going to get away with is my foot in their asses," Aunt Tillie said, roundhouse kicking for emphasis. "Here comes the thunder, girls!"

"SHE'S NOT REALLY GOING to kill them, right?" Terry asked, easily keeping pace with me and my shorter legs as we traipsed through the woods. It wasn't quite dark, so it was easy to pick our way through the underbrush. Coming home would be a different story.

"She won't kill them," I said. I was almost sure of it.

"She'll simply curse them into oblivion," Twila interjected. "There's not going to be a pair of pants big enough to fit them when they wake up tomorrow. Goddess have mercy on their souls."

"Don't pray for them," Aunt Tillie scolded. "They're thieves. Thieves should have their hands cut off."

"You stole a bunch of supplies from the stuff I bought last week," I reminded her. "You decided to make wine with it. Does that make you a thief?"

"I borrowed it," Aunt Tillie clarified. "Borrowing is allowed."

"You have to ask to borrow something."

"I did."

"You're lying."

"Don't ever call me a liar," Aunt Tillie warned, cresting the hill that led to the clearing. The four of us pulled up short, dumbfounded and irritated by the sight in front of us.

There they were, the three darlings of the Winchester family. Clove had a bottle of wine in her hand as she twirled … and twirled … and twirled. She would throw up soon if she wasn't careful. Thistle had her own bottle and was crawling along the ground, as if she was a dog or something. And Bay? Well, she was talking to a shrub. A shrub in which I had no doubt the ghostly visage of Constance Warren hid.

"And there they are," I said. "Our pride and joys."

"How should we do this?" Twila asked. "Should we yell or be sympathetic?"

Is that not the dumbest question you've ever heard? "We yell," Terry and I said in unison.

"But we did the same thing when we were kids," Twila said. "They're just acting like normal teenagers."

"And we got yelled at for it," I reminded her.

"Don't worry," Aunt Tillie said, stomping forward. "I'll handle this."

"I think that's a terrible idea," I said. "If you handle it there will be hurt feelings and tears."

"That's what I'm aiming for," Aunt Tillie said. "Hey, lushes, your Aunt Tillie is here, and she knows what you've done. You're in so much trouble they're going to have to think of a new word to explain the … um … trouble you're in."

As far as threats go, it wasn't Aunt Tillie's finest.

"I'd start running now," Aunt Tillie added.

Thistle, still on her hands and knees, turned. Instead of answering, she barked.

Clove, still twirling, mimicked the bark.

"That's going to get old fast," Twila intoned.

I pinched the bridge of my nose to ward off a headache. "Okay, girls, the party is over. Everyone back to the house. Your punishment will be severe."

Thistle barked again.

"I mean it," I said, my temper flaring. "If you don't start marching right now, Terry will arrest you."

"Is that true?" Clove asked, her eyes filling with tears. "I don't want to go to jail. Aunt Tillie says I won't survive jail if I ever go, and that's why I have to be really careful not to get caught when she gives me chores."

What chores was Aunt Tillie giving them? Wait, I don't want to know. "Well, it's too late," I said. "You're going to jail. You waited too long and didn't do as you were told. March!"

No one moved, but Thistle did muster another bark.

"Okay, Terry, that's it," I said. "Arrest them. Throw the book at them."

Terry was unmoved by the order. "Girls, go back to the house and drink a gallon of water each," he said. "Then have some aspirin and go to bed."

To my surprise – and resentment – all three girls fell in line and trudged toward the house, none of them uttering a word … or mustering a glare, for that matter.

"How did you do that?" I asked.

"It's the badge."

"Give me that badge," Aunt Tillie ordered. "I'm going to throw it at their heads."

"You go back to the house, too," Terry said. "This is mostly your fault."

"I didn't get them drunk!"

"You made the illegal hooch that they stole to get drunk," Terry pointed out. "Do you want to have a discussion about that?"

"Fine. I'll go back to the house," Aunt Tillie mumbled, flouncing away. "You're all on my list, though."

"What else is new?" I muttered.

FOUR

"How are the girls?" Terry asked, walking into the kitchen with a serious look on his face the next morning. "Are they sick?"

"I'm sure they are," I replied, mixing my pancake batter without glancing up. "I'm sure they've got headaches the size of wine bottles ... and then some ... this morning."

"I think they deserve it," Aunt Tillie said, strolling into the room.

I took a moment to study her camouflage pants and matching jacket. "Where did you get the coat?" I asked. "It has your name embroidered on it."

"This is U.S. Army issue. Therefore, I could tell you, but then I'd have to kill you."

"Of course," I muttered. I'd spent the better part of the morning trying to ward off my own headache without much luck. "Do we know if the girls are up yet?"

"They will be soon," Aunt Tillie said.

I narrowed my eyes. She was awfully sure of herself. "How do you know that? I would've assumed they'd sleep until noon given how they're bound to be feeling."

"Just call it a hunch," Aunt Tillie replied, averting her gaze. She was definitely up to something. I couldn't muster the energy to care, so I turned my attention to Terry. "What's going on?"

"What do you mean?"

"I mean ... not that I'm not happy to see you or anything, because I am ... but why are you here?" I asked.

"I'm here to give the girls a lecture," Terry replied.

"You should've done it last night," I said. "You should've arrested them and taught them a real lesson."

"I can't arrest them without explaining where the alcohol came from," Terry said, casting a pointed glare in Aunt Tillie's direction. "That would've put Aunt Tillie in hotter water than three underage girls."

"Yeah, we don't want that," Aunt Tillie said. "I think you should let me handle the punishment and forgo a lecture. Things will work out better if we do them my way."

"Not on your life," I said. "Your idea of punishment could kill them if we're not careful."

"You say that like it's a bad thing," Aunt Tillie sniffed. "Personally, I think we have one too many of them as it is. We should let natural selection take over and prune the number to two."

"No way!"

"You're only saying that because you know Bay and Thistle would be the ones to survive," Aunt Tillie challenged. "Admit it."

Sadly, it was true. I would never say it out loud, though. "You're not punishing them," I said. "I'll punish them."

Aunt Tillie arched a dubious eyebrow. "Really? What are you going to do? Are you going to spank them? Ground them? Oh, I know, send them up to their pretty little room and tell them they can't come out until they're eighteen and then we can kick them out."

"You're in a mood this morning," Terry interjected, putting the kibosh on the brewing argument. "I know they stole from you, but they're teenagers. That's what teenagers do when they're sowing their wild oats. I'm sure you remember, because you raised Winnie, Marnie and Twila. They were worse."

"We were not worse," I snapped. "We were good kids. Aunt Tillie was lucky to have us."

Aunt Tillie snorted, tickled by the statement. "Yes, I seem to remember the time you went skinny-dipping with the Travis boy, and his father caught you. He thought you were wearing a flotation device because your boobs were so big. When he came to the house he was horrified and said you refused to come out of the water. At least these girls weren't naked."

My cheeks burned, and when I risked a glance at Terry I found his face flushed with color. Apparently the "flotation device" comment embarrassed him as much as me.

"We didn't steal your wine and party in a field," I pointed out.

"Only because I was younger then and it was easier to keep my wine locked up," Aunt Tillie said. "You tried. I put a spell on the door, and it alerted whenever you tried to break in. Do you want to know how many times that spell alerted?"

Not even remotely. "I think you're exaggerating."

"Whatever," Aunt Tillie said, turning her attention to the door as a bedraggled Bay, Clove and Thistle trudged into the kitchen. They looked as if they'd seen better days.

"Well, there they are," I bellowed, internally laughing as the three of them cringed in unison, reaching for their foreheads. "It's the three lights of my life. How are you girls feeling this fine morning?"

"There's no need to scream," Thistle said, hopping up on one of the counter stools and reaching for the pot of coffee. "We can hear you fine if you whisper. In fact, I think we should have a silent breakfast this morning. How does that sound?"

"What was that?" I yelled. "I can't hear you."

"Mom, stop," Clove pleaded. "I think my head is going to explode."

"I think mine already did," Bay said. "I feel like toe lint."

Terry raised his eyebrows as he regarded the girls. I was mildly curious to see how he would handle this. Usually when approaching them he took a quiet tone. That wasn't the case this morning.

"Do you girls realize how incredibly stupid you were last night?" Terry exploded, causing Bay to shrink back.

For a moment I thought I saw regret on Terry's face. The last thing he wanted was for Bay to fear him. He regrouped, though, and didn't relax his stance.

"You stole wine that was illegally made," Terry continued. "That means it's stronger than the stuff in the store."

"Much, much stronger," I intoned.

"You drank yourselves silly in the middle of a field," Terry said. "First, what you did was illegal and I could've arrested you. Then you would've had records forever. Good luck getting a job with a record."

Thistle snorted. "Yes, I can see it now," she said. "I'm sorry, Ms. Winchester, but we can't hire you. I see here you drank in a field when you were sixteen. No job for you. Goodbye."

Terry ignored her. "Second, what would've happened if one of you fell and hit your head?" he asked. "You could've bled out and died. Would it have been worth it then?"

"No one fell and hit their head," Bay argued. "We were just … horsing around."

"Technically, I was a dog," Thistle said, laughing to herself despite Terry's serious tone. "Did I bark at you guys, or am I remembering that wrong?"

"You definitely barked," Twila said, striding into the room. "You were extremely obnoxious."

"No more obnoxious than you waking us up with a resounding rendition of 'Tomorrow,'" Thistle charged, scorching her mother with a harsh look. "Do you have any idea how horrifying that was to wake up to? I thought I'd died and gone to Hell."

Ah. So that's what Aunt Tillie was up to when she first came in. As far as payback goes, it was fitting.

"I'm thinking of playing Miss Hannigan in the town's production of 'Annie,'" Twila explained. "I think I have a real shot."

"I think I'm going to want to be shot if you sing like that again," Thistle said.

"Hey, I'm not done talking here," Terry said, glancing around the room. "I'm serious, girls. What you did last night wasn't acceptable.

Not only that, it was rude to your mothers and aunts, and it was disrespectful to me to boot. I'm ashamed of all of you."

Thistle didn't look bothered by the proclamation, and Clove merely shrank in her chair to escape detection. Bay, though, looked crushed.

"We're sorry," Bay said, her voice small. "We didn't mean to upset everyone. We only wanted to have a good time."

"And why did you think taking wine to drink in a field in the middle of the woods would be fun?" Terry pressed. "Who in their right mind thinks that's fun?"

Clove pointed across the counter, her finger singling out me. She always was a narc. "They do it once a month," she said.

"And they're naked when they do it," Thistle added. "At least we weren't naked."

Oh, crapsticks!

Terry shifted his eyes to me, narrowing them as he looked me up and down. I couldn't decide whether he was picturing me naked or trying to decide whether the girls were telling the truth. One was definitely preferable over the other. Actually, you know what? I'm fine with both of them. I look good naked.

"Do you and your sisters go to the clearing and drink wine?" Terry asked.

"Well … ." I wasn't sure how to answer.

"Are you naked when you do it?"

"Well … ."

"Do you do this in front of the girls?" Terry asked, his voice becoming increasingly shrill.

"We don't do it in front of the girls," Twila clarified. "They're supposed to be in bed. They've sneaked out a few times, though. I thought they would stop after the last … um … incident. They saw Aunt Tillie naked that time, and it traumatized them."

"I look good naked," Aunt Tillie snapped, causing me to realize that not only did I look like her, but I thought like her, too. That was … horrifying!

As if picturing Winnie, Twila and me naked wasn't enough, now

Terry had to grapple with the potential vision of full-frontal Aunt Tillie entering the fray. "Why would you do that?"

"We like to commune with nature," Aunt Tillie replied, unruffled. "It's better to commune with wine and nudity. It's … freeing."

"Oh, good Lord," Terry muttered, rubbing his forehead. "How can you expect these girls to behave when they're emulating you?"

"We're so not emulating them," Thistle said. "We left our clothes on. Seeing Aunt Tillie's boobs flopping around cured us of any desire to be out there naked. Did you know boobs could spin in different directions?"

"No." Terry was dumbfounded, frozen in his spot on the other side of the counter. He looked like the man whose face helped coin the term deer caught in the headlights. Whoops! Maybe "headlights" wasn't the right term given the topic at hand.

"Well, they can," Thistle said. "One spun this way and the other spun that way. I swear there was a moment where she had a third boob that hit her in the face."

"That was my hand," Aunt Tillie snapped, furious.

"That doesn't make it better," Thistle scoffed.

"Okay, this conversation has taken a turn I didn't see coming," Terry said. "From now on, you girls are not allowed to drink. It's illegal until you're twenty-one. If I see it again I'll arrest you. Do you understand?"

Thistle and Clove made faces as they nodded, but Bay didn't move. Terry locked his gaze on her. "Do you understand, Bay?"

"Yes," she said, her voice cracking. "I … didn't mean to disappoint you."

Terry's face softened. "You didn't really disappoint me," he said. I knew he'd give in if she turned on the waterworks. He's such a softie. "After hearing what your role models are doing, they're the ones who disappointed me."

Bay wasn't convinced. "So … you're not angry?"

"I'm not happy, Bay," Terry clarified. "We all know I can't stay angry with you girls, though. No more shenanigans. That's the rule."

"I didn't agree to that rule," Aunt Tillie said.

Terry scowled. "I can't even look at you," he said. "I'm going to have nightmares."

"It's probably the most action you'll see this month," Aunt Tillie said, patting his arm. "You should be thankful."

Somehow I didn't think that's what Terry was feeling.

"THERE'S A DELIVERY MAN HERE," Clove said, wandering into the kitchen a few hours later. She looked markedly better. The color had returned to her cheeks and she seemed almost chipper. "He says you have to sign for the box."

"That must be all of the ritual supplies," I said, wiping my hands on a dishtowel. "Thank you for telling me. You're still grounded for two weeks."

"I know," Clove said, making a disgusted face as she followed me out of the kitchen. "Would it help if I told you I'm sorry?"

"No."

"Would it help if I told you Thistle and Bay made me do it?" Clove tried again.

"Your cousins have strong wills, but you're not a doormat, Clove," I said. "Your cousins didn't make you do anything. You were a willing participant."

"Would it help if I told you that Thistle threatened to cut my hair off while I slept if I told?" Clove asked.

I actually believed that. There was only one problem with that scenario. "All you had to do was come and tell me what Thistle was threatening," I said, moving through the bed and breakfast and heading to the front door. "I would've taken care of Thistle. She wouldn't have done anything to you."

"She would've waited until you weren't looking and made me eat dirt," Clove argued. "That's not nothing. Have you ever tasted dirt? It's gross."

I couldn't argue with that. Winnie often wrestles people down and tries to make them eat dirt. "You've eaten a lot of dirt, Clove," I said. "You would've survived."

"But … ."

"No," I said, cutting her off with a shake of my head. "You're grounded for two weeks and you're a slave to my whims until this solstice celebration is over. That means you're going to be worked to the bone. I hope you enjoy it."

I greeted the deliveryman at the door and signed for the package before dragging it inside and opening it to make sure everything was present. Bay and Thistle joined Clove to check out the delivery, their eyes wide as they watched me count herbs and potions.

"What is all of that?" Thistle asked, intrigued. "Is that for the good luck spell on ritual night?"

"It is," I confirmed, replacing everything in the box. "It's for grownups. That means it's not for you guys. Do you understand?"

Clove solemnly nodded while Bay and Thistle exchanged quick looks. I smelled trouble.

"I'm not joking," I said. "This stuff isn't to be messed with. Don't touch it. Don't even look at it. In fact … ." I glanced around the room. "I'm going to lock it up."

"We're not going to do anything," Thistle argued. "You've made sure we can't. We're grounded, remember?"

I barked out a coarse laugh. "You got in trouble on our property last night," I reminded them. "You don't have to be out of the house to cause mayhem. I'm not an idiot."

"I don't think I like what you're insinuating," Thistle said. "You're assuming we're going to do something wrong when we haven't done something wrong yet. That's … convicting us before the fact." She looked to Bay for confirmation to make sure her phrasing was correct. When Bay nodded, Thistle continued her diatribe. "We're supposed to be innocent until proven guilty. You're assuming we're guilty."

I rolled my eyes. "That might work on Twila, but you're preaching to the wrong audience," I said. "I know you girls. You're always guilty. Don't touch this stuff. If you do, I'll make sure Terry arrests you."

"He won't arrest us," Thistle scoffed. "He loves Bay too much. He would never arrest her."

"He will if we disappoint him again," Bay said. I could tell she was still troubled by Terry's words. She's sensitive sometimes. It drives me batty. "We won't get in the magic stuff."

"We promise," Clove said, offering me a small smile. "Can we have a week off our grounding now?"

"Absolutely not," I said, hoisting the box and balancing it on my hip. "I'm watching you guys."

"Aren't you always?" Thistle asked.

"I am," I confirmed. "On top of that, Aunt Tillie is out for revenge. I would hate to be you girls right now."

Thistle balked. Aunt Tillie's wrath is the only thing that keeps her in line. "But ... we're already grounded," she said. "She can't punish us, too. You'll stop her, right?"

"Have you ever seen me stop her from doing something she really wants to do?" I challenged.

"We're dead," Clove said.

"You are," I agreed. "I hope you have a lovely funeral, girls."

FIVE

"Where are the girls?" I asked, joining Twila in the kitchen later that afternoon and scanning the room for mutinous faces. They were angry and plotting. I could feel it.

She looked up from the dough she was rolling, a blank look on her face. "I thought they were with you."

"Great," I muttered, stalking toward the rear door. "I'm going to kill them," I said. "I swear, if they're getting into trouble, I'm literally going to kill them this time. That way they can come back as ghosts and haunt Aunt Tillie."

"That sounds fun," Twila said, clearly absorbed with her work. She can focus only on one thing at a time. It's infuriating. Winchesters are multitaskers. She should get with the program.

I pulled up short when I saw the girls sitting on the back patio. Reclining in patio chairs, they appeared to be chatting. If they were plotting they would be whispering. Aunt Tillie has impressive ears for a woman her age.

"What are they doing?" Twila asked, refusing to turn from her dough. "Are they in trouble?"

I shook my head. "They're just sitting out there," I answered. "I guess that means they're not in trouble … for now. They have all their limbs, though. I'll call that a win."

Twila snorted. "I'm surprised we haven't seen any fallout from Aunt Tillie yet," she said. "I thought for sure she would curse them."

"I think that's still to come," I said, moving toward the counter. "Okay, what are you doing?"

"I'm rolling dough."

She's a master of the obvious sometimes. "What is the dough for?" I asked, tamping down my irritation. "Is it for bread or rolls?"

"Oh," Twila said, realization dawning. "It's for bread. I'm making vegetable, cinnamon, cracked wheat, white and regular wheat loaves."

"That sounds good."

"Do you think that's enough?"

"I think that's enough for twice the amount of people we'll be hosting this weekend," I said, rummaging under the counter for baking supplies. "I think we have enough for a town bread shortage, should it happen."

"Ha, ha," Twila said. "Are you baking cookies or pies first?"

"Cookies," I replied. "I'm going to gather the girls in a half hour or so to peel the fruit for the pies. That should put them in a terrible mood. It will keep them near us in case Aunt Tillie decides to curse them. I'm worried about what she'll come up with this time."

"Me, too," Twila said. "She was really angry."

"I don't know what she expects," I said, rolling up my shirtsleeves. "You can't keep homemade wine out in the open in a house with three teenaged girls and expect them not to get into it."

"Technically, I think you can expect that," Twila countered. "Probably only if you're in a different family, though."

"Probably," I agreed.

"Have you heard from Winnie yet?" Twila asked, not realizing the question set my teeth on edge. "She'll be angry when she hears about the drinking."

"Well, we don't want her angry," I said, adopting a breezy tone. "I think I'm going to wait until she gets back to tell her about the drinking. I don't want to worry her. She has a lot going on at the conference."

Twila giggled. "Do you expect me to believe that?"

Honestly? Yeah, I did. "It's the truth," I protested.

"You don't want to tell Winnie about the drinking because she left you in charge, and this proves you fell down on the job," Twila said. "I don't care whether you tell her. Personally, I'm not all that upset about what they did. I mean, I don't like the stealing and lying, but it's not as if we didn't do the same thing when we were their age."

I hate it when she has a point. It's rare, don't get me wrong, but it's irksome all the same. "I don't want to hear a thousand 'I told you so's' from Winnie," I admitted. "She expects me to fail. I don't want to fail. It's a vicious cycle, but there it is."

"We don't have to tell Winnie what happened," Twila said. "We can't ensure Aunt Tillie won't tell her, but we don't have to tell her. It's not as if the girls will volunteer the information, and Aunt Tillie is likely to forget when the other witches start showing up. The second they touch her stuff she'll forget all about being angry with the girls, and instead try to get them to help her pull pranks on our guests."

"They're grounded for two weeks," I reminded her.

"Oh, please," Twila scoffed. "That won't stick. It never does. They'll wear us down in three days, and we'll un-ground them just to get them out of our hair. Thistle is a master at wearing us down. Don't underestimate her."

I never do. "We'll figure it out as we go along," I said. "I … ." I didn't get a chance to finish because the phone on the wall started ringing. I knew who it was before I even answered. I let loose with a long sigh and then picked up the receiver. "Hello, Winnie."

"Hi, Marnie," Winnie said, her voice bright. "How are things?"

"They're fine," I lied. "How are things with you? Are you learning much at the conference?"

"I am," Winnie confirmed. "I have a lot of great stuff to show you. I'm anxious to get home, though. I miss Bay, and I'm excited about the solstice celebration. How are the preparations going?"

"They're on schedule," I said, opting to omit the speed bumps.

"Twila is making bread right now, and I'm about to tackle the desserts. Aunt Tillie is running around in camouflage, and the girls are on the back patio." None of that was a lie.

"That's good," Winnie said. "What aren't you telling me?"

Darn her. She has an innate instinct for knowing when I'm lying. I think it's what happens when you're the oldest. Bay can do it with Clove and Thistle, too. It's beyond frustrating. "I'm telling you everything," I said, earning a smirk from Twila. "Why do you naturally assume I'm keeping something from you?"

"You sound as if you're on edge."

"Well, I'm not," I said. "Things are going well. The girls and I cleaned up the clearing yesterday. We have everything stacked for the bonfire. The ritual supplies were delivered this afternoon, and I locked them in the linen closet to make sure no one gets their hands on them to pinch anything. Everything is under control."

"Are you worried about Aunt Tillie or the girls stealing from the ritual supplies?" Winnie asked.

"Actually both."

"I don't blame you," Winnie said. "Good move on locking that stuff up. I'll be home in time to help with the final preparations. Tell Bay I love her and to be good."

"I will."

After disconnecting, I had trouble lifting my head to meet Twila's gaze. When I finally did, her shoulders shook with silent laughter, and I knew I would never live this down. "I didn't technically lie."

"Yes, you did," Twila said, giggling. "You didn't mention the ghost. You didn't mention the drinking. You didn't mention Terry being here for the drinking. All of that would give Winnie an aneurysm."

"Well, I happen to love my sister," I replied primly. "I don't want to give her an aneurysm." The occasional migraine might be fun, though. "I don't want to upset her."

"It'll be fine, Marnie," Twila said. "You worry too much about this stuff. It always works out."

"That's easy for you to say," I countered. "You're the youngest. No one ever puts you in charge."

"And rightly so," Aunt Tillie said, appearing in the doorway. "If we put Twila in charge it would be absolute chaos. Now, don't get me wrong, I happen to love a little chaos. Twila's kind of chaos is not my kind of chaos, though."

"Thank you for that illuminating take on our current plight," I said. "What are you doing up here, by the way? I thought you would be brewing wine for the solstice celebration all day."

"I'm done with that," Aunt Tillie said. "I finished up yesterday. Even with the three bottles your children stole, we have more than enough."

Aunt Tillie's anger runs deep, but she must be really ticked off if she's taken to calling the girls "your children." She doesn't take credit for them at home, but in public she's full of pride. It's one of my favorite things about her. She can say whatever she wants about any of us, but if anyone else dares utter words tearing us down, she'll bring down a wrath fearful to behold.

"I think you should forgive them," Twila said, dropping a loaf of bread in a pan and placing a towel over it so it could rise. "They were just … testing out their boundaries. You should like that. You spend days on end testing your boundaries."

"Life has consequences, dear niece," Aunt Tillie replied. "Bay, Clove and Thistle are about to find out what those consequences are."

My heart painfully rolled. "What did you do?"

"What makes you think I did anything?" Aunt Tillie asked, feigning innocence. "I've been in here with you."

"Yes, but you were downstairs by yourself for hours," I shot back. "You just said you were done with your wine, so that means … holy crapsticks!" I left my cookie ingredients sitting in the bowl and hurried to the rear door. At first I was relieved when I saw the girls standing there. Then I noticed something odd about the way they waved their hands and talked excitedly to one another. "Oh, I'm going to hate this. I just know it."

I threw open the door and stepped outside, inhaling deeply and tilting my head to the side so I could listen to the Winchester teenagers and their inane chatter.

"This is so awesome," Clove enthused. "I feel like I'm floating."

"It's trippy," Thistle agreed, holding her hand in front of her face, almost as if trying to look through it. "I think this could be the best day ever."

"I just love you guys so much," Bay gushed, her blue eyes sparkling. "You're my favorite people in the world."

"No, I love you so much," Clove said, throwing her arms around Bay's neck. "You're the best cousin ever." If I wasn't mistaken, she slurred her words a little bit there.

"Nobody loves me," Thistle lamented. "No one wants to hug me."

"We love you," Clove said, holding out her arm and pulling Thistle in for a three-way hug. "We all love each other so very much."

"Oh, man," I muttered, turning when I heard laughter and finding Aunt Tillie videotaping the girls with her small handheld camera. "What did you do to them?"

"I like them," Twila said, watching from the open door. "They're so sweet and nice. It makes me think someone replaced our children with pod people, but I still like them."

"Do you know what we should do?" Thistle asked, breaking the hug first. "We should go down to the lake and go skinny-dipping. I heard Aunt Tillie talking about it yesterday, and it sounded fun."

"That's a great idea," Bay said, her blond head bobbing. "We can swim and swim and swim. I love swimming. Swimming is awesome. Swimming is ... what were we talking about?"

"Okay," Clove said, taking me by surprise. She was usually the last to agree to something like this. "Do you think someone will think my boobs are a flotation device?"

Why do they always listen to conversations they shouldn't?

"Only if we're lucky," Bay said.

"They're drunk," I said, shaking my head. "Or maybe high. Or maybe even a mixture of both. How ... why ... what ... when ... I don't understand." So many thoughts raced through my mind I couldn't grasp one and hold onto it.

"Hey, they wanted to be drunk," Aunt Tillie said, grinning when she saw the girls turn their backs and skip toward the woods. The lake was a good five-mile walk. There was no way I would allow that. "I only gave them what they asked for."

"Why are you taping it?"

"The Internet is full of fun videos," Aunt Tillie replied. "There's a site called YouTube. It launched a few months ago. I'm going to post it there."

"Yeah, that will pretty much kill them," Twila said. "I want a copy of that video to hold over Thistle's head, by the way. She'll do anything to keep that under wraps."

"This doesn't bother you?" I was incredulous.

"Should it?" Twila asked. "They're not doing anything harmful. They're being sweet and nice to each other. Quite frankly, they're enjoying the best part of being drunk. I'm not sure how much of a deterrence this will be."

Holy crapsticks! She was right. There is no way this was Aunt Tillie's intended punishment. I narrowed my eyes as I turned, extending a finger when I realized Aunt Tillie was trying to slink away unnoticed. "Don't even think about it."

"I have an appointment," Aunt Tillie said. "I can't be late. It's rude to be late."

"This isn't the whole curse, is it?" I pressed. "They're happy drunks now. They're going to turn into whining and crying messes at some point. That's going to be their payback."

"I have no idea what you're talking about," Aunt Tillie lied. "I really have to get to my appointment."

"Where is your appointment?" I asked.

"The lake."

I scowled. "You're going to go down there to tape them being idiots some more, aren't you?"

"I can't look a gift curse in the mouth," Aunt Tillie answered. "It will be fun. Trust me."

"They're drunk," I said, practically screeching. "They can't swim when they're drunk. They might drown."

"Oh, that's an old wives tale," Aunt Tillie said, waving off my concern. "They'll be perfectly fine. I'll be there to save them if something happens. I'll also have so much footage I'll be able to hold it over their heads for years." She kicked her heels together. "This is so much fun."

"This isn't happening," I said, reaching for her camera. "You're going to put a stop to this right now. If you want to curse them with something else, well, go nuts. This one could go very wrong."

"Oh, it's designed to go wrong," Aunt Tillie said, skirting my outstretched hand. "Now, get out of my way. I have teenage girls to embarrass. By the way, when the sobbing starts in about two hours, I'm going to tape them for exactly five minutes, and then they'll be your problem."

"Aunt Tillie!"

SIX

"Get in the house."

I shoved Thistle – probably harder than necessary – as I tried to force her through the front door of the bed and breakfast. She had half her shirt on and was thankfully wearing a tank top underneath. I managed to catch the girls before they got more than a quarter mile from the house. Getting them home proved problematic, to say the least. Bay and Clove were already inside, watching the spectacle from the living room with wide eyes. Thistle took more … wrangling.

"You get in the house," Thistle shot back.

"I will, right after you get in the house," I said.

"I don't want to get in the house."

"Thistle, don't make me wrestle you in this house," I hissed. "I will hurt you if I have to."

"You'd better be careful," Bay intoned. "She'll smother you with her boobs if you're not."

That did it. "You're all grounded for the rest of your lives!" I bellowed.

"Yeah, that will happen," Twila said dryly, walking into the room. "How are my drunk girls?"

"I'm happy," Clove announced, throwing herself over the end of the couch and falling on her back. "I'm really happy. I … ." She lost her train of thought and stared at her feet. "Have you ever noticed I have tiny feet? They're like little kid feet. I bet I could wear little kid shoes if I want. I like the ones that light up."

"That's good, Clove," I said, my temper ready to explode. "You sit there and stare at your feet. At least that way I know you're out of trouble."

"Okay," Clove said, happily wriggling her feet. She seemed to have absolutely no inclination to do anything else.

"Thistle, I will beat you to within an inch of your life if you don't move through that door," I seethed. It was an empty threat. I'd never done more than grab a handful of hair when the girls misbehaved. Aunt Tillie chased them with the flyswatter on occasion, but once they got fast enough to outrun her they turned it into a game. I was ready to hurt someone, though. Thistle seemed the obvious choice. "I will beat you! I swear to the Goddess I will!"

"What's going on?"

I froze when I heard the masculine voice behind me, swiveling to find Terry watching me from the front porch. I struggled to keep an arm around Thistle's waist, but she evaded me and made a break for it.

Terry nonchalantly snagged the back of her neck before she could bolt over the porch railing. "Where are you going, missy?"

"I'm going skinny-dipping at the lake," Thistle replied. "I need to do it now before I forget."

"She sounds drunk," Terry said, easily holding Thistle in place as he glanced around the room. "She can't possibly be drunk, can she?"

"That's a really hard question to answer," I hedged.

"Really hard," Twila echoed.

"It's not so hard," Aunt Tillie said, breezing into the room, camera in hand. "They're soused."

"Son of a … ." Terry gritted his teeth as he shoved Thistle into the house and slammed the door shut behind him. His chest heaved as he considered how to handle the situation. "What is the matter with you?"

Bay's lower lip began quivering at the vocal explosion, and while I knew some of the emotion was from the spell as it started to go bad, part of it was also because she was close to Terry and she hated when he yelled. "Are you disappointed in us?"

"You have no idea," Terry bellowed, planting his hands on his hips and shooting a dark look in Thistle's direction when she moved toward the door again. "I will handcuff you to the stair railing if you're not careful, Thistle."

Thistle stuck out her tongue and blew a loud raspberry. "You suck! You're a loser! Did I mention you suck?"

I was aghast. The girls were raised to treat Terry with the utmost respect, and not only because he was in law enforcement. He went out of his way for them on numerous occasions. Crapsticks! How would I explain this?

"Where did they get the alcohol?" Terry asked, ignoring Thistle's outburst. "Why didn't you lock it up last night? How irresponsible are you people?"

"Hey!" I extended a finger, the overwhelming anger coursing through me taking me by surprise. "We didn't leave alcohol out. They're not drunk like that."

"How many other ways are there to get drunk?" Terry asked, flummoxed. "Wait ... you're not saying they're on drugs, are you? If that's what you're saying, it's time for tough love. I'm dragging them all down to the station and booking them."

"Yay!" Aunt Tillie clapped her hands. "Can I ride with you and tape them for their perp walks?"

"Don't you dare," I screeched. "This is your fault. They were perfectly fine – heck, they were behaving themselves – until you got involved."

"How is this Aunt Tillie's fault?" Terry asked. "I would really like to know."

"Well ... ." I broke off, biting my lower lip. Explaining what Aunt Tillie did posed a conundrum.

"I don't want you to be disappointed in me," Bay wailed, bursting into tears and curling into a ball on one of the chairs. "I'm so sad."

"Bay's sad," Clove said, still happily wriggling her feet. "It's probably because she has huge feet and can't wear shoes with lights."

I rolled my eyes. Annoying as she was, Clove was the least of my worries right now. Thistle was intent on getting out of the house, and Bay was a sobbing mess. "They're not on drugs. In this instance, they didn't do anything wrong."

"That doesn't mean they're not starting to get loud," Twila said, absentmindedly patting Bay's head. "Don't worry, sweetie. Terry isn't disappointed in you. This will all be over soon."

"What will be over?" Terry asked.

I shifted my eyes to Aunt Tillie. "Do you want to tell him, or should I?"

Aunt Tillie shrugged, unperturbed. She honestly didn't care whether I told Terry the truth. "I'm not telling him anything," she said. "In fact, I think I'm hungry. I'm going to make a sandwich and watch my stories."

"No, you are not!" I grabbed her arm. "You need to remove this curse, and you need to do it right now."

"Oh, crud," Terry said, pinching the bridge of his nose. "Why can't you people be normal? You know I don't want to hear about this stuff. I like pretending it isn't happening. Is that what's going on here? Are they under a spell?"

I nodded. "Aunt Tillie thought it would be funny to give them a taste of their own medicine," I explained. "She made them drunk without having to drink."

"They were really happy when it first started," Twila supplied. "Clove still seems happy. Thistle is … Thistle. Bay, though, she's getting the bad part of the spell early. I'm not sure why."

"It's because Terry yelled at her," I said. "She can't take it when he's angry with her, so it tipped her over the edge early."

"I don't understand," Terry said. "Why is Bay upset and the other two aren't?"

"The spell was designed to make them drunk and lower their inhibitions," I explained. "That's why they want to go skinny-dipping. Aunt Tillie has been taping them so she can hold the footage over their heads for years to come."

"I'm going to upload it to YouTube," Aunt Tillie said. "It's this thing on the Internet where you can put embarrassing videos. Not porn, though. I checked. It was a little disappointing."

"I know what it is," Terry snapped. "What's the deal with the spell going wrong?"

"Well, as I'm sure you know, many people are happy when drunk," I replied. "A lot of people cry when they're drunk, though. That's what will happen to all of them eventually. They'll be wailing and crying messes."

"Like Bay," Terry prodded.

I nodded.

"I'm a bad person," Bay said, her face streaked with tears as she finally lifted it. "I'm a terrible person."

"No, you're not," Terry said, resting his hand on her shoulder. "I'm sorry I yelled at you. I didn't understand what was going on. You're a good person. It's your aunt who is evil." He scorched Aunt Tillie with a look. "You've had your fun. Lift the spell."

"Um ... no," Aunt Tillie said, shaking her head. "This is too delightful to give up."

"You're the only one having fun," I charged.

"I can live with that," Aunt Tillie said. "Did I mention I'm hungry? Who wants to make me a sandwich?"

"No one is making you a sandwich, you old bat," Thistle said, screwing her face into a nasty snarl. "Make your own sandwich!"

"What did you just say to me?" Aunt Tillie asked, knitting her eyebrows. "Did you just call me ... ?"

"An old bat," Thistle repeated. "That's what you are. Everyone knows it. They're all afraid to tell you, but I'm not. You're nasty and terrible ... like a bat!"

"I'm guessing Thistle is a mean drunk," Terry said, rubbing the back of his neck. "That figures."

"I don't need to take your lip," Thistle said, moving toward the stairway. "I'm going to bed. I don't want to see any of you again for the rest of the night."

"That sounds lovely," I said. "I think we'd all appreciate it if you went to bed."

Thistle flounced up the stairs as Bay continued to sob. I risked a glance at Clove and found her passed out. She was drooling, for crying out loud, but that was better than crying or screaming.

"You know she's probably going to climb out her window and head for the lake, right?" Terry asked.

"Crapsticks!"

"I'm on it," Twila said, hurrying up the stairs.

I turned on Aunt Tillie. "Take the spell off."

"No."

"Take it off or I'll never speak to you again," I said.

"That sounds like an incentive to keep the spell on," Aunt Tillie sniffed.

That was my breaking point. I couldn't take one more minute of this … responsibility. It was killing my soul.

"Fine! Leave the spell on," I shouted. "They're your responsibility now. I'm done. You did this, so you can clean up the mess."

"I don't want to clean up the mess," Aunt Tillie countered.

"That's not really my problem," I said, striding toward the stairs. "I'm going to my room to take a long bath and then go to bed. I don't care what the rest of you do. I'm officially on leave from this family. Have a nice night!"

Aunt Tillie's mouth dropped open as she watched me climb the stairs. I locked gazes with her, practically daring her to try to stop me. The last thing I heard was Terry taking care of Bay.

"Don't cry, sweetheart," he said. "Oh, Bay, please stop that. You know I can't take it when you cry. I'm not angry with you. I'm angry with Aunt Tillie. If you promise to stop crying you can see me yell at her."

I almost wanted to stay and watch that. Almost.

I WOKE up the next morning feeling surprisingly better. I knew exactly what I was going to do. I was going to let Winnie adopt Clove, and then join the circus. It was really the only option.

I made as little noise as possible as I descended the stairs. I figured everyone was still asleep, their adventures from the previous evening wearing them down. Instead, I found Twila serving the girls breakfast in the kitchen.

I watched for a moment, prepared to turn and run if they were still drunk. Twila caught sight of me too soon, though, and offered me an encouraging nod. "It's okay," she said. "They're back to normal."

"Well, back to normal for this family," Bay quipped. I was glad to see she appeared to be in good spirits, although her eyes were puffy.

"When did the curse lift?" I asked, rolling up my sleeves as I padded into the kitchen. "Was it before or after you went to sleep?"

"It was after I was asleep," Clove said. "Thanks for leaving me on the couch like that, by the way. My back is killing me."

"You're young. You'll bounce back."

"I was trying to climb out the window when the spell broke," Thistle supplied. "Then I was filled with rage and went looking for Aunt Tillie. Chief Terry made me go back to my room and think about better ways to control my temper."

"Did it work?"

"It put me to sleep in the middle of the afternoon, and I didn't wake up until this morning," Thistle replied. "It worked for that."

"Uh-huh. And what about you, Bay?" I asked. "How are you feeling?"

"I'm fine," Bay said, averting her eyes.

"You know Terry doesn't blame you for what happened yesterday, right?" I said. "He's not angry."

"I think she's embarrassed," Clove said. "She doesn't want to talk about it, though."

"Then we probably shouldn't talk about it," I said. "What about everything else? Where do we stand on the party preparations?" I thought a return to some semblance of normality was in order. No one wanted to dwell on yesterday's hijinks.

"I got the bread finished and did most of the cookies," Twila said. "We still have to bake the pies today, and someone needs to run to the market to get the rest of the stuff. We have a list, and it's a big one."

"That's not too bad," I said. "How do you want to tackle things?"

Twila glanced at each of the girls in turn. "Why don't you guys tell her how we're going to handle stuff?" she suggested.

"I'm going to the clearing to talk to Constance," Bay offered. "I hope she'll be able to lead me to her body. I'm not getting too close – so don't expect that – but I hope she'll move on when we find her body, and then we can tell Chief Terry where to find her."

"What if she won't talk to you?"

Bay shrugged. "I can't force her to talk to me, but if I'm patient and sit there she might come to me," she said. "I can only do what I can do."

"You sound like your mother."

"That's the meanest thing you've ever said to me," Bay said, making a face.

I couldn't help but chuckle. "Thank you for handling the ghost," I said. "I know it's not your favorite thing to do, but with everyone arriving tomorrow we have a lot to deal with. The ghost is at the top of the list. If you run into trouble … ." What? Who was supposed to help her?

"I'll figure something out," Bay finished. "I know Aunt Tillie won't help."

"I'm almost afraid to ask about Aunt Tillie," I said. "Where is she?"

"After Terry forced her to lift the curse, she took off, swearing she was leaving the family and joining the circus," Twila answered. "She's probably in her room … or out in the garden. She'll be fine."

"Okay, that's good," I said. "What about Clove and Thistle? What are you two doing today?"

"We're doing the shopping," Clove announced. "Twila thought it would be good for us."

"Yes, and we're really excited about it," Thistle deadpanned.

"Well, while you're in town, you should also stop by the police station and apologize to Terry," I said. "You said some really mean things to him last night."

Thistle's cheeks flushed with color. "I will."

Wow! If she wasn't putting up an argument she must know she was wrong. That was a first.

"Well, I guess we have a plan for the day," I said. "Thistle, can you go to the linen closet and get that box of ritual materials and bring it to me?"

It was a test. Thistle is usually the least helpful of the girls. She didn't give me an ounce of lip, though, instead accepting the key in my hand before getting to her feet and leaving the kitchen. I was really impressed. "She must feel pretty awful about the things she said last night."

"I think she's embarrassed and processing," Twila replied. "She feels bad about what she said to Terry. She knows he didn't deserve it. She doesn't feel bad about what she said to Aunt Tillie, though. I'm not sure she'll apologize for that."

"Probably not," I said, turning to the stove to dish up some breakfast. "If we all stay on task, we should be able to get everything ready in time. Winnie returns first thing tomorrow morning. We still have a shot at pulling this off without her finding out what a disaster everything has been."

Bay snorted. "She'll know. She always knows."

Unfortunately, she was right. "I'm not giving up hope," I said. "I … ." I lost my train of thought when Thistle reappeared in the doorway. Her face told me things were not as pleasant in the Winchester world as I thought this morning. "What's wrong now?"

"That box isn't in the linen closet," Thistle said. "It's gone."

Crapsticks! How did that happen? The universe must hate me. There can be no other explanation.

SEVEN

"What do you mean the box isn't in the closet?" I asked, my heart rolling. "I put it there yesterday."

"It's not there," Thistle said, shrugging. "There's only one linen closet, and the spot on the floor is empty. There aren't any other boxes in there."

"I just . . . ." I broke off, pursing my lips. "Aunt Tillie. She had to take it. The girls were drunk yesterday, so it couldn't have been them. That leaves only Aunt Tillie."

"She's our only option," Twila agreed. "Where would she take it?"

"More importantly, why does she want it?" I corrected. "It has to be in the house somewhere. My guess is she has it in the basement. That's the only place she would dare keep it in case it rains or something. The elements could ruin that stuff."

"What should we do?" Twila asked, rubbing her thumb over her bottom lip. I could practically smell the smoke from the gears grinding in her head. What? That's not mean. I love my sister. It will take forever if I let her figure this out, though.

"Okay, new plan," I said, clapping my hands together. "Bay, you go to the clearing and talk to Constance. Find her body if you can, but don't look at it. It's important."

Bay nodded.

"Twila, you're taking over shopping duties," I said. "It was a nice thought, but I need Clove and Thistle to do something else. That means you're the only one who can do the shopping."

"What are you going to do?" Twila challenged.

"I'm going to supervise," I answered. "I am the boss, after all."

I caught the amused glances passing among the girls. I would deal with them later.

"What are you going to have Clove and Thistle do?" Twila asked, biding for time. No one wanted to do the shopping. It was a massive list. That's why we'd been putting it off.

"I'm going to have them search the basement for the box," I answered, not missing a beat.

Thistle and Clove gaped in horror at the suggestion.

"Are you crazy?" Thistle exploded. "That old lady will kill us if she catches us going through her stuff."

"Like horror movie kill," Clove interjected. "She'll rip our jaws off and leave us in the median of the road like in that movie with the serial killer who drove the big truck."

"You're never allowed to watch television with Thistle again," I snapped. "Aunt Tillie won't kill you. She's cantankerous and mean sometimes, but she won't kill you."

"That's true," Twila said sagely. "She's far more likely to curse you again. She won't kill you, though. If she killed you, she wouldn't be able to torture you. She gets bored easily."

"I don't want to be cursed again," Thistle huffed, crossing her arms over her chest. "I don't like it."

"No one does."

"I kind of liked it," Clove said. "I still want those shoes."

She was my daughter and I adored her. I still wanted to smack her sometimes. Thankfully, child abuse is frowned upon in civilized circles. I don't want to draw attention to myself. "You can worry about the shoes later," I said. "You guys have to go downstairs and find that box. When you do, don't touch it. Come up and get me. I'll handle Aunt Tillie when it comes time to reclaim the supplies."

"Is anyone else worried she's concocting a really horrible spell that's going to turn us all into toads or something?" Bay asked.

"I'm more worried she's replacing ingredients with other things so we'll inadvertently cast our own bad spell," I said. That sounded just like her. "She had to know I would discover the box was gone. That means she planned to put it back before she thought I'd look in the closet."

"She's conspicuously absent from breakfast, too," Twila mused. "That can't be a coincidence."

"No," I agreed.

"What happens if she's down there when we go looking?" Thistle asked. "She'll know we're up to something."

"She has a sick sense," Clove said.

"Sixth," I automatically corrected.

"No, it's sick," Thistle said. "She'll know we're up to mischief if she sees us. Heck, she thinks we're up to stuff when we're really not. It's rare, but it does happen."

She had a point. I tapped my chin as I internally debated a solution. "Tell her you're gathering those canvas chairs for the ritual site," I suggested. "They're stacked in the far corner down there. Bring one chair up here at a time. That will allow you to search every nook and cranny without calling attention to yourselves."

Bay barked out a coarse laugh, causing me to scorch her with a look. "And I thought I had the worst job."

"Speaking of your job, you need to get moving," I prodded. "We all have tasks to do. Let's do them together."

Twila sidled toward me and lowered her voice. "Don't think I haven't noticed that you've conveniently given yourself the easiest job," she said. "I won't forget this."

"It's purely out of necessity," I lied. "Someone has to man things in the kitchen. I would be more than happy to do the shopping if you want to stay here and deal with the Aunt Tillie fallout should she realize the girls are snooping through her stuff. It's entirely up to you."

I didn't miss Twila's noticeable gulp.

"I'll do the shopping," she grumbled.

"I thought you would."

"You really know how to win an argument, don't you?" Twila said.

"It's taken years of practice, but yes," I confirmed. "Now, come on! We have a solstice celebration to save."

Bay and Thistle exchanged a dubious look.

"I was more excited that year we saved Christmas," Bay intoned.

"You and me both," Thistle said.

I waved my finger in the direction of the basement. "Go!"

MY HEART RATE was unnaturally high as I set about peeling apples for pies. Clove and Thistle made a seemingly endless series of trips into the basement, each one more nerve-wracking than the next. The basement appeared empty, but no one was taking any chances. If the basement was truly vacant, though, that prompted a terrifying worry: Where was Aunt Tillie hiding?

I lost track of time between trips, and before I realized what was happening I had six apple pies ready to go in the oven and two blackberry pies ready for fruit stuffing. That's when Thistle and Clove brought the last round of chairs to the main floor.

"We didn't see anything," Thistle announced. "If she has something down there, she's doing a good job of hiding it."

That's exactly what I feared. "Look again."

"You look again," Thistle shot back. "We're not going back down there. No way. No how. Nothing doing."

"Have I ever told you what a joy you are?" I asked.

Thistle shrugged, unperturbed. "Have I ever told you that forcing us to perform tasks that will get us cursed is mean and cowardly?"

I scowled. Thistle was the best button pusher in the business, no doubt about it. "Go back down there," I ordered. "If Aunt Tillie was down there, you would've seen her by now. That means she's out of the house. This could be our only shot."

"Why don't you just demand she show you where the box is?" Thistle countered. "You're in charge, right? She should have to listen to you."

"Give me a break," I snapped. "We both know that's not going to happen."

"We also both know that Aunt Tillie will do something horrible to us if she catches us going through her stuff," Thistle said. "I'm not going to do it." She crossed her arms over her chest for emphasis.

I turned my eyes to Clove. "You do it."

"I don't like it down there," Clove whined. "It's dark and scary. I think there are monsters hiding under the stairs. I saw a movie once where people were hiding under the stairs. They kind of looked like monsters, but they were nice. I think we have monsters, though, and I don't want to meet them."

"You're banned from television for the rest of your life," I snapped. "You both need to go down there and find that box. It's important."

"No," Thistle said, shaking her head. "I'm putting my foot down."

I was going to put my foot somewhere, and she wasn't going to like it. I sucked in a breath to calm myself, and then approached Clove and Thistle from a different tack. "I'll give you twenty bucks if you go down there and find that box."

Clove looked intrigued. "Each?"

I internally sighed. "Yes."

"Make it thirty and you're on," Thistle countered.

"Twenty."

"Thirty or it's no deal, and you can find the box yourself," Thistle shot back. "I'm not risking myself for anything less than thirty dollars."

"Fine," I muttered, resigned. "If you find that box I'll give you each thirty dollars."

"Great," Thistle said, gracing me with a bright smile, more evil than sweet. "It's a pleasure doing business with you."

"You just extorted your favorite aunt," I reminded her. "You might not want to look so smug when you take that into consideration."

Thistle shrugged, unbothered. "It's a capitalistic society, my friend," she said. "You have to play to win if you want to be let in the game."

"You watch too much television, too," I said. "Find that box." I wiped my hands on a dishtowel and moved toward the rear door. "I'll be back in a few minutes to start putting pies in the oven. If you find the box, hide it someplace up here where Aunt Tillie can't find it."

"You told us not to touch it," Clove protested.

"That's when I thought Aunt Tillie was in the basement," I said. "She's not. Bring it upstairs and hide it."

"What are you going to do?" Thistle asked.

"I have to check on Bay," I said. "Believe it or not, despite the theatrics from you two she actually has the suckiest job today."

"Yeah, we'll compare sucky jobs when the curses start landing," Thistle said. "Thirty bucks had better be enough to cover new pants if it becomes necessary."

"Just ... go!"

I FOUND Bay sitting in the middle of the clearing, her legs bent and her elbows resting on her knees. She looked forlorn.

"What's going on?" I asked, approaching her slowly. I scanned the clearing for a sign of whatever it was she studied, even though I knew there was no way I could see Constance's ghost. "Is she here?"

"She's here," Bay confirmed. "She's ... very confused."

"What do you mean?" I asked, flipping my fingers through Bay's flaxen hair to smooth it. "Is she having trouble accepting she's dead? She wasn't murdered, was she? It's going to be a pain if the cops are up here traipsing around and ruining the atmosphere for the solstice celebration."

"Yes, that's exactly what I was worrying about, too," Bay deadpanned, rolling her eyes. "I don't mean that she doesn't seem to accept that she's dead – although that may be true – I can't be sure. I mean she doesn't seem to know who she is."

I knit my eyebrows, confused. "How does that work?"

"I have no idea," Bay said. "She's been talking to me and stuff, but she kind of ... fades in and out. One moment she seems fine, although she keeps calling me Winnie. That's insulting. I look nothing like my mother."

"You look no more like your mother than Clove looks like me," I said.

"Oh, gross," Bay said, wrinkling her nose. Clove is an exact miniature of me, so I knew exactly where Bay's mind headed. "That's a depressing cherry on the top of an otherwise sucky day."

"Everyone thinks this is a sucky day," I said. "Tell me what's going on with Constance. I can't help if I don't know all the facts."

"She knows she's Constance sometimes," Bay explained. "Well, she knew she was Constance once. The rest of the time she keeps asking who she is. I told her and she kind of remembered, but then she forgot again."

"Hmm." I rolled Bay's words through my mind. "Terry said that Constance's daughter was worried because her mother had been acting strange. I wonder if she had a form of dementia."

"Do people with dementia know it when they have it?"

"That's a good question," I said. "I honestly don't know. My gut instinct is probably no, though. When your mind slips like that, you probably believe whatever reality confronts you."

"That's sad."

"It is sad, Bay," I agreed. "Does Constance know where her body is? It has to be around here somewhere. It has to be close. If she's as confused as you say she is, I don't think she's wandering. She stayed here, after all. I think that means she died close to this spot."

"That's sad, too."

"Why do you say that?" I wasn't arguing the fact that it was sad, but questioning the reason Bay thought it was sad. She's a melancholy little thing sometimes. It can get old pretty quickly.

"That means she died out here alone and probably didn't know who she was when it happened," Bay answered. "She could've fallen and hit her head … or twisted her ankle. Imagine how frightened she was when she died."

Sometimes I forget Bay has reason to be melancholy. She sees hard things that the rest of us don't have to deal with. "I think we should probably call Terry," I said. "He's going to have to get people out here looking for her. I'm not sure what to tell him, though."

"He knows I can see ghosts," Bay said. "I talked to his mother. She gave me a message for him."

"I know, and Terry would never turn on you," I said. "But how is he going to get a search party out here without telling them why we suspect Constance's body is near?"

"Maybe he should come alone first," Bay suggested. "He might have a better idea where to look for the body. Then he can say we found it, and call the ambulance people to get her."

"That's a good idea," I said, digging into my pocket for my cell phone. When Winnie suggested everyone get them, I thought it was a stupid idea. Now I couldn't imagine not having it – especially given this family's antics. "I'll have him come straight out here and then leave you two alone. If you get scared ... or if you find a body ... you can come right home. Terry won't expect you to stay. You don't need to see it."

"I'll stay," Bay said. "Constance needs someone to watch her until ... you know."

"I do know," I said. What I didn't say was how worried I was about Constance's ghostly future. If the woman couldn't remember who she was, or that she was dead for more than a few moments, how could she move on?

EIGHT

"What's going on?"

Terry's face was a mask of concern when he joined us in the clearing twenty minutes later.

"We have a problem," I said, helping Bay to her feet. "We should've told you sooner, but things have been really crazy. That's not an excuse, though. I'm sorry."

"Apologizing before you tell me what's wrong is a surefire way to get my hackles up," Terry said, running his hand over the top of Bay's head. He could read the stiff set of her shoulders and the sad look on her face. While I would prefer Terry favored Clove over the other girls – hey, she is my daughter, after all – I knew Bay needed him more. That's why Terry gravitated toward her. "Tell me what's wrong and we'll fix it."

"The other day – the day you stopped by to ask us about Constance Warren going missing, in fact – we came to this spot to clean it for our … picnic," I started.

"I know you guys aren't picnicking out here," Terry said, using air quotes for emphasis. "I don't want to know what you're doing out here, especially after finding out it will more than likely involve nudity, so I thank you for calling it that. Just tell me what's going on. You're starting to worry me."

"Bay saw something that day," I said.

"What?"

"Constance's ghost," I answered.

"Oh, man," Terry said, letting loose with a disgusted sigh and leaning his head down as he rubbed the back of his neck. He studied his feet for a moment and then shifted his gaze to Bay. "Do you know how she died?"

Bay shook her head. "She's ... confused."

"Is that normal for ... that type of person?" Terry asked, exhaling heavily. "I'm sorry. I don't like talking about this stuff. It's easier to pretend it isn't real."

"Well, we'd like you to get back to your fantasy world as soon as possible," I supplied. "Bay says Constance can't remember her name sometimes, has confused her for Winnie a time or two and doesn't seem to understand anything about death or why she would be out here."

"I guess that's not normal," Terry pressed.

Bay shook her head. "Most ghosts know they're dead," she answered. "It takes a little while for some of them to comprehend and accept it, but most of them know it whether they want to admit it or not. They stay behind because they want revenge for someone killing them ... or they want their body found. They generally have a reason."

"Why do you think Constance is here?"

"Because she doesn't know how to ask for what she needs," Bay replied.

"Okay," Terry said, placing his hand on her shoulder. "I guess you think her body is around here. Am I right?"

Bay nodded. "She's been here for days, which means she isn't wandering," she explained. "She's confused, so she probably doesn't know how to wander. I guess she's on an endless loop. She remembers where and who she is for brief periods and then she ... whatever ... she's trapped."

"Constance's daughter made it sound as if her mother's mind was slipping," Terry supplied. "I thought that was just normal mother and daughter stuff – like when Thistle says Twila is losing it – but now I'm starting to wonder whether something else was going on."

"She might've had dementia or early onset Alzheimer's disease," I suggested. "Constance was in her late fifties, so she seems young for that, but I've read about other cases in which it began at a young age."

"That's definitely possible," Terry said. "Okay, I'm going to take a look around. Just for my own edification, though, I'm not risking running into any naked people out here, right?"

The question was enough to draw a genuine smile from Bay.

"No," I said, chuckling. "The guests don't arrive until tomorrow afternoon. You're safe until then."

"Good to know."

"But Aunt Tillie is missing and could be out here for all we know," Bay said, an impish grin playing at the corner of her lips. "You definitely don't want to see that."

"You're such a comedian," Terry said, pinching Bay's cheek and giving it a good jiggle. "Why don't you go back to the house with Marnie? You don't need to stay out here for this."

Bay pressed her lips together and considered the offer, ultimately shaking her head when she made her decision. "Constance needs someone who can see her," she said. "I won't go close to the body, but maybe she'll be lucid for a minute and show us where her body is. She can't tell her story if there's no one here to hear it."

"You're very wise, young lady," Terry said. "Stay close to me and don't investigate anything on your own. If you think you see something, you point it out to me and then hang back until I check it out. Agreed?"

Bay nodded.

"I'm going to leave you to it then," I said. "I have pies that need to go in the oven, and I sent Thistle and Clove on a mission before I left. Hopefully they'll have what I'm looking for when I get back."

"Do I even want to know what that means?" Terry asked.

"Nope."

THE KITCHEN WAS quiet when I returned to the house. I poked my head through the open door that led to the basement and listened, but heard nothing. I hoped that meant Clove and Thistle were upstairs hiding the prized box of ritual goodies. In the wrong hands – and, yes, Aunt Tillie's are an example of the wrong hands – the supplies could do a lot of damage.

I set the oven to preheat before leaving, so I shoved four of the pies onto the hot racks and set the timer before moving to the counter to start filling the blackberry pies. I was lost in my own world, niggling worry about Bay and anticipation for Aunt Tillie's meltdown when she realized the supplies were gone warring for top billing in my mind. I was so lost in thought it took me a moment to register the banging noise coming from the stairway in the living room.

I frowned and waited. If Clove and Thistle were up to something they would make their presence known sooner, rather than later. I was almost content to return to my baking when I heard the banging a second time.

"What in the world?" I muttered, wiping my hands on my apron and running into the living room. "What's going on? Why are you making that racket?"

Clove and Thistle stood in the middle of the stairway, both gripping the railing intensely.

"Mom?" Clove sounded terrified.

"Of course it's me," I said, furrowing my brow as I moved closer. "Are you two playing a game? I'm not upping your pay. You get thirty bucks each. A deal is a deal."

"Mom, is that really you?" Clove asked, her voice cracking. That's when I realized that even though her eyes looked in my direction, she wasn't focusing on me.

"It's me," I said. "I just told you that. What's going on? Did you find the box?"

"Are you kidding me?" Thistle spat, flailing about as she attempted to keep her balance on the step. "Forget the stupid box! We have much bigger problems."

"Such as?"

"We're blind, you idiot!" Thistle shrieked, her tone shrill enough to cause Clove to burst into tears.

"What do you mean … you're blind?" I understood the words, yet had trouble comprehending the reality.

"We can't see," Thistle said, waving her hand in front of her face. "Nothing. Nada. It's all black in here."

"But … how?"

"How do you think?" Thistle snapped. "Aunt Tillie knows we found her box and she cursed us. You know how she feels about thieves. She thinks they should have their hands cut off and their eyes gouged out. This is the closest she could get to eye gouging without permanently maiming us."

That couldn't be right, could it? Aunt Tillie would never … . Oh, who am I kidding? I can't even finish that statement. "Okay," I said, hurrying toward the girls. "I'm coming to get you. Clove, stay right there. I'll help Thistle down the stairs first. Then I'll sit you on the couch and everything will be fine."

"Yes, everything will be peachy," Thistle said, sarcasm practically dripping from her tongue. "This is so not worth thirty bucks."

After a minor bit of grappling – and a heck of a lot of swearing that I pretended I didn't hear – I situated Thistle on the couch before retrieving Clove. My own daughter maintained she didn't trust me to help her down the stairs without cracking her head open, so she insisted on sitting on the steps and inching her way down herself. By the time I had them both settled, the timer in the kitchen went off and I had to save the pies before they burned.

When I returned to the living room, Thistle was plotting Aunt Tillie's demise.

"I'm going to sneak into her room when she's sleeping," she said. "I'm going to do it on a night when I know she's had wine so she won't wake up. She'll be snoring like the dickens, and then I'll put a pillow over her face and lay on it until she stops fighting. Then I'll lay on it another few minutes, because she's the type who would play dead to save herself."

"I'm just going to cry," Clove said. "That's what I feel like doing now. If I cry, will you make fun of me?"

Thistle hated crying. "Yes."

"Okay. I guess I won't do it then," Clove said, although I could hear the sniffle from here.

"Girls, everything is going to be fine," I announced as I walked into the room, cringing when both of them jolted at the sound of my voice. They really were helpless. "I'll find Aunt Tillie. You just sit here and don't move. I don't want you to hurt yourselves."

"I'm going to hurt that old lady," Thistle snapped. "She needs me to hurt her. She wants it. That's why she did this. There can be no other explanation."

I understood the inclination to attach reasons to Aunt Tillie's deeds, although they almost never proved true. Aunt Tillie simply does what she wants to do whenever the mood strikes. She has no boundaries, and there are times I think she never had a moral compass. If she hadn't taken us in after the death of our mother – and truly loved us for years – I'd consider embracing the fact that she has no redeeming qualities. Every time I think that, though, she surprises me.

One year she saved Christmas. Another year she took Bay trick or treating because the other kids were making fun of her. Funnily enough, all those kids ended up with fifty toothbrushes in their bags while Bay could barely carry her candy home. Six months ago Aunt Tillie taught Thistle how to cut the crotch out of her sworn enemy's pants in the gym locker room without even touching the clothing so she couldn't be blamed. Okay, that last one wasn't great for mankind, but it made Thistle happy.

What she did this time, though, is beyond words.

"I'll find her and make her reverse the spell," I said. "She'll do it because I won't give her a choice. I promise this is temporary."

"There's a chance it's not temporary?" Clove was bordering on panic.

"I'll handle it," I said. "I … huh."

"Now what?" Thistle snapped.

"I hope Aunt Tillie didn't curse Bay, too," I said.

"Yes, because poor Bay is too good to be cursed and we're not," Thistle hissed. "Bay, Bay, Bay. Everyone loves Bay!"

"It's not that, mouthy. It's just that Bay is still in the woods," I said. "Terry is with her, but if she was heading back to the house on her own … ." Crapsticks! "I'll be right back. Don't move."

"We couldn't if we wanted to," Thistle called to my back. "You're probably going to want to hurry up. I had three glasses of juice for breakfast and my bladder is going to start calling soon."

Well, great. As if I didn't have enough to worry about.

IT FELT as if it took me forever to find Bay and Terry. When I did, Bay was leaning against a tree and Terry was standing about twenty feet away, talking on his phone. He didn't look happy.

"Are you okay?" I asked, racing to Bay and searching her face. "You're not blind, are you?"

"What?" Bay was dumbfounded.

Terry disconnected his phone and shoved it in his pocket, fixing me with a questioning look. "Why are you so worked up? Why would Bay be blind? I didn't let her stare at the body, if that's what you're worried about."

"Aunt Tillie cursed Thistle and Clove, and now they're blind," I answered. "Wait … you found Constance's body? That's good, right?"

"Not for Constance," Bay said.

"Bay, I'm living on the edge right now," I said. "I can't take much more. I'm at my limit. You probably want to tread carefully right about now."

Bay had the grace to look abashed. "I'm sorry."

"Don't take whatever nonsense is happening back at that house out on her," Terry ordered. "She's had it bad enough."

Crapsticks! Now what? "She didn't see the body, did she? If she saw the body Winnie will never let me live this down. She'll never put me in charge again either. That means Twila will be in charge. Do you know how awful that will be?"

Terry's expression softened, but only marginally. "Bay spotted Constance's shoe and pointed it out to me," he said. "She didn't see more than that."

"Do you know how Constance died?" I asked. "I mean … was it hard?"

"I don't think it was easy," Terry said, choosing his words carefully. He made a point of not lying to the girls unless he thought it was in their best interests. He looked torn regarding what was best for Bay given the realities of her world. "I don't think she suffered long. It looks as if she fell down a little ravine and couldn't get out."

"How did she die, though?"

"I can't be sure, but I think she probably just went to sleep and didn't wake up during the night on the day she disappeared," Terry answered. "The coroner will have to answer that question. He's on his way."

"Okay," I said. "I have to get back to the house and find Aunt Tillie. She's hiding. Clove and Thistle are helpless as long as they're blind. Can I take Bay back with me to watch them?"

Terry nodded. "I think that's a good idea," he said. "Bay doesn't need to be around for what happens next."

"Cool," Bay said. "Does that mean I get to be in charge of Thistle and Clove? I mean … they are helpless, after all."

Of course her mind would jump there. She has a tiny bit of control freak in her. She gets it from her mother. "Sure," I said.

"Yay!"

"That also means you have to help them when they need to go to the bathroom," I added.

Bay's face fell. "Gross!"

"Responsibility comes with hardship," I said, turning back to the house. "Now, come on. If this day goes any further off the rails I'll need to find an entirely new train to hitch my caboose to."

NINE

"Are you guys still alive?"

I led Bay into the living room and frowned when I saw Clove curled up in a ball on the floor.

"What's your deal?" Bay asked, nudging Clove with her foot. "Are you pretending you're dead?"

"Can you see?" Thistle asked, shifting at the sound of Bay's voice. She was lounging on the couch and any outsider would think she didn't have a care in the world. I wasn't an outsider.

"I can see," Bay said, although she didn't look happy with the development now that she was in a room with her recently blinded cousins. "What's it like?"

"It's like staring into nothing," Thistle said. "So it's like staring into your head for asking that question … or like staring into Aunt Tillie's soul."

"What soul?" Clove asked, refusing to uncurl. "She has no soul. For a second, when I lost my sight, I thought the world ended. I thought I was dead and went to a bad place."

"You're not going to a bad place," I chided. Why do teenagers have to be so dramatic? Is it a law or something? "You'll be fine as soon as I find Aunt Tillie."

"I bet she got the idea from *Little House on the Prairie*," Bay mused. "She's been watching that on the Hallmark Channel. She said that Mary deserved to go blind because she was such a do-gooder. Oh, and she whined a lot, too."

"Well, that's just great," I said. "I'm glad to know she's watching something besides trash on television. Clove is convinced monsters live under the stairs in the basement. At least *Little House on the Prairie* has good family values."

"Because they don't have sex before marriage?" Bay asked.

"Yes. This should be a lesson to all of you. No sex before marriage."

"Why would we possibly want to learn that lesson?" Thistle asked. "We're already blind. Sex is all we have."

"I'm going to fix the blind thing," I snapped. "In fact … ." I didn't get a chance to finish because Twila picked that moment to walk through the front door, her arms laden with shopping bags.

"Well, I'm never doing that again," Twila announced. "I had the worst day ever."

"I bet I can top you," I said dryly.

"It's not possible," Twila said. "I got stuck in line behind a woman with twenty coupons and all of them were expired. She argued with the clerk about each and every one. Then she didn't start filling out her check until the very end, when she could've filled it out and just waited for the amount to finish it off. You know how I hate that. It was horrible."

"That's sounds horrible," I said, earning a raised eyebrow from Bay. "Do you want to know what I've been dealing with?"

"Not until all the groceries are in the house," Twila said. "Girls, go out to my car and empty the trunk and backseat. Take everything into the kitchen and put it away."

"We can't do that," Thistle said. "We're invalids now."

"That's nice," Twila said. "Hurry up, girls. I'm not joking."

"They can't get the groceries," I argued. "It's impossible. You'll have to get the groceries."

"Why can't they get the groceries?"

"Because we're blind," Clove wailed.

"Oh," Twila said, glancing around. "Aunt Tillie?"

"No, they randomly caught blindness," I deadpanned. "Of course it was Aunt Tillie. They found the box of magical supplies and brought it upstairs. When they were coming back down she paid them back and stranded them on the staircase."

"Well, get her out here and make her reverse the spell," Twila said. "I need help with the groceries."

"Why didn't I think of that?"

Twila shrugged, as if it wasn't a rhetorical question. "I don't know. Why didn't you think of it?"

"Because I can't find her, you nimrod," I snapped. "I've been baking pies, dealing with blind people, getting extorted to find a box, checking on Bay, calling Terry and dealing with a dead body on the property. Tell me about the freaking coupons again. Please!"

Twila's mouth dropped open. "Who extorted you?"

"You're just unbelievable," I hissed. "You need to get the groceries yourself. I'm sorry. That's just the way of the world today."

"What about Bay? She can help. She doesn't look blind. Why aren't you blind?"

"Because Bay is everyone's favorite," Thistle sneered.

"That's not why," I scoffed. "Bay was with Terry looking for Constance's body when these two pinched the box Aunt Tillie stole from us. Bay got out of punishment because she technically wasn't involved with the theft."

"Oh, well, that makes sense," Twila said. "I bet she got the idea from *Little House on the Prairie*. She really hates Mary."

"Is that important right now?" I snapped.

"I really don't like your attitude," Twila said.

"I will kill you if you don't shut up right this second!"

"Hey, I hate to interrupt this screamfest, but the coroner's van is out front and he's on the property," Terry said, appearing in the doorway between the living room and kitchen. He obviously entered through the rear door. "Does anyone want to tell me what's going on?"

"We're living in *Little House on the Prairie*," Clove answered.

"Okay," Terry said, not missing a beat. "Is there a reason you're on the floor?"

"I'll have less distance to travel when I trip over my own feet and fall to my death."

"That sounds very practical, Clove," Terry said. "You keep … doing what you're doing. How about you, Thistle? How are you feeling?"

"Evil."

"So … normal?"

Thistle scowled. "I need to apologize to you for saying those horrible things last night, but I can't if you're going to make fun of me."

"Hold on to the apology," Terry instructed. "I'm nowhere near done making fun of you yet."

Bay giggled, earning a murderous look from Thistle. Well, kind of. Thistle couldn't quite figure out where Bay was so she was actually glaring at empty space. It was close enough, though.

"I'm going to make you eat so much dirt when I get my sight back you're going to choke," Thistle warned.

"Leave Bay alone," I said. "She's been dealing with her own curse today. Her day hasn't been easy."

"You found Constance's body?" Twila asked. "How did she die?"

"We're still figuring that out," Terry answered. "If I had to guess, though, she fell into the ravine and injured herself. She was too weak to get out and … passed away in her sleep."

"He's only saying that to make me feel better," Bay said. "Constance is confused and doesn't know who she is most of the time."

"We think she had dementia," I supplied.

"That's awful," Twila said. "So, who's going to help me with the groceries?" Sometimes she has a one-track mind – and that's being very generous, because that one track gets stuck on repeat a lot.

"No one is helping you," I said. "Do it yourself. I need Bay to watch Clove and Thistle while I find Aunt Tillie. I can only deal with one crisis at a time."

"Aunt Tillie is on the back patio," Terry said. "She was drinking a glass of lemonade and had a big smile on her face when I let myself in.

If I had to guess, she knows exactly what's going on in this room and she's enjoying herself."

"That sounds just about right," I said, shaking my head. "Okay, I'm going to deal with Aunt Tillie. Bay, you watch Clove and Thistle. Twila, shut up and get the groceries. There! See! I'm in charge and things are going to work out just fine."

"And people say I'm delusional," Twila said, turning on her heel and stomping out the door.

"Come on, Terry," I said, grabbing his arm. "I might need you to be firm with Aunt Tillie again. We cannot have these girls wandering around blind with the coroner here. How will we explain that?"

"How do you explain any of the things you do?" Terry grumbled, although he followed me out of the living room and through the kitchen. He glanced longingly at the pies cooling on the counter as we passed. "You can have a pie if you help me," I offered.

"Sold."

Aunt Tillie didn't bother looking up when we joined her on the patio. "It's a beautiful day, isn't it? The sun is shining. The birds are chirping. It makes me glad to be alive."

"That's great," I said. "I'm going to put all of my cards on the table here because I'm about to lose it. I know you don't care about my mental health, and you're probably getting a kick over the fifty heart attacks I almost had today. Things have to be settled, though."

"I'm listening."

"You need to remove the curse you put on Clove and Thistle right now," I said. "That's the first thing."

"No."

"You have to," I snapped. "They're helpless."

"They shouldn't have gone through my stuff," Aunt Tillie said, finally bestowing a hard look on me. "I happen to know you instructed them to go through my stuff. You should be thankful I didn't curse you, too. I'm waiting to dole out your punishment until after Winnie gets back. We need someone in charge and Twila ... well ... she's just not up to the task."

"Because I ordered the girls to retrieve the box of items you stole, I think we should call it a draw," I suggested.

"They were in the wrong. You don't touch other people's stuff."

"That's my stuff!"

"I didn't steal it from you," Aunt Tillie clarified. "I borrowed it. There's a difference."

"Well, I borrowed it back," I said. "You have to take the curse off those girls. They're miserable, and with the coroner and his people running around the property we cannot risk them asking questions about why two of our teenagers have suddenly been rendered blind. What don't you understand about that?"

"Why is the coroner here?" Aunt Tillie asked, blowing off my question.

"Because Constance Warren's body was found on the property," I answered. "She fell in a ravine and died."

"That's a crappy way to go," Aunt Tillie said. "That will teach her to cheat at cards, though. Karma is a bitch."

"That will be just about enough of that," Terry said, taking me by surprise with his fortitude. "It looks like Constance Warren had early onset Alzheimer's. She didn't want anyone to know. Her daughter said her spells weren't bad enough to warrant a nurse, but I think she was deluding herself. Constance was confused, and walked out of her house and wandered around long enough to end up here. That's not something to be happy about."

"You talked to Constance's daughter?" I asked. "When?"

"When I was waiting for the coroner to arrive," Terry replied. "Constance Warren might well have cheated at cards. She might not have realized she was doing it, though. You know darned well what you're doing."

"I didn't know about the Alzheimer's thing," Aunt Tillie said, lowering her voice. "That's awful. Did Constance suffer?"

"We can't be sure, but if she died of exposure or from a lingering injury that kept her from being able to get out of the ravine, well, I can promise you it wasn't quick. I told Bay it was because I don't want her blaming herself or having nightmares, but there are much easier ways to go than the way Constance did."

"I didn't curse Bay," Aunt Tillie pointed out. "I should get points for that. I didn't know what was going on."

"Well, now you do know," I said. "Take the curse off the girls. Those are my supplies and I know why you wanted them. You're not putting one over on me. I'm testing the contents in each of those baggies before we use it."

Aunt Tillie scowled. "You ruin all of my fun."

"I often feel that way about you," I said. "We're on a clock here, Aunt Tillie. You've been nothing but a distraction for days. You've been worse than the girls … combined. Enough is enough."

"You can't talk to me that way," Aunt Tillie chided. "I'm still your elder."

"Then act like it," I ordered. "Clove and Thistle are miserable and frightened. They don't deserve this. I ordered them to do what they did. Quite frankly, I'm exhausted. I haven't had a moment's peace since Winnie left. I thought being the boss was all fun and games. Boy, was I wrong.

"I am tired, Aunt Tillie," I continued. "I've had to deal with drunken girls … Twila's singing … more drunken girls … crying girls … Bay seeing ghosts … missing supplies … baking … Thistle's mouth … and your shenanigans. I'm exhausted. I can't take one more second of this."

"No one asked you to be a martyr," Aunt Tillie pointed out. "When you need help, all you have to do is ask."

"I am asking."

"I'll consider it," Aunt Tillie said. "Talk to me about Constance's ghost. Is she still hanging around?"

"Bay said she's confused and has no idea who or where she is at any given moment," I answered. "I don't know what to do about that. I don't know what to do about any of this. What I really need is a bottle of aspirin and my bed. I don't think I'm going to get that, though, am I?"

"You can have anything you set your mind to, my dear," Aunt Tillie countered. "You only have to know how to get what you want."

"Well, I want to take some aspirin and lay down for a few hours," I said. "Then I want to finish the pies. When I come back downstairs, I want my daughter to be able to see again and you to be on your best behavior. Do you understand?"

"There's no reason to get whiny," Aunt Tillie said. "I'll fix Clove and Thistle. I'll handle Constance, too."

I was surprised by the second offer. The first was a grudging one and I knew I would get that … well, at least eventually. The second one was almost shocking. "You're going to take care of Constance? Why?"

"Because, if I don't Bay will take it upon herself to deal with Constance and she'll lose days out here on what might be a losing proposition," Aunt Tillie replied. "I know you think I'm stubborn and mean, but I don't want Bay to needlessly suffer. I can fix this so she won't have to."

"That's very nice of you," Terry said, earning a small wink from Aunt Tillie.

"Wait, are you saying you want Thistle and Clove to suffer?" I asked.

"I want them to suffer when they earn it," Aunt Tillie replied. "I'll fix this for you because I don't want you to suffer. I'm still going to get those little nitwits back when I have time to think of a fitting punishment."

"That would be lovely," I said. "Now, if you'll excuse me, my head really is pounding."

"Don't worry about a thing," Aunt Tillie called to my back. "I have everything under control. You can trust me. I'm in charge now and things will be rolling right along in the next five minutes. I'm the boss."

Now that was a terrifying thought.

TEN

When I woke from my nap, something felt off. I couldn't put my finger on what it was right away. When I shifted toward the window I was surprised. I thought for certain I would sleep until late in the afternoon. I expected shadows peeking through the curtains. The sun was bright, though.

"What the … ?"

By the time I made it downstairs and found everyone in the kitchen I'd moved from curious to worried. The girls sat around the kitchen table, happily chatting away as Aunt Tillie regaled them with some story from a previous solstice celebration. Twila served food to everyone, and it took a few moments for the people at the table to register my arrival.

"Good morning," Twila said, pulling out a chair. "I made French toast for breakfast. How many slices do you want?"

Did she just say breakfast? That can't be right. "Why are you cooking them breakfast for dinner?"

"Um … ." Twila glanced at Aunt Tillie.

"Because it's morning," Aunt Tillie replied. "You slept for almost eighteen hours. Congratulations! You're a slug."

"Aunt Tillie," Twila hissed, slapping her arm. "Don't mess with her. She's had a long week."

Actually, the week felt endless. This wasn't right, though. I couldn't possibly have slept for eighteen hours. "I don't understand," I said, slowly moving to the table and lowering myself into a chair. "How did I sleep for eighteen hours?"

"I believe it was on a pillow," Aunt Tillie said. "It might have also been because I put a sleeping spell on you to make sure you got some rest. Quite frankly, you've been really testy, and we all agreed you needed sleep to recharge."

"But … omigod!" Realization washed over me. "We have so much to do! The guests will start arriving in a few hours. I didn't finish the pies. What happened with Constance? Ugh, when will Winnie get here?"

"Calm down," Twila chided, pouring coffee into my mug. "Everything is under control."

How could she possibly say that? "Everything is not under control," I snapped. "Everything is pretty far from under control. I … this is a disaster." I buried my face in the crook of my elbow. "I'll never live this down. Winnie will never leave town again."

"Everything is done," Thistle announced.

I sucked in a breath. "What did you just say?"

"Everything is done," Thistle repeated. "We did it all."

"But … how?"

"After you went upstairs yesterday, I had a talk with the girls," Twila said. "We realized after the fact that you've had far too much responsibility heaped on you over the past few days and it wasn't fair."

"Notice she's leaving me out of that equation," Aunt Tillie interjected. "I didn't think you had too much responsibility. I was outvoted, though."

"Since when do you let people outvote you?"

"Since I decided to be the better person in this family," Aunt Tillie replied.

Bay snorted. "Don't you mean since Chief Terry threatened to confiscate all of your wine and hold it in evidence at the police station if you didn't help instead of hinder this weekend?"

"No one likes a fresh mouth," Aunt Tillie warned, wagging her finger in Bay's direction. "That's not what happened at all."

"That's exactly what happened," Twila said, doling two slices of French toast onto a plate and sliding it in front of me. "We know you've been running yourself ragged to make sure everything is perfect. The thing is, nothing is ever perfect. You have to understand that."

"This is an important celebration," I reminded them. "We have to do things the right way or Winnie will be really upset."

"Do you want to know something?" Aunt Tillie prompted. "Winnie will be upset if everything is perfect. She wants to think she's the only one who does anything right around here – Goddess knows where she gets that – so she'll be more upset that we got everything finished than she would be if everything was in tatters when she arrives."

She had a point. Still … . "How did you guys get everything finished on time?"

"I handled the baking and cooking, with Thistle and Clove's help, of course," Twila supplied. "Once they got their sight back it took only thirty minutes to talk them off the ledge and get them in gear."

"I'm still going to make you pay," Thistle said, leaning closer to Aunt Tillie and locking gazes with her. "I'm going to be your worst nightmare."

"You're cute when you're full of it," Aunt Tillie said, patting her head and chuckling. "I look forward to our upcoming war."

"No wars until after all the guests leave Sunday night," Twila warned. "You two agreed yesterday. Don't forget that."

"We won't forget," Thistle said. "The second the last car leaves our driveway, though, bam! I'm going to crush you like a bug."

"Sometimes you really are my favorite," Aunt Tillie said. "You make me laugh. You should be a comedian."

"I'm not joking."

"I know you're not," Aunt Tillie said. "That's what makes it all the funnier."

"You're not going to be laughing when I win," Thistle said. "I will win someday. Just you wait. I have a feeling it's going to be Sunday."

I had a feeling this conversation was going to get out of hand if I didn't put a stop to it. "I think everyone is looking forward to your war," I said. "It's not until Sunday, though, so retreat to your neutral corners."

"Yes, ma'am," Thistle said, taking me by surprise with her term of respect.

"So the food is taken care of," I said. "What about the ritual site? We need to get all of those chairs out there."

"That's taken care of, too," Twila said. "Aunt Tillie did it."

I narrowed my eyes. The mere idea of my aunt carrying thirty chairs into the woods was laughable. "Really?"

"She made them fly," Clove said, giggling. "It was like being in *Fantasia*."

"You definitely watch too much television," I said, although I was happy she seemed so tickled with Aunt Tillie's solution. "No one saw, did they? How long were the cops and coroner out here?"

"They were here until it was almost dark," Twila answered. "Aunt Tillie waited until it was completely dark to move the chairs. She even gave the girls rides."

"It was great," Thistle enthused. "It was like being on a roller-coaster."

"I didn't like it," Bay said. She had a weak stomach when it came to fast rides. "I did like watching Aunt Tillie chase Thistle with five chairs all at once, though. She made them bark."

"Yeah, that was annoying," Thistle said, her face falling.

I was sorry I missed that. "What about Constance?"

"She's gone," Aunt Tillie said, averting her eyes. "She's passed on. She's at rest now."

"How did that happen?" I was genuinely curious.

"Aunt Tillie talked to her for a long time," Bay said. "She said I could go with her and see how it was done." That sounded about right. "She was really nice to Constance. She never lost her temper."

"That didn't work, though," Aunt Tillie added. "Finally I had to enlist the girls to help me cast a release spell."

"What's that?"

"Aunt Tillie had us call to the four corners with her and put Constance's mind back as it was supposed to be," Bay explained. "She knew who she was at the end. She thanked Aunt Tillie for what she did and even apologized for cheating at cards."

"It seems she was lucid for that," Twila said. "Aunt Tillie wanted to undo the spell when she found out, but we talked her out of it."

"What about Terry?" I asked. "Is he going to show up with questions about the body being found here?"

"He's already asked all of his questions," Bay replied. "He said the case is closed. Constance's body is already at the funeral parlor."

"He said the coroner took a brief look at Constance and said she died of a heart attack," Twila said. "He called us with the news last night because he didn't want us to worry. She probably went pretty quickly."

"She would've been scared, though," Bay said, her eyes darkening. "She was trapped in that ravine and had no idea who she was. Then she died all alone."

"It is sad, Bay," I agreed. "She's where she's supposed to be now, though. That's the important thing."

"She's happy, Bay," Aunt Tillie added. "She knows who she is and she's moved on. She didn't have much life left to live here anyway. Don't be sad. Be happy because Constance is happy. That's the way it should be."

Bay nodded.

"So everything is done?" I said, amazed. "I can't believe you all worked together to do this … for me."

"I don't know why you're surprised," Aunt Tillie said. "That's what a family does. We torture each other until the last possible second and then we band together. That's always the way it has worked in this family. That's the way it always will continue to work."

"Even after I beat Aunt Tillie on Sunday," Thistle said.

"Dream on, smart mouth," Aunt Tillie said, arching an eyebrow.

I opened my mouth to thank them, a hundred different ways to express myself on the tip of my tongue, but a car honking out front ruined the moment. That's what I'm telling myself, at least.

"Mom's home," Bay said, wiping her hands and pushing herself up from the table. "I hope she brought me something."

"Winnie's here," I said. "Winnie's here and everything is done and on schedule."

"Exactly," Aunt Tillie said, smiling.

"I'm the best boss ever. Don't you think?"

"Don't get a big head," Aunt Tillie chided. "No one likes it when a person gets a big head. In fact, it's really annoying."

"She should know," Thistle said, giggling as she evaded Aunt Tillie's swat and skipped toward the front of the house. "I'll see you Sunday, old lady."

"I'll be waiting with curses on," Aunt Tillie shot back.

THE SOLSTICE CELEBRATION WAS A HIT. I knew it would be. What? I did.

After a picnic full of laughter and funny stories on the back lawn – Thistle and Aunt Tillie entertaining everyone with their antics – we moved to the clearing for our annual ritual. Technically, the Winchester family performs multiple rituals every year, but this was a special one. We were calling on the four corners to bless everyone with luck and love. The solstice made us strong, and we were stronger as a group.

"So, it seems everything went okay," Winnie said, moving up to my side. "I have to say that I'm impressed."

"You didn't think I could pull it off, did you?" So far, no one had spilled the beans about any of the week's trouble. I wasn't holding my breath that would last, but I was hopeful I would get a few days to bask in it before I had to own up to all of the … um … problems. Let's face it, no one wants to explain drunken curses and blind girls. Oh, and that's on top of the ghost with dementia and whatever Aunt Tillie had planned for that box of spell supplies. Whew! I'm tired just thinking about it.

"It's not that," Winnie said. I could tell she was lying by the way she averted her gaze and fixed it on the revelers as they danced around the clearing. "I was merely worried that I gave you a lot of responsibility. Most people wouldn't be able to handle that much responsibility."

"Would you have been able to handle it?" It was a pointed question.

"I think it would have been a definite chore," Winnie said. She was always so diplomatic. It made me want to wrestle her down and fill her mouth with dirt. What? The girls didn't think that little gem up on their own.

"What you're saying is that you would've handled it better than I did," I prodded. "Admit it."

"I'm saying nothing of the sort."

Why didn't I believe her? Oh, that's right, I know her. Humble isn't in her wheelhouse. "You're very good at the responsibility thing, Winnie," I said, choosing my words carefully. "I don't envy all of the organizing you have to do. Things still came together like they were supposed to. You can't possibly be unhappy with the outcome."

"Who said I was unhappy?" Winnie was all faux innocence and light. She actually wanted me to believe she was hurt by my assumption.

"You would've been happier if things were in chaos and you had something to fix when you got home," I said. "It's okay. I know you and the way you think. I don't take it personally."

"That's not true at all," Winnie said, smiling when she saw Clove turning cartwheels. "The girls all look happy. I was definitely worried they would get into it with Aunt Tillie and make your life difficult."

"That's coming Sunday."

Winnie knit her eyebrows. "What's coming Sunday?"

"Thistle and Aunt Tillie are going to war the second everyone leaves," I explained. "I'm telling you now so you can prepare yourself."

"Why are they going to war?"

I shrugged. "I think they like it."

Winnie snorted. "And this in no way has to do with them getting drunk or stealing Aunt Tillie's pilfered supplies and her cursing them to go blind, right?"

I stilled, my heart hopping. "Who told you?"

Winnie pressed her lips together in an effort to keep from laughing. "I know all and see all," she said finally. "Haven't I already told you that?"

"But … they promised."

"Yes, but Terry didn't," Winnie said, putting me out of my misery. "I saw him in town when I stopped to pick up a few things before coming home. He gave me a real earful about curses … and ghosts … and dancing naked and setting a bad example for three impressionable teenagers."

"Of course," I muttered. "I can't believe he turned on me."

"He didn't turn on you," Winnie clarified. "He only wanted to make me aware that it was unfair to dump everything on you at such a busy time. If anything, he was standing up for you."

That made me feel a little bit better. "That's because he likes me best."

"We both know he stopped me to catch up because he likes me best," Winnie shot back. "Don't kid yourself. I'm his favorite."

"Neither one of you should kid yourselves, because I'm his favorite," Bay said, giggling as she appeared at my side. I messed her hair, smiling despite myself.

"I think you're right, Bay," I said. "You're definitely his favorite."

"Does that mean I get to be the boss?" Bay asked, her eyes sparkling.

"I think you're already the boss … of your particular trio," I replied.

"Oh, puh-leez," Bay said, rolling her eyes. "Thistle is the boss. We all know it. She's too mean to be anything other than in charge."

"You're probably right," Winnie said. "Are you having a good time?"

Bay nodded.

"Did you miss me?" Winnie pressed.

"Of course," Bay said. I couldn't tell whether she was lying. "Marnie took good care of us, though. You shouldn't be angry. Things got out of control and she made sure we were safe. Don't make fun of her."

"When do I ever make fun of her?" Winnie asked.

"Every single day." Bay shot me a winning smile.

"No one panic, but we have a problem," Thistle said, racing up to me.

Uh-oh. I was waiting for this to happen. "What's the problem?"

"I'll fix it," Winnie said, causing my stomach to twist. "Just tell me what it is and I'll fix it."

"You can't fix it," Clove said, trailing behind Thistle. "Only Aunt Tillie can fix it."

Well, this couldn't be good. "What's wrong?"

Thistle pointed toward the clearing where ten witches were stripping down to finish their dance.

"Oh," I said, laughing. "I see what the problem is."

"No, the problem is that in three minutes we're all going to see everything again," Thistle said. "We need Aunt Tillie."

"What do you think she's going to do for you?" Winnie asked. "She'll be naked within the hour as well."

"We know," Clove said. "We need her to take our sight again before it happens. If she doesn't, we'll be scarred for life."

"We can't see boobs flying in a million different directions again," Thistle said. "It will turn us into deviants. We want to be blind again."

"I think you're just going to have to suck it up," I said. "I … ." I tilted my head to the side as I saw one of our Flint witches, Maven Dempsey – who is ninety years old if she's a day – removing her bra. "You know what? I want to be blind, too."

"Let's all be blind," Bay said.

"Indeed," Winnie added.

Everyone dissolved into laughter. All was right in the Winchester world – well, at least until Sunday. Then all bets are off.

WITCHDEPENDENCE DAY

A WICKED WITCHES OF THE MIDWEST SHORT 7/12/2016

ONE

"Is that a horse?"

I stopped what I was doing and shifted my gaze to the small boy hovering by Marigold's stall. He looked to be about eight, but short for his age. I had no idea how he found his way into the stable on his own.

"That is a horse," I confirmed, fighting the urge to laugh as the kid eyed the majestic animal with unveiled suspicion. "That's what we usually keep in a stable."

The kid didn't look impressed. "Does it do anything?"

"Like what?"

The boy shrugged, the sunlight filtering in through the high barn window glinting off his blond head. "I don't know. Can it do tricks?"

"Like fetching a ball?"

The boy enthusiastically nodded. "My dog Skippy can do that."

"Horses don't generally fetch balls," I explained, enjoying the kid's attitude despite the faces he made. "Marigold is very smart, though. She knows all the trails without having to be led. I don't know many dogs around here that can do that."

The boy wrinkled his nose. "She would be cooler if she could fetch," he said. "I don't like the name Marigold either. She should have a better name."

"Oh, yeah? Like what?"

The boy tapped his bottom lip as he considered the question. "Wonder Woman."

I couldn't help but snicker. "I'll take it under advisement," I said. "Where are you supposed to be? I don't recognize you. Do you belong to someone here in town?"

It was summer in Hemlock Cove, which meant the student population was free to wreak havoc. Still, I'd been around town long enough to recognize most of the regulars. Ever since Hemlock Cove rebranded itself as a magical destination a few years ago, tourism had exploded. That meant quite a few people traipsed in and out of town, and many of them brought their children.

"I live in Tawas," the boy said. "I'm Brett, by the way."

I extended my hand. "I'm Marcus Richmond. I own the stable."

Brett eyed my hand, suspicious. "You're not a pervert, are you?"

I worked overtime to swallow my laugh. Kids have no filters, which is what I like about them. Funnily enough, I'm also partial to adults who lack a filter. That's probably why I fell in love with a foul-mouthed witch with impulse control issues. I guess you could say I'm a glutton for punishment.

"Not last time I checked," I replied dryly, curious to see whether the boy would shake my hand or leave. Finally he extended his hand, his grip hesitant. "It's nice to meet you, Brett."

"I've never seen horses anywhere but at the carnival, and then they just walk around in a circle so the little kids can ride them," Brett said. "Can I ride this horse?"

"Marigold loves going for rides," I replied. "If you bring your parents here and they say it's okay, I'm sure she would gladly give you a ride through the forest."

For the first time since entering the barn, Brett looked excited. "Can I call her Wonder Woman?"

"Sure."

"Can she jump me over a big tree?"

"Probably not," I answered, opting for honesty. "She's a big animal and you're a small boy. You're safer just riding her to start."

"That sounds boring," the boy said, furrowing his brow as he crossed his arms over his chest. "I want to jump over the moon."

I chuckled. Kids and their whims always amuse me. "Well, we'll see what we can do," I said. "Find your parents and ask them if you can go for a ride. They might want to go with you."

"Blech." Brett made a disgusted sound in the back of his throat. "If they want to go with me they'll bring my sister. She's a real butthead."

I bit my lip and fought to keep my face neutral. "Is she younger than you, by any chance?"

Brett shook his head. "She's older … and she never lets me forget it."

"Sounds like a typical woman."

I shifted my eyes to an approaching figure, grinning when I caught sight of Landon Michaels. An FBI agent, his home office was in nearby Traverse City. I'd gotten to know him quite well since we began sharing the same roof several nights a week. You see, we're both in love with witches. I'm not being mean or rude. I've fallen in love with a legitimate witch named Thistle, and somehow the prickly name fits her personality. Landon is in love with her cousin Bay. The four of us spend more time together than apart now.

"How's it going?" I asked, tamping down the urge to laugh at Landon's face when he caught sight of Marigold doing her business in the stall. "Are you here for the weekend?"

"Oh, gross," Brett squealed, covering his eyes. "She just did a number two."

"You noticed that, huh?" Landon asked. "I thought I was the only one."

"How could I not notice?" Brett asked. "It's huge. It looks like an alien."

"I never really thought about that, but I guess you're right," Landon said, patting the kid on the head. "You're not Brett, are you?"

The boy wrenched his hand from his face and widened his eyes. "How did you know that?"

"I'm with the FBI," Landon replied, puffing out his chest for comical effect. "I know everything."

"He's 'The Man,'" I interjected, internally chuckling when I saw a dark look move over Landon's angular features. "He has unique powers of observation."

Brett remained unconvinced. "How did you really know?"

"Because your parents are outside calling for you," Landon replied. "They're starting to look a little worried. Did you sneak off when you weren't supposed to?"

Brett graced Landon with a sheepish smile. "My sister said she was going to put gum in my hair if I didn't shut up, and my parents took her side," he explained. "I don't want gum in my hair."

"I think you wanted your parents to worry as some form of punishment for taking your sister's side," Landon countered. "That's not very nice."

"I … ." Brett looked caught.

"You should go out to them now," Landon said. "Maybe if you apologize and mean it they'll let you ride the horse."

"Wonder Woman," Brett supplied. "That's her name."

"It's a good name," Landon said. "Now, run along and put your parents out of their misery."

Brett blew out a frustrated sigh. "Fine. My sister is still a butthead, though."

"Most women are," Landon said. "Eventually you'll find one that's not so bad, though."

"My sister?"

"Not unless you've got issues no one ever needs to hear about," Landon replied. "Ask your parents about a ride. I'll bet they'll agree to it."

"Okay," Brett said, hopping toward the door. "You should probably collect that poop alien and put it in a box, though. I know at least five girls in my class who would love to get that as a gift."

"You're kind of a sick little kid, aren't you?" I asked, shaking my head hard enough that my shoulder-length blond hair brushed against the top of my shoulders. "That's gross, man."

Brett didn't look particularly disturbed by the admonishment. "If girls don't want to be grossed out they should stay away from boys."

I laughed. "You'll change your mind one day."

"I doubt it."

We watched Brett scamper out of the barn, making sure we could hear him call out to his father before turning our attention to each other.

"Do you remember being as gross as that little guy?" I asked.

"I grew up with two brothers," Landon replied. "We were much grosser than that kid. Although, I have to be honest, I don't think we ever considered wrapping up horse droppings and then gifting the box to unsuspecting girls in our neighborhood."

"I'm thinking he's never going to find someone to date him if he's not careful," I said. "What's up with you? I thought you would be all over Bay right about now. Haven't you two spent three whole days apart?"

Landon's job kept him in Traverse City for the bulk of the workweek, although he often went out of his way to find an excuse to spend the night with Bay. When he wasn't around I made sure to keep an eye on her. Mostly it was for his peace of mind, but in truth, Bay has a tendency to find trouble, and she often drags Thistle along for the ride. They're a diabolical twosome, and now that they're living together without a buffer, things are getting rough.

"Bay is putting the paper to bed for the week. She told me I was distracting her," Landon replied. "She's … in a mood."

"I thought you liked her moods?"

"I like most of her moods, but she seems irritated today, and that's not what I was looking forward to," Landon said. "It's a holiday weekend, which means I get extra time off. I was hoping for smiles and kisses."

"Ooh, you're such a woman," I teased, although I got what he was saying. There's something about fireworks and picnics that put me in the mood for alone time with my witch, too. "Are you guys going to the festival this weekend?"

"I was willing to bypass it, but Bay says it's one of her favorite festivals of the year," Landon said. "Personally, I think this town has too many festivals. They should have one in the summer and one in the fall. That's it."

"It's a tourist town," I reminded him. "The festivals mean big crowds and money. That's why we have so many."

"I know." Landon tugged a restless hand through his long black hair. "I just had visions of a picnic basket, a bottle of wine and time alone with Bay. Now she's talking about pie-baking contests, kissing booths, funhouses, games and corn dogs."

"You usually love all of that stuff – especially the kissing booth."

"I still love it," Landon said. "Laugh all you want, but that kissing booth is awesome. Whoever thought of it is a genius. It's just ... I adore this family. I really do. I'm fond of every single one of them. Occasionally it would be nice to spend some time alone with Bay, though. I don't understand why we have to do everything as a group."

Bay and Thistle Winchester live in the guesthouse on their mothers' property. Their cousin Clove used to live with them, but she moved out a few weeks ago to live with her boyfriend. The move was proving to be more of an adjustment than I initially envisioned thanks to the ensuing power struggle between two belligerent witches.

Their three mothers own The Overlook, one of Hemlock Cove's most popular inns. They run it with the help of a recent town transplant named Belinda, who lives on the third floor with her daughter Annie, and the hindrance of their persnickety aunt, Tillie, who has more in common with a tornado than a typical senior citizen.

"It's the Winchester way," I said. "They can't go through life without one another. I think you either get used to it or ... ." Or what? I knew Landon was in it for the long haul. There really was no acceptable "or."

"I'm just complaining," Landon said. "Most of the time I enjoy the hijinks. It's just hot ... and I want some time alone with Bay."

"Why can't you spend time with the family and time alone with Bay, too?" I prodded. "Is there a reason you can only do one or the other? When I want time alone with Thistle we spend the night at my house."

"Yes, but my house is in Traverse City," Landon pointed out. "Bay is happy here. I love this town, too. I don't want her traipsing over there for half the week."

"Have you considered getting a place here in town?" I asked. "Heck, are you allowed to do that?"

"Not really," Landon replied, rubbing the back of his neck. "I would have to apply for a special dispensation, and to do that I need to have documented proof of a relationship."

I had no idea what that meant. "Can't you just tell them you're involved with Bay and want to be closer to her?"

"That's not quite how it works," Landon chuckled. "If we were married, it would be one thing."

"Are you ready to get married?"

"Not quite yet."

"So, what are your other options?" I asked, genuinely curious.

"I'm not sure yet," Landon said, shaking his head to dislodge whatever heavy thoughts weighed on him. "Don't say anything to Thistle. I don't want Bay getting worked up. We've had enough drama lately."

He wasn't exaggerating. About a week and a half ago, someone shot at Bay, Thistle and Clove while they were snooping in a senior citizen's back yard. They watched in horrified disbelief as the woman fell dead at their feet. The cousins are known for finding trouble – especially Bay. I knew, given everything they'd recently gone through, Landon would be happy with a few weeks of peace before the next dramatic upheaval.

"You'll figure it out," I said finally. "Do you believe in destiny?"

Landon shrugged. "This is a weird conversation to be having with another dude."

I snickered. "I get that," I said. "I believe in destiny, though. I think it was my destiny to move back to Hemlock Cove after being away for several years. I also think it was my destiny to fall in love with Thistle.

"The question you have to ask yourself is whether you think Bay is your destiny," I continued. "If you do, everything will happen the way it's supposed to. I'm a firm believer in that."

"You have an upbeat way of looking at life," Landon said. "I wish I wasn't such a downer all of the time."

"I don't think you're a downer," I clarified. "Your job is a lot harder than mine. You've seen some horrible things. Bay has, too. I still think you two were meant to find each other when you did.

"Think about it," I pressed. "What are the odds you would run into each other at a corn maze? What are the odds that you would keep crossing paths with her while you were under cover? If it's not destiny, you'd have to admit it's an incredible set of coincidences."

"I don't know whether I believe in destiny the same way you do," Landon said. "I do believe Bay is my heart, and I won't let her go."

"That sounded stalker-ish."

"I know," Landon said, flashing a rueful smile. "I didn't mean it to sound that way. I don't want to live my life without Bay. I'm not sure we're ready to get married quite yet. I have faith things will work out, though. Until then, I'm happy with how my life is going."

"Even though it's going to be a weekend full of Winchester hijinks?"

"Maybe even partially because of it," Landon conceded, glancing around the empty stable. "Do you need help with anything? I'm kind of on my own until Bay finishes up in an hour."

"Oh, are you lost without your blonde?" I teased.

"If I say yes, will you think less of me?"

"No," I said. "I feel the same way. I was wondering what Thistle was doing when Brett wandered in. I'm whipped, too."

Landon scowled. "Do you have to put it like that?"

"Come on," I said, clapping his arm to jolt him out of his doldrums. "I could use some help carrying that chest over there into the loft."

"Cool," Landon said, following me to the trunk in question and grabbing one of the ends. "Ugh, criminy. What do you have in here? It's not pot, is it?"

I rolled my eyes. Aunt Tillie's pot field was notorious in certain circles, and the fact that I help her cultivate it from time to time is hardly secret. Landon is convinced one day he will catch her in the act. I think the true problem for him is he has no idea what he'll do should that ever happen.

Landon talks a big game, and his fights with the persnickety Winchester matriarch are legendary, but I'm certain Landon will never do anything to hurt Bay. That includes arresting an eighty-year-old woman because she grows pot.

"It's old riding gear and tack," I explained, grabbing the other end and pointing toward the ladder. "This is going to be a pain to get up there."

"I'm strong and manly," Landon said. "You're almost as strong as me. I'm sure we can handle it."

"You make me laugh," I said, snickering as we shifted the chest.

It took some maneuvering – and a lot of swearing and sweating – but we finally managed to secure the trunk in the loft. Landon gave the large chest a final kick before his attention shifted to a spot on the loft floor.

"What are you looking at?" I asked, following his gaze. "Do you see a dead animal? They get up here from time to time. I can get rid of it."

"It's not an animal," Landon said, kneeling for a closer look before lowering his fingers into the straw. "I think it's blood." He lifted his fingers, the unmistakable dark stain shining on his fingertips.

"Really?" I arched an eyebrow as I moved closer to him. "Animal blood?"

Landon shrugged. "That would be my guess," he said, glancing around the expansive loft. "Maybe something got wounded and crawled up here to die."

"Let's look," I suggested.

We spent the next five minutes searching every corner but ultimately came up empty.

"If a wounded animal or bird died up here we might never find it," I said finally. "There are big enough scavengers in the area to drag it off."

"I guess," Landon said, although he didn't look convinced. "That's a lot of blood for a small animal."

"What do you think it is?"

"I don't know," Landon said. "I'd feel better if we had someone else look around this loft, though."

"Like who? Do you want to call Chief Terry?"

Terry Davenport is Hemlock Cove's chief of police. I was convinced an animal met a tragic fate in the loft, but I knew Landon well enough to respect his instincts.

"Not Chief Terry," Landon replied. "Let's call Bay."

I stilled, surprised. "Bay? Why do you want her?" The answer occurred to me after the question already escaped my lips. "You think a person might've died up here and want to see whether Bay can find a ghost, don't you?"

"I don't know," Landon replied. "Let's just call Bay. I'll feel better if we exert due diligence."

I shrugged. "Okay. Let's do it."

TWO

"What's the big emergency?"

Thistle Winchester, her short hair an odd shade of lavender this month, stepped into the stable and fixed me with a curious look.

She's hard to explain. Most people think she's mean and live in fear of her mood swings. They're probably smart to do that. I adore her, though. I like the way she smiles … and laughs … and plots to take over the world.

Thistle has a huge mouth, don't get me wrong, but she also has an enormous heart. She enjoys messing with her family – especially Aunt Tillie – but she would die for any one of them. She's brave and true. Did I mention she looks amazing in the bohemian skirts she wears?

"Landon found blood in the loft and he wants to make sure it's animal instead of human," I replied, leaning over to give Thistle a soft kiss. She returned the gesture, reaching her slim arms around my waist to give me a hug. The action was simple, but it completely took me by surprise. "What was that for?"

Thistle is sweet when no one is looking. In front of people, she likes to act tough. Of course, she is tough. I'm eight inches taller and sixty pounds heavier than she is, but I'm pretty sure she could take me in a fair fight. In an unfair fight? Yeah, she would mop the floor with me.

"Nothing," Thistle said, hurriedly shaking her head. "I only ... wanted to hug you. What? That's allowed."

I couldn't stop myself from chuckling. "It's definitely allowed ... and encouraged," I said, wrapping my arms around her waifish body and pulling her close. "You usually only hug me when we're alone."

"She's feeling vulnerable," Bay announced, stepping into the stable behind Thistle and shooting her cousin a dark look. "She knows I'm about to win the battle for the extra room and she needs someone to bolster her spirits."

"You wish," Thistle shot back. "That room is going to be for crafts. Period!"

Ever since Clove moved out, leaving an empty room in a building already cramped, Bay and Thistle have been engaged in something of a war to determine what to do with it. Bay wants to create an office and Thistle wants a place to do her craft projects in peace. I honestly have no idea who will win this one. It's fun watching the curses fly, though.

"No fighting," I said, flicking the ridge of Thistle's ear to get her attention. "We don't have time for that right now. You promised me a home-cooked dinner."

"Technically I promised you dinner," Thistle clarified. "I didn't say I was going to cook it."

"So, we're going to the diner?"

The Winchester women are some of the best cooks in the area. We often eat dinner at The Overlook. Two nights a week, though, Thistle requests a break. That generally means we get takeout from the diner and curl up on the couch to watch television at my place. The solitude offers solace and mental reprieve for both of us.

"Actually, I was thinking we could get dinner at the diner and then spend the night here," Thistle suggested, taking me by surprise.

"In the barn?" Bay asked, wrinkling her nose.

"No one is talking to you," Thistle snapped, her eyes flashing. "I believe your boyfriend is in the loft looking at blood. Why don't you join him?"

Because they grew up together, Bay and Thistle are used to each other's moods. "Why don't you bite me?" Bay challenged.

"I'm going to make you eat dirt and then sit on you and laugh while you choke if you're not careful," Thistle threatened.

This feud over the room was really starting to get out of hand. "Guys, that's enough of that," I ordered. "You're giving me a headache."

"Me, too," Landon intoned as he appeared at the edge of the loft opening and stared down at us. "Sweetie, can you please come up here and help me? I have a problem."

"It's probably in his pants," Thistle quipped.

Bay ignored her cousin and headed for the ladder. "I don't understand why you want me here," she complained. "An animal probably died up there. The odds of that blood belonging to a human are pretty slim."

"Thank you, Miss Expert," Landon drawled. "Can you look anyway?"

"That's Ms. Expert to you," Bay said, although she climbed the ladder, even accepting Landon's hand as he pulled her the final way up.

I couldn't help but smile when Landon whispered something to Bay, causing her to giggle. It was probably something dirty, but the FBI agent knew exactly how to soothe Bay's frazzled nerves. They're a good match.

"It was probably a raccoon or something," Thistle suggested. "Something bigger might have taken the carcass away. Or it could have crawled away and died out on the property."

"That would be great," Landon said. "I've learned that Hemlock Cove rarely yields easy answers, though. I want Bay to look for a … ." He didn't finish the sentence, worry someone might be eavesdropping forcing him to leave the implication hanging.

"A goat?" Thistle suggested, smiling evilly as Landon scowled. "Do you have Bay up there looking for goats?"

"Don't make me come down there, Thistle," Landon warned. "I will."

"Ooh, I'm so scared." I shook my head as Thistle turned her expressive eyes in my direction. "What? He started it."

"That doesn't mean you always have to finish it," I said, rubbing my thumb against Thistle's soft cheek. She's naturally beautiful, high cheekbones offsetting a pleasing face. She wears very little makeup and still manages to take my breath away. "What were you saying about dinner?"

"Oh, right," Thistle said, rubbing her hands together as she warmed to the topic at hand. "I was thinking we could get takeout and spend the night here."

"In the stable?" I was obviously missing something.

Thistle nodded. "I have blankets in my car and I thought we could watch the storm from the loft," she said. "It's supposed to be a big one. You know how I love storms."

She does love storms. She gets excited when she senses the change in the atmosphere. Thanks to her, I've grown rather fond of storms, too. I especially like the way she crawls into my lap during them. "We can do that," I said, still unsure whether I was missing something. "Do you want to tell me what else is going on?"

"I thought we could talk about the construction and how you're going to change things," Thistle admitted. "I … thought maybe I could help decorate."

Ah, there it was. Ever since I announced my intentions to expand the stable and turn the neighboring barn into a show house Thistle had been excited at the thought of decorating. She isn't much for outdoor work, and when it comes to the day-to-day tasks at Hypnotic, the magic store she owns with Clove, she shows varying degrees of interest. Creating candles and sculptures and decorating are a different matter entirely.

"We can do that," I said. "You've been telling me about these ideas you have for months."

"Well, we can't really do anything until the construction is finished, and that's not even starting for another three weeks," Thistle said. "It's just … I think both spaces could be really great. Then, by the time you add in the petting zoo you have planned, I think this could be one of the biggest draws in Hemlock Cove."

Her excitement was contagious. "I think that sounds fun," I said, cupping the back of her head and pressing a soft kiss to her upturned mouth.

"Good." Thistle did a little dance that was almost comical. "I brought catalogs."

The mention of catalogs would be enough to instill fear in most men. The idea of sharing time with Thistle and listening to her ideas filled me with delight. I love the way her mind works.

"Are you sure?" Landon looked annoyed as he appeared at the edge of the loft. "Look again, Bay. It's a big area."

"It might be a big area," Bay conceded, her blond head popping into view as she looked over the edge and shot Thistle an annoyed look. Something unsaid passed between the two women, and for the first time in days I realized their wordless communication had nothing to do with the battle over the spare room. This was pure man annoyance. "It's also a completely open area. Where do you think this … goat … might be hiding?"

"I don't understand why you're so convinced the blood is human," I said, slipping my arm around Thistle's shoulders as she leaned into me. "There's no reason the blood would be human. I lock the stables every night, and I'm the only one with regular access."

"I'm not saying the blood is human," Landon said. "It's just … if it is … I want to get ahead of it. I don't want a dead body popping up and biting us when we're trying to have a relaxing weekend. It's the Fourth of July. We should be having fun."

"If a dead body is popping up and biting you, we have bigger worries," Bay said, her tone serious even though mirth danced across her features. "That would mean we're in the middle of the zombie apocalypse and Aunt Tillie was right. It will be every witch for herself."

"Come here, mouth," Landon said, reaching for Bay and missing as she skirted his outstretched hands. "There's nowhere to run, Bay. I will catch you."

I smirked as I watched them cavort, Landon's earlier worry seemingly evaporating. Even when he was upset with Bay, or worried about their future, he always found joy in their everyday interactions.

"Oh, well, great."

I cringed at the new voice, turning to find Aunt Tillie standing in the open stable door.

She's hard to explain, too. She's four feet and eleven inches of raw power and sarcastic overtones. Today, for example, she's dressed in camouflage cargo pants and a pink hat with a flower sticking out of the top. She looks as if she's gearing up for trouble, which is never a good thing.

"What are you doing here?" Thistle asked before I had a chance to voice the question – in a much nicer way, mind you. I'm one of the few people who rarely fight with Aunt Tillie. Even I can't explain it.

"It's nice to see you, too, Little Miss Attitude," Aunt Tillie said, flicking the end of Thistle's nose as she passed. "Can't I stop in to see one of my favorite people without announcing my itinerary to the masses?"

Landon, his face red from the effort exerted to catch Bay, glanced down from the loft as he kept his wriggling blonde close. "I'm glad to see you admit I'm your favorite."

"I was talking about Marcus," Aunt Tillie scoffed.

I had a feeling Landon knew that, but he enjoys messing with Aunt Tillie whenever the opportunity arises. She gets immense joy from irritating everyone she comes in contact with, so whenever someone returns the favor everyone gets a kick out of it.

"You're welcome to stop by whenever you wish," I said, biting the inside of my cheek to keep from laughing at the annoyed look on Thistle's face. She doesn't get my relationship with her great-aunt. No one does. It's one of those weird, inexplicable things, yet I wouldn't trade it for anything. "To what honor do I owe today's visit?"

"I'm bored," Aunt Tillie announced, narrowing her eyes as Bay squealed and Landon struggled to keep his grip on her. "If you two are going to roll in the hay, you might want to wait until the rest of us leave," she shouted up to the loft. "That's what's done in proper circles."

"We're not rolling in the hay," Bay shot back. "Hay makes me itch."

"Cops do that to me," Aunt Tillie shot back, sending Landon a sarcastic thumbs-up. "Just ask 'The Man' there."

"I wish you would stop calling me that," Landon protested. "It's annoying."

"You're annoying, so that works out," Aunt Tillie said. "Seriously, what are you two doing up there?"

"We found blood in the loft and Landon wanted Bay to look around to see whether she sees anything," I supplied.

"She didn't, for the record," Thistle added.

"It was probably an animal," Aunt Tillie said, making a face. "Why would a person crawl up into the loft to die?"

"I just wanted to make sure," Landon said. "We're supposed to be having a nice weekend together. I don't want anything ruining it."

"You worry too much," Aunt Tillie said, shaking her head. "You're kind of a kvetch."

"I hate it when you use that word, too," Landon said, losing his grip on Bay and falling backward as she giggled. "You did that on purpose."

"I'm not rolling in the hay with you," Bay said, brushing a strand of her flyaway flaxen hair from her face. "It makes my arms break out and itch. You say you don't want the night ruined. That will definitely ruin our night because then you won't be able to touch me."

"Oh. Well, you should've told me that," Landon said, conceding defeat as he moved toward the ladder. "I would've stopped wrestling with you if I knew that was the case."

"Live and learn," Bay said, following Landon down the ladder. "There's nothing here, though. I think Marcus is right about the blood belonging to an animal."

"That's a relief," Landon said, waiting at the bottom of the ladder so he could snag Bay as she neared the bottom and twirl her around. "All I want to think about this weekend is food, fireworks and you."

"Men are simple creatures, like dogs," Aunt Tillie intoned, rolling her eyes. "Give them a hot meal and a woman and they'll happily wag their tails for hours. Speaking of dinner, though, you're expected to join your mothers at the festival. They're barbecuing, and I was sent to retrieve you."

"You said you came here because you were bored," Thistle argued.

"Yes, well, whenever people talk to me for more than a few minutes I get bored," Aunt Tillie said.

"I thought we were eating here," I reminded Thistle. "I thought it was going to be just the two of us."

"Attendance is mandatory," Aunt Tillie said. "That's why I'm here, too. Trust me. I didn't want to come into town, but Winnie said if I didn't she was going to start conducting regular contraband searches of my greenhouse.

"Now, I'm innocent, but I don't like my personal space being invaded," she continued. "She's such a busybody. I have no idea where she gets that from."

Landon scowled. "You're not fooling anyone," he said. "I know what you're doing in that greenhouse."

"Oh, please," Aunt Tillie scoffed. "You only think you know what's going on in my greenhouse. If you knew the truth you would be amazed."

"Yeah, I don't think 'amazed' is the right word," Landon countered. "Barbecue sounds good to me, though. I'm starving."

"You'll eat anything," Bay said, linking her fingers with his. "You don't care whether it's barbecue or bacon."

"Ooh, do you think they'll have bacon?"

I watched the couple leave the barn, shifting my eyes to Thistle once they disappeared. "What do you think? We could have dinner with your family and still spend the night here."

"I don't know," Thistle hedged. "I kind of wanted us to be alone."

"I think you should have dinner with the family," Aunt Tillie countered. "It's the right thing to do."

Thistle narrowed her eyes, suspicious. "Why are you saying that? You don't want to be there either."

"Yes, but at least I'll have someone to irritate if you put in an appearance," she replied. "I need to get my thrills somewhere. You'll do in a pinch."

I couldn't contain my chuckle as Thistle shot her great-aunt a murderous look.

"You really are a terrible person sometimes," Thistle said. "You know that, right?"

Aunt Tillie was unperturbed by Thistle's tone. "It keeps me young."

THREE

"Where's the bacon?"

Landon approached Winnie, Bay's mother, with a petulant look as he studied the assembled goodies on the picnic table in the middle of Hemlock's Cove's town square.

For her part, the generally amiable woman smacked his hand as he reached for a cookie and shot him a dark look. "Those are for dessert."

"I'm hungry," Landon whined. "Bay has been mean to me all day and I need a cookie to make me feel better."

Winnie pressed her lips together as she regarded her daughter's boyfriend. Even when she acted stern I could tell she liked Landon. He's too charming to dislike, and the way he dotes on Bay is every mother's dream. "Fine. You can have one cookie."

"Thank you." Landon snatched two cookies and pretended he didn't see Winnie's pointed glare as he handed one to Bay. "Don't say I never gave you anything."

"Yes, but that other stuff you gave her needed penicillin to knock out," Aunt Tillie interjected, grabbing her own cookie.

It took everyone a moment to grasp what she was insinuating.

"Aunt Tillie," Winnie screeched, disgusted. "Don't ever say

anything like that again! That is your great-niece … and the man who has saved your bacon more times than I can count."

"Speaking of bacon … ." Landon was unruffled by Aunt Tillie's comment.

"There's no bacon, Landon," Winnie said. "Suck it up. Aunt Tillie, apologize to Landon and Bay right now."

"I'm truly sorry," Aunt Tillie replied solemnly. The look on her face reflected sincere contrition, but I knew she had something else behind the look. "I've been a terrible great-aunt. As part of my punishment, I shall go home without supper and think about what I've done."

"Not so fast," Winnie said, grabbing the back of Aunt Tillie's collar and tugging her toward the picnic table. "I know what you're doing, and it's not going to work. This is a family dinner. That means the entire family is going to be here."

"Does that include me?" Sam Cornell, Clove's boyfriend, nervously approached the picnic table. He still felt like an outsider despite his new living situation and Clove's abject adoration. Sooner or later he would relax and embrace the family dynamic. It couldn't come fast enough for me. He was jumpy – and that made everyone else jumpy. No one needs jumpy witches. Trust me on that one.

"Of course it includes you," said Twila, patting Sam's shoulder as she moved closer to Thistle. "Why is your hair still purple? I think the color is all wrong for you. You need richer hues. The purples and blues wash you out."

Since Twila's hair was fire-engine red any dyeing advice generally fell on deaf ears.

"Thank you, Mother," Thistle replied, her irritation evident. "Just for that I'm going to dye my hair purple and blue next time. I hope you like it. I'm going to dedicate it in your honor."

Twila slapped Thistle's hand with a wooden spoon, taking me by surprise with her swiftness. "You're lucky I'm a good person," she said. "Otherwise I would punish you for being an insolent pain in the butt."

"Insolent?" Thistle arched a challenging eyebrow. "You've been watching *Wheel of Fortune* with Aunt Tillie again, haven't you?"

"It happens to be a wonderfully entertaining show."

"Yes, I've always wanted to watch a grown woman flip letters for a living," Thistle deadpanned. "It's a true gift to humanity."

I blew out a resigned sigh and pinched the bridge of my nose. Much like Landon, I love all of the Winchester women. When you put them in the same small area, though, headaches are inevitable.

"What's everyone doing at the festival tonight?" I asked, hoping to change the subject.

"I think that would be a cool job to have," Clove said, brushing her dark hair from her face as she reached for a cookie and earned a warning look from her mother, Marnie. "I would love to dress in an evening gown and turn letters on national television."

Thistle snorted. "You would."

"I think Clove would be great at it," Sam argued. "I think she's great at whatever she does."

"Thank you," Clove said, beaming widely as she blew Sam an air kiss. "I knew there was a reason I moved in with you."

"Yeah, he's full of it," Thistle said.

I opened my mouth to admonish her and then thought better of it. If I were the one who told her to take it down a notch she'd take her anger out on me and ruin our entire night. It was better to let someone else take her on – and then deal with the uncomfortable fall-out. I could be the sympathetic boyfriend making her feel better following what was sure to be an annoying verbal clash.

"Be nice," Twila chided, wagging a finger in her daughter's face. "I'm with Clove. I think it would be fantastic to dress up in sparkly evening gowns and turn letters. It would be an even better job if I could sing."

"I think it sounds boring," Bay offered.

"That's because you won't wear dresses," Winnie said. "The Goddess gave you legs. You should show them off occasionally. You always dress in jeans and cargo pants. It's … stupid."

Bay made a face only a mother could love. "Thanks!"

"I agree with your mom," Landon said. "I love it when you show off your legs."

"That's because you're a pervert," Aunt Tillie said, sticking her tongue out when Landon glared at her. "Don't look at me like that. Everyone knows you're a pervert."

"Have you ever considered you have a dirty mind?" Landon asked primly. "Perhaps I'm not a pervert. You probably think that because your mind is clouded with dirty thoughts."

"No, you're a pervert," Aunt Tillie shot back, unruffled. "How long until the food is ready? I'm starving. There are such things as elder abuse. You know that, right? I could report you."

"We haven't even started grilling yet," Twila said. "Dinner is at least a half hour away."

"Well, work faster," Aunt Tillie said. "If I don't eat soon my blood pressure will bottom out and then I'll go into hypoglycemic shock. You know what that means."

I had no idea what that meant, but was understandably curious. "What does it mean?"

"Oh, no," Thistle, Bay and Clove groaned in unison.

"Why did you ask her that?" Thistle asked, exasperated.

"I want to know if she's sick," I replied. "That hypoglycemic shock thing sounds serious."

"It is serious," Aunt Tillie said, nodding. "It can make a mind wander."

Well, that was a frightening thought. If Aunt Tillie's mind wandered any further it might not find its way back home.

"She's not sick," Thistle said. "This is like when she claimed she had glaucoma."

"I do have glaucoma," Aunt Tillie sniffed. "It's situational glaucoma. That means it comes and goes and I have no control over it. That's why I need my … herb garden."

"Keep it up," Landon warned, wagging a finger. "I'm going to burn that herb garden to the ground."

"And your oxygen allergy?" Bay prodded. "Whatever happened to that?"

Aunt Tillie squinted as she regarded her great-niece. "It comes and it goes … much like my glaucoma and your intelligence."

"All right, leave my Bay alone," Landon ordered, slipping his arm around Bay's waist. "I don't like it when you're mean to her."

"I do," Thistle said, earning a pinch on the wrist from Clove and a scowl from Bay. "What? Bay is being a pain. She won't let me turn Clove's old room into a craft room, and she's irritating me."

"You're irritating me," Bay shot back.

"You're both irritating me," Winnie said. "Who else is irritated by this never-ending argument between Bay and Thistle?"

I raised my hand before I ascertained the intelligence associated with the gesture.

"Really?" Thistle raised her eyebrows. "I can't believe you're turning on me after I planned a romantic night for us and everything."

"I'm not turning on you," I countered. "I'm just sick of hearing about the room."

"I think you should leave the room as it is," Clove said. "I think it looks pretty."

"Oh, puh-leez," Thistle said. "You want us to put a photograph of you in there so we can go in and worship your memory on a daily basis. You want that room to be a shrine. We're not wasting that space, so get over it."

"You get over it," Clove shot back.

"Can we all just get over it?" Marnie asked, her eyes flashing. "Good grief. Why does everything turn into an argument when we're all together?"

"I think it has a little something to do with your attitude," Aunt Tillie replied, reaching for another cookie and earning a whack on the hand from Winnie.

"If you try stealing one more cookie I'll make you eat the sheet we baked them on," Winnie warned.

"I think the whole family has PMS," Thistle announced. "That's the only explanation. It's probably situational, much like Aunt Tillie's glaucoma."

Landon groaned and covered his eyes. "Stop saying things like that. I'm going to have nightmares."

Despite the imminent Winchester meltdown – and it was imminent, make no mistake – I felt happy. This was a true family. This was true love. This was how a lazy summer night was supposed to be spent.

"Aunt Tillie, next time Landon ticks you off I think you should curse him with a never-ending supply of tampons," Thistle announced, earning odd stares from a few random festival guests who overheard the pronouncement as they passed the picnic table.

This is also a group of women – and a few men – who might know each other a little too well. There's absolutely no button they won't push.

"Who wants something to drink?" I asked, hoping to shift the conversation.

No one answered.

"Who wants family dinner to be over with?" Aunt Tillie asked, mimicking my voice.

Everyone's hands shot up in unison.

Okay, I love them. They're all major jerks sometimes, though.

"I THINK we should play some games," Landon said a few hours later, leading the way through the festival. "I want to win Bay a stuffed animal."

"Oh, how cute," Thistle enthused, sarcasm practically dripping from her tongue. "Bay finally found a boyfriend to win her stuff at a carnival. She only started dreaming about that when she was a fourteen, and now she's finally gotten her wish."

"Stop being a pain," I instructed, tugging on Thistle's hand to make sure I drew her attention. I'm not big on shouting. I've found being the quiet one in the Winchester world has its benefits. People have to strain to hear me, and I like that. "I think it's cute."

"I think it's cute, too," Clove said. "I want Sam to win me a stuffed animal so I can start a collection."

Sam looked uncomfortable with the suggestion. "Um … I've never been great at these games."

Thistle snorted. "All carnival games are rigged," she said. "No one is good at the games here. Don't feel bad. You're not meant to win. No one wins."

"I'm good at them," Landon argued. "I always win Bay something."

"Oh, you're so cute I want to gag," Thistle said.

Okay, it was time to take her ego down a notch or two. "I didn't hear you complaining when I won you that stuffed cat at the spring festival," I pointed out.

Thistle's cheeks turned crimson as Clove and Bay jerked their heads in her direction.

"Oh, really?" Bay looked intrigued – and like the shark in *Jaws* when it was about to eat someone while they were still alive and screaming. "What did this cat look like? It didn't happen to be orange with black stripes, did it?"

"And now goes by the unfortunate name of Mr. Whiskers?" Clove added.

"Who told you I named it that?" Thistle asked, mortified. "Did you tell them I named it that, Marcus?"

I held my hands up in a placating manner. "I didn't tell anyone about the cat."

"No, you just ratted me out in front of my cousins," Thistle grumbled, crossing her arms over her chest. "Where's the loyalty?"

"You love that cat and you know it," I said. "Bay loves the stuff Landon wins for her, too. There's nothing wrong with it. And Sam, well ... we'll help Sam win something for Clove."

"Thanks, man," Sam deadpanned. "I'll win Clove something on my own. I'm sure I can be a very effective carnival ... game thingy ... winner."

"Yes, you're going to terrify everyone when you play a game thingy," Landon teased. I searched his face for signs of distaste, but Landon's previous dislike of Sam appeared to be a thing of the past. I was glad for that. Clove clearly loved Sam, and he adored her. I wanted them to have some happiness, especially because Clove often gets shunted to the side thanks to Thistle and Bay's louder personalities.

"Let's all win something," Bay suggested, her eyes twinkling when they landed on Thistle. "I mean, the four of us, of course. Thistle is far too mature to watch Marcus win a stuffed animal for her."

I pressed my lips together to keep from laughing as I studied Thistle's conflicted features.

"I'm fine with that," Thistle gritted out.

"Great." Bay turned to the game aisle and pointed. "Let's do the balloon one first."

I purposely waited for Thistle to pick a pace and then fell into step next to her. I considered offering to win her a stuffed animal regardless, but sometimes it's better to let her make the suggestion. I had a feeling now was one of those times.

"I want a stuffed animal," Thistle whispered.

"Then you have to ask nicely."

Thistle rolled her eyes so hard I thought she might tip over. It took her a moment to collect herself, but when she did, she had an earnest expression on her face. "Will you please win me a stuffed animal?"

"I will," I confirmed. "Which one do you want?"

Thistle remained a few steps from her cousins as she perused the selection. "I want the dog on the shelf up there."

I studied the hound in question. He had a cute face and adorable floppy ears. "Consider it done," I said, moving to join Landon at the booth. "Just for curiosity's sake, though, what are you going to name him?"

"I'm not going to name him," Thistle scoffed. "I'm not ten. I don't name stuffed animals."

I arched a challenging eyebrow and waited.

"He's naming himself," Thistle clarified. "Mr. Paws."

I barked out a laugh and leaned over to press a kiss to the corner of her mouth. "Your secret is safe with me. One Mr. Paws coming up."

FOUR

"I think he looks dignified, don't you?"

Thistle happily snuggled her stuffed dog as we walked back to the stable shortly after dark. The air was moist and warm, almost oppressive. I could feel the oncoming storm building.

I glanced at the dog, his silly button eyes pointed directly at me, and smiled. "He definitely looks dignified," I said. "His hat makes him look like an elder statesman, or perhaps a duke."

Thistle snorted. "Thank you for winning him for me." I knew she was serious because she lowered her voice. When you date a blowhard, you learn to read the signs.

"You're very welcome," I said, gripping her hand as she slipped it into mine. "What did you think of the octopus Landon won for Bay?"

"It was not dignified," Thistle said. "He was kind of cute, though."

"And the panda bear Sam won for Clove?"

It was a silly conversation, but once Thistle is away from her cousins her internal sweetness always comes out to play. That's my favorite part of the day.

"I saw Landon pay the guy off to make sure Sam won that panda," Thistle said. "You were trying to distract us when he was doing it, but I saw. I knew when you had your heads together while watching Sam throw darts – and miss everything he aimed at, mind you – that you would do something to help him."

"There must be something wrong with his hand-eye coordination," I mused. "I've never seen anyone with poorer aim."

"It was still sweet," Thistle said. "Clove would've been heartbroken if we got stuffed animals and she didn't, and Sam would've gone broke trying to win her one."

"Yeah, I like how Landon flashed his badge and warned the game guy that he would shut him down if he didn't make sure Sam won an animal," I said, smiling at the memory. "He makes me laugh."

"You guys have grown pretty close," Thistle said, watching as I unlocked the stable. "I'm glad."

"I'm glad, too," I said, ushering her inside. "I wasn't sure I would like him when we first met, but I think he's good for Bay. I also think he's good for this family because he's willing to protect all of the people – and their multitude of secrets – with his life."

"I didn't like him when we first met him either, but that was because I thought he was going to break Bay's heart," Thistle admitted, moving toward the ladder to the loft. We'd carried the blankets up for safekeeping before leaving for the festival. Thistle didn't want to risk getting them wet in case we had to race back in the middle of a storm. "Now I know he'll never purposely break her heart, and I like him."

"What did you think when you first met me?" I asked, grabbing the dog before Thistle could climb the rungs. "I'll carry Mr. Paws. He's big and I don't want you to trip."

"You're such a strong protector," Thistle teased, beginning her ascent. I knew she was bargaining for time because she didn't want to answer the question.

"Tell me what you thought of me," I prodded. "I can take it."

"Well, if you must know, I thought you were the most handsome man I'd ever met," Thistle admitted.

Unabashed love washed over me. "I think that's the nicest thing you've ever said to me."

"I also thought you were kind of a goof."

"That's ... fine," I said, frowning. "How was I a goof?"

"You just kept tripping over yourself whenever I came into the stable to buy feed for animals we didn't have," Thistle replied, cresting the top of the ladder and disappearing from view. "I thought maybe you were a little slow or something."

I chuckled, memories of our first few meetings pushing to the forefront. "That's because I was nervous," I explained, handing her the stuffed dog as I finished my climb. "I knew I liked you, but I was completely out of my element. I wanted to ask you out but was afraid you would turn me down."

"I didn't turn you down."

"No, but I thought you might," I said, rubbing my finger over her forehead. The moon, which was almost completely obscured by the incoming storm clouds, managed to cast a green pall over her face, giving her an unearthly appeal. "I thought you were bohemian, brilliant and utterly terrifying."

"I am," Thistle said, grinning. "What do you think about me now?"

"I'm pretty sure the sun rises and sets on your smile."

"Ugh. You're so romantic it kills me," Thistle groused.

"You haven't seen anything yet," I teased, planting a soft kiss on her mouth before turning to study the stack of blankets. "We should get everything ready before the storm hits. Then you can tell me about your decorating plans while we wait."

"That sounds like a plan," Thistle said, happily grabbing a blanket and shaking it out. I grabbed one end and she took the other, following the effort with two more blankets before grabbing a fourth to cover us.

"That's weird," Thistle said, scanning the darkening loft. "I could've sworn I brought another blanket."

I followed her gaze but came up short. "I don't see one. Are you sure?"

"I ... ." Thistle snapped her mouth shut and shrugged. "I guess not. I probably left it on the couch back at the guesthouse. It's okay. We should be plenty comfortable."

We settled under the blanket, Thistle grabbing her catalog and resting her head on my shoulder as she got comfortable.

"I can't really see that catalog," I said. "It's too dark."

"That's okay. I can show it to you in the morning."

Thistle gets a bad rap from her family for being difficult to deal with. That's only true when she's around them. When she's around me, I never have issues.

"Tell me about your decorating plans," I prodded, tracing lazy circles on the back of her neck as she got comfortable. "What do you want to do with this place?"

"I'm a little worried you're going to think I'm taking over your project," Thistle admitted. "If I overstep my bounds, you need to tell me."

"I'll tell you," I said. "I still want to hear what you have in mind. You have a knack for this sort of thing."

"I do," Thistle agreed. Her ego was big, and sometimes out of control, but she could almost always back it up. "I was thinking you could expand to the front and back, and put display windows in the front. You have a lot of old riding tack, and we could set it up in scary scenes, as if we have ghost cowboys."

I chuckled, delighted with the idea. "How would we do that?"

"Oh, I can rig it with wire and paint really cool backdrops," Thistle offered. "No one would be able to see the wires and we could change out the backdrops every four months or so. We could do a different one for every season."

"That sounds like a lot of work for you," I said. "Are you willing to sign on for something like that?"

"I would love it," Thistle replied. "I love painting. I love decorating. I would spend every hour of every day doing it if I could."

"It would probably be easier if you were … closer … when it came time to do it," I said, momentarily worrying now was not the time to broach the subject of us moving in together. I knew it would eventually happen. The barn transformation was still months away, though. I was hoping to be living in it by Christmas. Still, even if it was early, I wanted to lay the groundwork. Thistle sometimes needed time to ponder a suggestion before embracing it.

"Maybe," Thistle said, licking her lips. "We have time to talk about that later, though."

That was an obvious sign she wasn't ready to discuss potential living arrangement changes just yet. I decided to follow her lead.

"You're going to help decorate Sam's new ship, right?" I asked, shifting the topic to something I knew she would be happy to discuss. "That will take up some of your time. When is he getting that, by the way?"

"It's not due to be delivered for another few weeks," Thistle replied. "I'm looking forward to decorating that, too. I have some outstanding ideas for ghost pirates. Ahoy, matey, I'm going to eat your guts for dinner!"

I laughed at her imitation of a pirate. "That sounds cool," I said. "I promised to help with any construction he needs."

"How are you going to do that and get everything handled here?"

"It will all work out," I replied. "I'm not doing the actual construction here so I can schedule time to help Sam between rides and taking care of the horses. I know he wants to have the boat up and running for Halloween, and I think it's going to be a cool draw.

"There are a lot of nautically-minded people in Michigan," I continued. "A haunted pirate attraction will draw more people to Hemlock Cove, and that can only help the rest of us."

"You have an incredibly pragmatic mind," Thistle said, brushing her lips against my chin. "I love you, Marcus."

I worried the first time I admitted I loved her she wouldn't say it back. She'd been surprisingly giving with the words – and emotions attached to them. "I love you, too."

"We'll talk about the other stuff when it gets closer," Thistle said. "I just ... later. Is that okay?"

"That's fine." I meant it. I'm a firm believer that things happen when they're supposed to, and you can't force destiny's timetable.

As if on cue, the storm picked that moment to arrive and the sky split with a terrifying bolt of lightning. We picked a spot far enough away from the loft hatch that we wouldn't get wet yet could still hear the storm as it rattled the stable's wallboards and watch it through the open hatch.

Beneath us I could hear a few of the horses shift in their stalls. The noise was somehow soothing, their presence relaxing.

"It's here," Thistle whispered breathlessly. "It's supposed to be a big one."

"What is it with you and storms?" I asked, genuinely curious. "You're always excited and want to watch when one hits."

"I just like them," Thistle replied. "They remind me that there's something bigger out there."

"Like what?"

"Power. Magic. Destruction."

It was a fairly profound statement from an entirely bewitching woman. "Well, relax," I said, pressing her head to my chest as we turned our eyes to the window. "I think we're in for one heck of a show."

"I think we're in for one heck of a life," Thistle said. "This is only the beginning."

WE SPENT a full hour watching the storm, my eyes growing heavier even as Thistle excitedly chattered away. It was an intense light show, but the sound of the rain beating on the roof lulled me, and eventually I drifted off.

I slept hard, my dreams filled with happy laughter. I couldn't see the woman giggling in my dreams, but I knew it was Thistle.

At some point the dream shifted, though, and I realized the sound wasn't laughter but screaming. I jolted awake, bolting to a sitting position and scanning the loft for Thistle. Her spot next to me on the makeshift pallet was empty, and my heart filled with dread.

A second scream filled the loft, followed almost immediately by a roaring rumble of thunder. I rolled to my side, glancing over the edge of the loft for some sign of Thistle – or imminent danger.

One of the horses – I couldn't be sure which one – stamped in its stall. The storm made all of them antsy, but the scream added to their discomfort.

"Thistle?"

I cocked my head to the side, praying for the reassuring sound of her voice. Perhaps she was down soothing the horses. Maybe she never fell asleep and got restless. When she didn't answer, my heart rate ratcheted up a notch.

"Thistle!"

She didn't answer a second time and I crawled for the ladder, swinging my leg over and quickly descending. I was barefoot, which is a general no-no in a stable thanks to errant nails and other debris, but a tetanus shot was better than the horrible things flying through my mind.

"Thistle!"

The storm answered for her, the thunder shaking the building. Then I heard the scream again. Whoever made the noise was outside. I raced toward the door, my toe hitting something sharp. I swore under my breath but ignored the pain as I threw the door open.

It took a moment for my eyes to adjust. The rain came down in heavy sheets, hitting the ground so hard it bounced. The outdoor area of the stable consisted of flattened dirt, which now resembled a mud pit.

"Thistle!"

The sound of footsteps jerked my attention to the right. Instead of Thistle, though, I found a sopping wet teenaged girl. For a moment I thought she was in trouble and I took a step in her direction, intent on offering help. A second figure bolted out of the bushes, though, and the girl screeched when she saw it. The sound didn't reflect terror, but glee.

She laughed as she darted away from him, giggling as he gave chase. It was just two teenagers messing around, which was a relief. That didn't answer the big question, though.

"Thistle!"

"What?"

I jolted at the sound of her voice, swiveling quickly to find her standing in the open doorway of the stable.

"You scared the crap out of me," I barked, striding toward her and pulling her in for a hug. "I thought that was you screaming."

"I'm sorry," Thistle said, patting my back. "I ... I'm sorry."

She looked confused, and a little frightened. "No, I'm sorry," I said, taking a step back. My clothing was completely soaked through. "I just when I woke up and you were gone."

"I went to the bathroom," Thistle said.

"I called for you."

"I didn't hear you," Thistle said, running her index finger down my wet cheek. "I didn't want to wake you when I came down. I'm sorry."

"It's okay," I said, grabbing her hand and pressing it to my chest. "I thought you were outside and I ran out when I heard the screaming. It turned out to be two teenagers messing around in the storm."

"Okay," Thistle said, reaching for the door to pull it closed. "It's okay. It was just a misunderstanding."

"Yeah." I exhaled heavily and then grabbed the door, pushing it forward so I could make sure it was locked. I cast a final glance outside, the hair on the back of my neck standing on end as I tried to shake the feeling of being watched.

I was being ridiculous. I was sure of it. The teenagers were probably out there laughing at me.

Still, something akin to dread crouched in the back of my mind. I stared out into the dark for a moment, but Thistle drew my attention away as she climbed back into the loft.

"Come on," she prodded. "The storm is still pretty active. We should get some sleep."

"I'm coming," I said, pushing the door shut and latching the lock. "I'm right behind you."

FIVE

I didn't think I would fall asleep, but the rain drove me under minutes after my head hit the pallet. I didn't stir again until my cell phone rang the next morning.

"I'm going to make you eat that phone if you don't answer it," Thistle grumbled, jerking the blanket over her head.

Her sweetness factor decreases the earlier the morning hour.

I fumbled around the top of the blanket until I found my phone. "Hello."

"It's the end of the world!"

I recognized the voice without checking the number. "Good morning, Aunt Tillie," I said, swallowing my weary sigh. "How are you?"

"Did you hear me?" Aunt Tillie barked. "It's the end of the world!"

I was used to her histrionic fits so I didn't put a lot of stock in her early morning meltdown. "Zombies or aliens?"

The silence on the other end of the call told me my joke landed on the wrong side of Aunt Tillie's funny bone. "You get more and more like Thistle and Bay the more time you spend with them," Aunt Tillie said.

"I think that's a compliment," I said, patting Thistle's head under the blanket as she growled.

"I'm going to kill that old woman," she threatened. "I'm going to hit her over the head with a shovel and bury her where no one can find her."

"Tell Thistle I heard that," Aunt Tillie said.

There was no way I was risking Thistle's wrath before she had her first jolt of coffee. "What can I do for you, Aunt Tillie? It's not even seven yet."

"Which means it's the middle of the night and she wants to die," Thistle hissed.

"I heard that, too," Aunt Tillie said. "Tell Thistle I'm going to curse her to smell like rotten potatoes if she's not careful."

"I will … relay that message at some point during the day," I said. "What's on your mind?"

Thistle pulled the blanket down and glared at me. "What did she just say?"

"She said she loves you and can't wait to see you today," I lied.

Thistle and Aunt Tillie snorted in unison, and not for the first time I wondered whether Thistle would evolve into the cantankerous matriarch as she aged. That was a sobering thought. "What were we talking about?"

"We were talking about the end of the world," Aunt Tillie said. "I need you out at my special garden right away. Civilization is breaking down. We have to prepare ourselves for Armageddon."

Most people would ask questions, or at least feign worry. I was fairly certain Aunt Tillie was spouting nonsense for dramatic purposes. I knew her well enough to realize she wouldn't let it go until I agreed to ride to her rescue. "Give me thirty minutes."

"Did you not hear me about the end the world?"

"I did hear you, but I can't get out there right this second," I replied. "I haven't even brushed my teeth yet."

"No one cares about that," Aunt Tillie barked. "I don't want to kiss you, just bend your ear and utilize your investigative talents. Swallow some mouthwash and move your butt. The world is about to end and I need a big stick to fight off evil."

Well, good. I love it when she carries around a big stick. She often whistles while she does it and makes growling noises at birds. The visual is hilarious.

"I'm on my way." I ended the call and glanced at Thistle, smiling at her mussed hair and murderous expression. "Good morning, Sunshine."

"Ha, ha," Thistle intoned. "What does that crazy old bat want now?"

"She mentioned something about the end of the world."

"Zombies or aliens?"

I chuckled. Thistle got my sense of humor and it was only one of the things I loved about her. "She says I have to meet her at her field."

"Oh, great," Thistle muttered. "Someone probably tripped the wards last night. Teenagers are always out there looking for pot. Aunt Tillie's field is the worst kept secret in Hemlock Cove."

"No one can find it, though."

"You can," Thistle pointed out. "She must've rigged the spell so you can see it. The only other people who can readily see it share Winchester blood ... and, well, Annie. She's a kid, though. She has no idea what she's looking at."

"I never asked why I'm able to see it," I said. "What do you have on your schedule today?"

"We're running a booth at the festival."

"Well, I'll run out to the inn and see what she's all worked up about and then meet you at the festival for lunch. How does that sound?"

"That sounds perfect," Thistle said, rolling over to rest her chin on my chest. "I'll make it worth your while if you stand that old lady up."

It was a tempting offer, but the idea of Thistle smelling like rotten potatoes for a week didn't exactly fill me with delight. "I'll take a rain check," I said, kissing the tip of Thistle's nose. "She'll take it out on you if I'm late."

"Good point," Thistle said. "Hit her over the head with a shovel while you're out there. I'll take care of the rest."

"You're a funny girl, Thistle Winchester."

"I should have my own comedy show," she agreed. "I'm not joking about this, though. Aunt Tillie is up to something. I can feel it."

Sadly, I could feel it, too.

I PARKED in front of The Overlook and skirted the inn instead of entering through the front door. I didn't want to explain my presence – or Thistle's absence – so I thought it better to avoid probing questions from Winnie, Marnie and Twila, and head straight to the source of my morning wake-up call.

I knew the Winchester property as well as my own by this point, and I was lost in thought as I walked the path that led to the pot field. I didn't pay much attention to my surroundings, and I was almost to my destination when Landon appeared in front of me.

I pulled up short, surprised by his sudden appearance. "Hey."

"Hey."

"Um ... good morning?"

"It is a lovely morning," Landon agreed, his hair freshly washed and still wet as it brushed against his shoulders. "How are you this lovely morning?"

Uh-oh. Something was off here. "I'm great," I replied, tilting my head to the side as I considered Landon's stance. He stood with his arms crossed over his chest as he blocked my way to the pot field. That had to be on purpose. "How are you?"

"I slept great," Landon replied, feigning brightness. "The guesthouse was quiet because Thistle wasn't there to get Bay going about that stupid craft room. The storm was loud and it knocked us right out."

"It was pretty much the same for us," I said. "Although ... we did have a slight incident."

Landon arched an eyebrow and remained silent.

"I woke up in the middle of the night because someone was screaming and Thistle was gone," I supplied, racking my brain for ways to get Landon out of my path without explaining where I was heading. I was fairly certain he would never arrest me, but I didn't want to give him a reason to try. "I ran outside, but it was two teenagers playing chase games."

"Where was Thistle?"

"In the bathroom."

"So that's really a non-story, isn't it?" Landon narrowed his eyes as he looked me up and down. "Where are you going?"

"Where are you going?" Crud. You're never supposed to answer a question with a question. Bay taught me that. It was too late now. "I mean, why aren't you up at the inn having breakfast?"

"Bay is still getting ready and had to handle something on her computer for the newspaper," Landon replied. "I came out to check out the storm damage and I saw the funniest thing."

Double crud. "What did you see?"

"I saw Aunt Tillie," Landon said. "She was wearing pajama bottoms and a sleeping cap. I didn't even know they still made sleeping caps. She had one on, though. She was whistling and swinging a big stick."

"Oh ... um ... maybe she was sleepwalking."

Landon rolled his eyes. "You're a terrible liar," he said. "There's only one reason she would be out here, and we both know what it is."

"I have no idea," I said, hoping my expression reflected confusion instead of subterfuge. "You have that keen investigative mind, though. You're probably one step ahead of me. Heck, you're probably ten steps in front of me."

"Knock it off," Landon said. "What's going on at Aunt Tillie's pot field? Why are you here?"

"I'm here because I love a good walk in the morning."

"Liar."

"I do," I said, committing to my story though it didn't make a lick of sense. "I find the best way to start a day is with a brisk walk."

Landon wasn't going to let it go. "Why didn't you walk around the stables?"

"The storm made it really muddy."

"It's muddy here."

"Not as muddy as the stables," I said.

Landon knit his eyebrows. "Just tell me what Aunt Tillie is up to," he said. "If something bad is about to happen, I need to know."

I got his worry. Something bad always seemed to happen. Trying to stay ahead of it was never going to work, though. Trying to stay ahead of Aunt Tillie was something akin to running through a vat of superglue. "I don't know what to tell you."

"You suck," Landon muttered, lifting his head when he heard Bay yell his name. "I guess it's time for breakfast. Would you like to walk up to the inn with us?"

"I should finish my walk."

"Right." Landon blew out a frustrated sigh. "I'm going to figure out what's going on. I hope you know that."

"Good luck with that." I clapped his shoulder, remaining rooted to my spot until I saw him join with Bay on the path leading back to the inn. She was giggly when she found him, her smile bright. They clearly had had a good night.

"They're gross, right?"

I jumped when I heard Aunt Tillie's voice behind me. She was near enough to crawl inside of me if she deemed it necessary. "You should wear a bell or something," I said, turning to face her. "By the way, Bay and Landon are very cute."

"I didn't say they weren't cute. I said they were gross."

"I don't think something can be gross and cute at the same time," I argued.

"How about bats?" Aunt Tillie never met an argument she was willing to lose.

"I stand corrected," I said, hoping to move things along. "What's the big crisis?"

"Someone tried to break into the field last night," Aunt Tillie said, leading me toward her private garden. "The wards held, but whoever it was meant business."

"How do you know that?" I asked, genuinely curious. I shivered as we crossed the magical barrier that shielded her field. I couldn't see it, but I always felt it.

"I put a spell on the field," Aunt Tillie answered, shooting me a "well, duh" look. "I already told you that."

"I understand that," I said, tugging on my limited patience. "I want to know how you're aware someone tried to cross the barrier. I mean … do you have an alarm?"

"Kind of," Aunt Tillie said. "It's more of a feeling than anything else. You can set an alarm, but it gets annoying if you forget to change the ringtone. There's only so many times you can hear Eminem talk about losing himself before you want to lose your mind."

Aunt Tillie's taste in music was as eclectic as her wardrobe. I took the opportunity to look over her lavender pajamas and matching sleep hat, marveling at her audacity to walk around in the outfit. She didn't care what anyone thought about her. It was an admirable – if sometimes annoying – trait. "So you just know they tried to cross the barrier multiple times last night?"

"Basically," Aunt Tillie replied, gesturing toward the far side of the field. "They came in from that direction and crossed the barrier at least four different times. The wards held, so they didn't find what they were looking for. They couldn't see what was right in front of them."

I followed her finger with my eyes. "Why would someone come on the property from that direction?" I asked. "There's nothing in that direction for miles."

"I know. That's what worries me."

"Are you sure it wasn't an animal?" I asked. "People claim wolves have been sighted in this area, although I've yet to see one. A wolf might be big enough to trip the wards."

"The wards don't work on animals," Aunt Tillie said, shaking her head. "The trespasser has to be human."

"So … what do you think is going on?"

"Well, I've given it some thought and I figured that we're either dealing with Bigfoot or zombies," Aunt Tillie said.

"I knew zombies would play into this," I muttered, rubbing the back of my neck. "What are your other options?"

"Teenagers out to steal pot – or something more nefarious."

"Like what?"

Aunt Tillie shrugged. "That's why I called you here," she said. "I can't figure out everything on my own. I need help occasionally."

"How am I supposed to figure out who is trying to cross your wards?" I asked, confused.

"I figured you could camp out here tonight and catch whoever is doing it," Aunt Tillie replied. "I would do it myself but … I don't want to."

Yeah, Thistle would just love that. "How do you know they will come back?"

"I have a feeling."

"Kind of like the feeling you had that led you to believe someone tried to cross the wards last night?"

Aunt Tillie shook her head. "It's a different feeling. I can't explain it."

That's part of the problem with her. She always tells me she has "feelings" and then expects me to blindly follow her orders. I wasn't in the mood to play games today. "Can't we come up with a different solution?"

"Like what?"

"I don't know," I hedged. "Maybe you should have Landon stake this place out. He would love to catch someone doing something. In fact, I think that's about the only thing that's going to relax him right now."

"Yeah, he's wound a little tight this weekend, isn't he?" Aunt Tillie wrinkled her nose. "I don't want to involve the Fed. He'll start asking questions and threatening to arrest me if I don't burn the field. He's a real killjoy sometimes."

"I thought you liked him," I countered. "You even said it yourself."

"I like him just fine," Aunt Tillie said. "That doesn't mean I want to take him into my confidence. You're special. You get special treatment. Landon isn't ready for the treatment."

How did I get so lucky? "I can't stake out the pot field tonight," I said. "I have plans with Thistle and a bunch of stuff to do for the festival. Can't you set a different spell to track the person trying to cross over?"

"That's an interesting idea, but I don't want to do that."

"Why not?"

"It's too much work," Aunt Tillie answered. "I'm an old woman and my energy only lasts for short bursts. You're young. You should jump at the chance to catch evil-doers."

"I ... can't," I said, making a face. "I promised Thistle I would hang out with her."

"Okay," Aunt Tillie said, her tone cool. "If something terrible happens, it's on you. I won't take the blame for it."

I forced a smile. "I think I'll take the risk."

"May the Goddess have mercy on all of our souls," Aunt Tillie intoned, resting her hand against her heart. She looked so serious I considered giving in. She got distracted before I acquiesced. "I'm starving. Let's get up to the inn before Landon eats all of the bacon. That boy is a glutton."

"Sure," I said, resigned. "Let's eat breakfast."

"And then we'll talk about you staking this place out," Aunt Tillie said. "You'll probably feel different on a full stomach. Your mind will go back to its usual peak performance and you'll realize that saying no to a defenseless old lady is cruel and unusual punishment."

What is it with the women in this family knowing exactly how to manipulate me? I'm starting to think it's a pattern.

SIX

"How was your morning with Aunt Tillie?" Thistle asked later that afternoon, settling next to me on the picnic table bench as she slid a plateful of food in my direction. "Are you ready to join the circus yet?"

"Ha, ha." I rolled my eyes. "She's a piece of work."

Thistle arched an eyebrow, surprised and amused. "You rarely speak badly about Aunt Tillie. She must've been a real pill this morning."

"Yes, I think she was a stool softener," I deadpanned, earning a belly laugh from my girlfriend. "I'm sorry. I shouldn't say anything negative about her. She's … a lovely woman."

"Yeah. She's a real goddess amongst men," Thistle said.

"Who are we talking about?" Landon asked, settling in across from us with his own heaping plate. "Did she happen to be walking around the property in pajamas and a sleep hat this morning, by any chance?"

"Ooh, intrigue," Thistle said, leaning forward. "What was Aunt Tillie doing out in her pajamas? She usually saves that behavioral gem for when she's trying to make Winnie's head implode."

Landon snorted. "That would do it," he said. "Winnie caught her coming back inside with Marcus before breakfast and had a fit. Aunt

Tillie said she and Marcus were meeting for a secret liaison and not to tell you because jealousy is an ugly beast."

My cheeks burned as Thistle shifted an annoyed gaze in my direction. "Did she really say that?"

"She might have insinuated it," I conceded. "She was clearly joking."

"Yes, I wouldn't worry about Marcus leaving you for Aunt Tillie," Landon said. "No man wants to wake up to that sleeping hat."

"What did she really want?" Thistle asked.

I didn't miss Landon's pointed gaze as it landed on me. "Oh, well, she just wanted to talk about fertilizer options." I really am a terrible liar. I get why everyone says that. I'm not immune to my shortcomings.

"You had to talk about fertilizer before Aunt Tillie was out of her pajamas?" Landon challenged. "Why don't I believe that?"

"Because you're smart and handsome," Bay supplied, dropping a kiss on Landon's cheek before sitting next to him. "Did you miss me?"

"I cried the entire time you were gone," Landon replied.

"Ugh. You guys make my stomach turn," Thistle groused. "Do you have to be so cutesy all of the time?"

"You're just jealous," Landon said, grabbing a french fry from Bay's plate and popping it into his mouth. "You wish you could be as cute as us."

"Yes, it's my hidden dream," Thistle said, her tone droll. "How did you ever figure it out?"

"You make me tired," Landon muttered, rolling his neck until it cracked. "I'm not going to let this early-morning excursion go until you tell me what's going on. It would be easier on everyone if you owned up to it."

"Yeah, Marcus," Thistle said, poking my ribs and grinning. "Tell everyone what you were doing during your clandestine meeting with Aunt Tillie this morning. We're all dying to know."

"I … ." Crud. I hate being put on the spot. "I noticed you took a sample of the blood you found in the loft yesterday, Landon. Did you send it in to be tested?"

"Smooth," Landon said, shaking his head. "I did send it to the lab. It's not exactly a priority, but they said they should be able to tell whether it's animal or human before the end of the day. It's going to bug me if I don't know."

"That was a great swerve," Thistle said. "Now how about we go back to your morning with Aunt Tillie."

I love the woman, but she's a real pain in the … .

"Oh, leave the boy alone," Aunt Tillie chided, taking everyone by surprise as she popped up at the end of the table. "There's no need to torture him because you're jealous of our legendary love affair, Thistle.

"I'm old and don't have the energy I used to have," she continued. "I'm sure we can share. Marcus has enough affection to spread the wealth. I'm a gifted lover, but I'll only be able to muster the strength to entertain him once a week."

Landon choked on whatever he was trying to swallow and hit his chest to clear the blockage. Bay couldn't stop herself from giggling, and the look on Thistle's face was one for the ages. As for me, well, I wanted to crawl into a hole and die.

"Aunt Tillie called Marcus to come out to her pot field this morning because someone tripped the wards," Thistle announced, narrowing her eyes in a challenging manner as she locked gazes with Aunt Tillie. "I'm not sure how things went – or how far anyone got – but that's what Marcus was doing out there."

"Thistle," I groaned, leaning my head back so I could stare at the sky. Sudden onset blindness thanks to the bright sun would be welcome at this point. "Why did you say that?"

"Because Aunt Tillie knows exactly how to get under her skin," Bay supplied, smirking. "She's very good at it."

"It's a gift," Aunt Tillie agreed.

"I knew that's what you were doing," Landon said. "I don't know why you bothered lying to me given the circumstances. The woman was walking around in her pajamas and swinging a big stick while whistling."

"That's how I hunt," Aunt Tillie shot back. "It's very effective."

"Whatever," Landon muttered. "Was anything stolen? If something was stolen you have to tell me. I need to know whether people are creeping around the property stealing marijuana. Drug dealers can be dangerous."

"You're a real pain this weekend," Aunt Tillie said. "I think it's because things have been quiet for an entire week and a half and you've convinced yourself something bad will happen because you have a long weekend. Chill out."

"You chill out," Landon shot back. "I have an awful feeling something is going to happen. I can't shake it."

"Maybe you're clairvoyant," Bay said, patting his arm. She didn't appear particularly perturbed about Landon's admission. "Aunt Tillie is right, though – wow, there's a sentence I never thought I'd say. You need to relax. Nothing bad is going to happen."

"Except for the blood in the loft and someone trying to cross the wards in that field," Landon argued. "How can I be the only one who sees this?" Landon looked to me for support.

"I'd like to help you, man, but I think you're overreacting, too," I said, offering him a rueful smile. "I get that you're antsy given everything that happened the week before last. Bay almost died and you've been hyper-vigilant ever since. There's no reason to freak out, though."

"Thank you for your support," Landon muttered, shifting his eyes to Bay. "Do you really think I'm overreacting?"

"Yes, but I love you anyway," Bay said. "It's going to be okay. I understand where you're coming from. If history is any indication, something bad is due to happen. It usually happens to one of us when the time comes.

"I promise to be careful, though," she continued. "We can spend the day together and you can watch my every move."

Thistle snorted. "That doesn't sound co-dependent or anything."

"No one was talking to you," Bay sniffed. "It's going to be fine, Landon. Nothing is going to happen. We're going to eat lunch and then wander over to the pavilion to check out the pie contest. All of our mothers have entries."

"Yeah, that's why I'm here," Aunt Tillie said, wrinkling her nose. "They keep trapping me into agreeing to things I would rather die than attend. I think I must be slipping."

"Oh, no, don't say that," Thistle said. "I think wandering around in your nightgown with a stick is totally normal. You keep doing it."

"No one needs your fresh mouth," Aunt Tillie warned. "I'm here to see the pie contest and then I'm going to search for the creeper."

I stilled, confused. "Who is the creeper?"

"The person who tripped my wards," Aunt Tillie replied, irked. "Haven't you listened to anything I've said?"

"Yeah, Marcus," Landon teased, his earlier bad mood lifting. "The creeper is a real threat. He could throw the entire balance of Hemlock Cove out of whack."

"You're on my list," Aunt Tillie threatened, extending a finger in Landon's direction. "You probably don't want to push me. I'm not in the mood for games."

Tension roiled between Aunt Tillie and Landon for a moment, and I got so uncomfortable I decided to alleviate it. "So, you're going to the pie contest?"

Aunt Tillie finally jerked her eyes from Landon and focused on me. "I am," she confirmed. "Personally, I don't see why you would bake a pie and let someone else eat it. That seems a real waste of time."

"I'm right there with you," Landon said. "They should've just given me the pies."

"Well, at least we agree on something," Aunt Tillie said. "Hurry up and eat your lunch. If I have to watch that stupid contest, you're coming with me. Someone needs to entertain me or I'll die of boredom."

"Well, at least we have something to look forward to," Thistle said.

"You're on my list, too."

"I CAN'T BELIEVE how many people are here," Landon said, glancing around the crowded pavilion. "Who cares about pie this much?"

"You," Bay replied, resting her head against his chest as he wrapped his arms around her waist. "The only thing that would get you more excited than a slice of Marnie's blackberry pie is if someone could figure a way to make one out of bacon."

Landon's eyes lit up. "Do you think that's possible?"

"Only if you want all of us to throw up," Thistle answered, slipping my arm over her shoulders so she could move in front of me to see the action. "Oh, look. All three of our mothers made the finals. This should end well."

"You have a wonderfully witty outlook on life today," I said, poking her stomach and earning a grin. "What's with you?"

Thistle shrugged. "I don't know. The storm invigorated me."

"How did sleeping in the barn go?" Bay asked. "I don't think I could've done that. I prefer a bed."

"Yes, you're a terrific prude sometimes," Landon said, skirting her hand when she playfully slapped him. "I heard you guys had some excitement when Thistle disappeared, though. I wouldn't have liked that setup."

"I went to the bathroom," Thistle argued. "It's not like I left town."

"I wouldn't have even noticed if the screams didn't wake me up," I said. "It was just … eerie. I know it was teenagers fooling around, but I swear I felt as if someone was watching me when I shut the stable doors."

"You didn't tell me that," Thistle said. "Why didn't you say something?"

"I didn't want to make you nervous. I was just … overreacting."

"And running around barefoot when you shouldn't have been," Thistle said. "How is your toe?"

"Sore and bruised, but otherwise fine. There's no reason to worry, Mom. I didn't break the skin."

"Okay, I've been scoping out the competition, and we don't have any," Aunt Tillie said, pushing between Landon and me to give herself room. "The only other person who made the finals is Denise Tipton. We all know her pie tastes like cardboard."

Meadow Tipton, Denise's daughter, stood on the other side of Landon and shot Aunt Tillie a dirty look. Aunt Tillie ignored her.

"I thought you didn't care about the contest," Bay challenged, tilting her head to the side as she watched her mother carry her pie to one of the pedestals on the far side of the stage. "Now all of a sudden you're acting as if winning a blue ribbon instead of a red one is important."

"Hey, I don't care about the contest, but your mothers do," Aunt Tillie said. "If they want to win, I want them to win."

"You just like beating people," Thistle said. "Admit it. You're happiest when you can claim victory, even if it's for a pie you didn't bake."

"There's nothing wrong with winning," Aunt Tillie sniffed, rolling her eyes when Twila took the time to wave at her. "Things are going to get ugly when one of your mothers is judged to have better pie than the others."

Thistle pressed her lips together to keep from laughing, the double entendre proving too hilarious to ignore.

"I know what you're thinking, and you're a pervert," Aunt Tillie chastised. "Stop being a buffoon, and focus on your mothers."

"I'm a little worried," Bay admitted. "If Mom wins she's going to be unbearable."

"Don't kid yourself. If Marnie or Twila win they'll be unbearable, too," Aunt Tillie said. "No matter what happens, there's going to be a fight. It's going to make all the squabbling you two do look like the junior leagues."

"I think that sounds fun," Thistle said. "We should've brought a camera."

"Some days I really like you," Aunt Tillie said, patting Thistle's head. "You make me very proud."

"Why do they keep entering these contests if they know it's going to spark a fight?" I asked, earning dumbfounded looks from Aunt Tillie, Thistle and Bay. "Er … forget I asked."

"Nice save," Landon said. "Where are Clove and Sam, by the way?"

"They're working at the Dandridge today," Thistle answered. "They're going to come into town later. Marcus wants to have a bonfire by the stables."

"That sounds fun," Landon said. "We're probably going to want a place to hide once the pie contest goes south. Do you think I'll still get a slice?"

"I can't believe you're not fat," Thistle said. "All you talk about is food."

"And Bay," I added.

"Hey, where did Mom's pie go?" Bay asked, craning her neck to study the empty pedestal. "I ... did Mom move her pie?"

"That could be misconstrued as dirty," Thistle said, although she studied the empty pedestal, too. "Seriously, I didn't see her move the pie. Did anyone else?"

"I ... ."

"Where is my pie?" Winnie's angry screech was loud enough to cause everyone under the pavilion to cringe.

"I guess that answers that question," I said, exchanging a glance with Landon.

"I'm on it," Landon said. "If I find it, I'm eating it, though."

"Yes, that should go over well."

Curiosity got the better of everyone and we followed Landon to the pedestal.

"What happened, Winnie?" Landon was all business. He's the only guy I know who can make pie theft seem like a legitimate FBI case.

"I put my pie there two minutes ago and someone stole it," Winnie snapped. "I demand a mistrial!"

"This isn't a courtroom," Landon said, circling the pedestal. He frowned when he got to the far side, which happened to be by the far flap, and hunkered down for a closer look. "Well, crap."

"What is it?" I asked, walking to him. "What do you see?"

Landon refrained from touching the pedestal and merely pointed. "What does that look like to you?"

I followed his finger and frowned when I saw the red smudge against the white paint. "I ... um ... ." There was no way that could be what it looked like.

"It's blood," Bay said, her eyes widening.

"Just like I found in the loft," Landon said. "I told you something terrible was going to happen. I was right!"

"Yes. We're about to be inundated by pie thieves," Thistle deadpanned. "Everyone run for your lives."

"It's the creeper," Aunt Tillie said sagely. "He's more fiendish than we initially envisioned."

"Who is the creeper?" Winnie asked, frustrated. "Where is my pie? Can someone bring me my pie? I'm lost without my pie."

Thistle opened her mouth to respond but I slapped my hand over her mouth. She would only make things worse. "You can let some of them go."

SEVEN

"I can't believe someone stole Winnie's pie." Clove, snuggled in Sam's lap as we congregated around the bonfire outside the stable later that night, was dumbfounded. "Who steals a pie?"

"Someone with excellent taste," Landon said. "I had to eat cake. It wasn't the same."

"Something tells me you'll live," Bay said, laughing as Landon tickled her ribs.

"You've got a mouth on you," Landon muttered, although he didn't look particularly perturbed. He expected something bad to happen – and it did – but in the grand scheme of things, a pie thief wasn't going to cause him to lose sleep. "Do you think your mother is still pouting?"

"Oh, Mom will never going to let this go," Bay said. "She tried to call a mistrial on the pie contest, but Marnie won anyway. I think Marnie should probably sleep with one eye open."

"And her bedroom door locked," Clove added. "Winnie was spitting mad at dinner."

"Yes, I noticed," Landon said. "The hamburgers tasted funny."

"That's because they pour their emotions into their cooking," Clove supplied. "They're kitchen witches. It's what they do."

"And what about you three?" I asked. "What do you pour your emotions into?"

Clove shrugged. "I think I probably do that with gardening."

"Which is why the flowers she planted three months ago look as if they've been growing for years," Sam said. "They're really beautiful ... like Clove."

It was relatively dark around the bonfire ring, but Clove's blush was obvious.

I shifted my eyes to Thistle. "What about you? You pour everything into your art. That's why you're always keen to decorate, isn't it?"

"Probably," Thistle said. "We're not exactly accomplished kitchen witches. We find our inspiration in other places."

"Oh, I don't know," Landon said. "Bay burned toast the other day. I think that's an accomplishment."

Bay scowled. "You're on my list."

"I'm happy to be on your list," Landon said, wrinkling his nose as he kissed her cheek.

"If Clove pours her heart into gardening and Thistle pours hers into art, what does Bay pour her heart into?" I asked, lightly rubbing Thistle's back as she reclined against me.

"Trouble," Landon answered, not missing a beat.

Bay slapped his knee. "That's not true," she protested. "I don't go looking for trouble."

"Yes, it's merely drawn to you," Landon said. "It's like you're the refrigerator and trouble is those magnets representing the cities you visit on vacations."

"Are you saying I have hips like a refrigerator?"

Landon realized his mistake too late to take it back. "I'm saying I love you more than anything and absolutely adore your hips."

I chuckled. I couldn't help myself. "Nice save."

"This isn't my first rodeo," Landon teased, although he turned serious after a moment. "You pour your heart into helping people, sweetie. It's a nice gift. Personally, I wish you weren't so giving, but I also realize that's one of the reasons I love you."

"Oh, he's so sweet," Clove cooed, pressing her hand to the spot above her heart.

"Yes, just like drinking a bottle of corn syrup," Thistle said, rolling her eyes. "Both make me want to puke."

"Leave them alone," I chastised, poking her ribs. "Everyone is having a good time. Why do you have to ruin it?"

"Because that's what's truly in her heart," Clove replied. "She shares a heart with Aunt Tillie."

"You take that back," Thistle hissed. "I'm nothing like that woman. Marcus, tell her I'm nothing like Aunt Tillie."

Now I was the one caught. "I think you have many wonderful qualities," I said, choosing my words carefully. "One of them is a tendency to dig your heels in, which shows you're determined. The other is your delight in irritating your family, which makes you very entertaining and a true slave to your muse."

"Wow," Landon intoned, making a hilarious face. "That was a masterful turn of a phrase. I am impressed."

"Me, too," Sam said.

"Yes, this isn't my first rodeo," I said, sputtering as Thistle elbowed me in the stomach and scorched me with a murderous look. "That was a compliment, Thistle."

"You're on my list," Thistle warned, although she settled her head against my chest and focused on the fire. "What do you guys think is really going on around here? Between the blood in the loft, the attempts to get into Aunt Tillie's field and Winnie's stolen pie, something weird is happening."

"We don't know that everything is related, though," Bay cautioned. "They could be three separate instances. People are always trying to find Aunt Tillie's pot field, and a holiday weekend when everyone is looking to party would make the field doubly tempting."

"That's true," Landon said, brushing Bay's hair from her face. "I think whoever was in Marcus' loft is the same person who stole the pie, though."

"Because of the blood?" I asked.

Landon nodded. "I think it's too much of a coincidence."

"You don't know that the blood in the loft was human, though," Bay pointed out. "As far as we know, an animal died up there and got dragged off by a bigger predator. It could've been a smaller bird or even a cat or something killed by an owl."

Landon opened his mouth, and for a moment I thought he was going to call her on her assumption. He changed his mind mid-course, though. "You're right," he said finally. "We don't know anything yet. I'm still waiting for confirmation from the lab. So far we have a stolen pie."

"Yes, and great memories," Thistle enthused. "I will never forget Winnie screaming 'Someone put their grubby hands on my pie!' I almost died."

"That's because you have a demented mind," I said, although I couldn't help but chuckle at the memory. "I liked when she realized why we kept snickering and threatened to unleash unholy hell on us if we didn't find her pie."

"Then we just laughed harder," Landon said. "I'm not going to get bacon all weekend. I know it."

We lapsed into amiable silence for a few minutes. I wasn't surprised when Clove was the first to break it. "What are your plans for the stable expansion?"

"I'm going to double its size out the back," I replied. "We're going to keep more than horses in there. I also want a dedicated storage area so the other barn will be completely open for home renovations. Thistle wants to add display windows on the front so we can draw people in with haunted scenes in the front area by the door."

"That sounds like a great idea," Bay said. "People will love that. How are you going to do it?"

Despite their argumentative ways, Thistle, Bay and Clove loved each other beyond reason. Even though they were mid-fight about the spare room in the guesthouse, Bay enjoyed bolstering Thistle's creative endeavors.

"Well, Marcus has a bunch of vintage riding gear in the loft,"

Thistle said, leaning forward. "I figure I can paint different backdrops on two big canvases, put them on either side of the main door, and then use wire to make it look as if the outfits are being held up by ghosts."

"Ooh, that sounds neat," Clove said, getting in on the action. "We're going to be ordering some lighting stuff for the ship when we get it. You should get in on the order because we'll save if we do it in bulk. You can get some of those eerie lights."

"That would be cool," Thistle said, taking me by surprise when she hopped off my lap. "Come look inside. I want to show you a couple of others idea I've been toying with."

"I thought you were going to enjoy the fire with me," I complained.

"We'll be back," Thistle said, making a face. "I want to show them my ideas."

"Let them go," Landon said. "Don't get in the way of women and decorating. It never ends well."

I considered offering s'mores to keep them close – for some reason the idea of letting them wander around the stable alone didn't sit well with me – but I had a feeling Landon wanted to talk away from their prying ears.

"Be careful," I said. "Don't separate."

"Yes, we don't want anyone to steal our pie," Thistle teased.

I fought the urge to laugh but joined in with Landon and Sam when they began chuckling. She knew her target audience.

Bay and Clove happily fell into step with Thistle, decorating plans spilling out of my tiny witch as she practically hopped toward the building. I waited until they disappeared from view before turning to Landon. "What's up?"

He balked. "What makes you think something is up?"

"Because you looked as if you were going to argue with Bay when she declared that an animal probably died in the loft, and then you purposely wanted them out of earshot so we could talk," I replied. "I'm not an idiot."

"No," Landon agreed, ruefully rubbing the back of his neck. "I forget how observant you are sometimes. You could be an investigator."

"I like horses better than criminals."

"Hey, I noticed you were acting weird, too," Sam interjected.

"You're brilliant, too, Sam," Landon said, glancing over his shoulder to make sure the women were still happy with their decorating talk before continuing. "I lied when I said I hadn't heard from the lab. I got results back on the blood from the loft. It's human."

I stilled, legitimately surprised. "How can you be sure?"

"The lab ran it," Landon answered. "They know what they're doing. I didn't ask for extensive tests because I wasn't sure what I was dealing with. I didn't want to seem like an alarmist, so I passed it off as due diligence."

That was probably smart. "Did they give you any other information?"

"They did," Landon said. "That's why I didn't want to mention it in front of the girls."

My interest was piqued. "And?"

"It belongs to a male," Landon said. "I have no idea of age or anything, but this individual is in serious trouble."

"For stealing a pie?" Sam didn't look convinced. "I admit it was wrong to steal Winnie's pie, but come on."

"Not that," Landon said, his irritation bubbling up. "I think whoever is behind this has a serious wound. That explains leaving a trail of blood. I have no idea how they got it or how serious it is. Until we find who it is, we're in the dark there.

"What I do know is that this man has a blood infection," he continued. "This wound is literally making him sick and putting his life in jeopardy."

"How does a blood infection work?" I asked.

"It depends on the infection," Sam answered, taking me by surprise with his fortitude. "It's probably sepsis. He could've been injured, maybe he ran into a something or even stubbed his toe. The bacterial infection can grow out of seemingly small injuries.

"If left untreated he could have organ failure or it could even travel to his bones, depending on the wound," he continued. "He's probably very sick."

Landon's mouth dropped open. "How do you know that?"

"Clove makes me watch *Grey's Anatomy* reruns on Lifetime," Sam admitted, not ashamed in the least. "I like it because a lot of the women are hot."

"Well, that makes it perfectly okay," Landon said, turning his thoughtful eyes to me. "Have you seen anyone limping ... or holding their side ... or hanging around the stable when they shouldn't be?"

I shook my head. "I would've noticed that," I said. "I keep a relatively good eye out because I'm afraid someone might steal an animal. It always seems like a good idea to go horseback riding when you're young and drunk. I don't want to risk the animals being injured because some idiot decided to take them for a joyride."

"Your teenage experience and my teenage experience were vastly different," Landon said. "It always seemed like a good idea to steal a four-wheeler when we were teenagers."

"Horses are better."

"Whatever," Landon said, checking over his shoulder again to make sure the girls weren't returning. "I didn't say anything in front of them because I don't want to ruin their weekend. Odds are someone is very sick and might not even realize it."

"You don't want them to be afraid," I surmised. That was the last thing I wanted, too. I also didn't want them caught off guard. "I understand why you're keeping this to yourself, but wouldn't they be better off knowing what's going on?"

"I don't know," Landon said. "Bay is so happy and she's been having a great time at the festival. She thought the pie theft was funny. I don't want to ruin that."

"I don't want to ruin it either," I said. "I wouldn't forgive myself if something happened to Thistle because we didn't tell them, though."

"I'm with Marcus on this," Sam offered. "Sepsis can play tricks on the mind due to fever and other factors. If this man is suffering from it, he may be extremely delusional. He could accidentally hurt one of them without meaning to do it."

Landon held up his hands, resigned. "Okay. We'll tell them. I don't want them getting worked up, though."

"No, you don't want them getting it in their heads to find whoever this individual is and take off on their own to do it," I corrected. "There's no shame in wanting to protect them."

"There is if you hear them tell it," Landon grumbled. "I … ."

Whatever he was about to say died on his lips as a bone-chilling scream filled the night air. I exchanged a look with Landon, surprised. "What was that?"

"Clove!" Sam jumped to his feet and raced toward the stable.

Landon and I followed, my heart pounding as I fought to keep up.

"Clove?"

No one immediately answered, and my mind drifted to my panic the night before when I thought Thistle went missing in the middle of the storm. An unfortunate suspicion crossed my mind.

"Thistle, if this is a joke because of what happened last night … ."

"Landon, we're over here." Bay's words cut me off, and I could tell by the tone of her voice she was serious.

We hurried to the far corner of the stable, pulling up short when we saw Bay and Thistle holding pitchforks and pointing them toward the office.

"What's going on?" Landon asked, hurrying toward Bay as I moved behind Thistle. Clove was unarmed, and she threw her arms around Sam's neck when he approached.

"There's someone in here," Thistle said, pointing toward the office. "He ran in there."

"Are you sure it was a man?" Landon asked, briefly locking gazes with me.

"He was too big to be a woman," Bay answered. "He was tall. Like … Bigfoot tall."

"I thought it was Bigfoot," Clove admitted.

"Oh, my poor Clove," Sam said, kissing her forehead.

"We were just wandering around talking," Bay explained. "We didn't see him at first. He was hiding behind that big wooden thing."

"That's a tool bench," I said, running my hand down the back of Thistle's head. "He didn't touch you, did he?"

"No," Thistle answered. "He ran into the office when he realized we saw him. We kind of froze for like twenty seconds. I swear that's what it felt like. Then he took off and ran into the office."

"Okay," Landon said, grabbing the pitchfork from Bay. "Move over there with Sam, Clove and Thistle. Marcus and I will check out the office."

Bay, her face white, shook her head. "What if he hurts you?"

"It's going to be fine, sweetie," Landon said, brushing a quick kiss against her forehead before pushing her toward Sam. "I'm trained for this."

"Then you should do it alone and leave Marcus with me," Thistle interjected.

"Yeah, that's not going to happen," I said, cupping Thistle's chin and giving her a light kiss. "Go over there with your cousins."

Thistle didn't look thrilled with the suggestion, but she followed my instructions and shuffled to Bay's side.

Landon reached inside the office, feeling around on the wall for a light switch. "Are you ready?"

"Let's do this."

Landon flicked the switch and the overhead lights in the small office flashed on. I steeled myself for action and found … absolutely nothing.

"Well, do you see him?" Thistle asked.

"The office is empty," Landon replied, striding toward the open window and scanning the field behind the stable. "He must have hopped out the window."

"There's more blood," I said, pointing toward a spot near the corner. "He must be seriously hurt."

"I don't know what to do," Landon admitted. "He clearly needs help, but he's acting like a criminal and is hiding from law enforcement for a reason."

"Maybe we should get dogs out here," Sam suggested. "They should be able to track him."

"I don't know anyone willing to send dogs out here for a guy stealing pies, especially on a holiday weekend," Landon said, extending his hand so Bay would take it and then pulling her close. I jumped when Thistle appeared next to me and wrapped her arms around my waist. "I think you and Thistle should spend the night at the guesthouse, Marcus. Don't risk staying here again."

"What about the animals?"

"He doesn't appear interested in the animals," Landon said. "I think he's just looking for a place to sleep."

"Should I let him sleep here?"

Landon shrugged. "I have no idea. I don't know what to think."

EIGHT

"What are you doing?"

Landon found me sitting on the side patio of the guesthouse the next morning, my feet bare as I studied my injured toe under the bright sunshine.

"I'm trying to decide whether I have sepsis," I admitted, flashing a sheepish smile. "That stuff Sam said about organ failure kind of freaked me out."

I thought Landon would make fun of me. Instead he was all business as he sat on the paver stones and leaned forward. "Let me see."

He was gentle as he reached over and touched my toe. It was bruised and sore, but it didn't look particularly life threatening.

"Do you think it's going to fall off?" I asked, offering a lame chuckle. "Do you think my organs will fail?"

"I think you stubbed your toe and it looks sore," Landon replied. "There's no broken skin, though. Sam also said it generally starts with a bacterial infection. I don't think you have that problem because there's no open wound."

"That's good," I said, relieved. "Were you surprised he knew all that stuff?"

"Bay makes me watch home renovation shows and I now know

more about putting ceramic tile in bathrooms than I ever would've imagined," Landon replied. "I have to keep reminding myself that he's smarter than I give him credit for."

"He lied when he came to town," I said. "I can see being leery."

"Yes, but he's proved himself in multiple ways since then – including getting shot while trying to save Bay," Landon said. "He deserves a clean slate."

"Plus, he makes Clove really happy."

"There is that," Landon agreed. "I worry about Clove because she seems somehow … needier … than the other two. Sam seems to understand that, and gives her what she needs to feel secure."

"I worry about Clove because Thistle and Bay get mean," I admitted. "Sam takes it in stride and bolsters her confidence."

"They are mean little cusses sometimes," Landon said, smirking. "I think your foot is going to be fine. If you're really worried, though, you should see a doctor."

"I thought you were my doctor," I teased.

"I don't care what you do, Bay and I are not playing nursemaid," Thistle said, popping around the side of the guesthouse and fixing us with a curious look. Landon instinctively snatched his hand away from my foot, and for a reason I couldn't fathom, my cheeks burned. "Do you want to tell me what you two are doing?"

"I … Marcus stubbed his toe the other night and he wanted to make sure it wasn't serious," Landon explained.

"Uh-huh." Thistle arched an eyebrow as she locked gazes with me. "Do I have to be worried about this little relationship?"

Landon and I shot her twin scowls of mortification. "No."

"What's going on?" Bay asked, exiting the guesthouse and pulling up short when she saw us sitting together on the patio. "I'm almost afraid to ask."

"Landon and Marcus are playing doctor," Thistle said, her eyes sparkling. "I think my heart may break."

"We're not playing doctor," Landon snapped, brushing the seat of his cargo shorts off as he stood. "Don't be gross."

"It's okay," Thistle said, her expression earnest. "We'll cry a little bit, but we truly wish you the best."

Bay giggled. "I don't wish you the best. I can't fight it, though. Follow your hearts."

"You're in trouble," Landon said, grabbing her around the waist and swinging her in the air. "You're not funny."

"Is there something seriously wrong with your foot?" Thistle asked, turning sober as she knelt down. "Does that hurt?"

"Some," I replied, refusing to admit I was in agony whenever I stepped wrong on it. I was too much of a tough guy for that. "Landon says the skin isn't torn, though, and it's not infected."

"Is it broken?"

I shook my head. "I stubbed it when I was looking for you the other night," I replied. "It will be fine in a few days. There's nothing to worry about."

"I'm not worried," Thistle said. "I think you might be, though. We can have Winnie look at it. She should be able to give you a healing poultice."

"I'm fine," I said, tugging my sock over my foot and then gingerly pulling my tennis shoe on before climbing to my feet. "I'm perfect. See."

"You are perfect," Thistle agreed, squeezing my hand. "I still think we should have that looked at just to be on the safe side."

"I'm fine."

"Oh, let her play nurse, man," Landon said. "She might put on an outfit or something."

"You really are a pervert," Thistle said, flicking the spot between Landon's eyebrows and causing him to growl. "Aunt Tillie says you're all hormones and hunger. I'm starting to think she might be right."

"I'm also manly and strong," Landon said. "Don't ever forget that."

"How could we?" Thistle teased. "You tell us every day we're together."

"You know what? You're on my list today," Landon said, grabbing Bay's hand and turning her toward the inn. "Let's get breakfast. I'm starving."

"I'm starving, too," Bay said. "Dinner last night was terrible. I hope breakfast is better."

"It won't be if Winnie is still stewing," Thistle said, falling into step next to me and slipping her finger through my belt loop to stay close. I'm not big on grand romantic pronouncements. Thistle isn't either. The little things she does to show her affection get me every time, though. "I hope Marnie and Mom cooked breakfast if Winnie is still in a funk."

"No one had better burned my bacon," Landon said. "I'm going to join Aunt Tillie's 'end of the world' prediction bandwagon if my bacon is bad."

"You're nothing if not predictable," Bay said.

"Are you calling me boring?"

"I'm calling you the handsomest man I know," Bay replied.

"Nice one," Thistle said, laughing as Landon rolled his eyes. "All men love a good ego boost in the morning, especially if they're contemplating a career change."

"Career change?" I was confused.

"Landon wants to be your nurse," Thistle said. "I hear he's going to try giving you a sponge bath before he makes his final decision."

Thistle delightedly darted out of my reach as she did a little dance on the pathway. Bay joined in her laughter as Landon locked eyes with me.

"I blame you for this," Landon said. "You're the one who made me look at your toe."

"No one said you had to get on the ground with me," I pointed out. "That's what made the whole thing weird."

"You have a point," Landon muttered.

We lapsed into comfortable silence as we made the trek to The Overlook, Bay and Landon swinging their joined hands as Thistle carefully drew closer to me. I think she was worried I would pay her back for the "sponge bath" comment, but I was already over it. Er, well, mostly.

The entry to the family living quarters at the back of The Overlook is generally quiet in the morning. Winnie, Marnie and Twila busy themselves with breakfast preparations early, and Aunt Tillie likes watching the morning news programs so she can hurl insults at the anchors and tell them how stupid they are.

This morning was different.

"That did it," Winnie barked. "Call the police. I'm pressing charges."

"Against who?" Twila asked. "We have no idea what happened. For all we know a dog could've taken it."

"Or Aunt Tillie," Marnie added. "She might be messing with us."

"I hadn't considered that," Winnie said. "Aunt Tillie!" Her screech was loud enough to jolt me, and when I risked a glance in Landon's direction I found his face twisted with confusion.

"What's going on?" Bay asked, increasing her pace as she approached the back patio. "Did something happen?"

"Yes, something happened," Winnie said, gracing her daughter with a look that would've been comical under different circumstances but was outright frightening now. "We've been robbed."

"Is this about the pie again?" Landon asked, releasing Bay's hand and moving his fingers to her hip. He looked ready to run if the morning conversation didn't shift in a more appealing direction. "I understand losing the pie contest has upset you, but … it's a pie. You can make another one. I suggest blackberry … and make it big so I can have three slices."

"Listen, glutton, no one is talking to you," Winnie snapped. "This is much bigger than the pie. I've come to grips with losing my pie and never seeing it again. Stop smirking, Thistle! This is not about my pie!"

"Oh, good, it's meltdown morning at The Overlook," Aunt Tillie drawled as she sauntered out the back door of the house and joined her nieces on the patio. "Does anyone want to tell me why all this screeching is going on? I'm trying to watch the news. They're being real idiots this morning, and I don't want to miss my daily laugh."

Winnie was in no mood for games, and when she swiveled in Aunt Tillie's direction the persnickety elder aunt had the grace to look abashed. Winnie clearly meant business. "Did you steal my bread?"

"Oh, man. Now the bread is missing? It really is the end times," Landon intoned.

Winnie ignored him as we joined everyone on the patio, her attention remaining fixed on Aunt Tillie. "It would be just like you to steal the bread as a joke. If you did, you'd better tell me. I'm not in the mood for games."

"Oh, and here I thought we were about to join in a rousing game of Ring Around the Rosie," Aunt Tillie deadpanned. "Why would I take your bread? That really sounds nothing like me. I can't list the 'Bread Heist of 2016' on my resume."

"Maybe not," Mom conceded. "You do enjoy torturing me, though. That's right up your alley."

"Well, I can't deny that," Aunt Tillie conceded. "I didn't steal your bread, though. I have no interest in stealing bread. Wait … there's no bread? What am I going to put my jam on? This day went down the toilet quick."

I bit my lip to keep from laughing at the dejected look on Aunt Tillie's face. Since no one asked the obvious question, I took it upon myself to do so. "Why was the bread was on the patio?"

"I'd like to hear the answer to that, too," Landon admitted. "Don't you usually keep the bread in the kitchen?"

"Yes, but the counters were full and we needed a place for the bread to cool," Winnie explained. "We put towels over the pans and put them on the edge of the table. They were only going to be out here thirty minutes. They were perfectly fine."

"And what?" I prodded. "You came outside and they were gone?"

"No, Marcus," Winnie deadpanned. "They're right here. They're just invisible."

This family has a serious snark problem. "Are you sure one of the guests didn't take it?"

"Why would they?" Marnie challenged. "None of the guests ever cross into this portion of the yard because they know it's our private area."

"We have signs," Twila added, pointing for emphasis. "Even if they did somehow manage to wander over here, why would they steal the bread?"

That was a pretty good question.

"It was the creeper," Aunt Tillie said, her tone ominous. "He's gone from trying to steal my ... herbs ... to stealing bread. He must have the munchies."

"Yes, that sounds totally plausible," Landon said, his eyes flashing. "The creeper climbed up into Marcus' loft to bleed, left that area and came out here to break into your pot field, went back to the festival to steal Winnie's pie, showed up at the stable last night to scare the girls and then came back here to steal bread. That's completely normal."

"It does sound strange when you put it like that," I admitted, rubbing my chin. "What if this guy is confused because of the blood poisoning thing?"

"What blood poisoning thing?" Winnie asked, confused.

Landon related his discovery from the day before, explaining about the man in the stable. When he was done, Winnie's demeanor instantly shifted.

"He's sick?" Winnie asked. "Why not ask for help if he's sick?"

"Sam says he might be confused because of a fever or something," I replied. "We're not sure why he's not asking for help."

"Or what he really wants," Landon added. "We simply don't know what's going on right now. Given that fact, though, I want you locking the back door until we catch this guy. If he gets bolder, he might enter the inn."

"I'm not particularly worried about that," Winnie said. "We have bread in the freezer, and if this man honestly needs help I'd like to offer it. There has to be something we're missing here."

"I agree," Landon said. "I'm going into town after breakfast so I can talk to Chief Terry. He might have an idea I've overlooked. Until then, I want you all to be careful. I don't think this guy is dangerous, but if he panics ... ."

"Then all bets are off," Winnie finished. "Okay. We'll get the bread out of the freezer and finish breakfast. I hope you find this man. If he really is hurt ... or dying ... we could be running out of time."

"That's exactly what I'm afraid of," Landon said, ushering Bay toward the inn. He stilled when something else occurred to him. "He only stole the bread, right? The bacon is still okay, isn't it?"

"You make me tired, Landon," Winnie said. "I need a nap."

I DROPPED Thistle off at Hypnotic, promising to meet her at the festival for lunch. She offered to go to the stable with me, but I declined. If someone was inside the last thing I wanted to do was put her in danger.

I opened the door to the stable as quietly as possible, scanning the horses in their stalls. They were calm, Marigold's dark eyes solemn as I gazed into them.

I glanced around the stable to see if anything looked out of place. Nothing had been moved or appeared to be missing. I set about my morning tasks, forcing my thoughts to something more entertaining – like tomorrow's fireworks – and almost stepped on something as I passed the grain bin.

I frowned when something red caught my attention out of the corner of my eye and I leaned over. I pressed my fingers to the ground, lifting them so I could study my fingertips under better light. It was blood ... and it looked fresh.

I shook my head as I studied the ground, finding a small trail through the stable leading to the back door. There, the telltale signs of a bloody print against the doorframe – almost as if someone braced himself there to gather strength – told me someone fled in that direction.

I considered calling Landon, fingering my phone in my pocket, but ultimately decided to search on my own. For some reason – and I had no idea why – my inner danger alarm wasn't flashing. All I could think was that someone was in trouble and needed help.

That's exactly what I intended to do.

NINE

The blood trail was light, and I lost it in the underbrush behind the stable pretty quickly. I considered my options, but ultimately decided searching on my own was the best way to go.

I approached my task pragmatically, mentally squaring off the property into grids, and searched any spot capable of hiding a grown man. After forty minutes I was tired … and frustrated … but I refused to give up.

That's when I caught a hint of movement in a small gathering of trees about fifty yards away. I narrowed my eyes as I studied the location, not realizing I was holding my breath until the need for oxygen overwhelmed me. I exhaled heavily, and that's when I saw the movement a second time.

I approached the area carefully, giving the spot where I saw the activity a wide berth until I could ascertain what I was dealing with. I rounded to the opposite side of the , frowning when I realized what I saw.

The man resting on the ground, his back to one of the trees, looked as if he was in rough shape. He was tall, his long legs splayed out in front of him, and his clothing looked tattered and ragged as he clutched a familiar blanket – I recognized it from the guesthouse – to his chest. His face was drawn, his features waxen and unbelievably pale. He had a grizzled look about him, a salt-and-pepper beard covering the lower portion of his face.

I cleared my throat to get his attention, and he jolted when he realized he wasn't alone. He moved to get up – probably to run – but he grimaced instead and fell back against the tree. He gripped his side, where I saw blood soaking through his clothing.

"I'm here to help you," I said, holding up my hands so he wouldn't mistake me for a threat. "My name is Marcus Richmond. You look as if you need medical help. I'm going to call someone."

"Don't do that," the man rasped, his eyes furtive as they glanced toward the field. If he tried running he wouldn't get far. He probably knew that, and didn't attempt to rise again. "Please, don't do that."

"Okay," I said, licking my lips. I wasn't ruling out calling for help, but I wanted to talk to him first. If I could get him to agree with my suggestion, things would be easier. "What's your name?"

"Dutch Jenkins."

"Hello, Dutch," I said, hunkering lower so I could have an easier sightline to his injury. "Were you hurt?"

"I fell," Dutch gritted out, his breathing labored. "It happened four days ago. I didn't think much of it. I was sleeping in your stable and I rolled off that bed you have in your office and I fell on the toolbox. I cut my side. It wasn't bad, though, so I ignored it. A day later I started feeling really sick. It's gotten progressively worse."

I pictured the toolbox in my head. "That thing is old and rusted," I said. "It used to belong to my grandfather. I've been meaning to throw it out, but … it somehow felt disrespectful."

Dutch barked out a laugh, the sound hollow. "You have respect for your elders. That's nice to see in a man your age."

"I believe in having respect for everyone," I said. "Some people lose that respect, don't get me wrong, but in general I like to think of myself as respectful."

"You are. Don't worry about that. I've been watching you for days."

"Have you been sleeping in the stable every night?" I asked, carefully lowering myself to the ground so I could get more comfortable. "Are you homeless?"

"I never really considered myself homeless," Dutch clarified. "I'm more … nomadic … by nature."

"Is that by choice or necessity?"

Dutch shrugged. "It's not a choice."

"Okay," I said, confused about how to handle the situation. "Are you from around here? Did you grow up in Walkerville?"

"I'm from Traverse City," Dutch replied. "I grew up there and I spent two years living in the veterans hospital before they shut it down a month ago. I had nowhere else to go … and I was just kind of wandering around the city … but they kept threatening to arrest me for loitering so I left."

The declaration made me inexplicably sad. If he was a veteran, that meant he served our country. Now he was homeless and treated with disdain. "Dutch, you should've asked for help," I said. "This town is full of warm people. I know quite a few of them who would've liked to help you."

"That's a nice sentiment, boy, but I don't know you and I have trouble believing anyone would help a stranger out of the goodness of their heart."

"Then you don't know the same people I do," I said. "I know some very helpful people. I would like to call one of them now so we can get you checked out at the hospital. That wound looks bad … and I think you're very sick."

"I'm definitely sick," Dutch acknowledged. "I think I'm dying. I don't have money for a hospital, though. This is a nice spot. I can die here. I even got some fresh bread for the end of my run."

I glanced at the bread pan next to him. He'd been digging in and eating with his fingers. "I know the woman who made that bread," I said. "She would like to help you, too."

"I stole it," Dutch said. "I'm a thief. She wouldn't help me."

"You might be surprised," I countered. "Although, to be fair, you should've waited until the pie contest was over before stealing the pie."

"That was good," Dutch said, grinning weakly. I had no idea how he managed to traipse all over town in his condition. "That was the best pie I've ever eaten. She should've won an award or something."

I bit the inside of my cheek to keep from laughing. "I'm sure she'll be happy to hear that," I said. "You should be around to tell her, though. I need to call for help, Dutch. We had your blood tested when we found it in the loft. You have blood poisoning. If it's left untreated ... well ... you're definitely going to die."

I didn't want to scare the man, but I needed him to see the bigger picture.

"Maybe it's my time," Dutch suggested. "There's no one here left to mourn me. I'll go to sleep looking out at this field and ... move on."

"You don't have any family?"

"I have family," Dutch answered. "They cut ties with me long ago. The doctors at the hospital said I had that PTSD thing. They tried to help me – and I was getting better – but then the bottom dropped out.

"I drank to numb myself for too many years," he continued. "I lost my family because of it. No one will miss me. Don't fret, boy. There's nothing you can do to help."

I didn't believe that for a second, and I refused to let Dutch die without at least trying to save him. "I have to call for an ambulance," I said. "You need help."

"They'll arrest me," Dutch argued. "I'll go to jail for stealing the pie and bread. I'll go to jail for breaking into your stable."

"I won't press charges," I promised. "The woman who made the pie and bread won't either. We can help you."

"And what about the woman at the unicorn store?" Dutch pressed. "I stole from her shop, too. She had candy and I was hungry."

Crap. Margaret Little owned the porcelain unicorn shop. She wouldn't be nearly as forgiving as Winnie. "We'll cross that bridge when we come to it," I said. "You need help, though. I won't just sit here and watch you die."

"I'm not spending my last days in jail," Dutch said. "No hospitals."

"But ... ." His defiance irked me, but somehow I understood his pain. No one saw him. No one took the time to look for him. He was a forgotten man ... and he was running out of time. Then something occurred to me. "What if I could get you help without taking you to a hospital?"

Dutch lifted an eyebrow. "And how are you going to do that?"

"You're going to have to trust me," I cautioned. "I need to take you back to the stable and get you comfortable, but I'm pretty sure I know someone who can help."

"Do you happen to hang out with angels, boy?"

"Not angels, but I do know a fair number of witches. The head witch can fix this. I know it."

"**WHAT'S** THE BIG EMERGENCY?"

Aunt Tillie breezed into my office, an annoyed look on her face. Her demeanor shifted the moment she saw Dutch.

"He needs help," I said, fluffing the pillow under his head. "Do something."

"You must be the creeper," Aunt Tillie said, moving closer. "What's your story?"

"This is Dutch Jenkins. He was at the veterans hospital in Traverse City until they shut it down," I explained. "He's been stealing food to stay alive. He fell and cut himself when he was sleeping in the office. Now fix him."

"I need to look at your wound," Aunt Tillie said, leaning over and reaching for Dutch's shirt. "Just for the record, if you hit me or bite ... I bite back."

"I like her," Dutch said, chuckling as he leaned back to stare at the ceiling. "I'm warning you. It looks awful."

"I'm sure I've seen worse," Aunt Tillie said, moving the fabric and making a disgusted face. "It's infected."

"Oh, well, thanks. We couldn't have figured that out on our own," I deadpanned, irritation washing over me.

Aunt Tillie widened her eyes, surprised. I rarely yelled or snapped at her. That's one of the reasons we get along so well. "Calm down, Marcus," she comforted. "It's going to be okay."

"He says he's dying."

Aunt Tillie shifted her eyes to Dutch, her expression thoughtful. "Do you really think you're dying?"

Dutch nodded. "It's only a matter of time. I don't expect you to help."

"Why haven't you called an ambulance?" Aunt Tillie asked. "Doctors might still be able to help him."

"No doctors," Dutch barked, grimacing. "God, that hurts something fierce."

"He's afraid of being arrested," I supplied. "He doesn't want to go to jail."

"We're not going to press charges," Aunt Tillie countered. "He won't go to jail."

"He stole from Mrs. Little, too."

"Oh, well, that woman is evil," Aunt Tillie said. "She'll press charges. We'll deal with her once we get Dutch here on his feet. I'm going to need some supplies, though."

"I figured," I said. "What do you need? I'll get it."

"I'm also going to need help," Aunt Tillie said. "He's very sick. I need a … power boost … for what I have planned."

"A power boost?" Dutch looked alarmed. "You're not going to cut my stomach out, are you?"

"Hardly," Aunt Tillie scoffed. "That's not the sort of power I need."

I understood what she was getting at. "Which ones do you want?"

"Get me the three young ones," Aunt Tillie replied. "They're easy to boss around. Clove should have the supplies I need at the shop. I'll get you a list."

"He doesn't have much time," I said. "I … don't know how I know that, but I can feel it."

"I feel it, too," Aunt Tillie said. "That's why you need to hurry. Get the girls and my supplies. Don't dawdle. While you're gone, I'll keep Dutch company. He's going to enjoy my stories."

"I'm already looking forward to it," Dutch said, pressing his eyes shut. He looked as if he could slip away at any moment.

"Hurry, Marcus," Aunt Tillie prodded. "We need to do this now!"

"**ARE WE** sure this is a good idea?" Clove asked, her eyes huge as she took in Dutch's prone form. He'd passed out during my absence and his breathing was shallow. "We need to get him to a hospital."

"He doesn't want that," I argued. "He's afraid. Can't you help him?"

"We'll do our best," Aunt Tillie said, sorting through Clove's herbs and handing her three bags. "Mix that into a poultice and pack it on his wound. We need to start the chant soon."

Chant? "Can you stop him from dying?"

"We don't have power over life and death, Marcus," Thistle said. "You know that. We might be able to do something else, though." She held up the fabric poppet Aunt Tillie instructed her to bring. "We're going to direct his illness into this. If it works, he'll be weak but hopefully recover."

"And if it doesn't work?"

Thistle shot me a pained expression. "He'll die."

"We're not going to let that happen," Aunt Tillie said. "Everyone get moving. We're almost out of time."

Bay, Clove and Thistle sprang into action, seemingly knowing what Aunt Tillie wanted them to do without her uttering a word. I held Dutch's limp hand as they readied the area, taking a step back but refusing to release my grip when Clove applied the poultice.

"Okay, Marcus, you need to step away," Aunt Tillie instructed. "We can't have you messing up our energy field."

"But … I don't want him to die alone." Tears burned the back of my eyes. I barely knew the man yet I was invested in his survival.

"Then take a step back," Aunt Tillie pressed. "If we do this right, he won't die."

I tugged a restless hand through my hair and did as she asked, leaning against the office wall as Aunt Tillie placed the poppet in the center of the floor and then joined hands with her great-nieces.

"Are you ready, girls?"

They nodded.

"You remember what to do, right?" Aunt Tillie asked. "We have only one shot at this and you haven't done it since you were kids."

"We remember," Bay said.

"We could never forget," Clove added.

The women pressed their eyes shut, and a chill swept over me as something powerful moved through the room. I couldn't see anything, but I could feel everything.

"We call upon the power of the north," Clove intoned. "Stay true. Stay solid. Stay the course. Stay watchful."

"We call upon the power of the east," Bay said. "Be strong. Be courageous. Be true. Be diligent."

"We call upon the power of the south," Thistle said, her face a mask of concentration. "Earth. Air. Fire. Water. To all of you we take heed, and ask for help."

"We call upon the power of the west," Aunt Tillie said. "We're out of time. We're out of options. Make haste and do your best."

Nothing happened, and I felt a severe pang of disappointment. Then they repeated their chant over one another. I was dumbfounded as wind whipped through the room and four voices ceased standing out as unique entities and instead melded.

It felt as if the spell would never end. My heart ached, and when I looked at Dutch I couldn't help but wonder whether he was already gone.

Then, as the whispers grew to a feverish pitch, a light flashed and the poppet on the floor exploded, causing me to jump as small fabric fragments flew across the room.

The women released each other's hands and cleared the way so Aunt Tillie could move to Dutch's side.

"Is it over?" I asked.

"It's over," Thistle said, leaning over to offer me a hug. I gladly accepted it as I pulled her body flush against mine.

"Is he okay?"

"I don't know," Aunt Tillie answered, resting her hand against his forehead. "Now we have to wait. We're not out of the woods yet."

TEN

We waited.

Bay took to pacing, while Clove sat on the floor with her back flat against the wall, and Thistle leaned her head on my shoulder. At first I thought Thistle needed solace, but then I realized that's what she offered me.

We waited some more.

Bay became antsy and called Landon. None of us knew whether that was the right decision, but she had to follow her heart, and she could never justify lying to Landon.

We continued waiting.

Dutch never moved, and by the time Landon let himself into the office I'd pretty much resigned myself to losing the man. I'm not a pessimist, but he was still far too long.

"How is he?" Landon asked, opening his arms so Bay could step between them and pulling her tight against his chest as he hugged her.

"It's too soon to tell," Thistle answered. Part of me thought she was lying to protect me. Hurting me was the last thing she wanted to do. The other part remained hopeful.

"What do we know about him?" Landon asked.

"His name is Dutch Jenkins," I supplied. "I found him by some trees out behind the stable. He admitted to stealing food, including the bread and pie. He also slept in here some nights. I'm not pressing charges, so don't even think you can talk me into it."

Landon arched a challenging eyebrow. "Did you really think I would try to make you press charges against him?"

I shrugged, flustered. "No. I just … I'm sorry."

"It's okay," Landon said. "Everyone looks beaten down here. Can someone explain to me why he's not at a hospital?"

"He didn't want to go," Bay replied, her voice small as she glanced up to lock gazes with Landon. "He told Marcus no one would miss him, and he was terrified of going to prison. He didn't have much fight left in him, but that was his final wish."

Landon brushed a strand of hair from Bay's face as he studied her somber blue eyes. "Okay," he said. "We're going to have a lot of questions to answer if he dies."

"He's not going to die," Aunt Tillie said. She hadn't moved a muscle since concluding the spell, her hand wrapped tightly around Dutch's as she offered him comfort only she could see. "He's going to be okay."

"Is that witch's intuition?" Landon asked.

"It's faith," Aunt Tillie replied. "You should know all about that. I see it reflected in your face every time you look at Bay."

Landon exhaled heavily as he shook his head. "You know, every time I think I have you figured out you do something that throws me for a loop," he said. "You'll go weeks on end being evil and plotting against everyone, and then you do something like this. I don't understand you."

"And you never will," Aunt Tillie said, winking at him. "All you need to know is that Marcus needed help and I was happy to give it."

"I don't know how long I can let this go on, guys," Landon said. "He needs to go to a hospital. I know he doesn't want to go to jail, but if Marcus and Winnie don't press charges … ."

"We have another problem," Thistle interjected, cutting him off. "He stole from one other place."

Landon rested his chin on the top of Bay's head and waited.

"It was Mrs. Little," I supplied. "He stole candy."

"Oh, well, of course," Landon hissed, rocking Bay as he considered our options. Several weeks ago the Winchester witches had a showdown with Margaret Little that almost left several people dead. Her nefarious deeds were made public, but there was nothing left to blackmail her with. "I'll talk to Chief Terry and see if she filed a report."

"She did." Hemlock Cove's police chief, Terry Davenport, strolled into the office. He didn't appear surprised to find a homeless man near death on my cot, or four of the Winchester witches in attendance. "She wants the culprit prosecuted to the fullest extent of the law. He stole three bucks worth of candy."

"I'll take care of her," Aunt Tillie said, her eyes flashing. "She and I have some unfinished business to settle."

"She thinks you stole her candy," Chief Terry said.

"I'm going to set that candy on fire and shove it up her … ."

Landon cleared his throat and shook his head in warning. "Now is not the time for that," he said. "How did you know we were here?"

"Well, let's see," Chief Terry began ticking off items while running his hand over the back of his neck. "I saw Clove and Thistle take off from their store a couple of hours ago. They looked to be in a hurry. Then I saw Bay running over from the festival. It's a little hot to run … and she never runs."

Bay's smile was rueful. "He's right. I'm really lazy."

"I'll fix that later," Landon said, petting her head. "So you knew something was going on just because they all ran to the stable?"

"Oh, no. You're the one who tipped me off to that," Chief Terry said.

"How?"

"You got a call from Bay, and instead of being all flirty and gooey you got a weird look on your face and went outside," Chief Terry answered. "That usually means trouble. I decided to follow you … and listen outside because I was curious … and then I decided to help."

"Really?" Clove looked relieved.

"Did you really think I wouldn't help, Clove?"

"I don't know," Clove replied. "Aunt Tillie told me to work up some tears just in case I had to cry to manipulate you."

Chief Terry scowled. "Don't tell her to do stuff like that. It bugs me."

"You bug me," Aunt Tillie said. "It evens out."

"Whatever." Chief Terry glanced at me. "You did a good thing here, son. I would've preferred him going to a hospital, but I understand why you did what you did."

"You might not say that if he dies," I pointed out.

"Probably not, but we'll cross that bridge when we come to it," Chief Terry said. "Right now I want to move forward on the assumption that he's going to survive. How much care is he going to need?"

"He should be fine after a couple of days," Aunt Tillie replied. "He'll be weak and need a lot of rest, but he should make a full recovery. I'm an excellent doctor. I could do it professionally if I wanted."

"Yes, and what a bedside manner," Chief Terry said. "Do you guys have a room at The Overlook?"

"He won't like that," I argued. "He's big about paying his own way and not owing people."

"He stole pie and bread," Chief Terry argued. "He's going to have to learn to accept help, whether he likes it or not." Chief Terry can be gruff, but he has a giving nature. "We need to find him a job and cover for why he's in town."

"You want to lie?" I was stunned.

"That's the wrong way to look at it," Chief Terry said. "We need to be sure that Margaret Little never finds out who he is because she'll press charges just to spite Tillie."

"I said I would take care of her," Aunt Tillie said. "She's had something special coming from me for as long as I can remember."

"Oh, well, that's good," Bay deadpanned. "We won't have to worry about Dutch going to jail. We'll just send Aunt Tillie in his place."

"Listen, spaz, I've had just about enough of you for one day," Aunt Tillie snapped. "Don't worry about Margaret Little."

"I agree with Chief Terry," Clove announced. "I think we should lie."

"I don't know whether to smack you or proclaim how proud I am," Aunt Tillie said. "Why do you think we should lie?"

"I don't think we should tell a big lie," Clove clarified. "I think we should just lie about when he got to town."

I caught on to what she was saying right away. "You think he should recuperate out of sight and then miraculously show up in Hemlock Cove to start his new job at the stable."

Thistle shifted toward me. "At the stable? Are you going to hire him?"

"You said yourself I need help," I reminded her. "He can help. He can stay in the office once he's feeling better and earn enough to get back on his feet."

"I've got some work for him, too," Aunt Tillie said. "I need to find out why he was trying to steal from my ... herb ... garden, though." She darted a look in Chief Terry's direction and pretended she didn't see his pointed scowl. "I still don't understand what he was doing out there."

"I asked him while I was waiting for you to show up," I supplied. "He had no idea what I was talking about. He had no idea you were growing ... oregano ... on the land. You don't have to make up something to cover that. He said he went out to the inn because they always had food and the women were hot."

"Hey." Chief Terry shook his head. "Those are my women."

"Excuse me?" Landon made a face and pulled Bay closer. "This one is mine."

"I was talking about the other three," Chief Terry countered. "If he thinks the younger ones are hot we're going to have a problem. They're children."

"Oh, now I feel dirty," I said, earning a reproachful look from Thistle. "Don't worry. I'll get over it."

"I'm already over it," Landon said. "We need to get a plan in place before he wakes."

The fact that he didn't mention the possibility of Dutch not waking warmed me. "We need to get him to the inn without anyone seeing," I said. "Mrs. Little probably knows everyone is here. I wouldn't be surprised if she figures out a reason to stop by."

"I wouldn't put it past her," Chief Terry said. "If she sees Dutch, the game is over. She's going to put two and two together and realize what's happening. She's not stupid."

Aunt Tillie snorted. "Yes, she is."

"We need to protect this man, Aunt Tillie," I pleaded, hating how weak I sounded. I wasn't used to begging, but I was willing to do it if necessary. "Please help us."

"Of course I'm going to help," Aunt Tillie sniffed. "You don't need to worry about Margaret, though. I said I would handle her."

"And how are you going to do that?" Landon challenged.

"Don't you trust me?" Aunt Tillie pasted an "I'm old and you have to believe what I say" smile on her face. "Don't you have faith in me?"

Landon locked gazes with her as he ran his tongue over his teeth. "Okay," he said finally. "You need to distract Mrs. Little. We're going to get Dutch in my Explorer because it has tinted windows. We just need time to get him from here to my vehicle. Can you give us time?"

"Of course," Aunt Tillie said, squeezing Dutch's hand one more time before releasing it. "I already have a plan."

"Oh, well, good," Bay said. "I can't wait to see this."

"You will," Aunt Tillie said. "I'm going to need help."

"Oh, man!" Bay made a face. "Why me?"

"I think it's karma," Thistle said, grinning.

"Keep it up, mouth," Aunt Tillie said, sliding her a dark look. "I need your help, too. Before you think you're getting away with something, little kvetch, your assistance will also be necessary."

Clove didn't look bothered by Aunt Tillie's conversational shift. "Fine."

"I have a great plan," Aunt Tillie said, beaming.

"Of course you do," Thistle grumbled. "I can already tell this is going to bite."

"And yet I know you'll do it anyway because you love Marcus," Aunt Tillie said. "That's one of the few things I never doubt when you're around."

Pride and love washed through me as Thistle shifted her eyes to me. I knew she was on board before she uttered a word.

"Thank you," I whispered.

"Of course," Thistle said. "I was always going to help. I just hope Aunt Tillie's plan doesn't land us in jail."

"That would be nice for everyone," Chief Terry said. "Okay, let's move. Aunt Tillie ... you're on."

FOUR HOURS later Thistle sidled up to me on the sidewalk in front of the police station, her eyes weary but her smile genuine.

"There you are," I said, grinning. "I was wondering when you would make your way back to town. I didn't know whether you were in hiding."

"Feathers are harder to get off than you might imagine," Thistle replied. "Especially when Aunt Tillie sticks them on you with magic."

I had no idea how Aunt Tillie and her great-nieces distracted Margaret Little. I heard rumors. One included an absurd story about a tribal dance in the middle of Main Street. If it was true, part of me was sorry I missed it. Dutch's smile when he woke – and the look on his face when Marnie, Twila and Winnie doted on him – more than made up for it.

"Feathers, huh? Did you look like a chicken?"

"Aunt Tillie used chicken bones in her voodoo curse," Thistle replied, stepping closer and tilting her chin up so she could meet my gaze. "That's what she told Mrs. Little we were doing, by the way. Supposedly we put a voodoo curse on her so the dead would rise and stalk her. The tourists loved it."

"And how about you?"

"I hated it."

"I figured," I said. "Thank you for doing it anyway. Dutch is ... overwhelmed ... with how everyone is treating him."

"He's a good guy," Thistle said. "I think he'll make a great addition to the town, once we can introduce him the right way. I stopped in and saw him before I left the inn. He's doing well, and our mothers are fattening him up even as we speak. I think everything is going to turn out okay."

"I think so, too." I cupped the back of her head and pressed a warm kiss to her forehead. "Still, you went above and beyond with your chicken dance."

"I don't know, but the look on Mrs. Little's face made the dance worth it," Thistle said. "She ran into her store and pulled the curtains to hide. She kept screaming that Aunt Tillie was trying to kill her."

"I wish I'd seen it."

"Chief Terry filmed it with his phone after helping load Dutch into Landon's Explorer," Thistle replied. "I have a feeling you'll get to see it eventually."

"And that's the highlight of my night."

Thistle pressed a soft kiss to my lips, her face unreadable. "Can I ask you something?"

"Always."

"Why didn't you call the ambulance this afternoon? Dutch was in no position to fight you."

"He served our country and all he wanted was a little respect," I replied. "I needed to give him that."

"You're a good guy, too."

"And you're a great woman," I said, tightening my arms around her. "Do you want to celebrate the Fourth of July holiday with me? The fireworks start in an hour, and I'll win you another stuffed animal if you ask nicely."

"I don't need the stuffed animal, but the fireworks sound nice," Thistle said. "I would love to spend the holiday with you."

"That's good," I said. "I wasn't going to let you out of it no matter what you said."

Thistle sighed. "Happy Fourth of July."

"Oh, no," I said, shaking my head. "Happy Witchdependence Day."

And, in the end, it was a marvelous holiday for all of us.

HAPPY WITCHGIVING

A WICKED WITCHES OF THE MIDWEST SHORT

10/11/2016

ONE

TWELVE YEARS AGO

"What the … ?"

I glanced down at my foot, disbelief washing over me. That couldn't be … nah, no way. I had to be dreaming.

"Your foot went through your front deck and there's a big hole." Ronnie Duncan, Walkerville's lone mail carrier, leaned over so far his big bag of envelopes and flyers tipped him to one side so he had no choice but to put both hands out to steady himself. He hissed when his bare hands met the cold wood.

Fall was officially here – and the mornings were much cooler – but it hadn't turned downright cold yet. At least I had that going for me. My mother used to call me an optimist – but I think she was an optimist and that was wishful thinking on her part. I definitely lean toward pessimist – or at least "meh-ist." That's a thing … which I just totally made up, by the way.

The fact that my foot was lodged in the deck would never be a good thing, but it could be worse because snow might've gotten in my boot a month from now. That's upbeat thinking, mind you. My mother would be proud – if she was watching from up above, that is.

"Thank you, Ronnie," I intoned, working overtime not to snap at the man – and then cuff him up the backside of his head for good measure just because I could. As the newly minted police chief I have a certain reputation to uphold, and cuffing people … or shoving them … or outright kicking them … was frowned upon by the good residents of Walkerville. Even good things have drawbacks. For example, I get more money now, but I can't do the things I really want to do, like shove Ronnie's face into the deck until he ceases stating the obvious.

"You're welcome," Ronnie said, completely missing my sarcasm. "Why do you think there's a hole in your deck?"

That was a good question. I had no idea. "I don't know. Maybe the wood just rotted." I've had this house ten years and never done anything but waterproof the deck that circles the entire front and two sides of my home. Something like this was bound to happen eventually. Er, at least that's what I'm telling myself. "It probably just has a weak spot."

"What are you going to do?"

"I thought I would just stand in this spot all day and work from here," I replied, my temper getting the better of me. "How does that sound?"

Ronnie shrugged. "It doesn't sound particularly constructive to me, but then again, I'm not you, so maybe you could get a lot done working that way, Chief Davenport." He scratched the side of his head as he studied the hole. "What if your foot is stuck in there and it's never going to come out? Maybe there's an animal in there. Ooh, maybe there's a demon. I saw that in a movie the other day. That would be creepy, wouldn't it?"

That was the most ridiculous thing I'd ever heard. The only reason I was even out on the deck is because I heard Ronnie dropping the mail in the box on the side of the house and decided to collect it before heading to work. In reality, this was his fault. Sonovabitch! Now I can't stop thinking there's something brushing against my foot down there. I know there's no demon but … is that a horn slipping under my pant leg?

"Help me get my leg out," I barked, the frayed reins of my sanity slipping.

Ronnie isn't known as one of the great thinkers in this world, but the look he sent me was downright smug. "Do you feel the demon?"

"I feel pain because I scraped my ankle going down," I replied, irritated. That technically wasn't a lie, by the way. My ankle did hurt ... and there might be a demon down there. I want to get this entire town drug tested one day. That's not an exaggeration.

"Oh, sorry," Ronnie said, instantly contrite. He leaned closer so I could use his shoulder as leverage, and when I tried to pull my foot free I found resistance. I tried another angle and came up against the same problem.

"Son of a ... ."

"It's probably the demon working against us," Ronnie said with an air of certainty.

"There is no demon down there," I barked, frustrated. "Stop saying that."

"There's no reason to be testy," Ronnie said. "You're the chief of police. You should be able to call the station and have a hundred different men come out to rescue you."

That sounded like the worst idea I'd ever heard. I would never live that down. Rescued from my own deck? No thank you. "We're going to try again," I said. "This time I want you to grab my ankle and really give it a tug."

Ronnie didn't look thrilled with the idea. "What if the demon gets me?"

"You need to worry about me a lot more than a demon," I snapped. "Now ... grab my leg."

"Sheesh. I hope no one sees this," Ronnie whimpered as he wrapped his hands around the part of my calf remaining above the splintered deck. "People might talk about what we're doing."

"You're helping me get my leg out of the deck."

"Yeah, but it could look like something else from a distance."

It took me a second to grasp what he was saying, and it wasn't until I caught a glimpse of our reflections in the nearby window that I realized what he was implying. He was on his knees in front of me and ... oh, man. A demon would be so much better than this. "Just help me," I snapped, gripping his shoulder and giving my foot a vicious yank as Ronnie jerked on my pant leg to help.

"Turn your ankle to the right just a bit and then poke your toes down," Ronnie ordered.

Under any other circumstances I would've ignored his advice but I wasn't in a situation that warranted putting up a fight. I did as I was told, momentarily smiling when I felt my foot come free. The smile didn't last for more than a split second because I realized that I was falling backward thanks to my newfound momentum.

I hit the deck hard – my rear end almost bouncing from the impact – and I fought the urge to yell at Ronnie for letting me fall. Hey, I didn't say the inclination was rational.

"You fell over," Ronnie said.

I gritted my teeth. "I hadn't noticed. Thank you."

"I'll bet you're glad there's not a demon down there," Ronnie said, warily eyeing the hole. He remained on his knees, seemingly in no hurry to get back to his route.

"I'm thrilled there's not a demon down there, Ronnie," I said. "I want to throw a party just because of it."

Sarcasm is wasted on someone like Ronnie. He either doesn't get it or pretends he doesn't understand it. Either way the effort is never put to good use. "I wouldn't throw a party just yet," he said.

"I wasn't really going to throw a party, Ronnie."

"That's good," Ronnie drawled. "The demon isn't down there, but a whole bunch of termites are."

"That can't be right." I moved closer to the hole, staring down into the darkness. I couldn't see one particular bug, but I could see a decent amount of movement. "Son of a … !"

"**YUP, THOSE** ARE TERMITES."

I stood next to the side door of the house, checking email on my Blackberry and messaging instructions to the office. Just because I had a domestic disturbance didn't mean I could shirk my duties. I was the chief, after all. Terry Davenport, chief of police and lunatic wrangler. Termites couldn't stop me. Of course, the mere idea of those things crawling over my body while I slept was freakier than Ronnie's demon. Thankfully he'd returned to his route and I didn't have to worry about more demon talk – or him mentioning our peculiar position when he helped me out of a jam. I moved closer to Jim Stinson as he held a flashlight high and stared into the hole. That hole really sucks, by the way. I was having a great day before that hole.

"Is it bad?" I asked.

Jim shrugged. "I guess that depends on how you feel about millions of tiny monsters with huge mouths – for their size, I mean – eating the very foundation of your house."

He's such a comforting soul sometimes. "What should I do about it?" I asked, tamping down my irritation. Walkerville is the size of a pinprick. You don't have a lot of options when you need certain things done. If you need food, you're good because there are five restaurants in town. If you need varmint eradication, though, you're in a pickle because Jim's the only game within a fifty-mile radius. You can't tick him off, no matter how much you might want to shove your boot in his butt and … huh, what were we talking about again?

"I meant … never mind what I meant," I said, rubbing the back of my neck as I shifted my eyes to the driveway. The morning was quiet – as they so often are in Walkerville – but my head was mired in noisy tumult. "What happens next?"

"Well, it depends," Jim said, rubbing his chin. I could tell already whatever he was about to unveil would be a sarcastic masterpiece. It was too late to stop it, though. I'd already asked. "You can continue living here and adopt the termites as pets – that's your first option, although I don't really recommend it. You would probably have a decent six months before the house completely falls down, though. Maybe that's your thing."

"What's my other option?" I asked, hating that I had to play the game.

"Your other option is tenting the heck out of it and then getting my team in here to fix things," Jim said. "You might miss the termites.

I have no idea if you're an animal lover, but I hear they make cuddly bed friends."

He's a sick man. "I'll take option number two," I said. "I need an estimate and a schedule. If you need to tent first, do you do that today?"

"Probably not until tomorrow," Jim replied. "I need to get all of the equipment ready and my crew is over at a house on the south side of town."

I couldn't really expect him to drop everything and bump me up the list, but it was still disheartening information. "Fine," I said. "So you tent tomorrow. If you do it in the morning, can I be back in by the afternoon?"

Jim snorted as if I'd said the funniest thing imaginable. "No."

I blew out a sigh, resigned. "How long?"

"Well, we'll tent tomorrow and you usually need to stay out three days," he replied. "That's a minimum of two nights, but I recommend three. I also recommend packing up some belongings and spending the night someplace else this evening because you won't be able to sleep in here now that you know there are bugs running around."

"Weren't the bugs running around yesterday, too?"

"Yes, but you didn't know about them then so you didn't imagine them crawling all over you," Jim replied. "I've seen this happen a million times. Trust me. You're going to want to get out of here tonight."

I considered putting up an argument, but he wasn't wrong. "I'll figure something out," I said. "It's not like this place isn't bursting at the seams with inns. It's freaking Walkerville, for crying out loud. Inns we have in excess."

Walkerville is a touristy town, and the number of inns scattered around the general area outnumbered just about everything else. I'd have no problem finding a bed for a few nights.

"Yes, but it's Thanksgiving weekend," Jim reminded me. "That means all the inns probably filled up weeks ago."

Crud. I hadn't thought about that. "I'm sure that … ." What am I supposed to do?

"I'm guessing if you're a good boy and go charm those Winchester women you're so fond of they'll give you a place to stay," Jim said. "I'm thinking that's your best bet."

The mere mention of the Winchester women was enough to make me smile – and then internally cringe. That essentially sounded like three days of heavenly food accompanied by loud women arguing about absolutely nothing whenever they get bees in their bonnets. The food more than makes up for it, but there's a lot of estrogen flowing free in that house – and that's on top of the rumors about them being witches.

"I guess I'll have to give it some thought," I said finally. "I'm sure they could find room for me, but … ."

"Yeah, they're crazy," Jim said. "That Tillie is a … whew!"

Tillie was another problem. I hadn't even gotten to her yet. "I'll figure it out," I repeated, glancing toward my driveway as one of Walkerville's dedicated police cruisers pulled in. "Get this place tented as soon as possible. I don't want this mess dragging into more than three days."

"Yeah, I love it when the guy being eaten alive by bugs puts me on a timetable," Jim deadpanned, smirking when I darted a dark look in his direction. "It's almost as if you think you're in charge, but … no offense, Chief Davenport."

Yeah, that's me. Chief Terry Davenport. I'm the top cop in Walkerville, yet I have absolutely no power over the guy slaughtering termites. This day bites. "Just get it done," I repeated, moving toward the driveway to greet my officer. "I don't have a lot of time to mess around with this stuff. Like you said, it's a holiday weekend coming up. That means we'll have a lot of drunks to deal with the night before Thanksgiving, and a lot of family fights on Thanksgiving Day. Those family gatherings are usually worth a few stabbings."

Jim smirked. "I do love a holiday free-for-all," he said. "Make sure you get everything you need out of the house before leaving. You can't go back inside when it's tented. You could die from the fumes. I don't think that's how you want to spend your holiday."

He's such a pain. "Thanks," I replied dryly. "I'll keep that in mind." I turned my attention to David Parker, a local graduate who joined my team only two months ago. He was green and gung-ho – a terrible combination. "What's going on, Officer Parker?"

"Well, Chief, we got a BOLO," Parker said, tipping his hat back on his head as he handed me a sheet of paper. I think he saw that move on some cop show and thinks it makes him look distinguished. He reminds me of Barney Fife when he does it. "A BOLO means to be on the lookout, by the way."

I frowned. Did he think I didn't know that? "I'm well aware of what a BOLO is," I said, studying the sheet. "This says they're looking for a con artist who may be in the area. They say he bilked some women out of their money in a land fraud deal."

"I know," Parker said. "I thought if he's here, we should find him."

The boy is nice – and the local teenage girls seem to love his looks – but he's not the sharpest tack in the bulletin board. "How do you suggest we find him?" I kept my tone even so as not to embarrass him.

"We should look," Parker said, his expression completely serious.

Wow. That was almost profound. Or … not. "Okay, I think that this should be great for your first solo case," I said. What? It's not like he's going to find anyone. The guy could be anywhere in the state. The odds of him landing here have to be astronomical. If Parker spends the next few days looking, though, that keeps him out of my hair. "Just keep me updated on your search efforts."

Parker looked thrilled. "Thank you for trusting me with this, sir!"

"You're welcome," I said. "By the way, if you guys need me I'll be at the Winchesters' bed and breakfast. This place needs to be tented and I can't stay here. So if you run into trouble and can't find me in town, track me down there."

Parker's face clouded. "People say the Winchesters are witches, sir. Are you sure that's safe?"

I scowled. "People have too much time on their hands," I said, even though I'd seen the witch rumors proven myself. "Don't worry about the Winchesters."

"But … Tillie," Parker said, lowering his voice. "She threatened to turn my thing green once because she caught me talking to Bay. I think she meant it. Don't let her turn your thing green, sir. Pick another inn."

I did the math in my head. Parker was young – only twenty-two – and dumb, but Bay Winchester was only seventeen. I took the opportunity to vent my morning aggression and cuffed the back of Parker's head, taking him by surprise. "Bay is still a child," I said, extending a finger. "If Aunt Tillie turns your thing green for looking at her, I honestly have no problem with it."

Parker swallowed hard. "I was just talking to her, sir."

"Well, don't do it again," I said. "I'll be fine at the Winchester place. No matter what anyone says, they're just women. Sure, they're loud women, but they cook like angels and I'm sure I'll get a good night's sleep there."

"Maybe we should come up with a code in case you get in trouble," Parker suggested. "You could call me with a safe word or something."

I pressed my lips together as I fought the urge to roll my eyes. "I think I'll be okay," I said. "It's just seven women, after all. How terrible can they be?"

TWO

"You are a terrible person."

"No, you are a terrible person."

"You're the queen of terrible people!"

"You're the … ."

"Knock it off, girls." Winnie Winchester lightly tapped the back of her niece Thistle's head and directed the girl to move from behind the front desk as I walked into the bed and breakfast with my overnight bag.

Thistle clearly wasn't happy with the reprimand. Her argument associate – her cousin Clove – looked smug thanks to her ability to avoid her aunt's busy hands. Winnie beamed when she saw me, and I couldn't help but feel a warm giddiness wash over me. What? She's quite the looker … and she cooks like a Zagat chef. If I didn't think it was a one-way ticket to living in this madhouse full-time I would ask her out. Er, well, maybe.

"Hello, Terry," Winnie said. "What's going on?"

"We didn't do it," Thistle said automatically, her dark blond hair glinting under the overhead light. She's been making noise about dying her hair funky colors – something her aunts and mother are fighting – but she's such a terror I know she'll get her own way eventually.

"What didn't you do?" Winnie asked, confused.

"Whatever he's here to arrest us for," Thistle replied. "I'm innocent and I demand a lawyer."

That kid … I swear, she's going to make some man miserable one day. Oh, don't get me wrong, I think she'll eventually make him happy, too. She is work, though. She's like sixty-five inches of acid reflux rolled into a compact one-hundred-pound package. Oh, and if you poke the package it's like pouring soda on an Alka-Seltzer tab. It grows exponentially fast and if you try to put it in something too small to contain it everything explodes.

"I'm not here to arrest you," I said dryly.

"Oh, don't be hasty." Clove flashed me an impish smile. She's unbelievably cute … and she knows it. She shares a smile full of dimples whenever she wants something, and if that doesn't work she can turn on the waterworks in less than five seconds. "I happen to know Thistle has done at least ten illegal things this week. I can give you information on all of them if you agree that my testimony cannot be used against me."

Winnie smirked at their antics, causing me to shake my head. I love the girls – and the chaos that often surrounds them – but I have no idea how anyone could live with the noise – and mischief – they bring to one house.

"I want to testify against Clove," Thistle announced. "She's the one who should go to jail."

"You liar!" Clove wrinkled her ski-slope nose and tucked a strand of dark hair behind her ear. "I'm an angel."

"A dark angel," Thistle shot back. "I'll have you know that just this week she stole flowers from the cemetery. She took a big bouquet of roses."

Clove's face drained of color as she darted a furtive glance in my direction.

"Is that true?" I asked.

"It had better not be true," Winnie warned. "Why would you do that?"

"Thistle was there, too," Clove said, chewing on her bottom lip. "She acted as lookout, so she's just as guilty as I am."

Oh, geez. What is it with female teenagers? Why do they always have to make things so difficult? "Why would you steal flowers from the cemetery?" I asked, although I was pretty sure I already knew the answer. "That's against the law ... and rude."

"Well ... ." Clove looked caught as Thistle arched a challenging eyebrow, practically daring her cousin to own up to everything.

"They did it because Aunt Tillie wanted the roses and she made us go to the cemetery with her." Bay Winchester, the oldest of the teenaged tempests, trudged into the room. She brightened when she saw me and hurried over, giving me a quick hug. "What are you doing here? Are you going to arrest Thistle?"

Thistle scowled. "He's here to arrest you," she shot back. "You and your big mouth are going to be locked up for narcing."

"Yeah," Clove intoned. She's rarely the instigator, but because there are three of them – and Bay and Thistle are often at odds – she's the deciding vote. She enjoys having so much power at her tiny fingertips. She will make some man very happy one day, but that's mostly because he probably won't realize he's being manipulated. When you're less than five feet tall and have those dimples you can get away with murder and no one notices.

"It's not narcing when a police officer asks," Bay argued. "Isn't that right, Chief Terry?"

She's my favorite. I know you're not supposed to admit things like that, but she is. She's so blond she looks like an angel some days, and her smile lights up a room. Her eyes are bright blue, and sometimes clouded with a hint of sadness. She's a good kid who gets terrorized by other kids for being different. That's the witch thing I don't want to talk about and prefer to pretend doesn't exist, despite all evidence to the contrary.

"That's why you're my good girl," I said, resting my hand on her head. "You always follow the rules."

Thistle snorted. "She was there for the theft, too."

That was disappointing, although not altogether unsuspected. I glanced at Bay, purposely keeping my face neutral. "Did you help steal flowers from the cemetery?"

Bay's expression was benign. She knew I would never do something mean and lock her up, although I had yelled a few times – and each incident caused her to cry. Yes, some people might think she's manipulating me. I think she's just sensitive, though. What? I'm not a sap.

"Aunt Tillie made me do it," Bay said.

"I didn't make them do anything," Tillie said, appearing in the doorway between the lobby and main hallway. "They had a choice whether they wanted to do it or not, and each one of them opted to do as I asked."

Tillie Winchester is ... there are no words. She's terrifying. She's as short as Clove, and even boasts the same coloring as her mini-me, although Tillie's hair is shot through with gray. She's blustery, full of herself, and unbelievably loyal. Most people avoid her once they learn about her – and that's exactly how she prefers things – but I kind of like her. I couldn't help but wonder if that would change once I was living under the same roof with her for a few days. Perhaps I only liked her from a safe distance.

"What kind of choice did they have?" Winnie asked, legitimately curious. "That sounds ... odd ... to me."

That made two of us.

"They had a chance to help me or not help me," Tillie replied. "They chose to help."

"Yeah, we chose," Thistle muttered, shaking her head and causing me to narrow my eyes. I wasn't particularly worried about cemetery flower theft. It's not a good thing, mind you, but there are bigger things to worry about. Besides, everyone in town knows Tillie takes a weekly shopping trip to the cemetery. If people didn't want their stuff stolen, they wouldn't leave it out to be pilfered.

"See, it doesn't sound as if you chose anything," Winnie argued. "It sounds like you're insinuating that Aunt Tillie made you do something. Is that the case?"

Tillie snorted. "How could I possibly make them do anything? I'm an old lady."

Here's a tip: Tillie is only old when she's trying to distract people. If anyone calls her old on a normal day when she's not up to something – okay, she's up to something every day, so that argument doesn't really hold up, but you know what I mean – the curses start flying. And I mean that literally.

"You are an old lady," Thistle agreed. "You're a mean, nasty .... "

"Thistle!" Winnie smacked the back of Thistle's head again. Clove may be the one who will end up looking like Tillie, but Thistle has her attitude. There's a frightening future in this household, let me tell you.

"Bay, why did you girls help Aunt Tillie steal flowers?" Winnie focused on her daughter. "You said that the last time would be the last because she convinced you that zombies were coming out of a crypt and then left you stranded there and you had to walk home. Why did you go again?"

"They volunteered," Tillie interjected, her eyes thoughtful as they locked with Bay's. "Isn't that right, Bay?"

Bay's gaze bounced between faces, briefly latching onto mine, before she shrugged. She looked helpless. "Sure. We volunteered."

"You didn't volunteer, but I don't have time to mess with you right now," Winnie said. "I'll figure out what you were doing later. Terry, what can I do for you?"

I hadn't explained my presence yet. I'd almost forgotten. I related my day so far, telling everyone about the termites – earning disgusted "ews" and "yucks" from the teenaged crowd – and then asked if they had a room.

"You're extremely lucky," Winnie said. "We had one cancellation. It's all yours."

"Thank you." That was a relief.

"You're really staying here for three nights?" Bay looked excited at the prospect. "Will you tell us stories about dead bodies and stuff?"

I frowned. "Why would you want to hear about that?"

"She wants to be a reporter," Thistle said dryly. "She likes hearing about crime stuff. Personally, I think it's weird. But I want to hear about the dead bodies, too."

She's a strange kid. You can't help but like her, though. Of course, that's easy to say when you're not on her bad side. When that happens she's almost impossible to like.

"I'll consider it," I said, accepting the key from Winnie and smiling. "I'm going to go upstairs and get my things settled and then I have to make some calls for work. I'll be around if anyone needs me."

"And if anyone needs to be arrested," Clove added, grinning as she poked Thistle's side.

"You're an instigator," I said, tapping the end of her nose. "You know that, right?"

Clove shrugged, unbothered. "I am many things, and I can't be pigeonholed."

"Truer words were never spoken," I said. "You girls be good until I come down for dinner. I don't want to miss any arrest-worthy crimes."

"No promises," Thistle called to my back. "We'll see what we can do, though."

"You do that."

BY THE TIME I hit the main lobby for a second time I was exhausted. I thought working from my room would be easy and painless. I was wrong, mostly because Parker called every hour to update me on his lack of progress finding the con man. I should've thought that assignment through before doling it out, but honestly, who could see this coming? It was almost dinner time when I finally finished all of my paperwork.

The lobby was empty, but I found Clove, Thistle and Bay hiding close to the wall that led to the dining room. They were partially obscured by a large potted plant, and they whispered to one another as I approached.

"I think he's weird," Clove said. "He's probably a pervert. Aunt

Tillie always says that perverts come in all shapes and sizes. She probably meant that guy when she said it."

She wasn't talking about me, was she? I glanced over my shoulder but no one was there. The girls all stared at the same spot in the dining room, so I was reasonably assured they were talking about someone else.

"I don't think he's a pervert," Thistle said. "I'll bet he's a criminal, though. He looks like a thief."

"You've got stealing on the brain because of earlier," Bay said. "Let it go."

"You're the one who almost told," Thistle shot back. "You need to let it go."

"Chief Terry could've helped us," Bay said. "I know he would've helped us. Now we're stuck with Aunt Tillie blackmailing us. Who knows what she's going to make us do next."

That was interesting. Why was Tillie blackmailing them? I filed that topic away to revisit later.

"As long as it doesn't involve nudity and dancing, I don't care," Clove said. "I don't mind stealing flowers."

"Oh, that's such crap," Thistle said. "You swore you saw a zombie."

"That turned out to be a raccoon," Bay added.

"Hey! It could've been a short zombie," Clove argued. "You don't know. It's never been proven that the zombie virus won't jump from species to species."

"There's no such thing as a zombie virus," Bay snapped. "It's not real."

"It could be real," Clove grumbled.

"Well, it's not," Bay said, crossing her arms and returning her gaze to whatever held their interest in the dining room. They were interesting to watch. A few hours earlier they were scrapping. Now they were together working against a common enemy – although I had no idea who – and they were still scrapping. I will never understand the female group dynamic. "I don't think he's a pervert or a thief."

"Do you think he's a criminal?" Clove asked.

"Oh, he's definitely a criminal."

I cleared my throat to get their attention, delighting at the way they all jumped and turned to face me. Thistle was the first to speak.

"We didn't do it."

I scowled. "Why is that always your opening greeting?"

Thistle shrugged. "Because most people in this house usually accuse first and ask questions later."

"She's not wrong," Bay said, smiling. "I'm glad you're still here. I was worried when we didn't see you all day."

"We're stuck here because it's a holiday week and we had to help," Clove grumbled. "It sucked."

I chuckled as I patted her shoulder. "I'm sure you'll live. Just out of curiosity, what are you guys looking at?"

"The couple in the corner," Bay said, pointing. I moved so I could look over her shoulder and stared at the portly man who bore more than a striking resemblance to Dom DeLuise. He was rounder than he was tall and he had a huge, fluffy beard. His wife was a string bean of a woman, no curves to speak of, and her dishwater blond hair hung lifelessly around her shoulders. "We're pretty sure they're criminals."

"Why do you think that?"

"Because they look like criminals," Thistle answered. "I think they look like Boris and Natasha from *Bullwinkle*."

"I think they look like Bert and Ernie," Bay said. "We all agree they're evil, though."

I couldn't love these three girls more if they were my own, but the things they come up with sometimes are just … out there. "Ladies, did you ever think that maybe they're just regular people?"

"No," Clove answered. "They're not regular people. They keep watching everyone else and acting normal, but that means they're not normal."

That made absolutely no sense. "Well, how about I keep an eye on them over dinner just to be on the safe side? How does that sound?"

"Like we'll be trying to solve your murder next episode," Thistle answered, not missing a beat. "That's how these things work. The law enforcement official coddles the little kids and doesn't believe them and he ends up dead. It's karmic retribution."

"Yeah," Clove said.

"Well, I'll take my chances," I said. "It's dinner time. Sit down."

"Fine, but we're not sitting next to the criminals," Clove said, flouncing into the dining room with Thistle at her side. Bay remained with me, her face unreadable.

"What's wrong?"

"Nothing is wrong," Bay replied. "It's just nice having you here." She impulsively reached over and hugged me. "We usually only have female family members here. Now you'll be the only male."

The fact that she considered me family made me a little misty, although I would never admit that in front of an audience. "I'm glad I'm here, too," I said, patting her shoulder. "We need to sit down if we don't want to miss dinner, though. Your mother is a stickler for the rules, and it's almost seven."

"She'd let you slide," Bay said. "Can I sit next to you?"

I nodded.

"Good," Bay said. "I want to help you watch the criminals. Maybe we can nab them together."

I opened my mouth to admonish her and then snapped it shut. Really, what harm could come of her watching the guests? They would never know. "That sounds like a great idea," I said. "I'm going to need your eyes when I'm focused on the chocolate cake."

"Deal." Bay extended her hand and I shook it. "Now we're like partners."

I couldn't help but grin. "I think that's the best offer I've had all day."

THREE

"Good morning, ladies."

For some reason, entering the family kitchen instead of the guest dining room for breakfast the next morning held special meaning for me. The guests would eat breakfast in the other room in an hour. Because I had to get to the office early I planned to forego breakfast until I got to town. Winnie wouldn't hear it – and then her sisters Marnie and Twila wouldn't hear it when they caught wind that Winnie was trying to curry favor with me – so I was invited to a private family breakfast before retiring the previous evening. The Winchesters always go all out, so I was more than happy to oblige.

"There's nothing good about a morning," Thistle murmured, rubbing her forehead as she rested her elbows on the table. "They suck."

"Get your elbows off the table," Winnie scolded, tapping Thistle's arm for emphasis. "I have no idea why you're so tired. You girls went upstairs at ten."

"Yeah, what were you doing?" Marnie asked, narrowing her eyes as she scanned the three teenaged faces in the room. "You'd better not have left this house."

"We didn't leave the house," Clove said. "Why do you always assume we did something wrong?"

"Because history is not in your favor," Marnie replied. "Seriously, what is up with the three of you?"

They looked tired. They were young girls, yet they all had dark circles under their eyes. I sat between Bay and Winnie – earning a scowl from Twila, who was saving me a seat on the other side of the table – and fixated on Bay. "Are you sick?"

Bay shifted her eyes to me. They were their usual bright color, and she didn't look pale or waxen, so I figured I was overreacting. "We didn't get a lot of sleep," she said.

"And why is that?" Winnie asked.

"You weren't spying on that couple, were you?" I shot Marnie a thankful smile as she pushed a mug of coffee in my direction. "I told you last night that I thought you were barking up the wrong tree."

"They're evil," Thistle said. "I can feel it in my bones."

"Oh, geez," Twila muttered. "You sound like Aunt Tillie."

Thistle made a face. "That's the meanest thing you've ever said to me."

"You'll live."

I had indulged Bay, Clove and Thistle's game for a decent amount of time the previous night. Caroline and Charles Garvey were boisterous and sometimes brash, but they seemed perfectly normal to me. They were in the area visiting relatives one town over, but no matter how much information they shared about their trip the teenagers remained convinced they were up to something nefarious. I think teenagers need constant stimulation or they get bored, and that's what's going on here.

"They're over-sharers," Thistle said. "That's always a sign that people are hiding something."

"I don't know what that means," I said, grabbing some bacon from the center plate. "What's an over-sharer?"

"A person who shares too much," Bay automatically answered. "That means they volunteered a bunch of information to us. It was full of details, but it told us nothing."

"Uh-huh." I rubbed my forehead. Living full time with teenagers must be baffling – and tiring. Winnie, Twila and Marnie seemed mildly irritated with the girls, but not surprised by their suspicions. That told me this wasn't the first time they'd done something like this. "Perhaps they're just excited to see family. Charles told me that he hasn't seen his brother in almost five years. Maybe they talked so much because they couldn't help themselves from being excited."

"How are you still alive?" an incredulous Thistle asked. "If this was a horror movie you would be the dead blonde in the shower. Although, your breasts aren't nearly big enough."

"Thistle!" Twila slapped the table as I swallowed my laughter. The things Thistle came up with sometimes were downright hysterical. I was pretty sure the girl could have a future in stand-up comedy if she so desired. "Don't say things like that."

Thistle was unperturbed by her mother's tone. "He knows he doesn't have breasts. He's not offended."

"She's right," I said, grinning. "I still don't understand why you're convinced these two people are criminals."

"Bay read an article that said one out of every ten people is a criminal," Clove supplied. "There are ten guests staying here right now. That means one of them has to be a criminal. We've been watching all of them, and the Garveys are the only ones who seem suspicious."

"Oh, I don't know. I think the guy who kept picking his nose and coughing into his hand to cover it is kind of shady," Bay said. "The Garveys just have a weird vibe"

"That's another thing," Thistle said. "Their names are Charles and Caroline."

Did she just explain something? "I don't know what that means."

"It's from *Little House on the Prairie,*" Bay explained. "Charles and Caroline Ingalls."

"Okay, but their last name is Garvey."

"Yes, but there was a Garvey family in *Little House on the Prairie,*" Thistle said. "It's all a little ... *Law & Order: SVU.*"

"On the prairie," Clove added.

Wow. "You guys watch way too much television," I said, shaking my head. "I think we should assume that the Garveys are telling the truth and their names are a coincidence. Charles and Caroline are common names."

"I think you're never going to survive the end of the world when it comes because you're far too trusting," Thistle said. "Don't worry about it, though. We're watching them. We've got everything under control."

"Uh-huh." I didn't have time to make sense of teenage logic. "Well, just don't do anything until you run it by me first, okay?"

"We would never," Bay said solemnly. "We're partners in this."

"Okay." I sipped my coffee and then turned my attention to the mothers at the table. "What does everyone else have going on today?"

"Normal stuff," Winnie replied. "We're going to get a leg up on our Christmas baking. That takes a month to finish and then we freeze stuff. We pick one recipe a weekend between now and then. Today it's Christmas tree cookies."

"Oh, yay!" Bay clapped her hands as her expression brightened. It was almost enough to chase the circles from beneath her eyes.

"Can we have some?" Clove was interested, too.

"We will keep one plate out for you girls," Winnie replied. "You have to be good to get them."

"Are they those little sugar cookies with the green frosting?" I asked.

Winnie nodded.

"Those are damn fine cookies," I said. "You girls better be good today or I'll eat all of them myself."

"We'll be good," Bay said.

"Mostly good," Clove added.

"Speak for yourself," Thistle countered. "I'm going to be me and just steal cookies from everyone else. That sounds easier."

And that summed up this trio. "Well, I'll be getting a full report from your mothers when I get back tonight," I said, winking at Winnie. "They're going to let me dole out the cookies, so you'd better be on your best behavior."

Thistle snorted. "That's not saying much in this house," she said. "Next to Aunt Tillie, we're practically angels."

She had a point. "Speaking of Tillie, where is she?" I almost missed it, but I was positive Bay and Thistle exchanged a quick look before focusing on their plates. That couldn't be good.

"She's upstairs getting ready," Twila replied. "When the seasons change it's always a big deal for her to shuffle her wardrobe."

That sounded ... preposterous. "She always wears the same thing."

"Not really," Thistle said. "She wears green camouflage during the summer because it fits in and allows her to stalk the woods for evil-doers without anyone noticing she's there. When all the leaves die in the fall, she switches to brown camouflage so no one can see her coming."

"She's the invisible marauder," Clove said, parroting back what I'm sure was a Tillie claim from their childhood.

Yeah, I should've realized it would be something like that. "Well ... ."

As if on cue, the distinctive sound of Tillie throwing a fit upstairs assailed my ears. It didn't sound as if words were the only thing she was throwing, because something definitely hit a wall on the second floor.

"Someone is in big trouble!"

This time there could be no denying the look Thistle and Bay exchanged.

"We're done with breakfast so we're going to go," Bay said, wiping her hands and throwing her napkin on the table. "We have that garden shed work we promised to finish for you. We'll be out there."

"Yeah," Thistle said. "We love outdoor work."

I expected Winnie to halt them but she was too busy staring at the ceiling. She didn't notice as the girls raced out the back door, slamming it behind them in their haste to get outside. No wonder the three scamps get away with murder. Tillie confounds things and their mothers are more worried about keeping her in line than their offspring.

"Where are they?" Tillie appeared at the bottom of the stairs, her hair standing on end. Sure enough, she was dressed in brown camouflage pants. You learn something new every day.

"Where is who?" Winnie asked.

"Toil, Trouble and Thistle." Either Tillie couldn't think of a name for Thistle or the girl's moniker already struck fear in the Winchester populace all on its own. "I know they were just down here."

"I think they said they were going outside to clean up the garden shed," Winnie said. "I can't remember exactly what they said, though."

"Who cares?" Marnie added. "We want them outside. Pretty soon it's going to snow and then they're going to be inside twenty-four hours a day. Then we'll all need to be committed."

"What's wrong anyway?" Twila asked. "Why were you yelling?"

"Someone has been in my room," Tillie intoned. "Unless it was one of you – which I very much doubt – it was one of them. Or, most likely, all of them."

"Why would they go in your room?" I asked. "Isn't that off limits?"

Tillie glanced at me. We didn't have an especially close relationship, but we shared mutual respect and admiration. "Why are the Keystone Cops here?"

Or maybe that was just me.

"He's staying at the inn while his house is tented for termites," Winnie answered. "We told you that last night."

"Yes, but sometimes you yammer on so long I just nod and pretend I'm listening," Tillie said. "It's not my fault you talk so much. If you could get your point across in fewer sentences I think it would benefit all of us."

Winnie narrowed her eyes and crossed her arms over her chest. Tillie ruled the roost – until she didn't. She could push Winnie only so far before she pushed back. "What was stolen from your room?"

Tillie tilted her head to the side and glanced at me. Whatever was missing she didn't want to own up to it in front of law enforcement. That meant it was probably some of her homemade wine. "I don't recall."

"Then how do you know something is missing?" Marnie challenged.

"Perhaps I'm psychic."

"Perhaps you're psycho," Twila said. I think she believed she was thinking her comment because when she realized she said it out loud her cheeks colored. "I mean ... you're psychotic."

"That's worse, Twila," Marnie said, shaking her head. "Either tell us what's missing and we'll ask the girls or let it go, Aunt Tillie. We don't have time to mess around with you all day."

"Don't you worry about me," Tillie said. "I will handle this matter on my own."

"How will you do that?" I asked, genuinely curious.

"I'm nothing if not gifted," Tillie replied, stalking toward the door. "You said they went out back, right?"

"They're supposed to be in the garden shed," Winnie supplied.

"That means they'll be someplace else," Tillie said, throwing open the door before bellowing. "I'm coming, girls!"

I expected Winnie, Twila or Marnie to follow their aunt and stop her from doing whatever it was she had planned. Instead they ignored the mayhem.

"So, what are you doing today, Terry?" Winnie asked, flashing a flirty smile.

"Just normal stuff," I replied, casting a worried look at the door Tillie disappeared through. She wouldn't kill her great-nieces, right? "I don't expect anything big to cross my desk."

"Well, don't be late for dinner. We're having roasted chicken tonight."

"I'll be here with bells on."

"Oh, don't do that," Twila said. "Aunt Tillie hates bells. She'll curse you."

Yeah, there's never a dull moment in the Winchester house of horrors.

BY THE TIME I was ready to leave the office that afternoon I'd almost managed to put the morning's antics out of my head.

Whatever Bay, Clove and Thistle did to Tillie would most likely be remedied by the time I hit the bed and breakfast, and after a crazy day dealing with Walkerville's finest – and I use that term loosely – I was ready for a glass of bourbon and a spot in front of the fireplace.

That's when Parker appeared in my office, making an easy escape out of the question.

"What's going on?" I asked, trying to hide my disappointment when he blocked the office door. "Is something wrong?"

"Nothing is wrong, sir," Parker said. "I'm glad I caught you before you left for the day, though."

"And why is that?"

"Because you've been busy all afternoon, sir," Parker said. "I saw Norman Peterson in here and I thought he wouldn't stop talking for the entire night at the rate he was going."

"Yes, he's convinced that Selma Baker is stripping down next door and trying to entice his son by walking past her window naked," I said dryly.

"Isn't Selma Baker eighty?"

I shrugged. "Norman's kid is sixteen. We're all animals at that age. I told him I would talk to her."

"Are you going to talk to her?" Parker looked horrified at the prospect.

"I sent you an email," I said, internally chuckling. "You can add it to your list of duties tomorrow."

Parker tried to swallow his disgust but couldn't hide his revulsion. "Anything I can do to serve the town, sir."

"I'm glad to hear it," I said. "How is your investigation into the con man coming along? I can't remember his name." To be fair, I couldn't remember anything about the guy. That's how far down on my list of worries it was.

"It's Adam Edwards, sir."

"And how is your search for Adam Edwards going?"

"Well, the state police sent this over." Parker handed me an updated BOLO and I scanned the information, arching an eyebrow when I got to the interesting part. "This says the man appears to be traveling with a woman now and possibly heading in this direction."

"I know, sir. Isn't that great?"

I pressed my lips together and focused on Parker. "I'm not sure 'great' is the word I would choose, but what's your plan of attack?"

"I'm going to monitor all of the inns in the area for new visitors and conduct constant surveillance on the town."

"Constant surveillance?"

"I'm dedicated to keeping this town safe, sir." You couldn't fault Parker's work ethic. His gung-ho attitude was another story. That was so fervent it bordered on annoying. Oh, who am I kidding? It passed annoying two weeks after I hired him.

"Well, keep me updated," I said, grabbing my coat from the back of my chair and switching off my computer monitor. "I'll be out at the Winchesters' place if you need me."

"Have you seen anything ... witchy?" Parker asked, too interested to maintain his reserve.

"I've watched three teenagers drive their mothers crazy and convince themselves that two of the guests are evil," I replied. "I'm pretty sure they stole some wine from their great-aunt, too, so I'm waiting for something to happen with that, and I'm pretty sure it will be loud. That's about it, though."

"Well, if you need help with them, don't forget to call," Parker said. "Did we ever settle on a safe word?"

"We did," I said, forcing a smile. "Have a nice night."

Parker obviously didn't grasp the sarcasm. "Which one of those words is the code, sir?"

FOUR

"Where is everyone?"

Marnie was standing behind the front desk when I entered the inn, her face blank as she daydreamed about something. Perhaps she wasn't daydreaming, though. Perhaps she simply wanted a break from her sisters … and daughter … and nieces … and her aunt. Especially her aunt. Time alone in this place must come at a premium.

"They're around," Marnie said, her smile turning flirty. She and her sisters play a game in which they like to entice me. I'm not sure if they really like me or if they just want to win, although I'm leaning toward the latter. Everyone gets along, don't get me wrong, but winning is a highly valued in this family. "Winnie and Twila are finishing up the cookies."

"And the girls?"

Marnie smirked. "They're outside. I think they're still hiding from Aunt Tillie. It's been a long day of slamming doors and people running through the inn."

That couldn't be good for business. "Have the guests been complaining?"

"They think it's a show," Marnie replied. "Someone even called it 'family theater.' I'm not sure what that means, but no one has complained."

I dropped my files on top of the desk and glanced around. It was quiet. Too quiet. Part of the appeal of staying here is the noise. "I'll go outside and find the girls," I offered. "If they're getting in trouble I'll put an end to it."

Marnie snorted. "They're always getting in trouble. Knock yourself out, though."

I turned back toward the door but Marnie stopped me before I stepped outside.

"Oh, and if you could remind them to make sure the dog does his business before they come inside, that would be great."

The dog. How could I forget Sugar? I was the reason they had him. He was a big-breed mutt that watched and loved all three of them. He was getting up there in age, although the girls didn't seem to mind that he preferred sleeping in front of the fireplace more than playing these days. When he passed – which was hopefully still a few years off – they would be crushed.

"I'll remind them."

Winters in northern Lower Michigan are brutal, and they come on fast. Summers are blessed with long days of sunshine (and sometimes cursed with heavy humidity). Autumn is my favorite time of year, the temperature remaining comfortable even as the leaves turn. Once Halloween hits, though, anything after that could be considered winter. We didn't have snow on the ground yet – although a few flurries fell the other night without sticking – but it was inevitable.

With the days getting shorter, it was almost dark. The bed and breakfast is located in an isolated portion of town. The parcel of land the Winchesters own is huge, and while Marnie, Twila and Winnie don't seem to worry about the girls running around after dark with so many trees to get lost in, I can't help but debate the intelligence associated with that. Sure, the girls are teenagers and capable of taking care of themselves, but they are still technically children.

I pulled up short when I caught sight of Bay's blond head. Even though the sun was almost gone, a whisper of light remained, bouncing off her flaxen highlights and drawing my attention to bushes located at the corner of the house. Sure enough, Clove and Thistle were with her. Sugar was, too, although he was asleep at their feet as they stared into the back yard.

I was quiet as I approached, hoping to get a line on their conversation before they noticed me. They were probably hiding from Tillie. I didn't blame them.

"What do you think they're doing?" Clove whispered.

"I think they're scouting the house and all of the exits so they can rob us at gunpoint and make their getaway," Thistle said. "They'll probably shoot us before they go."

They definitely watch too much television, and they clearly weren't hiding from Tillie. That left only one thing.

"Chief Terry won't let them shoot us," Bay said. "They're probably afraid now that they know he's here. He'll shoot them before they can shoot us. He would never let anything bad happen to us."

I puffed out my chest at her words. Bay's faith warmed me even as a chill descended with the departure of the sun.

"Chief Terry won't shoot them," Thistle scoffed. "They'll kill him first. Don't you pay any attention to the movies we watch?"

"I try not to," Clove said, shuddering. "That last one was terrible. That girl climbing out of the well was freaky."

"I thought it was freakier when she climbed out of the television," Bay said. "It was still cool, though."

"I think we should watch more chick flicks," Clove said. "Those are never scary and they never give me nightmares."

"They always give me nightmares," Thistle intoned. "I mean … do you hear how whiny those chicks are? That's the stuff of nightmares right there."

"They're not whiny," Clove protested. "That's crap."

"You're crap," Thistle shot back.

"You're both crap," Bay interjected. "Now keep your voices down. They'll hear us if you're not careful."

"And then shoot us," Thistle added.

Okay, I'd heard just about enough of that. I closed the rest of the distance and clamped a hand on Thistle and Clove's shoulders. "What's up?"

"Holy crap!" Clove practically jumped out of her skin, swiveling quickly and slapping my hand away. The noise was enough to draw the attention of Charles and Caroline Garvey, who were sitting on the patio drinking coffee and chatting. Yeah, they looked like criminal masterminds. "Don't do that again!"

"I'm sorry," I said, removing my hands. I wasn't remotely sorry. That was kind of funny. "What are you doing?"

Thistle, who handled the surprise better than Clove (or at least masked it better), made a face. "We were watching the bad guys in case they made a move," she replied. "Now they know we're here, so they're not going to let us in on their evil plan."

"Yeah, you ruined it," Clove said, wrinkling her nose. "I'm starting to think Thistle is right about you being the first to die when they attack. You might want to rethink your undercover technique."

I didn't bother hiding my scowl as I shook my head. "I'm not undercover."

"You're definitely not good at it," Thistle said.

Sugar raised her head and graced me with what looked like a doggy grin. "You're not much of a guard dog, are you? I walked right up to these guys and you didn't stir."

"He knows you," Bay argued. "He knows you would never hurt us."

I wasn't convinced, but it didn't really matter. The girls were in no danger from me. Their great-aunt was another story. "Are you guys going to spend the whole night stalking the guests? I thought maybe you were hiding from Aunt Tillie."

Bay and Thistle exchanged a look – it was one I was beginning to recognize – and Thistle opted to answer. I shouldn't have been surprised. When it comes to subterfuge, she's the go-to liar.

"I have no idea what you're talking about," Thistle said. "Why would we be hiding from Aunt Tillie?"

"Yeah, we love her," Clove said. She's a terrible liar most of the time, by the way. She might be able to fool a stranger, but anyone who knows her can't help but read the naked emotion on her face when she's full of crap.

"I didn't say you didn't love her," I pointed out. "I said you were hiding from her."

"We were hiding from them," Thistle said, jerking her thumb in the direction of the Garveys. "I know you don't think they're evil – and when that comes back to bite us I'm going to want an apology – but we know they are."

"Okay, why do you think they're evil?" I asked. I had to be missing something. It couldn't just be the *Little House on the Prairie* references. "What is your evidence?"

"We don't like them," Thistle replied. "Charles grabbed my cheek and jiggled it. He said, 'Aren't you cute!' I'm not cute … and I'm also not three years old."

I had to bite my lip to keep from laughing. I was sorry I missed that. The girls were trained never to backtalk guests, but that had to be an exercise in control for Thistle. "That's it? That hardly seems like evidence that they're evil."

"What about their names?" Clove pressed. "That can't be normal."

"I think that's just one of those things that happens," I said. "Do you know how many Andy Taylors I've met who are cops?"

"No."

"Tons."

"What does that have to do with anything?" Thistle asked, confused. "Who is Andy Taylor?"

"From *The Andy Griffith Show*," I prodded, getting three blank expressions in return. "Oh, come on. Barney Fife? Opie? Aunt Bee?" The three girls shook their heads in unison. "So you watch every horror movie under the sun but a television classic is mentioned and you draw a blank? That seems criminal."

"Is Aunt Bee like Aunt Tillie?" Clove asked.

"Definitely not."

"Then that would be a horror show," Thistle said, laughing. "I crack myself up."

"You're the only one," Bay said dryly.

"Speaking of your great-aunt, why does she think you stole something from her?" I asked.

"Oh, wow, look at the time." Thistle glanced at her bare wrist. "We should probably get inside. We don't want to be late for dinner."

"Yeah, it's roasted chicken and potatoes," Clove said, rubbing her stomach. "Yum!"

"Yum, yum," I said, bobbing my head, "but you're not leaving until you answer the question. That trick you pulled this morning when you raced outside while your mothers were distracted was cute, but I'm not falling for it."

"What trick?" Clove feigned innocence. "We had a job to do and we always want to make our mothers happy. You can't dillydally in this family. No, sir. That's not allowed."

"Yes, you're a diligent worker, Clove. I've never doubted that for a second."

"He thinks you're lying," Thistle said. "You laid it on too thick. You always lay it on too thick. We've talked about moderation. You need to remember that."

These kids … holy crap! How does anyone keep up with them? "What did you steal from Tillie? She seemed adamant that you stole something, although she didn't want to tell me what."

"We didn't steal anything," Thistle said. Unlike Clove, you can never tell when she's lying. She's a master. "That's a terrible thing to say. I want a lawyer."

"We all want lawyers," Clove said.

I rolled my eyes until they landed on Bay. When it came to lying, she was somewhere in the middle. She was perfectly fine lying to most people, but for some reason she drew the line at lying to me. "What did you steal, Bay?"

"I … ." Bay's mouth worked but she couldn't find the words she needed. I almost felt sorry for her.

"They didn't steal anything." I jumped at Tillie's voice behind me, glancing over my shoulder to find her detaching from the house. I had no idea how long she'd been listening.

"You said they took something," I pointed out. "Did you find what they took?"

"I was ... mistaken ... about them taking something," Aunt Tillie said. She's an enigma when it comes to lies. When she commits she can sell anything. She wasn't trying to sell this, though. She was backing up the girls, but only because she didn't want to give me ammunition against them. It was an interesting development. "I found what I was looking for earlier."

I didn't believe her. I'd known her far too long to do that. I couldn't call her a liar on her own property, though. "Okay," I said finally. "I guess we should go inside and get ready for dinner. Girls, Marnie said to make sure Sugar does his business before going inside."

"Got it," Bay said, clapping her hands to get Sugar on his feet. She looked relieved. I figured it was because Tillie saved her from having to make a hard choice. "We'll see you inside."

I watched them go, amused as they whispered and chattered as they turned the corner of the house. Then I fixed my attention on Tillie. "Why are you covering for them if they stole from you?" I was genuinely curious.

"I never said they stole from me." Tillie averted her eyes. "I thought I was missing something this morning, but I found it."

"Do you want to know what I think?"

"Not really."

I plowed ahead anyway. "I think they stole a bottle of your wine," I said. "I think they do it all the time and have turned it into something of a game. I think you don't want to admit it because you illegally make that wine and you don't want to get in trouble."

Tillie snorted, taking me by surprise. "You're a good guy and I like you," she said. "I'm not worried in the least that you'll arrest me, though. You're too fond of my nieces – and you love my grandnieces. You would never hurt them."

She had a point. "So what are you doing?" I prodded. "Are you saving this as more blackmail material? That's how you got them to go into the cemetery the other night. I know it."

"Our family has some ... peculiar ... traditions," Tillie said. "I can't explain them in great detail because you would never understand. Don't worry about it."

"I do love those girls," I said. "I would hate if something happened to them."

"You worry too much," Tillie said, slapping my arm. "They're all destined for greatness in one form or another. Something little like a pilfered bottle of wine – and I'm not saying that's what's going on here in case you're wired and 'The Man' is listening – won't derail them.

"They're spirited girls and they like getting in trouble," she continued. "That's what makes them interesting."

"You're a hard woman to understand, Tillie," I said. "You make me laugh, don't get me wrong, but even as you're terrorizing those girls you're also protecting them. I just don't understand it."

"I love them, too."

"I've never doubted that."

"Loving them and letting them off the hook are two different things," Tillie said. "I can love them and still want to mess with them. That's the way of family. Heck, that's the best thing about family."

"I guess I've missed out on that," I said, my mood turning melancholy. "Maybe I don't understand how a real family operates."

"Oh, that's horse pucky," Tillie said. "This is your family. It doesn't matter that you're not married to one of the older girls, you're still the closest thing to a father those younger girls have, and every one of them loves you, no matter what they say."

It hurt to swallow over the lump in my throat. "I ... um ... ."

"Oh, geez, don't get mushy," Tillie said. "You need to put your foot down when it's important, but this isn't important. Bay especially needs you, but don't put her in a position where she has to choose between loyalty and you. It's not fair to her."

"That's not what I was doing," I protested.

"That's not what you were purposely doing," Tillie clarified. "You love Bay dearly. She's your favorite."

"I don't think I'm supposed to have a favorite."

"I have a different favorite depending on the day," Tillie said.

"Right now you're my favorite because your heart grew about ten sizes when I mentioned the girls love you. That's what I like about you. Just ... don't force Bay to tell the truth when you know it's going to cause a rift between her and Thistle.

"If it's a big thing, I have no problem with you doing that," she continued. "This is not a big thing."

"Are you sure?" I wasn't entirely convinced.

"I'm sure that I'll handle the three menaces and things will be fine," Tillie said. "Buck up. You're here to enjoy yourself for a few days. Do that. Don't focus on the negative stuff. That's my job."

And like that, she was off. She had a little extra zip in her step as she moved to the front of the house, and I knew she was going after her grandnieces. She acted tough on the outside, but on the inside she loved all of her girls. That's why I liked her.

"I can feel you being schmaltzy from here," Tillie called out. "Knock it off and hurry up. You don't want to miss the chicken."

FIVE

"This smells amazing."

I inhaled the heavenly aroma and smiled. As a bachelor, my idea of cooking is whatever I can pop in the microwave or pick up at a diner in town before going home every night. The meals I share with the Winchester family are always better, and the food is only part of that.

"Thank you." Winnie beamed from across the table. "I know how much you love chicken."

"I made the chicken," Marnie snapped.

"Yes, but I watched while you were doing it to make sure it was done right," Winnie said.

"I made the potatoes," Twila offered, running her hand through her flame-red hair. "I added rosemary because I know how much you love it."

"Good grief," Tillie muttered, shaking her head as she reached for her glass of wine. "I made a mess out in the garden shed. If anyone cares, that is."

Thistle made a face. "We spent half the day cleaning that."

"Huh, I didn't notice." Tillie sipped her wine. "I guess you'll have to go back out there and do it again tomorrow, huh? Whoops."

"But ... we just did it," Clove whined.

"What a complete and total bummer." Tillie looked pleased with herself, which is never a good thing.

Winnie narrowed her eyes as her gaze bounced between her aunt and the girls, some internal dilemma busying her mind as she decided if she wanted to get involved. Finally, she did the only thing she could. "You'll clean it again tomorrow."

"That's not fair," Thistle snapped.

Winnie extended a warning finger in Thistle's direction. "We all know why it got messed up a second time. Do you want to talk about that?" Thistle pursed her lips but remained silent. "I didn't think so. Eat your dinner, Thistle."

"This meal looks glorious. I can't wait to dig in." Charles Garvey sat at the end of the table with his wife, his cheeks flushed from either too much time outside or too many glasses of Tillie's wine. I couldn't be sure which. "Do you always cook like this?"

"We love cooking," Twila replied. "It's something of a family gift."

"Oh, do you cook?" Caroline smiled indulgently at Tillie. "I'll just bet you were a great teacher."

Winnie, Marnie and Twila snorted in unison, earning a murderous look from Tillie.

"I'm a lovely cook," Tillie said. "I could do it professionally if I wanted. I decided to take a different route, though, and focus my efforts on other things."

"Oh, really?" Caroline was either clueless for not picking up on Tillie's tone or purposely obtuse. "What did you focus your efforts on?"

"Evil," Thistle replied, reaching for the breadbasket at the center of the table. "She rose to the top of her field, too."

I knew it was wrong to encourage her, but I couldn't stop myself from laughing. Tillie didn't appreciate my contribution to the situation.

"I take back everything I said to you outside," she hissed.

"What did you say to him outside?" Winnie leaned forward, intrigued. "Did you tell him what's going on with you and the girls?"

"Nothing is going on with me and the girls," Tillie said. "We're one big happy family."

"Kind of like the Mansons," Thistle said, bobbing her head. The smile she offered the guests came off more deranged than anything else.

"And we know how it worked out for the Mansons," Bay said, her eyes thoughtful as she studied Charles and Caroline. "You said your brother lived over in Alden, right?"

"On Torch Lake," Charles confirmed, smiling. He obviously thought Bay was being polite and making dinner conversation, but I knew otherwise. "I haven't seen his house yet, but I've heard it's fantastic."

"Why haven't you been there yet?" Thistle asked. "I mean, you've been making such a big deal out of it and you've been here two days, but you still haven't visited."

If Charles noticed the hint of tension in Thistle's question, he didn't comment on it. "We're going Thanksgiving Day."

"And where do you live?" Clove asked. "I know you told us, but I forgot."

"We live in Grand Rapids."

"And what do you do?" Bay asked.

"I'm a plumber," Charles replied, chuckling. "Boy, you guys are curious little things, aren't you?"

"You know what they say about curiosity, right?" I said, shooting a pointed look in Thistle's direction.

"No, what do they say?" Tillie asked.

"That it killed the cat," Clove answered for me. "We don't have a cat, though. We'll be fine."

"We have a cat," Thistle said. "It's evil and it stalks us all of the time. It even messes up sheds after we've spent hours cleaning them."

"If you're referring to me, I'm hardly a cat," Tillie said.

"I think it's your spirit animal," Thistle countered.

"My spirit animal is a shark," Tillie shot back. "A great white."

"Ooh, I love sharks," Caroline enthused. "We went on a cruise several years ago and they let us go out on boats and get up close and personal with the sharks. It was neat."

"Obviously they didn't eat you," Thistle said. "Aunt Tillie is the type of shark who would eat you."

"And spit you back out, Mouth," Tillie muttered.

"Okay, let's stop talking about sharks," Winnie suggested. "I think that's an inappropriate – and entirely weird – topic."

"I agree," I offered. "Let's talk about something else. What are you girls going to do with your extended weekend?"

"I'm going shark hunting." Thistle's eyes never left Tillie's face. "Do you know that scene in *Jaws* where the really tan guy blows up the shark? Well, smile you … ."

"Thistle!" Winnie had reached her limit in front of the guests. "If you say one more word you're going to your room without supper."

I had no idea what was going on between Thistle and Tillie, but somewhere between our time together outside and dinner things turned serious. It had something to do with the garden shed. I couldn't question them about that now, though, so I picked a different topic to smooth things over.

"Bay, what are you doing this weekend?" I asked, shifting my eyes to her.

"I don't know," Bay replied. "I think I'll probably just read. It's supposed to snow this weekend."

"We can go sledding," Clove suggested. "We always do that during the first big snow."

"We can do that," Bay said, nodding.

I risked a glance at Thistle and found her staring Tillie down. The unspoken standoff wasn't going unnoticed by anyone, although the guests appeared to think it was part of a game. In a weird way, it kind of was a game. This game had bigger stakes than I initially envisioned, though.

"If you guys come into town this weekend I'll take you for hot chocolate and doughnuts," I offered. "That's our usual first snow outing, right?"

"Can we get sprinkles?" Clove asked.

"Don't I always get you sprinkles?"

She seemed happy with the answer. "Then can we go to the office with you and see the hot new officer?" Clove asked. "He's very cute."

I rubbed my cheek as I glowered at her. "He is much too old for you."

"He's not that old," Thistle argued, finally dragging her eyes from Tillie. "He's only four years older than Bay. That's nothing."

"Five," I corrected. "He's five years older than Bay."

"And I already warned him I would turn his thing green if he didn't stop sniffing around here," Tillie said. "And I don't mean in a cool Incredible Hulk kind of way."

I snorted. It was rare that Tillie and I found ourselves on the same side of an argument. "I'll help you."

"Oh, I don't need help," Tillie said. "Just motivation. He's too old for you, Bay."

"I don't want to see him," Bay said. "Clove has the crush on him."

"He's definitely too old for you, Clove," I said. "Plus, he's very intense. His job is the most important thing to him. You don't want a guy who focuses on his job rather than you."

"I bet I could get him to focus on me," Clove said, her eyes taking on a far-off quality. "He has nice … dimples."

"She's talking about his butt," Thistle offered. "That's just code."

"Thistle!" Winnie looked as if she was going to crawl over the table and take Thistle out. She didn't care if she had an audience.

As if sensing that the tension was about to spill into uncharted territory, Bay took control of the conversation. "What did you do today, Chief Terry? Is anything exciting going on in Walkerville?"

I wanted to hug her for being so in tune to her family's wacky ways. "Well, it seems Selma Baker is getting naked and walking past her upstairs bedroom window and Norman Peterson doesn't like it," I offered. "He thinks she's doing it to lure his son away."

Winnie made a face as she turned from Thistle. "Ryan? He'll stare at anyone. I caught him out here peeping through the windows one day. At first I thought he was looking for the girls, but then I realized he was looking for anyone. He got Aunt Tillie's room."

Now that was a sobering thought.

"Oh, yeah," Thistle said, laughing. "When you caught him he wasn't even embarrassed. He did ask why she wore socks on her chest, though, and you had to explain those weren't socks. I think he was terrified by the time you were finished."

"He's a schmuck," Bay said.

"I think he's cute," Clove interjected. "He has a nice smile."

She worries me. All of the girls are boy crazy in their own way, but Clove always has to take it to a freaky level. "If Ryan Peterson is out here peeking at your aunt, then he's definitely not good enough for you."

"Hey!" Tillie was offended. "He would be lucky to get a gander at my … ."

"Socks?" Thistle challenged. Of course she would manage to turn a mildly obnoxious conversation into a potential declaration of war.

"Mouth, you don't want to push me right now," Tillie warned. "I've had just about as much as I can take from you."

"We all have," Winnie said. "If you're going to continue to be obnoxious, Thistle, go to your room."

"I haven't eaten dinner yet."

"I don't care."

Thistle tilted her head to the side, considering. Finally she blew out a long-suffering sigh only a teenager who thinks she's being mistreated can muster. "Fine. I'm sorry."

"That's better," Winnie said.

"What else happened at work?" Bay asked. She appeared genuinely interested in my day. She seems starved for attention at times, which is ridiculous because this family showers attention on each member at every turn, but she never gets enough of hearing me talk. She doesn't care how mundane the conversation.

"Well, it seems Mrs. Little has been putting a bag over the parking meter in front of her store and pretending it's out of order so she can reserve the spot for herself," I said. "I asked the guy who collects the coins to figure out what was wrong with the meter and it turns out nothing was wrong."

Tillie snorted. "That sounds just like that … ."

"Aunt Tillie!" Winnie was not having a good meal. I'd forgotten how much Tillie and Margaret Little hated each other. That one was on me.

"Oh, and everyone's favorite new police officer is convinced some con man is coming to town, so everyone should be on the lookout for him," I said.

"Con man?" Bay was intrigued. "Like … he steals from people?"

"This guy had a fake land deed deal in the Upper Peninsula," I replied. "He sold deeds for very little money – although I guess it added up to a goodly sum eventually – but when people went to check out the land it was in the middle of a swamp … and he didn't own it. It was government land."

"Wow," Bay said. "How much money did he get?"

"The alert didn't say," I replied. "It would have to be a decent amount to warrant the attention he's getting. The first alert said he could be anywhere in the state. The second seemed to indicate he was traveling in this direction.

"The first alert also said he was alone," I continued, "but the second one said he was traveling with a woman."

"Really?" Bay's eyes shifted to the end of the table where Charles and Caroline sat. They seemed interested in the conversational shift, but oblivious to Bay's pointed gaze.

"Is that a big deal?" Caroline asked. "I mean … will the cops go out of their way to find these people so close to the holidays?"

I shrugged. "It's big enough for the state police to get involved," I answered. "I think the odds of someone trying to hide out in a town the size of Walkerville are small. There's no money here and everyone knows everyone's business.

"Just in case, I put Officer Parker on it," I continued. "He's very keen on catching these two, so if they do happen to come through here I have every confidence he'll catch them."

"What's he doing to find them?" Bay asked.

For a moment I thought she was interested because she had a crush on Parker. Then I realized what she was really doing. I wasn't sure which scenario bothered me more. "He'll alert me if he does find them and then we'll handle it. That's the police handling it, Bay. No one else."

She ignored the pointed statement. "Do you think they could be … I don't know … staying at one of the local inns?"

"Surely not," Charles said, laughing. "All of the inns booked up early."

"That's true," Winnie said. "All of our reservations were taken months ago."

Bay seemed disappointed. "But … what about the guy who cancelled?"

"He didn't cancel, Bay," Winnie replied. "He got a divorce, so there was no way he wanted to keep a reservation his ex-wife made. They just forgot about it."

"I hope they do come here," Thistle said. "It would be neat to catch a con man."

"Oh, yeah? What are you going to do if you catch him?" Tillie asked.

"They're not catching him," I interrupted. "Don't encourage them to do stuff like that. They'll get in over their heads. They're little girls. They're not investigators."

Bay was miffed. "I'm not a little girl."

"I didn't mean it like that, sweetheart," I said. "It's just … you have to be trained to do work like this."

"Yeah, Bay," Thistle said. "You have to be trained to die first in the horror movie. It takes more than just big boobs."

"Okay, that's it." Winnie slapped her hands on the table. "You're going to bed early, Thistle. Say good night to everyone."

Thistle opened her mouth to argue with her aunt but the look Winnie shot her meant business. "Fine," she said. "I want you all to know I'm not going to forget this, though. I'll remember … and I will get my revenge."

Marnie, Twila and Winnie looked mortified by Thistle's announcement, but Tillie barked out a laugh, drawing everyone's attention to her end of the table.

"Okay," Tillie said. "Today she's my favorite. That was just priceless."

Like I said, never a dull moment in the Winchester house.

SIX

Sleeping in a strange bed isn't a problem for some people. I'm a creature of habit, though. As homey and welcoming as the Winchesters are, the strange noises accompanying a different house woke me in the middle of the night.

I took a moment to listen, resting flat on the bed and staring at the ceiling. It was probably one of the other guests getting up to use the bathroom, I told myself. I wasn't the only one in the guest area of the inn. I'd almost convinced myself that I'd imagined it when I heard the noise again. This time there was definitely a bump.

I tossed the covers off and climbed out of bed, glancing down at my flannel sleep pants and T-shirt, debating whether I wanted to get dressed. The outfit was perfectly modest, but if something bad was going on and I had to make an arrest I'd prefer not doing so in pajamas. On the flip side, Bay believed I would stop someone from hurting her and I couldn't very well do that if I was late because I was primping before a mirror.

I opened the door that led to the main hallway, tilting my head to the side as I listened for the telltale signs of someone walking … or perhaps even breaking into the inn. The only thing I heard was the furnace kicking on. I waited for what felt like forever, and then I heard another noise – a door opening farther down the hallway corridor.

I peered out, frowning when I saw a dark figure emerge from the room and pad into the middle of the hallway. I couldn't make out any features, but the shadow seemed to be looking in the same direction as me, so it wasn't aware of my presence. Not yet, at least.

I cleared my throat to make the shape aware it wasn't alone in the hallway, and when it jumped I realized I was looking at slight shoulders. It had to be a woman.

"Is something going on?"

The voice was definitely female and I risked moving closer for a better look. "Mrs. Hillman?" I was pretty sure that was the woman's name. In all the excitement over dinner – Thistle's meltdown, Bay's grilling of the Garveys, Tillie being … well, Tillie – I didn't get a chance to talk with many of the guests.

"I heard a noise," I replied. "I was coming to check it out. Was that you?"

"I heard it, too," the woman replied. "I thought … I don't know … maybe someone was breaking in."

"I had the same thought," I admitted, rubbing my chin. "It could also be Tillie running around doing something illegal." I wasn't talking to myself – and that probably wasn't a smart thing to say – but being wakened before I'm ready always muddles my brain.

"I would lay odds it's the teenagers rather than the old lady," Mrs. Hillman said. "She seems like the type who is in bed before ten. The others seem somehow … rowdier."

The comment rankled, though I had no idea why. "They're good girls."

"I didn't say they weren't," Mrs. Hillman said. "They're wild, though, and their mothers let them get away with murder. They've got you wrapped around their little fingers, too. The blonde one especially."

"They're kids," I said, working to tamp down my irritation. "They're not doing anything wrong. They're just … testing their boundaries. That's what teenagers do."

"If I talked to my mother the way that one did tonight I would've been smacked upside the head," Mrs. Hillman said. "She was rude and mean."

I really couldn't argue with that, so I decided to ignore it. "I'll go and check the main floor," I said. "You can go back to your room. If I find something, I'll handle it."

"If you find those girls being rowdy, you should probably handle it with a good belt to the behind," Mrs. Hillman said. "That always worked when I was a kid. I think it would do those girls wonders."

"I'll keep it in mind," I said dryly, leaving Mrs. Hillman to her judgmental attitude as I headed for the stairs. Even as I discarded her statement, however, I couldn't help but wonder if she was right. Not about beating them, mind you, but they did appear to be on a mission to see how many people they could push to the brink in a three-day period.

I never had children. Would I have liked a family of my own? Perhaps, but the thing I always wanted most was to be a police officer. Getting to the point where I could be the boss, too, was like a dream come true. The idea of having children of my own diminished the older I became.

That's why spending time with Bay, Clove and Thistle turned out to be a blessing. They stopped by once a week, I spoiled them rotten, and then they went on their merry way. Every once in a while they had a big problem they needed to talk over, but those times were rare. Most of it was fun and games, and that's the way I liked it.

Bay had the most trouble, and although I didn't bring it up because the family seemed to rally around her in an effort to keep certain things a secret, I knew what her big problem was. She talked to ghosts. When she was really young I thought she was imagining things. I believed she had an imaginary friend she chattered with when she was on her own.

The reality shifted when she relayed a message from my mother, a woman long since buried. I didn't want to believe what the girl was saying, but when everything she told me proved true I couldn't help myself. I believed in her, which, it turns out, was the one thing Bay needed most. She attached herself to me after that, and I was happy for the company. There were times I wished Bay was my daughter. Sure, I knew she had a father out there she saw on rare occasions, but I liked spending time with her. I liked hearing how that busy brain worked.

Thistle and Clove look upon me more as an occasional uncle who scolds them. Clove is much more interested in getting attention from the Winchester females and Thistle prefers soaking up as much negative attention as possible because she enjoys ticking people off. Bay is different, and she was the one I worried about as I hit the main floor. If someone was in this house … .

I heard the distinct sound of something scraping against the floor. It took me a moment to get my bearings. With the only light coming from the lamp by the front desk, illumination was dim. I kept my feet as light as possible as I turned the corner, pulling up short when I saw movement at the bottom of the second set of stairs, which ended close to the kitchen.

"Pick it up."

"You pick it up."

"I can't pick it up alone. It's too heavy."

Crap. It was the girls. I'd recognize Bay and Thistle's voices anywhere. The question was: What were they doing?

"You guys need to be quieter." Oh, good, Clove was with them, too. It wasn't really a surprise, mind you. Where one went, the other two followed. Still, I would've preferred refraining from yelling at one of them tonight.

"You need to help or shut your hole," Thistle shot back. "This is your fault. I told you that old lady would find the spot in the shed where we hid the first batch."

"And I told you hiding it in the shed in the first place was a bad idea," Bay hissed. "It will freeze out there. It will explode if it freezes. We should've picked a better spot from the start."

"Thank you, Bill Nye," Thistle snapped. "I have this under control. I'm the boss."

"You're not the boss," Bay scoffed. "I'm the boss."

"I don't want to be the boss," Clove said. "I don't want to get caught either. You need to shut your mouths. If Aunt Tillie finds out we stole a whole box this time ... ugh ... she's not going to be happy."

"She's never happy," Thistle said. "And, oh, I am totally the boss."

The conversation was going nowhere, so I decided to help things along. I flipped the switch on the wall, flooding the room with light. Bay and Thistle froze, a wooden crate perched between them, and Clove's eyes widened to the size of saucers.

"Uh-oh!"

"I'm pretty sure I'm the boss," I said. "Does someone want to tell me what's going on here?"

"We didn't do it," Thistle said automatically.

"I see you doing it right now." I pointed toward the crate. "Is that Tillie's wine?"

Thistle tried again. "I want a lawyer."

I blew out a weary sigh. "Why can't you girls just behave for one night? Is that too much to ask?"

"We can't answer that question on the grounds that we may incriminate ourselves," Clove said. "Of course, if you were to let this go ... ." She batted her brown eyes for emphasis.

"I can't let this go," I said, my gaze locking with Bay's. She seemed resigned. "You girls are going to get in big trouble for this one. You know that, right?"

Thistle shrugged. "It will hardly be the first time."

And I had no doubt it would be the last.

"**WELL,** everyone looks ... chipper ... this fine and lovely day."

I accepted the mug of coffee Winnie handed me as I walked into the family kitchen the next morning. Waking Winnie to tell her what I found on the main floor wasn't high on my favorite memories list. Still, I figured it had to be done. I felt like a rat whenever Bay, Thistle and Clove looked at me, though.

"Yes, we're very chipper," Marnie grumbled, rubbing her cheek as she stared at the girls. "We're all so chipper we can't stand it."

"That's a stupid word," Thistle said. "What does it even mean? Shouldn't chipper refer to doing something to wood?"

"I heard you did that when you visited the boys' locker room last week," Clove said, taking me by surprise with her venomous attitude. Even on bad days she fakes being the sweet one.

"Knock it off, Clove," Marnie warned. "You're already in trouble. Do you want to make things worse?"

Clove shrugged. "I haven't decided yet," she said. "Can you give me a moment to think about it before responding? I would prefer to do my thinking in silence, too. Great. Thanks."

Sarcasm is my weapon of choice when dealing with stupid people. Clove apparently planned to turn it into an art form today. "Listen, I'm sorry I had to tell on you … ."

"Narc you mean," Thistle interrupted. "You narced on us."

"That's so not cool," Clove said, shaking her head. "I thought you were our friend."

Bay remained silent in her seat, staring at nothing. That was somehow worse. At least if she joined her cousins' petulance I knew she'd eventually get over it. Her refusal to even look at me was annoying … and hurtful. Yeah, I said it. A seventeen-year-old girl hurt my feelings. Oh, geez, what has happened to me?

"I'm not your friend," I said finally, choosing my words carefully. "A friend is a peer. I'm not your peer any more than your mothers and aunts are. I am, however, someone who cares about you dearly. I had to tell what I found you doing. You could've gotten yourselves in trouble."

Bay finally shifted her eyes in my direction, her expression thoughtful. She didn't look angry as much as hurt. That was definitely worse. "Bay … ."

"Don't apologize to her," Tillie said, sashaying into the room. She was dressed in combat boots and pants that were … something I didn't know how to identify. They were almost track pants but they looked somehow bigger. They were also hot pink. "She did wrong and needs to suck it up."

"He shouldn't have told on us," Thistle snapped. "You don't tell on us when you catch us doing stuff."

"No, I blackmail you," Tillie said. "I teach lessons my way. Chief Terry teaches them his way. Stop giving him a hard time."

I was surprised. Just yesterday Tillie told me not to get involved if it was a small matter. Because I had a feeling the three youngest Winchesters pilfered her wine regularly, I didn't think she'd consider that a big matter. She's an enigma, that woman.

"He narced on us," Thistle complained.

"Oh, please," Tillie scoffed. "You guys were making enough noise to wake the dead. I knew exactly what you were doing. You're just lucky he stopped you before you drank it, because I knew you were coming and cursed it."

I frowned. I know they're witches. I know they believe they're witches. Heck, I know Bay can do some out-there things. I don't want to be part of a conversation in which they talk about being witches, though. I draw the line there. Yeah, it doesn't make sense to me either. I can't explain it.

"What do you mean it was cursed?" Clove asked, widening her eyes. "What would've happened to us?"

"I'm not telling," Tillie replied. "I figure I'll keep that little secret for next time you tick me off. Suffice to say, though, Chief Terry saved you from a very unhappy day. Do you remember the Great Gas Extravaganza from last spring, Thistle?"

Thistle scorched her elderly great-aunt with a dark look.

"That was child's play," Tillie said. "This one would've embarrassed you until Christmas."

"You're mean," Clove said. "We only took it because you stole our stash in the garden shed."

"What stash?" Winnie asked.

"You have such a big mouth, Clove," Thistle complained, reaching for her juice. "Now, because of you, we have to weed the gardens today. It's the day before Thanksgiving. Who weeds gardens in Michigan in November? It's supposed to snow in two days. The weeds are going to die."

"It will keep you guys out of trouble," Winnie said. "That's all we care about. We have more baking to do."

"We didn't even get Christmas tree cookies yesterday," Bay said, her voice low and pitiful. "Thistle got us in trouble at dinner and then Chief Terry got us in trouble last night. We'll never get cookies now."

I knew she was trying to manipulate me but I didn't care. I … crap. I care. She knows exactly how to grab my heart and squeeze until I fall to my knees. Stupid teenagers. I swear.

"You'll get cookies when you act like proper young ladies and not wild witches out to torture your family," Winnie said. "Now finish your breakfast and get to weeding."

"Woo-hoo." Bay's inflection was lifeless. "What are you doing today, Chief Terry?"

Well, at least she was still talking to me. Kind of. "I'm spending a few hours at the station, Bay. Tonight is usually bad because this is one of the biggest party nights of the year and there are a lot of drunks on the road. I'll be on call in case anything happens on that front. Other than that I should be done early. Why?"

Bay shrugged. "Are you going to learn more about the con man?"

Were we back to this? "I … ." I couldn't take her sad face. I'm a sap. The moods of a seventeen-year-old affect me way more than they should. "I am, Bay. I'll keep you updated if I find any information."

She looked markedly happier, although nowhere near her normal self. I hoped that would be remedied by the time I returned tonight. "I'll bring you girls doughnuts when I come since you missed out on your cookies," I added.

Tillie made an exaggerated face that would've caused other men to feel shame. I wasn't other men. I was at the mercy of three teenaged terrors. I can admit it.

"You're a total wuss when it comes to these girls," Tillie said. "You know that, right?"

I shrugged. "I like being loved. Sue me."

"They're going to love you no matter what," Tillie said. "Although, I certainly love you more thanks to the doughnuts."

I couldn't hide my grin. "I guess my work here is done."

SEVEN

I was barely in the front door of the station when I got a call from Margaret Little. She was beside herself, ranting and raving to the point I couldn't understand what she was saying. By the time I got to her kitschy knick-knack store (seriously, it's full of porcelain unicorns and Precious Moments statues) she was standing on the sidewalk talking to Officer Parker. She did not look to be in a good mood, although that's not exactly newsworthy.

"What's going on?"

Parker glanced up from his notebook as I approached. "There's been a robbery, sir."

A robbery? That's practically unheard of in Walkerville. "What do you mean? Did someone shoplift something?" I had no idea who would want to steal a statue of a unicorn driving a lawnmower, but stranger things have happened.

"Not that kind of robbery," Parker replied.

"They had a gun," Margaret shrieked. "They pointed it at me and told me to empty my cash register."

This had to be some sort of mistake. "A gun? Like a water pistol?"

Margaret narrowed her eyes to dangerous slits. "No, the kind that fires bullets and that I want to shoot you with," she snapped. "A water pistol? Why can't we have a decent police presence in this town? It's undignified."

She's a pill on a regular day. Clearly she was about to go nuclear, which means everyone should assume crash positions because she's likely to bring a cement wall down with her tone alone.

"Okay, slow down," I instructed. "Tell me what happened from the beginning."

"I told you over the phone," Margaret shrieked.

"Yes, and I couldn't understand you any better then," I said. Patience truly is a virtue when you're in law enforcement. Even I can't muster patience when Margaret Little is on a tear. She sounds like she's inhaled the helium from eight balloons and then smoked a carton of cigarettes all so she can make the most annoying sound known to man. "Just take a deep breath and tell me what happened."

Margaret sucked in a steadying breath, all the while glaring at me, and then launched into her tale. "I was sitting in the rocking chair by the fireplace," she said. "I didn't expect to be busy today – in fact I was considering closing down early, but I thought someone might stop in needing a last-minute hostess gift so I held off – and I heard the bell over the door jangle.

"A couple came in and they were very friendly," she continued. "They said they were staying at one of the inns and just wanted to look around. They seemed delighted with the town and how it was set up and couldn't stop talking about how cute it was. The woman loved my stuff. They fooled me because I thought anyone who liked quality stuff like I have must be good people.

"Anyway, the man talked to me a little when I got up to stand behind the counter," she said. "He seemed friendly – kind of gregarious almost – and he asked about the town and what kind of business it did. I explained how everything was seasonal, and he seemed interested. He said he was a businessman and loved hearing about small businesses thriving."

"Okay," I said. "When did they pull the gun?"

"I was just standing there talking and he was fidgeting with something in his pocket," Margaret said. "The next thing I know there's a gun in my face and he's telling me to empty the cash register."

"Was it a real gun?"

"No, it was one of those blaster things from *Star Wars,*" Margaret deadpanned. "It shot lasers and they made 'pew' sounds as they ran around the store explaining how they were going to save the galaxy with the money. How the heck should I know? It looked like a real gun to me."

She was even testier than normal today, not that I could blame her. "What did the woman do while he was holding a gun on you?"

"She watched through the front door to make sure no one headed in this direction," Margaret replied. "She kept chatting the entire time. She was really friendly."

"Did you hear names?"

Margaret shook her head. "They just referred to each other as 'honey' and 'dear.' It was as if they were trying to be cutesy and annoying."

That was interesting. "Did they threaten you?"

"He said he would shoot me if I didn't give him the money in the register," Margaret said. "There was only fifty bucks in there, and he was miffed. He asked if I had a safe, but I told him this was Walkerville and safes aren't really necessary in this area."

"Hmm." I glanced at Parker. "Do you think this has anything to do with the case you're fixated on?"

"It could very well, sir," he replied. "We obviously can't know until we find them, though."

He had a point. "Can you describe them?"

"Well, the woman was tall and had black hair, and the man was short and bald," Margaret answered. "The thing is … I don't think the man was really bald."

I stilled. "Why do you say that?"

"Because up close I could see, like, this line right here." Margaret gestured to a spot close to her hairline. "I think he was wearing a bald cap. He had a full beard and everything, so I just don't think he was really hairless. He wanted me to think that was the case, you know, give me something memorable to focus on."

"What about the woman?" I prodded. "If you think the man was wearing a disguise, it only makes sense that she do the same."

"I couldn't see her clothes or anything because she wore a trench coat, but I don't think her hair was real either," Margaret said. "Real hair has a certain way of flowing and this just seemed too … heavy … or something. I don't know how to explain it."

Generally I wouldn't pay much heed to Margaret's instincts, but what she said this go around actually made sense. I know. It boggles my mind, too. "What color was the man's beard?"

"Brown with some gray."

"How old do you think they were?"

Margaret shrugged. "I would guess they're in their forties or so. Maybe fifty, but they didn't seem quite that old."

"Okay," I said, licking my lips. "Officer Parker is going to take your statement and give you a copy of the report for your insurance company. I'm going to go back to the station to see if I can get more concrete information on that BOLO. Is there anything else that you can think to tell me, Margaret?"

Margaret held her hands palms up. "Just that for some reason when I looked at them they reminded me of Fred and Wilma Flintstone. They had cartoon proportions. She was tall and thin and he was shorter and fat. I have no idea why I can't get that out of my head, but I can't."

Something about that observation wormed its way into the back of my brain, but I couldn't decide why. "Okay. I'll be in touch."

I WAS FOCUSED on my computer screen an hour later, waiting for an in-depth report and sketch to come across from the state police, when a light knock at my open office door drew my attention.

Bay, bundled in her winter coat, with a knit hat pulled low to cover her ears, shifted from one foot to the other in the doorway.

"What's up?"

"I … ." Bay looked conflicted. "I came to apologize."

Part of me was surprised by the statement. The other part wasn't at all. She was sensitive, and when she felt as if she hurt someone's feelings she couldn't let it go until she got it off her chest. I gestured toward one of the chairs across from my desk. "Sit."

Bay did as instructed, resting her elbows on top of her knees as she regarded me. I briefly wondered what was going through her mind. Did she think I would yell? Was she afraid I was angry? Was she still upset because she thought I betrayed her? I decided to tackle the problem head-on. "Bay, why do you think I woke your mother up to tell her what you were doing?"

Bay blinked rapidly three times. "Um … because we broke the law." She was searching for the answer she thought I wanted to hear.

"Be honest, Bay," I prodded. "Why do you really think I did it?"

"Because we were bad and deserved to be punished."

"You're not bad, Bay," I said, annoyed she would think anything of the sort. I cannot fathom the mind of a teenaged girl. It is a swampy and dangerous place. "You're just … spirited."

It was weird to use that word, mostly because she could actually see spirits. My mother used that word to describe me a time or two when I was a teenager. It annoyed me at the time – as it probably did Bay – but now I thought it was funny.

"Here's the thing, Bay. You come from an extremely loud and energetic family," I said. "You have seven women in your house and everyone is competing to be the top dog. Family likes to needle each other. They know exactly what to do to irritate everyone else and push their buttons.

"I don't think you guys were stealing Tillie's wine because you couldn't stand to be without it or wanted to hurt someone," I continued. "I think you stole it because you think it's funny and you want to do what all teenagers do and enjoy something taboo.

"Your biggest problem is that Tillie is a terrible role model," I said. "She's the oldest one in the family, but she often acts as if she's the youngest. She gets off on wreaking havoc. Thistle is that way, too. You're kind of in the middle. You like having fun and making trouble, but you're also happy with a book and being quiet. Can you guess which one I prefer?"

Bay's smile was rueful. "The book?"

I leaned back in my desk chair and rubbed the back of my neck. "You'd think that, wouldn't you? I like it when you get in trouble, though. You have fun when Thistle thinks up devious ways to mess with Tillie."

Bay was surprised by my answer. "You want me to get in trouble?"

"I don't want you to get in big trouble," I clarified. "I always want you to have fun, though. What you girls did last night was not big trouble. That doesn't mean it couldn't have led to big trouble, though. Do you understand what I'm saying?"

"That we're bad and it's okay."

I shook my head. "Stop saying you're bad," I ordered. "You're a good girl. Clove is a good girl, too. Thistle ... well ... she's a piece of work, but when it comes down to it she's always going to be loyal and she has a good heart. She's just like your great-aunt."

Bay's blue eyes widened as she tried to hide her smile – and failed miserably. "That would kill Thistle if she knew you said it."

"That means you're going to tell her, right?"

Bay shrugged, noncommittal. "I haven't decided yet."

"Do you feel better about our talk?"

Bay nodded.

"That's good," I said. "What are you doing in town, though? I thought you were supposed to be weeding the garden."

"Mom sent us to the store to pick up some flour, sugar and milk that she forgot to get yesterday," Bay replied "Thistle and Clove are doing it, but I thought I should apologize for being mean to you this morning. I shouldn't have done it."

"You weren't mean," I said. "You were ... ."

"Mean," Bay finished. "I wanted to hurt your feelings because you hurt mine."

"Bay, I never want to hurt your feelings," I said. "I can't ignore something I know to be wrong, though. The most important thing to me is that you girls are safe. I had to tell your mother. It was the right thing to do."

"It's okay," Bay said, grinning. "In the end you saved us. I'm sure Aunt Tillie's curse would've been terrible."

"I'm sure you're right," I said. "What do you think it was?"

"Probably zits … or pants that won't fit … or she would probably make us smell like cabbage or something," Bay replied. "It's hard to know, because she has an evil mind and Thistle says evil is impossible to predict."

"She would know," I said, chuckling. "We're good, though, right? You're not angry anymore, are you?"

"No. Are you mad at me?"

"No."

Bay's smile was wide and heartfelt. "That's a relief," she said, getting to her feet. "You're still bringing doughnuts home, right?"

Ah, yes, all was right with the world. She was back to shaking me down for sweets. "I am," I confirmed. "I'll buy ones with extra sprinkles just for you girls."

"Yay." Bay clapped her mitten-clad hands. "I should probably get going. We have to finish the garden before nightfall."

"Okay. Be careful going home," I instructed.

"Oh, don't worry about us," Bay said. "This is Walkerville. Nothing exciting ever happens here."

Something occurred to me. I didn't want to encourage her to spy on the guests, but I also wanted her to be wary, just in case. "Bay, will you do me a favor?"

Bay nodded, her expression solemn.

"I need you to watch the Garveys for me," I said, knowing I was opening a box the contents of which I couldn't predict but not seeing another way around it until I could get back to the inn and watch them myself. "Don't approach them or talk to them, but keep an eye on where they go. Oh, and if you happen to eavesdrop on a conversation or two, that wouldn't hurt either."

"Okay," Bay said, wrinkling her forehead. "But … why?"

"Something happened at Mrs. Little's store today," I replied, debating how much to tell her. "She was robbed at gunpoint."

Bay's mouth dropped open. "By the con man?"

"I don't know yet," I said, holding up a cautioning finger. "Mrs. Little believes the people who came into her store were wearing disguises. She described a short man with a big belly and a willowy woman."

Bay was incredulous. "Like the Garveys? I told you!"

"Yes, I know you told me," I said, fighting to keep my temper in check. "Do not approach them and don't ask them any questions. I don't know if it's them yet. I need more information from the state police before I can act. Do you understand?"

Bay mock-saluted and clicked her heels together. "I do understand, sir. I will watch the suspects until you return for dinner. I won't let them out of my sight."

I frowned. "That's not what I said, Bay."

It was too late. She was already gone. Crud. What did I just do?

EIGHT

"Where is everyone?"

I was anxious to get back to the inn once the state police came through with sketches and grainy video footage from an Upper Peninsula gas station. While I couldn't say with certainty that the Garveys were our culprits, I couldn't rule them out either. That made me antsy. It also embarrassed me because I might've been out-investigated by three teenagers. I would never live down the shame.

"Who is everyone?" Twila stood behind the front desk, a blank look on her face. I wish I could say that wasn't her normal expression, but she's a dreamer. She's the nicest member of the Winchester family, but she's also the daffiest – and that's saying something.

"Well, for starters, where are the girls?" I held up the box of doughnuts I carried for emphasis. "I promised them sugar."

"Oh, well, they stole a plate of Christmas tree cookies, so the last thing they need is more sugar," Twila said. "That won't stop them, though. I think they're in their room or outside."

That didn't really narrow things down for me. "Did you see them go upstairs?"

"No."

"Did you see them go outside?"

"No."

"Then what makes you think they're in either place?" I asked, struggling for patience. Living under the same roof with the Winchesters is a lot of freaking work. Good grief. I was starting to miss the termites.

"Listen." Twila tilted her head to the side and cast her eyes toward the ceiling. "Do you hear any screaming?"

"No, but … ."

Twila cut me off. "Do you hear any fighting?"

"No."

"If they were on the main floor we would hear both of those things," Twila said. "That means they're either outside or upstairs. I'm not sure which."

I wanted to ask her if she thought that was an example of solid parenting but I figured that would be overstepping my bounds. "Okay. Thanks. I'll check upstairs first."

I moved to the second set of stairs, which led to the family living quarters at the back of the bed and breakfast, and bounded up them two at a time. Guests aren't allowed to use them, but I wasn't a normal guest and I didn't think anyone would question me when I hit the second floor. I was wrong.

"Are you looking for a peep or something?" Tillie, a pink robe cinched at her waist, walked out of the bathroom on my left and fixed me with a bright smile. Her hair was damp from a shower and her smile was evil. "I guess I can give you one if you're desperate, but I might need some caffeine to work up the energy if you want more than that."

Speaking of people who know exactly how to needle someone … . "That's a very kind offer," I said. "I'm good, though."

Tillie didn't look bothered as much as amused by my presence. "Who are you looking for?"

"The girls."

Tillie narrowed her eyes. "Why?"

"I bought them doughnuts."

"You always buy them doughnuts," Tillie said. "You spoil them rotten. Of course, they're already rotten, so you're not making things worse. You're not here about the doughnuts, though."

She's extremely perceptive when she wants to be. It's incredibly annoying. "I could be here about the doughnuts."

"And I could be the world's shortest supermodel," she said. "Let's come back from La-La Land and put our cards on the table. Tell me what's going on."

Now I was the one on the defensive. "How do you know anything is going on?"

"Because you're a terrible liar and you never come up to this part of the house in case you accidentally get a gander at females doing chick stuff," Tillie replied. "Spill."

I wasn't sure how much to tell her. I was afraid I'd already overstepped my bounds with Bay. Still, when it came down to it, Tillie might be a good ally to have. "Mrs. Little was robbed today."

"Oh, you came up here to make me happy," Tillie said, pressing her hand to the spot above her heart. "Did someone steal her life?"

I scowled. "That's not funny and I know you don't mean it."

"It's very funny and I most definitely mean it," Tillie countered. "If she was dead you wouldn't be here, though. I know I'm not that lucky. So Margaret was robbed, huh? Did someone break out of a nuthouse and suddenly feel a need to pad their ceramic unicorn collection? If so, those are not the sort of people we want running around Walkerville. They're likely to bite their own faces off." She mimed what she was talking about for reference. "Do you need me to help you track them down?"

That was such a roundabout tangent I almost lost my train of thought. "I … no," I said, shaking my head. "She said the people who robbed her had a gun and wore disguises. The people she described to me, though, could be guests at this inn."

Tillie was intrigued. "The Garveys? Oh, if that's the case we're never going to hear the end of it from those girls."

I had the same worry. "I made the mistake of telling Bay my suspicions. I … it was wrong."

Tillie waved off my concerns. "It wasn't wrong. It was smart. The girls can watch them without tipping the Garveys off. They're teenagers. Even if it looks like they're up to something funky that can be ignored because teenagers are often up to something funky."

"I need to find them, though," I said. "I don't feel good about this. I'm worried they're going to do something wonky."

"Oh, they're definitely going to do something wonky," Tillie said, patting my arm. Unfortunately when she did that, the robe parted slightly and I had to hurriedly avert my gaze lest I see something traumatic. "You're so cute I can't stand it. I wish you would get it together and date one of my nieces. Do you want me to open the rest of my robe and rock your world or give you an easy escape?"

"Escape," I sputtered in a weak whisper.

"That's what I thought," Tillie cackled. "Check the back yard. I'm sure that's where the girls are. They're supposed to be weeding, but I'll bet that's not what they're doing."

I stumbled over my own feet twice descending the staircase, and it was a relief to feel the cool breeze hitting my cheeks once I made it outside. I headed toward the side of the house once I caught my breath – and the danger of passing out dissipated – and I found Bay, Clove and Thistle in the exact spot they were hiding the day before. They were staring at the back patio.

"Where have you guys been?" I asked, annoyed as I approached. "I've been looking for you everywhere. I even checked upstairs and found Tillie … in a state I'd never seen her before."

"Was she dead?" Thistle asked with faux excitement.

I scowled as I shook my head. "She was getting out of the shower."

"Oh." Thistle nodded sagely. "Now you just wish you were dead because you caught a nip slip, huh? Don't worry. You'll forget it if you drink enough. Why do you think we wanted the wine in the first place?"

That girl is a total menace. I swear she just … . "What are you doing?"

Bay pressed a finger to her lips to quiet me and pointed toward the back patio. "It's the Garveys." She was taking her investigative position on my team to heart. It was extremely cute … and a tad worrisome.

"What are they doing?" I asked, peering over Bay's shoulder. Charles and Caroline Garvey appeared to be drinking hot cider on the back porch and … staring at the trees. That wasn't even remotely evil, which was somewhat disappointing.

"They're plotting their next move," Clove intoned. "I think they're about to blow up the town."

She's so dramatic she puts the other two to shame. "You think they're going to blow up the town, do you? Why is that?"

Clove shrugged. "Why do evil super villains do any of the things they do? I mean, if Lex Luthor really wants to end the world, where does he think he's going to live?"

I had no answer, mostly because it was an absurd question. "How long have you been watching them?"

"Since we got back," Bay replied. "We told our moms that you gave us a special mission but they didn't believe us, so we still had to weed the gardens while we were working for you. We set up a system, though."

Oh, I couldn't wait to hear this.

"It mostly consisted of making Clove hide in the bushes and tell us what they were saying," Thistle informed me. "It wasn't a very ingenious system, mainly because she whined all of the time and we couldn't hear what they were saying over her snotty tears."

"You're all heart, Thistle," I said, patting her shoulder. "Did you hear them say anything?"

"Just that they were going to do it tonight," Bay replied.

"Do what?"

She shrugged. "They didn't say, but I think they're going to kill someone."

Oh, well, good. No one's imagination had run away from them in fifteen minutes. We were about due for an overreaction. "I don't think they're killers. Even if they are the people we're looking for – and I'm not saying they are – they haven't killed anyone."

"I think they were talking about something else when they said they were going to do it," Thistle said, her eyes flashing with devilish glee. "I think we all know what it is. Well, maybe not Chief Terry. It might've been too long for him. He probably forgot."

I scowled as I stared her down. "You are so … delightful."

"What did you forget?" Clove asked, lost and confused.

"Nothing," I replied, grabbing her shoulder and pushing her toward the front of the house. "Surveillance is over. It's time for dinner. I'll take over all forms of the investigation from here on out."

"But … we're a team," Bay protested, her lower lip jutting out.

Great. I can't take that stupid lip. "We're still a team," I said. "We're just a team regrouping after dinner. That's what all the great investigators do when they have a case."

"Yes, I particularly like reading the stories of when Sherlock and Watson discovered a clue and then spent a chapter regrouping," Thistle deadpanned. "To me that was the best part of the book."

I pointed toward the front of the house. "March."

"This investigation stuff is hard," Clove said. "It's nowhere near as fun as I thought it would be either. I don't think I want to ever do it again."

Well, at least I had one bright spot in an otherwise dreary day.

"OOH, PORK CHOPS." I was delighted when I took my seat at the dining room table shortly after bribing the girls with doughnuts to keep their mouths shut about what I told them. The last thing I needed was them spilling the beans to their mothers or the other guests.

"I can't eat pork," Mrs. Hillman said, crossing her arms over her chest. "I don't eat pig."

"That's good news for you if we ever turn into a cannibalistic society, Chief Terry," Thistle offered, earning a smack across the back of the head from her mother.

"That was rude, Thistle," Twila admonished. "Apologize or go up to your room right now. We will not have a repeat of last night."

I was glad for the distraction, but I thought that was the wrong message to send to Thistle. She really was bucking for Santa's naughty list this year.

"I'm sorry," Thistle said, and she looked as though she meant it. "That was too far."

I widened my eyes, surprised. I didn't think Thistle was capable of recognizing a line until she was ten steps beyond it. "I accept your apology," I said. "Now hand me the mashed potatoes."

"We have other things if you can't eat pork, Mrs. Hillman," Winnie offered. "We also made red wine-infused chicken breasts, and there are some vegetarian offerings, too."

"I'm happy with the chicken," the woman said. "I just can't eat pork."

"Why?" Clove asked. "Are you allergic to pigs?"

"I'm Jewish."

Walkerville isn't what you'd call a religiously progressive town, so Clove's face flashed blank at the news. In this part of the state you're either Christian or Winchester. "Oh. Are there other things you can't eat?"

"Clove, that's not an appropriate question," Winnie warned.

"It's fine," Mrs. Hillman said, waving off Winnie's concern. "I think it's nice that she's curious. We can eat almost anything except pork and shellfish."

Thistle's eyes widened. "So … no bacon?" She looked distraught at the thought.

Mr. Hillman, a portly man with a friendly face, chuckled at Thistle's reaction. "I know. It sounds terrible, doesn't it? I've never tasted bacon, but I have smelled it. I think I'm on the losing end of that one."

"You should just sniff a bacon burger once a week or something," Bay suggested. "Maybe you'll be able to taste it through osmosis."

"I'll consider it," Mr. Hillman said, grinning.

"So what's the deal here tomorrow?" Charles Garvey asked. "When is dinner served?"

I pursed my lips and glanced at Tillie, both of us thinking the same thing. "I thought you were eating with your family at Torch Lake?" I asked the question before Winnie had a chance to respond.

"We are," Charles said. "Their dinner is early, though. We thought if we could make it back in time we could eat twice. Thanksgiving is my favorite meal of the year."

"Mine, too," I said, offering up as much fake enthusiasm as I could muster. "I believe dinner here starts at four."

"We'll have appetizers out front all day, though," Winnie said, smiling. She took Charles' comment as a compliment. I was starting to suspect it was something else, although I still couldn't figure out the couple's end plan in all of this.

"What time will you be leaving for your brother's house?" Bay asked. "How long will it take you to drive there?"

"Oh, we plan to leave before the sun even comes up," Charles replied. "You probably won't even see us. You don't have to clean our room or anything, though. Tomorrow is a holiday, and we'll be back before dinner so we can eat twice."

"Yes, we're really looking forward to it," Caroline said. "We definitely don't need maid service, though."

Well, that was downright suspicious. They were basically saying they planned to get up in the dead of the night and sneak out of the inn. And they don't want anyone in their room while they're gone. What are they hiding? The money from Mrs. Little's store, perhaps? Fake land deeds?

"Well, I'm sure it will be a great day for everyone," I said, reaching for my glass of wine. "Personally, I can't wait to get a load of the turkey these ladies are going to whip up. Their cooking is legendary."

"Oh, thank you, Terry," Winnie said, preening.

"He was talking to me," Marnie snapped.

"Not even close," Winnie shot back.

"You're both wrong," Twila interjected. "He was talking to me."

Marnie and Winnie snorted in unison. "In your dreams!"

I ignored the feigned catfight and glanced at Tillie. Her eyes were thoughtful when they locked with mine. It was obvious we were in agreement. Whatever the Garveys had planned, it was going down tonight. There was no doubt about that.

Now we only had to figure out their plan, catch them in the act, and make sure the turkey wasn't ruined. What? Priorities, people.

NINE

"Is everyone in bed?"

Tillie, a combat helmet firmly in place on her head and black boots to match on her feet, met me at the bottom of the family staircase shortly before ten. The fact that I was going on an investigative mission with her was … dumbfounding. I didn't have a lot of options, though. I had no proof Charles and Caroline Garvey were criminals. I had to catch them in the act for that. I needed backup, and I couldn't call in Parker in case I was wrong. That left Tillie. What is the world coming to?

"The house is quiet," she replied. "That hardly means everyone is in bed, though."

"What does that mean?"

"I can't speak for the guests, but I'm guessing most of them – except the ones we're looking for – are down for the night," Tillie explained. "My nieces are in their bedrooms reading – or drinking in Twila's case. She likes a bit of the nosh before sleep."

"That's good, right? That means they won't come down here for the rest of the night."

"Probably not," Tillie confirmed. "Our problem is the three younger ones."

How did I know she was going to say that? I pinched the bridge of my nose to ward off what I'm sure would be a monster of a headache if it took hold. "What are they doing?"

"I stopped in their room to mess with them, let them know I would be watching if they tried to steal my wine; you know, put a good scare in them," Tillie answered. "I thought if we could keep them in there plotting revenge it would be worth it."

"And?"

"And they're suspicious and I think expecting them to stay in their room is probably more than they can handle."

"Well, great," I muttered. "What should we do? Should I go up there and order them to stay in their room? That might make things worse."

"Unless you want to see teddy bear pajamas and more Clearasil than should be allowed under law, I'd steer clear of that room," Tillie said. "Don't worry about it. I locked them in."

I stilled, confused. "You locked them in? Are you telling me you locked that door from the outside so they can't get out? That's a fire hazard. What if something goes wrong? They could be hurt."

"Not that way, drama queen," Tillie said, rolling her eyes. "I used these." She wiggled her fingers for emphasis.

"Do I want to know what that means?"

"Probably not," Tillie replied. "You like pretending everything happening in this house is normal. You know it's not and yet ... it is."

"Yes, well, great," I said. "Just for clarification, though, what happens to them if there's a fire?"

"They're allowed out if there's an emergency," Tillie said. "It's not just a fire. Say bad people went up to that room. They're allowed to fight back and run if need be. They just can't leave if they're planning to break the rules."

"That's actually fairly ingenious."

"I know." Tillie puffed her chest out. "I could win Jeopardy if I wanted."

"Sure. Whatever. Where do you think they'll hit? Should we split up? Maybe one of us should go to the lobby and hide and the other to the kitchen. How does that sound?"

"Like you want to handle the kitchen so you can eat cookies."

I pressed my tongue against the roof of my mouth to stop myself from saying something snotty. "I'll take the lobby."

"That's good," Tillie said. "There's still a doughnut with sprinkles in that box you brought home and I think it has my name on it."

We separated in the dining room, me heading in one direction and Tillie the other. It was odd being in the big house alone so late at night. I enjoyed visiting as often as I could – Winnie insisted I eat dinner with the family at least twice a week – but I never realized how quiet it was without teenaged Winchesters bouncing around and excitedly telling me about their days.

In truth, that was my favorite part about visiting for dinner. Oh, sure, the food was phenomenal. I liked the camaraderie, though. I love listening to Bay tell me about the book she's reading, even though I might not get why she wants to read it. I like Clove waxing poetic about whatever boy struck her fancy this week. Then, of course, I like telling her why that boy is a bad idea and how she should stay away from him. I even like listening to Thistle plot how to take down her enemies – mostly because it revolves around that sneaky snake Lila Stevens, who goes out of her way to make Bay miserable at every turn. It's mundane and magical at the same time.

I crouched in the small alcove in the archway between the dining room and one of the lobby chairs. Given the limited light, I was completely hidden and there was no way the Garveys would risk turning on more lights and drawing attention to themselves.

I remained in my spot for what felt like forever. In real time it was probably only fifteen minutes, but my knees ached as though they belonged to a man twenty years older and finally I had no choice but to stand. That's when I heard a noise from the bowels of the house. It sounded as if it originated from the kitchen.

I took a chance and left the lobby, carefully navigating around the chairs and table in the dining room. I pressed my ear to the door in the kitchen, sucking in a breath when I heard a drawer opening and then closing. Then it happened with another drawer.

Someone was ransacking the kitchen. Where was Tillie? Why hadn't she made her move? Perhaps they discovered her and knocked her out. She was elderly, no matter how much she hated people pointing that out. I wasn't armed – which was probably a mistake, but I didn't want to risk shooting anyone in the dark. I carefully pushed open the swinging door that led to the kitchen, keeping as quiet as possible as I patted my hand on top of the counter, finally coming up with a weapon I could use. Then I sucked in a breath, squared my shoulders and flicked on the kitchen light.

"Gotcha!"

Tillie jumped out from behind the chair in the corner when I made my move. I lifted the rolling pin I had grabbed from the counter over my head, ready to strike. Instead of the Garveys, though, I found three wide-eyed teenagers clinging to one another as they stared back at me.

"I didn't do it," Thistle automatically announced.

"Don't kill us," Clove said. "We'll be good. I swear."

Bay's reaction was something else entirely. "I knew it! You're investigating without me!"

"Oh, geez," I grumbled, rubbing the back of my neck as I lowered the rolling pin. "What are you doing down here? You're supposed to be in bed."

"We wanted a midnight snack," Clove lied.

"What's all over your faces?" I narrowed my eyes.

"That's moisturizer," Bay said, hurriedly rubbing her cheek and causing Tillie to snort.

"That's Clearasil for the zit patrol," Tillie corrected. "I warned you about that when I saw you last."

I'd forgotten about that part of our conversation. I was pretty sure it was on purpose. I hadn't forgotten about the other part of our talk, though. "I thought you said they were locked in their room."

"Hey, that's right," Tillie said, wrinkling her nose. "How did you get out of that room?"

"I have no idea what you're talking about," Clove replied, averting her eyes. "We just walked out."

"Liar."

"I am not a liar," Clove sniffed, crossing her arms over her chest. "That's a horrible thing to say to your own flesh and blood."

"You're not even a good liar," Tillie said, shifting her eyes to Bay. "How did you get out?"

"We opened the door and walked out," Bay said, meeting Tillie's gaze without flinching. "It wasn't hard at all."

"Yeah," Thistle said. "Maybe you're slipping in your old age."

"The only thing that's slipping is my foot and it's going to slip right into your . . . ."

I held up my hands to cut her off. "Okay, everyone has had their fun," I said. "You three need to go back up to your bedroom right now. I'm not messing around."

"No." Bay's answer took me by surprise. I expected tears, maybe a little foot stomping to get her point across, but I also thought she would capitulate quickly. That didn't appear to be the case.

"You have to go upstairs," I argued. "You can't be down here."

"You can't make me go upstairs," Bay shot back. "We're partners. You said so yourself."

I glanced at Tillie for help.

"Don't look at me," Tillie said dryly. "I warned you this would happen if you played both sides of the fence. You can't say no to her, and she knows it. You agreed to this, now you're stuck with the follow-through."

I was incredulous. "You can't be serious," I complained. "They're children. We have no idea what we'll be up against if the Garveys come down here. Of course, they probably heard the argument and high-tailed it back to their bedroom. We've probably already lost our shot."

"We haven't," Thistle said. "Er, well, I don't think we have just yet."

I knit my eyebrows, suspicious. "What is that supposed to mean?"

"Don't tell him," Bay said.

"Yes, tell me."

Bay shook her head and gripped Thistle's arm, squeezing as hard as she could to get her point across. Thistle stared right back, seemingly oblivious to the pain. Finally she couldn't take it for another second, though, and jerked her arm away.

"That hurt, Bay!" Thistle slapped her cousin's arm for good measure.

"Ow!"

"I'm going to ow both of your butts if you're not careful," Tillie warned. "Lower your voices. We're on a mission. What have I told you about missions?"

"That it's every witch for herself if the cops come and you're not going to bail us out," Clove answered, not missing a beat. "You don't care if we cry, but if we narc on you we'll never have jeans that fit again."

"You're such a kvetch," Tillie muttered. "No. In missions we are silent but deadly."

"Like a fart," Thistle said, giggling at her own joke. Truth be told, I had to bite the inside of my cheek to keep from laughing myself.

"Listen, fresh mouth, I often find you funny," Tillie said. "Now is not one of those times."

"You girls need to go back to your room and behave yourselves," I snapped. "I'm the boss here. That's an order."

The three girls – and Tillie, for that matter – snorted in unison.

"That's not going to work," Tillie said.

I couldn't take much more of this. Seriously. How much is one man supposed to put up with? "What will it take to make you go up to your room?"

"You can't make us go up to our room," Bay replied, causing my stomach to twist. "We, on the other hand, can help you."

"Oh, yeah? And how is that?"

"Well, we know something you don't know."

"What?" I gritted out, fighting desperately to contain my temper. The last thing I wanted was to yell and frighten her. She wasn't giving me a lot of options, though.

"The Garveys snuck out the side door and headed toward the garden shed," Clove supplied, earning a loud slap from Thistle.

"You moron! That was our leverage."

"You said we were going to tell them," Clove argued.

"After he agreed to take us, dummy," Thistle shot back.

"Wait … the Garveys are already moving?"

Bay nodded. "They left about five minutes ago."

"Holy crap!"

I WANTED to put up an argument about the girls going with us, but I didn't have the time, and Tillie refused to put her foot down and make them obey my orders. We were totally talking about that later, by the way. So, against my better judgment, I walked out the back door of the inn with one senior citizen at my side and three teenagers with Clearasil all over their faces serving as my backup. Yeah. It wasn't one of my finer moments.

As we approached the tool shed, the back porch lamp offered limited light. I could see the metal door was open. I could hear someone rummaging around inside and hush-hush voices echoing against the thin walls. That meant the Garveys were in there together. That was good news.

"You guys stay here," I whispered.

Bay grabbed my arm and shook her head. "It's too dangerous. You need me."

Her earnest expression caused my heart to roll. "I think I'll be okay. You stay here with your aunt."

Bay opened her mouth to argue but I clamped my hand over it to silence her.

"Promise me you'll stay safe," I ordered. "Stay with your aunt."

Bay mutely nodded, her eyes conflicted. I left her with Tillie, exchanging a curt nod with the curmudgeonly matriarch, and closed the distance to the shed. I waited until I was positioned in front of the open door to flick on the flashlight I grabbed before leaving the kitchen.

"Boo."

Charles and Caroline were so startled they dropped the clay pot they were holding and held their hands in the air.

"We surrender."

I stilled, surprised. I wasn't holding a gun but these two were nervous wrecks. They hardly fit the profile of criminal masterminds. "You surrender?"

Caroline bobbed her head. "We're sorry and we won't do it again."

"You're supposed to say you didn't do it and ask for a lawyer," Thistle called out helpfully from behind me. I growled as I forced myself to ignore her.

"What are you looking for?" I asked, keeping my expression neutral. "If it's money for your little land deal, I'm pretty sure the Winchesters don't keep it in a gardening pot."

"That's not entirely true," Tillie clarified. "I make quite a bit from my wine business and I stash it all over the place. In fact, half the time I forget where I stash it. That's why these imps were so eager to clean this place the other day. Other than hiding my wine out here, they thought there was a possibility they would stumble upon money. I collected it before they could, though."

"Great," I growled. "That was really important to this conversation. I'm so glad you enlightened me."

"What is going on here?" Bay asked.

"That's a very good question," I said. "Who wants to answer it?"

Clove's hand shot up in the air.

"Not you, sweetie," I said, shaking my head. "I was talking to Charles and Caroline."

"Oh, well, we heard there might be some pot out here and we came to see if we could find it," Charles offered. "My brother doesn't allow drugs in his house – and he's a real downer most of the time – but we thought a joint would be nice for the road."

I stilled, confused. "I … what?"

"Who told you about my pot?" Tillie asked, irritated.

"What pot?"

"Never you mind," Tillie replied. "It's none of your concern. I see someone has loose lips, though."

"Don't look at me," Thistle said. "If we told Chief Terry about the pot he'd burn the field and then we wouldn't be able to steal it."

"You're grounded," I snapped, extending a finger.

"Oh, geez," Thistle muttered, shaking her head. "This night bites."

She wasn't wrong. I was about to suggest everyone return to the inn and get out of the cold to finish the discussion where it was warmer when a twig snapped behind the girls. Two more figures joined the scrum, and for some reason an overwhelming sense of dread washed over me when they appeared.

"I'm afraid it's going to get worse."

I couldn't see our new guests, but the glint of the moonlight off the barrel of the gun the man held was unmistakable.

What now?

TEN

"What's going on?" I tried to keep my voice neutral but the fact that a man I couldn't identify was holding a gun and standing behind Tillie, Bay, Clove and Thistle was enough to make my head explode. I had to remain calm. I knew that. But if something happened to one of them … .

"I was just about to ask you the very same question," the man said.

"Why don't you step a little closer so I can see who I'm dealing with and we'll talk about it?" I suggested.

"I don't think that's necessary."

"It's Mr. and Mrs. Hillman," Bay offered, her voice squeaky. "They have a gun."

"I know, sweetheart," I said, swallowing hard as I gestured for her to head in my direction. "Bay, why don't you and your cousins come this way?"

"I don't think that's a good idea," Hillman said, resting his hand on Bay's shoulder to still her. His wife remained silent at his side. "I think we should all stay right where we are."

"Take your hand off her," I growled. "Don't touch her."

"Don't worry, daddy bear," Hillman said. "I have no inclination to hurt the girl. I just want her to stay close so you don't get out of line."

"Chief Terry?" Bay's face was a mask of fear and confusion.

"Stay there, Bay," I said. "Stay close to your aunt."

"You'll be fine," Tillie said, grabbing Bay's arm and dragging her a few feet from Hillman, practically daring him to call her on the action when she shot him a challenging look. "We'll all be fine. I'll make hot chocolate once we get inside."

"You don't cook," Clove pointed out.

"Then I'll watch you make it and show you where your mothers hid the Christmas tree cookies," Tillie countered. "Now … be quiet."

"You know, I'm pretty sure this doesn't involve us," Charles said. "Maybe we should … I don't know … go back inside and let you guys sort this out. How does that sound, Roger and Carol?"

Were those the Hillmans' first names? I couldn't recall ever hearing them. All I remembered of the couple was a general unpleasantness whenever they spoke. Well, actually that wasn't true now that I reflected upon it. The husband seemed nice and the wife seemed nasty. It was probably an act on both of their parts.

"I think you should shut up, Charles," Roger said. "You're not a part of this, but you really did cause this whole thing. If you'd stayed in your room Carol and I could've made our getaway and no one would've been the wiser.

"Instead you had to make a spectacle of yourself and get these girls all riled up," he continued. "That got the cop riled up because he thinks they walk on water. This is really your fault when you think about it."

"We just wanted some pot," Charles complained. "We didn't mean to get involved in this."

"I still want to know how you found out about that," Tillie said. "If someone has been talking out of turn … ."

"We heard a few of the teenagers talking at the coffee shop downtown," Carol offered. "They claimed you had a lot of it. We didn't think you'd miss it if we pinched a little."

"Which kids?" Tillie narrowed her eyes. "I'll just bet it was that Stillwater kid. I caught him poking around the other day. I thought he was here sniffing around the girls, but I think I might've read him wrong."

"Is that really important?" My voice sounded unnaturally high. "We need to focus on the problem at hand."

"Relax," Tillie said. "Don't freak out. Everything will be okay."

Was she trying to calm me down? I was the professional here. I forced my eyes back to Roger. "What's your plan? Why are you even out here?"

"We hid a few things in the shed," Roger replied. "We had no idea that they would punish these … children … by having them clean it. It was too late to do anything about it, though, so we were hopeful they didn't find our stash."

"We checked, though, and the money is gone," Carol said. "They took it. We were trying to get them alone, but they're never alone. They're either fighting with adults or talking to you."

"And we're out of time," Roger added. "So, girls, where is our money?"

I was furious. There was no way around it. The girls found money in the shed and didn't tell anyone. Instead they kept it and put all of us at risk. I was going to ground all of them before the night was over. As long as everyone survived, that is.

"We didn't take your money," Bay said, making a face. "There was no money in there."

"Someone took our money," Roger argued. "You were sent out here to clean the shed. Do you think I believe your lie for one second?"

"Don't call me a liar," Bay hissed. "We didn't take your money."

"Heck, we didn't really clean the shed," Thistle said. "We sat out here and gossiped for two hours and rearranged the pots. There was no money. Trust us. We looked."

"Yeah," Clove said. "We thought Aunt Tillie might've put money out here, but she took it before we got a chance to look."

That's when things shifted into place. The girls weren't liars. They were still my little angels. Well, er, kind of. Tillie was the one to blame. I turned my attention to her, trying to read her blank features.

She was a master liar when she wanted to be, and it looked as if she was about to put on a show.

"I took your money," Tillie announced.

Seriously? Every single time I think I have her figured out she proves me wrong. I just ... quit. I'm done. I can't deal with this.

Bay's eyes locked with mine and she offered me a small smile. It was almost as if she was encouraging me, telling me everything would be okay. I was the one who was supposed to be protecting her. She had faith in me. What the heck was I going to do?

"You took our money?" Roger asked, dubious. "How did you manage that?"

"It's quite simple really," Tillie replied. "The girls stole wine from me and hid it out here. I knew they did it, and I also have a tendency to hide my money in odd places and then forget about it.

"I came out here before they were assigned to clean the shed and reclaimed my wine," she continued. "I also searched for money so they couldn't steal it. I found some. I assumed it was mine."

That actually made sense. How frightening is that? I cleared my throat to draw Roger's attention. "I'm sure Tillie will return your money if you leave the girls here," I said. "There's no need to make this worse than it is. You can get the money from her and take off. I'll give you an hour to get out of town."

"That's cute," Roger said. "I'm not sure I believe you, though."

"You don't have to believe him," Tillie prodded. "You have to believe me. Don't I look trustworthy?"

"You look like a hobbit," Carol said.

"Hey!" Thistle scorched the woman with a dark look. "I'm the only one who can say things like that to her."

"It's okay, Mouth," Tillie said, resting her hand on Thistle's forearm. "I have a feeling they're going to learn a thing or two about karma before the night is over. Calm yourself."

"So are you going to give us our money?" Roger asked.

I was relieved. He sounded reasonable. If Tillie handed over the money everyone would be safe.

"Not a chance," Tillie replied. "You stole it from innocent people. It's not your money. You didn't work for it. I'm not giving it back."

Seriously? The powers above must hate me. There can be no other explanation. "Tillie," I gritted out, shooting her a warning look. "Do as they ask."

"Um, no." Tillie shook her head hard enough her combat helmet shifted off-center, making her look even more ridiculous than before.

"Um, no?" Roger was irked. "How about I shoot you? Will you tell me where my money is then?"

"Nope."

"Tillie!"

She ignored me and remained focused on Roger. I didn't miss the almost imperceptible shift as Bay, Clove and Thistle joined hands behind her. They were up to something witchy. I just knew it.

"I want my money, old lady," Roger seethed, leveling the gun on her. "If you don't give it to me, I'm going to shoot those brats behind you. I'll start with the mouthy one."

"You'll have to be more specific," Tillie said. "They're all mouthy."

"I think he's talking about me," Thistle said.

"I'm definitely talking about her," Roger agreed.

"Well, in that case, I'm going to have to say … bite me."

Bay, Clove and Thistle giggled as Roger's temper flared.

"Don't make me kill those kids, lady!"

As if on cue, a huge roar of thunder filled the night air and I shifted my eyes to the sky as surprise washed over me. The darkness lifted as lightning flashed three times in quick succession. A thunderstorm in November? That never happens.

"What the … ?" Roger turned his attention to the heavens, which gave me the opening I needed. I threw myself in his direction, knocking his hand up and away from the girls should he squeeze the trigger and unleash a stray bullet. Carol screamed out a warning, but it was too late. "Oomph."

We hit the ground hard and I slammed my knee into Roger's stomach to knock the air out of him before pounding his wrist against the ground to dislodge the gun. Carol watched the scene with wide eyes for five seconds before turning to flee. Tillie was having none of that, which was a godsend because I couldn't control both of them. Instead of unleashing magic, though – which I was thankful for – she instead picked up the flashlight I discarded while attacking Roger and lobbed it in Carol's direction.

Now, granted, I never figured Tillie for a softball player, but she had some nice arc. I'm sure magic helped, but it wasn't so obvious I would have to make up a lie for a report. The flashlight clobbered Carol on the back of the head, pitching her forward. She didn't move once she hit the ground face first.

Roger sputtered as his mouth met dirt, and I wrestled him to a supine position, using my bigger frame to pin him in place. Once I was sure he wasn't going anywhere, I glanced at the Winchesters, who seemed more excited than frightened. "Is everyone okay?"

Bay beamed. "That was so cool."

"You're all in trouble when I get this settled," I said. "Each and every one of you is going to be punished severely for not staying inside like I told you."

"We can't wait," Thistle deadpanned. "I think it's going to be the highlight of our night. After this awesome storm, of course."

I scowled. "Go inside and call the station. Have them send backup."

"I'm on it, partner." Bay saluted before racing toward the house. She seemed downright giddy.

"Good job," Tillie said. "We're quite the team."

"Yes, I was just thinking the same thing," I said dryly.

"I'll handle the hot chocolate and you handle the cleanup," Tillie said, turning on her heel and walking toward the house. "I think that's the best way to divvy up the labor."

That sounded like a great idea to me.

BY THE TIME I reentered the inn I was exhausted. Tillie stood next to the couch where the girls were sprawled and staring at a blank space on the wall, their eyelids heavy and dark circles under their eyes.

"What are you girls doing up?" I asked. "I thought you'd be in bed."

"We want to hear what happened," Bay said, brightening, but only marginally. She looked exhausted.

I heaved out a heavy sigh as I sat next to her, smiling as Clove made enough room so I could get comfortable but not so much that she wasn't resting her feet against my thigh. "The Hillmans have been taken into custody," I replied. "The Garveys – and that is their real name and they had no idea it has ties to *Little House on the Prairie,* so you were wrong there – have headed to Torch Lake early. I let them off with a stern warning."

"I'll handle them," Tillie said. "Don't worry about that."

Funnily enough, I was more than happy to let her handle that problem. "Sure. Whatever."

"What about the Hillmans?" Thistle asked, yawning as she rolled to rest her head in the spot next to Clove's. "Will they be locked up forever?"

"Yes."

"Will we get to testify?" Bay looked excited at the prospect.

"Probably," I replied, stifling my own yawn. "Seriously, though, why are you girls still up?"

"They wanted to see you," Tillie said. "Bay refused to go to bed before you came inside. That meant the other two wouldn't leave her. As for me, now that you're here, I'm going to retire. My old bones can't take much more creaking."

"You're going to need to give me that money in the morning," I said. "There are people up north who need it."

"I have no intention of stealing," Tillie said. "I honestly thought it was mine."

"Thank you." I watched her head toward the stairs, my mind screaming for sleep as my body protested the idea of getting up. "Thank you for keeping them safe and … doing whatever you did out there."

"I didn't do anything," Tillie countered. "You saved them. You're the one who put your life on the line to take out the man with the gun."

"And you're the one who made it storm." It was an absurd statement, but I knew it to be true.

"I have no idea what you're talking about," Tillie said, winking. "Get a good night's sleep, though. Winnie, Twila and Marnie woke up long enough to see what all the fuss was about and then went back to bed. They plan to cook up a storm for their hero tomorrow."

My cheeks colored at the "hero" reference. "I'm nobody's hero."

"Oh, no?" Tillie cocked a challenging eyebrow. "Look around, Terry. You have three fans who say otherwise."

I shifted my eyes to both sides of me, finding Bay already asleep with her head on my shoulder and Thistle and Clove slumbering on my other side. They looked like angels – even though I was pretty sure they were really devils in angel costumes. Despite that, my eyes misted.

"Take care of our girls," Tillie said, climbing the stairs. "They're going to be unbelievably obnoxious tomorrow."

"Why is that?"

"They were right about someone evil staying at the inn. We're never going to hear the end of it."

"Yes, but they were wrong about who was evil," I pointed out.

"They won't remember that part," Tillie said. "All they'll remember is the way their blood pumped and how happy they were to curl up with their hero on the couch for the night."

For the entire night? Did she expect me to stay here with them until morning? I didn't get a chance to ask the question because when I got up the nerve she was already gone. I turned back to the girls, their light snores and sighs lulling me.

Oh, what the heck, right? There are worse ways to spend a night. I slid lower on the couch and smirked when Bay shifted her head to get more comfortable. She never moved it from my shoulder. Okay, this wasn't so bad. It was actually kind of nice.

Tomorrow was Thanksgiving after all, and after tonight I was more thankful than I'd ever been.

"Goodnight," I murmured.

No one answered, but I knew they were already happy in dreamland, thinking up ways to torture their family tomorrow. I was just happy I managed to land on the family list. I was even looking forward to the torture.

What a day. What a night. What a life.

I wouldn't trade it for anything.

MERRY WITCHMAS

A WICKED WITCHES OF THE MIDWEST SHORT

12/6/2016

ONE

18 YEARS AGO

Do you hear that noise? Probably not, but let me tell you something: It's insipid. No, it's worse than that. It's infernal racket that should be outlawed. That's right. No one really cares about a holly, jolly anything. I certainly don't. And chestnuts roasting on an open fire? Yeah, that's a good revenge technique. It certainly doesn't give me warm fuzzies about the holiday season.

No, in truth, the only good thing about winters in Michigan is the snow. Ah, you might be wondering why a woman my age – I'm in my prime sixties, thank you, and I get younger every single day – would like snow. That's because I've picked up a new side business over the past few years. I plow snow. I have a big truck with a blade and everything.

Yes, that's right. My name is Tillie Winchester and I plow snow for a living. Okay, I'm also a witch and I make my own wine. I have a pot field on the back of the property, too, but I don't sell the product. I give it away to those in need and use a bit myself. It's medicinal. No, I swear it is. In truth, I don't make a lot of money plowing snow. I used to have paying clients, but they fired me because I had a few problems leaving mailboxes unscathed. They thought it was because I couldn't see properly. I let them believe that because they might press charges if they knew why I really run them over.

The government is out to get us, people. Mailboxes are merely a way to keep track of our locations until they can inject us with chips and watch our every move. I'm not making it up. I thought about becoming a spy before the notion of plowing great big piles of snow (and potentially burying evidence when hiding from the police) appealed to me, but the idea of helping the government is abhorrent. I would be a great spy, though. Don't kid yourself. I could definitely do it for a living. As for the mailboxes, I find most of them ugly and I'm merely trying to prevent my neighbors from enabling the government to complete its takeover. I'm doing them a service.

No, really.

"Aunt Tillie!"

My niece Winnie is a good girl but her voice reminds me of fireworks in November. It's simply too loud and grating. It's also often unnecessary. I hear her calling me from the kitchen, but one of the good things about getting older is that you can fake hearing loss and no one will dare call you on it in case you find it insulting. I find everything insulting – and sometimes nothing insulting, depending on my mood – so my three nieces wisely refrain from pushing my buttons. They treat me like their goddess, which I heartily encourage.

"Aunt Tillie!"

I rolled my eyes as I flipped pages in the catalog. My three great-nieces, Bay, Clove and Thistle, thoughtfully left it behind – open to a page with some castle thing they desperately want to open under the tree Christmas morning – and I needed a distraction. Winnie sounded as if she wanted to give me a chore. I'm too old for chores. I can accomplish them, mind you. I'm still as fit as one of those tennis players I see whacking balls on the television – that sounds like a fun job, doesn't it? Whacking balls. I could do that professionally – but I have no interest in completing chores. I'm not lazy, I'm just smart about delegating my time. I only have so much of it left on this planet -- a good eighty years or so, I'm sure -- and I have no intention of doing what anyone else wants me to do with my time so limited.

"Aunt Tillie!" Winnie was exasperated as she poked her blond head through the door that separates the living room and kitchen. Despite having a kid – and a husband who abandoned her – she's held up well in the looks department. I'm positive she gets that from me. "Did you hear me calling you?"

I feigned surprise as I lifted my eyes and tilted my head to the side. "Did you say something to me?" Sometimes it's fun to mess with my nieces. They all handle things differently. Winnie is a planner and control freak, so the idea of me ignoring her is enough to send her over the edge.

"I've been calling your name," Winnie replied, wiping her hands on a dishtowel. She wore a pink apron to keep her clothes clean as she toiled in the kitchen with her sisters. We all share the same roof – that's three adults, three children and me (who defies categorization) in one space, if you're keeping count – and even though the house is big, it feels small when everyone is bustling around at the same time.

"I didn't hear you, dear," I said, feigning confusion. "Perhaps I've gone temporarily deaf for the day. It's probably because of that noise in the kitchen."

Winnie narrowed her eyes. "What noise?"

"Something about some grandmother being run over by a reindeer," I replied. "Oh, and some kid wants a hippopotamus for Christmas. Don't get that for the girls, by the way. I bet they stink."

Winnie made a face, clearly trying to control her temper. She believes patience is a virtue, or some such crap. I can't really remember. She likes to exert quiet control whenever she can. Her efforts double around the holidays. She doesn't like big fights. I tend to thrive on them, so we're complete opposites. Sometimes I wonder if she was switched at birth with some other infant. Of course, she was born at home so that's not very likely. Still, I'm not ruling it out.

"Aunt Tillie, I would like to discuss something with you in the kitchen," Winnie said. "Do you think you could come this way for a few minutes?"

Ooh, I smell a trap. She's using her fake "I love and respect you" voice. I'm not going to fall for that. "I'm good."

Winnie pursed her lips and increased the intensity of her stare. "I would really appreciate it if you would come in here and talk with me. I promise it will only take a few minutes."

That stare works on everyone but me. "Um … no." I flipped a page in the catalog. "Oh, hey, they have pink beepers in here. I would love a pink beeper."

"What do you need a beeper for?" Winnie asked. "Those are for drug dealers and pimps."

"I've been considering expanding my business base." That will drive her nuts.

"Aunt Tillie … ."

"I'm not getting up," I said. "I'm old and my hip hurts. You should respect your elders, for crying out loud. Don't make me put you on my list."

I'm good with a threat, but Winnie is bad at fearing them.

"Get in this kitchen right now!" Winnie barked. "If you don't come in here I'm going to bring everyone out there. If you thought the Christmas music was bad, wait until we start serenading you."

Winnie disappeared through the swinging door without a backward glance. As far as threats go, that was a fairly good one. I heaved out a sigh as I pushed myself to my feet. She isn't winning, mind you, I simply refuse to push the issue until she asks me to do something I really don't want to do. Then you'll see me win … in any manner necessary.

I found Winnie behind the counter, her sisters Twila and Marnie flanking her, when I walked through the door. I didn't miss the furtive glances Marnie and Twila exchanged before I spoke.

Twila is something of a free spirit who many of her cues from me. She'll make a great crazy old lady one day. She likes to do things like glue eyelashes on ceramic frogs and paint murals and canvases in the yard while naked. I encourage that. She's also something of a kvetch. She won't shut up.

As for Marnie, she has Middle Child Syndrome. She's constantly trying to live up to Winnie's expectations – and beat her whenever possible. She's a complainer, but she also has an … um … witchy streak I find more than delightful. She can make a grown woman cry in less than thirty seconds with only one insult and two glares in her arsenal. It's quite the sight.

"What do you want?" I asked, adopting a gruff tone. "I'm old and tired, and you're bugging me." What? They know they're bugging me. They're doing it on purpose. I'm hardly hurting their feelings.

"We want to talk to you about your attitude," Winnie replied. "We feel you've been something of a … what's the word I'm looking for?"

"Jerk," Marnie supplied, earning a dark look from me.

"I haven't been talking about you behind your back," Twila announced. "I refused to do it. If you're going to punish someone, I suggest punishing them. I'm the innocent party here. They've wronged me."

I was going to wrong her right onto my list if she didn't stop babbling. "What's wrong with my attitude?" I asked, ignoring Twila's jabbering. "I think my attitude is delightful."

"That's part of the problem," Winnie said. "You think you can do no wrong and you walk around making sure everyone else thinks that way, too. You're giving the girls the wrong impression about following rules."

"How so?" I asked. "I don't believe rules should be applied to everyone. There's an exception to every rule. That exception is usually me. What 'wrong impression' am I giving them?"

Winnie pressed her lips together as Twila shuffled from one foot to the other. Marnie simply stared me down. She's smarter than Winnie in some ways. She was waiting for Winnie to tick me off so she could swoop in with a compromise and look like the hero. I'm on to all three of these witchy wonders.

"The girls have started adopting some of your attitude," Twila said, licking her lips. "I heard Thistle telling Bay and Clove that they were on her list last night."

I snorted. That sounded just about right. "Thistle is a mouthy pain," I said. "I like her … some of the time. I don't see what the problem is. If Thistle wants to make a list, I think it's a great idea.

"It improves her writing skills … and planning skills … and organizational skills," I continued. "There's really no downside to Thistle starting a list."

"It also improves her revenge skills, tyrant skills and unfiltered mouth skills," Winnie pointed out.

She said that like it was a bad thing. "I still don't see the problem," I said, planting my hands on my hips.

The grim set of Winnie's jaw told me she was done playing games. "Listen, we love you," she said. "You know that. We wouldn't trade you for anything. You've got to stop being a bad role model for the girls, though."

"You raised us after Mom died and we will be forever grateful," Twila added. "But Thistle is turning into a real handful. She sees you acting out and thinks it's okay."

If they thought for one second they could blame Thistle's willfulness on me, they had another thing coming. "I'm not the one who lets her get away with murder," I pointed out. "I punish her when she gets out of line. You're the ones who let her run roughshod over this household. I can't believe you think I'm the root of her issues."

"That's not what we said," Winnie clarified. "It's just ... she's getting worse every day. She says whatever comes to her mind and, well, frankly ... um ... she's channeling you for most of this bad behavior."

"She's never been a sweet girl, but she used to be controllable," Twila said. "I don't know what to do with her. She bosses Clove and Bay around as if they're her slaves. It's not healthy."

"I think you're worrying too much," I said. "Thistle only acts this way because she gets away with it. Eventually Bay and Clove are going to get fed up and give her a dose of her own medicine. That's what you want."

"That's the last thing we want," Winnie argued. "This house isn't big enough for World War III."

"It won't come to that," I said. "Thistle only acts up because no one pushes back when she does. If you would let Bay and Clove off their leashes, they would teach Thistle a thing or two about getting too big for her britches.

"As it stands now, Bay and Clove follow the rules and they're handicapped because Thistle doesn't follow the rules," I continued. "You have to even the playing field."

"That sounds dangerous," Twila said.

"That sounds like the way of the world," I corrected. "Don't worry about it, though. I'll have a talk with the girls and figure things out. If that's what you want me to do, I'm more than willing to step in and do my part to fix Thistle's attitude."

What? That won't take more than two or three minutes, right? I'll just lay down the law with Thistle and then leave the room when she melts down. By the time dinner rolls around she'll be fine again.

"That's not why we called you in here," Winnie said. "We don't want you to talk to the girls. Quite frankly, whenever you do that you give them harebrained ideas about controlling the world, and then I get a call from Lila Stevens' mother because they've ganged up on her and done something truly awful and are in danger of being expelled or something."

"Hey, Lila has it coming," I said. I was pretty sure that kid was Hitler in a past life or something. She's evil incarnate. "If Lila doesn't want the girls going after her, she should leave them alone."

"That's hardly the point," Winnie said.

"And what is the point?" I was losing track of the conversation.

"We need you to be on your best behavior for the next couple of weeks," Twila said. "We're going to try to teach the girls by example instead of words. If everyone in the house gets along, then they'll get along."

"Have you been watching Oprah?"

Winnie made a face as her world-famous patience wore thin. "That's our new plan and you're going to stick to it. Do you understand?"

"Have you gotten into the eggnog early?" I challenged. "You can't tell me what to do. I'll act as I see fit."

Winnie crossed her arms over her chest and scorched me with a harsh look. "Do you understand?"

She clearly meant business. That meant I could either fight with her or capitulate and operate behind her back. The only question was:

What was I in the mood for today? Decisions, decisions. "Fine. I'll be on my best behavior."

"That's great," Winnie said, exhaling heavily. "We really appreciate it."

"Yes, I'm always happy to help," I said. "So ... um ... is that all? Can I go back to the living room and take a nap?"

"Actually, we were hoping you would spend some time with the girls this afternoon and put your new attitude on display," Marnie hedged. "We thought it would be a good example for them to see you acting in a certain manner first."

That sounded absolutely terrible, and I didn't even know what they were trying to trick me into doing yet. "I think I'm good. I can show them how to act while taking a nap, too. I'll definitely be on my best behavior then."

Winnie wrinkled her nose. "That's not what we have in mind."

I could tell I was going to hate whatever plan they cooked up while I was distracted by the catalog in the other room. "And what did you have in mind?"

"Walkerville's tree-lighting ceremony is this afternoon," Twila said. "We thought you might want to take the girls to it."

The only way they could have thought that was a legitimate possibility is if they started smoking crack when I wasn't looking. "I think I'll pass."

This time Twila and Marnie crossed their arms over their chests and joined Winnie in a no-nonsense stance. It was supposed to be terrifying. It made me want to laugh.

"I still think I'll pass," I said.

Apparently Winnie wasn't going to give me the chance, because she opened her mouth and bellowed to the second floor by way of forcing my hand. "Girls, your Aunt Tillie is going to take you to the tree-lighting ceremony. Get bundled up and down here in five minutes."

"Yay!"

I heard Clove's enthusiastic clapping through the ceiling and rolled my eyes. "Do you think that's going to work on me?"

"Are you really going to disappoint them?" Winnie challenged. "They'll cry."

She had a point. Still .... "Fine," I said, blowing out a resigned sigh. "I'll take them."

"And you'll be on your best behavior," Marnie added. "You need to set an example for them."

"And I'll be on my best behavior," I conceded, striding toward the living room door before staring down all three of them. "You're all on my list, though. Prepare yourselves for war."

Yeah, I've got your jingle bells right here, people. Christmas is coming and I'm taking charge of the entire holiday. It's going to be a bumpy sleigh ride. Strap in.

TWO

"Are you ready?" I secured Clove's pink combat helmet under her chin before pointing toward my plow truck. "Get in."

My nieces worked under the misguided notion that I was a menace behind the wheel. They only agreed to allow the girls into my truck if they were well protected. That meant I had to purchase helmets and knee pads for them (in case they flew into the dashboard when I rammed a snow bank). I think their mothers were overreacting. The girls had a great time when we plowed.

Clove sat in the spot closest to me and Thistle and Bay fought over the window seat, as they always do. Instead of listening to them work things out on their own, I made the decision for them.

"Bay gets the window seat."

Thistle, her blond hair sticking out in odd places under the helmet, made a face. "Why does Bay get the window seat?"

"Because I said so."

That was never a good enough answer for Thistle. "Why else?"

"Because Bay is the oldest and I don't have to worry about her opening the door when I'm plowing," I replied. "I seem to remember someone opening the door two weeks ago because she wanted to see if she could hook it on to Mrs. Franz's mailbox."

"I did that once," Thistle groused, hopping into the truck. "It didn't work. I don't see why you're complaining."

That kid cracks me up sometimes. I would never tell her, of course, but I love her attitude. Bay is much more serious than her younger cousin. I like her, too. She thinks things out before she does something stupid. That doesn't mean she won't do something stupid, mind you. She simply prefers thinking out all of the ramifications before embarking on mayhem. She has a pragmatic mind and a wild streak rolled together. It's an interesting combination. As for Clove, well, these days she's going through life relying on the fact that she's cute. She's smaller than both of her cousins and she's found she can manipulate people if she fakes tears. I find that trait annoying, but it's come in handy a time or two ... or twelve. I'm not one to look a gift personality defect in the mouth, especially if it proves helpful.

"It's only funny to take out mailboxes when no damage can be done to my truck," I told Thistle as I climbed onto the driver's seat and slipped the key into the ignition. "I don't want my truck wrecked. Your mothers will find a reason to take it away from me if that happens. Mark my words."

"You're an adult," Clove pointed out. "They can't take something away from you if you don't let them."

"Don't kid yourself," I said. "I may be an adult and their elder, but they're real pains in the behind when they want to be. They know how to get what they want ... just like you."

"Do they cry, too?" Thistle asked.

"I don't cry," Clove snapped, fastening the middle seat belt around both her and Thistle. "My eyes leak. There's a difference."

The kid may be young, but she's a master at manipulation. "That's a very good argument, Clove," I said, putting the truck in reverse. "You keep that one handy when someone accuses you of crying to get attention. Tell them your eyes leak because your heart hurts. That will work until you're at least twelve and start puberty."

"That's a great idea," Clove said, smiling prettily.

I wasn't paying attention to where I was going, so when the back of the truck rammed into a snow bank it took me by surprise. All three girls jerked forward. Thankfully the seatbelts – which I had to get installed and prove were in good working order before my nieces would let their daughters ride with me – kept them from flying into the dashboard.

"That came out of nowhere," I muttered.

"How is that possible?" Thistle sputtered, rubbing her neck. "You're the one who put the snow bank there."

"And it's a really good place for it," I shot back. "I think it moved or something, though."

"How?"

"You live in a house filled with magic, Thistle Winchester," I reminded her. "How do you think it moved? I'm pretty sure your mothers did it as payback for that thing I did the other night."

"Are you talking about when you stole all of their fresh cookies and replaced them with store-bought ones and then told Mom that we must have a cookie gnome?" Thistle asked.

"Cookie gnomes are real."

"I think they're as real as the house-trashing fairy you told us about this summer," Thistle said. "You said that was real, too, but Mom says you made that up because you dirtied up the kitchen and didn't feel like doing your dishes."

"Your mother says a lot," I said. "I had no idea she flapped her gums to that magnitude when I'm not around. What else does she say?"

Thankfully Thistle had no qualms about narcing on her mother. Most kids would balk at that. Thistle was her own person, though. "How much time do you have?"

"It will take me twenty minutes to get to town if I do some plowing along the way," I said, shoving the gearshift into drive and pressing my foot to the gas pedal. "Start talking."

"Well, she also says you're lying when you say you're going for a walk during the summer," Thistle said. "She knows about your oregano field and thinks you put magic enchantments on it to keep her out."

The front of the truck caught the edge of the large snow bank at the lip of the driveway, causing the truck to fishtail and bounce against the other bank as I overcorrected.

"Did they move that, too?" Clove asked.

I shrugged. "They must've. Keep going, Thistle. I'm dying to hear what else your mother told you when I wasn't listening."

Thistle happily recited a nonstop litany of terrible beliefs her mother held during the ride to town. I stopped to clear out Dorothy Sanderson's driveway – swearing I would make Twila pay the entire time – and then I took the snow from her driveway and planted it in the already cleared spot in front of Margaret Little's driveway across the street. The girls knew what I was doing but refrained from commenting. That was good. I trained them right – unlike their mothers.

By the time I hit town I was in an awful mood. It seems Twila, Marnie and Winnie want me to act a certain way and then tell lies behind my back when I don't do as they want. Yes, lies. There really is a house-trashing gnome. I had a feeling they were going to meet it up close and personal before Christmas if they weren't careful.

Walkerville was bustling with activity as I parked. The girls scrambled out of the truck, being sure to leave their helmets behind so the other kids wouldn't make fun of them. I thought they should leave the helmets in place so they could go after their enemies hard and fast, but the girls thought differently.

They gathered on the sidewalk outside of the police station and waited for me to join them. I was about to tell them to run off and play (and not bother me for at least two hours) when their favorite police officer, Terry Davenport, walked out of the station's front door. Bay immediately ran to him and threw her arms around his neck as he bent lower so he could be on her level.

A stranger passing by might assume Terry was Bay's father – perhaps even Clove and Thistle's dad as well – but he was merely a strong presence in their lives. He adored all of them, but he especially doted on Bay.

"Officer Terry," Bay squealed excitedly. "I didn't know you were going to be here."

"Are you here to give us presents?" Clove asked expectantly.

Unlike other adults who melted when they saw Clove's big brown eyes, Terry was wise to her machinations. "It's not Christmas, Clove," Terry said. "You don't get gifts until Christmas."

Clove jutted out her lower lip. "There's no rule that says that. That's just what everyone decided and they made it a rule. It's not a real one."

"Well, I'm a rule follower," Terry said, pointing toward the badge on his uniform jacket. "I'm a police officer. I have to follow the rules – whether they're real or imagined."

"Now, wait a second," Thistle said, tapping her lip as her mind worked overtime. "I'm not a big fan of agreeing with Clove, but she might be on to something. We should have, like, ten days of presents before Christmas. I think that would be best for everyone."

"You would," Terry said, ruffling her hair and causing me to snicker as he turned his attention to Bay. "Have you been good girls this year? Will Santa leave you a lot of presents ... or just one or two?"

"I've been good," Clove announced. "I'm the best-behaved one, so I'll get the most presents."

Terry made a face. "Oh, yeah? What makes you think that?"

"Karma is a real thing," Clove supplied. "My mom told me. That means I'm going to be rewarded."

"I'm not quite sure it works that way," Terry said dryly. "What about you, Thistle? Have you been good?"

"I don't believe in karma," Thistle replied. "I've been bad and I'll get just as many things to open as Clove. Just watch. I'll count to be sure."

I pressed my lips together to keep from laughing. The kid's attitude was a thing of beauty. Er, unless you were her mother, that is. I could see why Twila was worried. If Thistle puffed out her chest any further she'd fall over.

"Uh-huh." Terry didn't look convinced. "I know my Bay has been good," he said, tickling her ribs. "What did you ask Santa for?"

"We want a special fairy castle," Bay replied. "We want to share it, but I'm not sure Santa will bring it. It's expensive."

"Is that the ugly thing you marked in the catalog you left on the living room table?" I asked, furrowing my brow. "Why do you want that?"

"Because it's pretty and it's for witches," Thistle replied.

"I thought you said it was a fairy castle?"

"Yes, but fairies are just pretty witches," Clove said. "We all talked about it and that's what we believe."

"So don't try changing our minds," Thistle added. "If you can believe in the house-trashing fairy, we can believe that fairies and witches are the same thing."

"I would never try changing your minds," I said. "I don't care either way. Why don't you girls leave Terry to do his job and go get some hot chocolate or something? If we're going to be stuck down here until they light up the tree, we might as well add chocolate and sugar to the mix to liven things up."

Clove and Thistle were excited by the prospect, but Bay looked torn.

"I want to stay with Officer Terry," Bay said. "I can help him work." I love the kid, but she has a needy quality where Terry is concerned. He feeds into it.

"Officer Terry will be around," I prodded. "Get some hot chocolate." I handed a few dollar bills to Thistle before shooing Bay with my hands. "Go on."

"We need more money than this," Thistle said.

"That's more than enough for three hot chocolates."

"Yes, but you rammed us into ten snow banks on the way here," Thistle said. "I counted. We want doughnuts, too. If you don't give us doughnuts, we might accidentally tattle to our mothers about the snow banks."

I was wrong. That kid is a menace. Can you believe she's actually shaking me down for more money? "No one is going to believe I ran into ten snow banks on the way here."

"Everyone who has ever seen you drive will believe it," Terry countered. "Buy them the doughnuts."

"You're just a big softie where they're concerned," I grumbled, digging into my purse. I handed Thistle more money and narrowed my eyes. "If that gets out, you're going to be at the top of my list."

Instead of cowering, Thistle matched my stare with a menacing one of her own. "You're not supposed to have a list," she shot back. "You're supposed to be leading by example."

"You were listening by the heat vents again, weren't you?"

"You said it was a classic for a reason," Clove said. "Why would we stop?"

I really wish these kids would stop listening to me sometimes. "Fine," I said, waving them off. "Do what you want. I really mean that. If Lila Stevens gives you guff, do something terrible to her."

Thistle's eyes gleamed at the prospect. "I'm on it."

I shook my head as I watched them scamper away. When I finally shifted in Terry's direction, I found him glaring at me. "What?"

"You shouldn't tell them to do things like that," Terry admonished. "They're good girls, but they manage to find trouble on their own. They don't need you helping them."

He was so earnest I could do nothing but snort. "Don't kid yourself," I said. "They may look like angels, but there's a little devil in each of them."

"Especially Thistle," Terry muttered.

"You've got that right," I said, moving my eyes to the town. "When are they supposed to light the tree? I don't want to be down here all night."

"I'm surprised you're down here at all," Terry admitted. "You generally shun town activities."

"Yes, well, I got tricked into being the dutiful aunt today," I admitted. "Winnie, Marnie and Twila are on the warpath because they think Thistle takes her cues from me when it comes to having attitude."

"I can believe that."

I ignored him. "Personally, I think the entire thing would work itself out if they would stop making Bay and Clove follow the rules and unleash them on Thistle to exact their revenge," I said.

"It's probably a good thing you weren't a parent," Terry said, shaking his head. "I'm going to run over to the festival area and then make a loop around town. Keep an eye on the girls, will you? It gets dark early these days."

"They're little girls, not sunshine," I said. "They don't disappear just because the moon comes out."

"Ha, ha," Terry intoned. "They're still children. They need to be watched."

"You're only saying that because you're fond of them," I said, falling into step next to him. "It's a little pathetic the way you let them wrap you around their fingers."

"I don't care what you say," Terry said. "I like spending time with them. They make me laugh."

"They're not bad kids," I grudgingly admitted. "They'll probably even be half-decent adults."

"That's the nicest thing you've ever said about them," Terry deadpanned, making a face. "I still don't understand why you're on babysitting duty. That would seem like the worst possible choice if you ask me."

"I'm an excellent babysitter," I countered. "I could do it professionally if I wanted. As for the rest, I think my nieces are wrapping Christmas presents but they don't want to admit it. Getting me and the girls out of the house for a few hours frees them to wrap and hide gifts."

"Well, I guess that makes sense," Terry said. "I … ." He didn't get a chance to finish what he was saying because Bay, Clove and Thistle were making a ton of noise as they raced in our direction. They looked as if someone was chasing them, but the path behind their small bodies was clear. Terry's eyes filled with concern as he caught Bay before she could skid and fall on the sidewalk. "Slow down. You're going to hurt yourselves."

"What's going on?" I asked. "Did Lila do something to you? I'll help you get her if you want. I'm bored anyway."

"It's not Lila," Bay said, struggling to catch her breath as her chest heaved. "It's something else."

"What?"

"There's a dead body over there," Thistle volunteered, pointing toward a clump of trees on the other side of the town square. "Someone is dead!"

"Are you serious?" I asked, doubt washing over me.

Thistle licked her lips and nodded. "I swear there's a dead guy over there!"

Well, merry freaking Christmas.

THREE

"What do you mean you found a dead body?"

I'm not calling my great-nieces liars, mind you, but they have active imaginations. Clove has been convinced that a ghost lives in their closet for the past year. For the record, that's me. Sometimes I like to move their stuff around just to mess with them. Some people might call me mean. Life is boring if you don't get your kicks somewhere.

"I mean there was a man on the ground and he wasn't moving," Thistle said, drawing her words out so slowly it was almost excruciating. "It was almost as if he fell but didn't get back up. Oh, wait, it was exactly like that."

"Why are you talking like that?" Terry asked.

"So the old people will understand me," Thistle replied. "By 'old' I mean you and Aunt Tillie."

Terry scowled as he rested a hand on Thistle's shoulder. "I'm not so old that I'm stupid," he said. "How can you be sure this man was dead? Maybe he just fell down."

"Because most people who fall down get back up," Thistle answered. "Oh, they also breathe."

Terry slid a dubious look in my direction. "What do you think?"

"I think they're prone to dramatic fits," I replied, not missing a beat. "I have no idea where they get it from."

"I know exactly where they get it from," Terry shot back, his eyes flashing. "Okay, girls, how about you show me where this dead body is?"

"I don't want to go back," Clove said. "I don't want to see it again."

"Fine. Then stay here alone." I put my hand to the back of Bay's neck and prodded her in the direction of the woods. Terry did the same with Thistle, and the look on Clove's face as she considered remaining behind was priceless.

"You're a mean old lady," Clove grumbled as she scurried to keep up with us. "You knew I wouldn't stay back there alone, didn't you?"

"I had a hunch," I replied, casting a glance at a few curious onlookers who stared at us from the festival area. I recognized one as Margaret Little. I couldn't be sure if she'd discovered that the end of her driveway was buried in a foot of hard snow yet, but I looked forward to the showdown when she did. We'd known each other since our school days, and the hate was entrenched in us early. When she lifted her eyes I saw recognition flash in the depths of her hateful orbs and I knew she was well aware what of the state her driveway was in. I couldn't stop myself from smiling and waving, launching her into a march in our direction.

"Why are you waving at her?" Terry asked, suspicious. I forget sometimes that he has keen eyesight. It's both a blessing and a curse, depending upon what he's investigating at any given moment. "You hate Margaret."

"Yeah, she's a real turd," I agreed, causing Thistle to snort. "She's one of those hard ones left to bake on the sidewalk in hundred-degree weather. She stinks, too."

"I think she's nice," Clove interjected. "She gave me a piece of candy at the summer parade this year. It was shaped like a unicorn."

"What did I tell you about taking candy from old crones who live in glass houses?" I challenged.

Clove wrinkled her nose. "Nothing. You told me not to throw water balloons at anyone other than dirty busybodies who had nothing better to do than spy on you when you were gardening, but you never mentioned anything about old crones and glass houses."

"Well, I'm mentioning it now," I said. "Don't take candy from them."

"What's a crone?" Thistle asked.

"Margaret Little."

"Don't tell them that," Terry snapped. "Margaret Little is a perfectly … ." He broke off, unsure how to proceed. I was fairly certain he was going to say "nice" and then realized how ludicrous the statement sounded. "She's your elder and deserves respect," he said, changing course. "Don't listen to your aunt."

"She's our elder, too," Bay pointed out. "Shouldn't we respect her?"

"And that's why you're my favorite today," I said, patting her shoulder. "You're a good girl."

"She's our elder but she's batshit crazy," Thistle supplied. "We don't have to respect batshit crazy. That's her rule."

"Don't swear, Thistle," Chief Terry ordered, taking her by surprise with his vehemence. "You're a lady. You're not supposed to curse like that."

"That's not a curse," Clove argued. "A curse is when we wake up and none of our shoes will stay tied."

"Or our hair won't stay braided," Bay added.

"Or we can't stop farting and falling down," Thistle said.

Terry is aware of the Winchesters' witchy ways, but he goes out of his way to pretend otherwise. My nieces make a big deal of fawning over him in an attempt to get him to invite one of them on a date. I know they really like him, but they would chew him up and spit him out if he ever dated one of them. He's smarter than I often given him credit for, though, because he refuses to play that game. He does, however, enjoy the casseroles and cakes they throw at him.

"Stop talking about that stuff," Terry ordered. "I'm not kidding. That's a … well … that's a home conversation. Do you understand what I'm saying?"

Clove shook her head. "No."

"I do," Thistle volunteered. "It's like when we're not supposed to talk about our mothers being attacked by the menstruation monster when we're around strangers."

Terry stilled as he grabbed the back of Thistle's coat and tugged her toward him. "What did you just say?"

Thistle was too oblivious to be embarrassed. "The menstruation monster," she said. "Aunt Tillie told us about it. It visits once a month at the same time for everyone. It could be worse because we could have three smaller monsters visiting at different times. Instead we get one big monster in the middle of the month."

Terry's face was full of outrage when he focused on me. "What is wrong with you?"

"You'll need to be more specific," I replied. "Answering that question could lead us in a hundred different directions."

"And none of them are good," Terry muttered, shaking his head. "I just … how could you tell them that?"

"The menstruation monster is real," I said. "It lives with the house-trashing fairy and the sock-stealing gnome. No, that's a true story."

"You make me so very tired," Terry grumbled, pinching the bridge of his nose. "Girls, which way is the body?"

Thistle pointed toward the woods. "Just on the other side of those trees," she said. "You can't miss it."

Something occurred to me. "Why were you in the trees in the first place?" I asked. "You were supposed to be getting hot chocolate and doughnuts. That's why you shook me down for extra money."

"We were on our way there but we saw Lila was going inside so we decided to get something to give her as a Christmas gift before joining her," Thistle answered. "It was only going to be a short side trip."

"Uh-huh." I wasn't sure I wanted to know where this story was going. Oh, who am I kidding? The kid's mind is a masterpiece when it comes to payback. She's a joy to watch when she gets down to business. "What gift?"

"I'm not sure I should answer," Thistle replied, darting a nervous look in Terry's direction. "That might be a home conversation, too." She tapped the side of her nose to give me the secret signal I had taught them years ago. It was for when she knew she was doing something naughty and didn't want to own up to it.

"Gotcha," I said, grinning.

Terry didn't look nearly as happy with Thistle's admission. "Gotcha? No, that's not how we're going to play this game. What were you going to give Lila, girls?"

"It was nothing big," Clove answered. "It was just ... snow. We were going to put it in a globe."

"Snow?" Terry was understandably dubious. "I don't get it."

"Yellow snow," Bay clarified. "We weren't so much going to put it in a globe as her hair."

"Ah," Terry said. Even though he was trying to be serious, the corners of his mouth tipped up. "Did you find any?"

"We found a body instead."

"Bummer."

"Yeah, total bummer," Bay said, her expression serious.

I was about to tell her not to worry about a body – it was far more likely they stumbled over a bag of garbage or even a half-drunk elf who lost his way to the tree-lighting ceremony – but I didn't get the chance because that's when Margaret finally caught up to us. Drat! I was hoping she would forget and turn around.

"Tillie Winchester!"

"She looks angry," Terry said, stopping on the sidewalk before following the obvious trail in the snow the girls left during their yellow snow hunt a few minutes earlier. "What did you do to her?"

"Why do you think I did something to her?" I challenged. "I'm clearly the victim here."

"Yes, I'm sure you are."

I swiveled to face Margaret head-on, adopting a bored expression before she even opened her mouth. "Hello, Margaret. It's so lovely to see you."

"Oh, don't even start with that," Margaret snapped. "I'm not in the mood to mess around with you. I'm not playing games."

"That's probably good," Thistle said. "You don't look as if you'd be very good at them."

I wanted to laugh, but Terry lightly swatted the back of Thistle's head to quiet her. "What seems to be the problem, Margaret?"

"The problem?" Margaret's face was so red I worried she'd pass out. "The problem is that you plowed in the end of my driveway -- like you always do -- and I almost got stuck."

"That doesn't really sound like a problem to me," I countered. "In fact, I think the fact that you got out of the driveway is the real problem. The people of Walkerville would be much happier if you hibernated for the winter rather than left the house. I know. I took a poll."

"Tillie." Terry's voice was low and full of warning. We were on a mission, after all.

"I was already late when I noticed the problem," Margaret snapped. "I had to bring my world-famous Christmas cookies to the baking area to be judged, but they didn't make it because I tried to drive through the snow and it's too hard. The second I hit the bank they flew across the seat and ended up on the floor."

"That sounds as if I saved the innocent people of Walkerville from botulism," I said.

Margaret narrowed her eyes. "My cookies are famous."

"You've said that twice now and I still don't believe it," I said. "How are they famous?"

"People love them."

"People love street thespians, too. That hardly makes them famous."

Margaret stomped her foot and made a shrill growling noise. She was clearly at her limit. I prefer when I push her over the limit and she explodes. I wonder what I can do to make that happen.

"I want her arrested, Terry," Margaret announced. "She plowed in my driveway. That has to be a felony."

Terry tilted his head to the side. "I don't think so," he said. "Plus, um, do you have proof it was her? Did you see her do it?"

"Well, no," Margaret conceded. "She obviously wasn't alone, though. These three ... ruffians ... were with her. Ask them what happened."

Terry shifted his eyes to Thistle, Clove and Bay. He clearly didn't like Margaret calling them names. He also looked worried about what they might say. I wasn't worried in the least. I knew exactly what they would say.

"Ask them," I prodded. "It's okay."

Terry cleared his throat. "Girls, did you see Aunt Tillie plow in Mrs. Little's driveway?"

"No, sir," Clove replied solemnly. She really is the best little liar in the world. "Aunt Tillie would never do that. She has a kind heart and a giving soul. It hurts my heart and makes my eyes leak to think someone would accuse her of doing something so wrong."

Oh, that was priceless. I was going to have to get that kid a better Christmas gift.

"Thistle?" Terry prodded.

"Aunt Tillie didn't do any plowing today," Thistle replied. "I was with her the whole time."

"Uh-huh." Terry shifted his eyes to the small blonde in front of me. "Bay?"

If there was a weak link in this lying trio, it was Bay. It wasn't because she couldn't lie. She could tell whoppers to almost anyone. She couldn't seem to bring herself to lie to Terry for some reason, though.

"I didn't see her do anything wrong," Bay said. It was sort of an evasion, but it did the trick. "Honest."

"Well, you heard them," Terry said. "They didn't see Tillie do anything to your driveway."

Margaret was annoyed. "Well, obviously they're lying," she said. "Girls, did you know it's a crime to lie to a police officer? Terry is going to throw you in jail for lying."

"Don't tell them that," Terry admonished. "I'm not putting them in jail. I don't appreciate your threats."

"That makes two of us," I volunteered, smiling evilly when Terry turned his attention to the woods. "Now, if you'll excuse me, we were on a mission when you approached."

"So, nothing is going to happen to her?" Margaret pressed.

"She didn't do anything, and she has three walking alibis," Terry said. "I'm not going to do anything to her. Besides that, we need to look in those trees. The girls swear they saw a dead body."

"A dead body?" Margaret was taken aback. "I ... why would there be a dead body in the woods?"

"Probably because that's where he died," Thistle replied.

"But ... that makes no sense," Margaret said.

"Neither does the fact that you call your cookies 'world-famous' even though no one outside of Walkerville has ever eaten them," I pointed out.

"They're still delicious."

"I heard they taste like butt crack," I said, causing my three young charges to giggle as Terry rolled his eyes. "I'm a better cook than you've ever dreamed of being. I could do it professionally."

"That's a laugh," Margaret said. "When do you ever cook?"

"I cook all of the time," I shot back. "Girls, tell her I cook all of the time."

That was apparently too far to push my partners in crime.

"Mom says all you cook up is trouble," Thistle said.

"You and your mother are on my list," I snapped, extending a finger. Thistle didn't look particularly worried. "As for the cooking, well, I guess I'll just have to show you."

"Oh, yeah? How are you going to do that?" Margaret scoffed.

"I'm going to join the cookie contest," I replied.

"I think it's a baking contest," Clove supplied.

"No one asked you."

"Go ahead," Margaret said. "I look forward to you falling on your face in public."

"That makes two of us," I fired back. Er, wait. I think that came out wrong.

Thankfully for me I didn't get a lot of time to dwell on it because Terry drew my attention back to him by coughing and then pointing at the woods.

"We need to see if someone is in there," Terry said.

"I already told you someone is in there," Thistle said.

"Well, I need to see for myself." Terry stepped off the sidewalk and marched into the trees, Thistle close to his side. I kept Bay in front of me as I followed. I wasn't surprised to find Margaret following Clove and bringing up the rear. She always was a busybody.

"Where?" Terry asked when he got to the end of the footprints.

"He was right there," Thistle said, pointing to an indentation in the snow. It did sort of look as if something had been resting there, but there were no footprints leading away.

"He's not there now, though," Terry said. "You don't see him, right?"

"Duh." Thistle rolled her eyes. "I'm not imagining things. I swear he was right there."

"He was," Clove said solemnly. "We all saw him. He had pink socks and everything."

My forehead creased. "Pink socks?"

"I swear we saw them," Clove said.

"Well, he's obviously gone," Terry said, forcing a bright smile for the girls' benefit. "I doubt he was dead. He was probably just … resting."

"No, he was definitely dead," Thistle said.

"And I'm definitely bored," Margaret said, turning to return to the sidewalk. "If this is their idea of the truth, I don't know how you can believe them about Tillie and my driveway, Terry. I'm very disappointed in you."

"Somehow I think I'll live," Terry said dryly.

Her tone irritated me. "I'll see you on the baking court, Margaret." Baking court? Is that a thing? Oh, well. It's too late to take it back.

"I can't wait," Margaret said, huffing as she trudged through the snow.

I waited until I was sure she was gone before turning back to the girls. "I'm sure no one is dead. You probably made a mistake and didn't understand what you were seeing."

"The only thing we made a mistake on was lying about your plowing," Thistle grumbled.

"What did you say?" Terry asked.

"They didn't say anything," I said hurriedly, motioning for them to come to me. "Come on, girls. I'll get you some hot chocolate and doughnuts, and then we'll head back to the house. I need to ask your mothers a favor."

"Yeah, well we want candy now, too," Thistle said.

"I think hot chocolate and doughnuts is more than enough," Terry said.

Thistle ignored him and stared me down. I recognized the potential mayhem in her gaze. She would tell Terry the truth if I didn't capitulate.

"Fine," I gritted out. "Candy, too."

Thistle was all smiles after that. "I think my work here is done."

Well, she finally found something we could both agree on.

FOUR

"Absolutely not."

My nieces weren't nearly as keen to help me in my cookie endeavor as I initially envisioned. In fact, they were angry. Who saw that coming?

"Why not?" I asked, grabbing a piece of fudge from the platter on the counter. "I thought you liked baking."

"I do like baking," Winnie said. "I love baking, in fact. We have a ton of baking planned for the next week."

"So give me some of those cookies."

"No way." Winnie shook her blond head and rested her hands on her hips as she stared me down. It was almost as if she was trying to send me a subliminal message. I wish she would just say whatever was poking at that busy brain of hers, because I'm not a mind reader.

"I don't see what the problem is," I said, breaking off a corner of my fudge brick and handing it to Clove. Marnie widened her eyes when she saw that. I'm not known for being much of a sharer. "Just give me a plate of your cookies and I'll take them to the contest and pretend I made them.

"Then, when they hand out the blue ribbon, I'll do a little dance to make Margaret Little feel like an idiot, and spend the purse on some new combat boots," I continued. "I've had my eye on a pair in that catalog you brought home last week. They're camouflage. I think they'll make a statement."

"And what statement is that?" Marnie asked, resting her hand on Clove's shoulder. "While we're at it, why did you give Clove a piece of your fudge?"

"I'm a giving soul."

"Why really?"

I shrugged. "I guess I wasn't thinking," I lied. "What were we talking about again?"

My nieces grew up with me, so they know when I'm skirting the truth. I hate that. For the bulk of their childhood I was the kooky aunt who made them go on cemetery outings in the middle of the night. I was adventuresome and adored. I loved that. After their mother died, I had to be the disciplinarian. That ate away at some of the love. I loathed that, but I never once regretted taking them in. I like to think they're strong and proud because of me.

"Why did Aunt Tillie give you fudge, Clove?" Marnie asked, pointedly focusing on her daughter.

"Because I lied to Officer Terry when Mrs. Little accused her of filling in the end of her driveway with snow," Clove answered immediately, causing my stomach to flip. This wouldn't end well.

"Hey, I bought off you little gluttons with hot chocolate, doughnuts and candy," I reminded them. "I didn't do that out of the goodness of my heart. It was a bribe. That means you need to shut your mouths."

"I thought that was the rule when we were in front of other people," Clove said, feigning innocence. "Whoops."

"Yeah, well, I'm going to put that whoops up your behind if you're not careful," I warned.

"Oh, I feel so loved," Clove deadpanned, earning a stern look from her mother. "What? I think my eyes are leaking."

"Knock that off," Marnie warned, wagging a finger in her daughter's face. "That might work on other people, but it doesn't work on me."

"Nope. They're definitely leaking." Clove made a big show of swiping at her dry cheeks. "I think I hurt my heart."

"Your butt is going to hurt if you don't zip it," Marnie shot back. "Good grief."

"Why are you making them lie to Terry and Mrs. Little?" Winnie asked.

Was that a serious question? I can never tell. Winnie's sense of humor comes and goes like a fart in a car when the window is cracked. Sometimes you're certain it's there and other times you think it escaped out the window. That's how I felt today. "I didn't tell them to lie." That's technically the truth. "They just did it. I have no idea why."

"Why did you do it?" Winnie asked Bay.

"Because Aunt Tillie says that we should always protect family over everyone else, and that Mrs. Little is a crone who lives in a glass house," Bay answered. "I've seen that house, though. Only the windows are glass."

"That's not really helping, Bay," I said.

"I didn't know that's what I was supposed to be doing," Bay said. "Can I go upstairs and read for an hour before dinner?"

"Sure." Winnie smoothed Bay's hair before the girl hopped down from her stool.

Bay flashed a smile in my direction as she headed for the stairs. "I'm sorry you're in trouble, Aunt Tillie," she sang out.

She didn't sound sorry.

"I'm sorry, too," Thistle said, touching my arm as she passed. "The doughnuts were delicious, though."

"We'll talk about the doughnuts when I track down you little turncoats later," I said.

"I'm looking forward to it."

Once it was just my three nieces and me, I found something fascinating to stare at on the wall. There was nothing there, but I've found that pretending I see things helps avoid an argument if I play the game correctly.

"Stop doing that," Winnie said, lightly slapping my arm.

Apparently I was off my game today. "I don't know what you want me to say," I said. "I was actually helping clean out driveways ... you remember Mrs. Franz, right? ... and somehow the snow accidentally made it from the end of her driveway into Margaret's yard. It was an accident."

"You know we don't believe that, right?" Marnie challenged. "I honestly don't care about you filling in Mrs. Little's driveway. That's the least destructive thing you've done to her all year. I care about you teaching the girls to lie to Terry."

"Technically only Clove and Thistle lied to Terry," I said. What? If they're going to turn on me, I'm going to pay them back. "Bay kind of talked around the situation. She didn't tell an outright lie."

Winnie seemed pleased with the knowledge. "Well, I guess that's not bad for her then."

"Yes, she's a regular angel," I deadpanned. "Now will you give me some cookies to take to the contest?"

"No." Mean Winnie was back with a vengeance. "We're not doing that. If you want to win the baking contest – and I think it would be great for you to get involved because it might keep you out of trouble for an afternoon – you need to make your own cookies."

That didn't sound like any fun at all. "Why would I bake my own cookies when there are piles of them in this house just waiting for me to pretend I baked them?"

"Because that's cheating."

"Since when do I care about that?"

Winnie scorched me with a look. "Since you're supposed to be on your best behavior and leading by example," she replied. "Your actions today weren't what we had in mind."

"Hey, the day was going fine until they claimed they saw a dead body in the woods," I said. "I maintain they derailed things. I was an innocent bystander."

"Yeah, that's weird, right?" Twila said. "Do you really think there was a body out there?"

I shrugged. "It looked like something had been resting in the snow, but for all we know it was a bag of garbage," I said. "Also, maybe someone did fall down. Maybe one of the elves got drunk. I have no idea what they really saw. It clearly wasn't a dead body, though."

"Well, that might be the only bit of good news we've gotten today," Marnie said. "You need to be careful about what you say in front of those girls. Remember what we talked about before you left. Set a good example."

"Yeah. I'll never forget that conversation." Mostly because it was so excruciating it was seared in my mind forever, I silently added. "Is that all?"

"Yes," Winnie answered. "Dinner will be ready in an hour."

"Can I steal some cookies?" Asking one more time couldn't possibly hurt.

"No."

"Fine," I huffed. "I want you all to know you're on my list, though."

"We were on your list this afternoon," Twila pointed out.

"Yes, but this time I'm going to do something about it," I said, stalking toward the door. "You're all going to pay for ruining my day. Mark my words."

Winnie appeared completely disinterested in my threat. "Wash your hands before you come to dinner. I can see you've been busy with the fudge, and you refuse to use a napkin unless we make you."

I narrowed my eyes. Clearly they'd gone too long without having to pay for their transgressions. I would fix that right up.

I FOUND the girls getting dressed in their bedroom the next morning, the smell of bacon wafting through the vents and informing me that their mothers were already downstairs cooking. They seemed surprised by my appearance, mostly because I generally showed up in their room only after they vacated the premises and I wanted to mess with them.

"What do you want?" Thistle asked, instantly suspicious. "If you're here to pay us back for yesterday, I'm prepared to scream and call for my mother."

"Oh, like that really terrifies me," I said, rolling my eyes. "Your mother frightens me least of the three."

"I'll scream for my mother, too," Clove warned.

"I'm still not frightened." I looked to Bay. Her expression was unreadable.

"I'm too tired to scream," Bay said. "I didn't sleep well."

Now that I gave her a good once over, she did appear paler than usual. I pressed my hand to her forehead as I studied the dark circles under her eyes. "Are you sick?"

"Eww. If you're sick, get away from me," Thistle said, shoving Bay's arm. "I don't want to get sick right before Santa comes. That would be the biggest holiday bummer of them all."

"I'm not sick," Bay said, glaring at her cousin. "I just didn't sleep well."

"Why not?" I asked, pulling my hand away. "You don't feel warm."

"I had nightmares," Bay said. "I saw the man in the woods, and he was haunting us."

This was a difficult situation because Bay could actually see and talk to ghosts. It was a family gift she inherited from me. Unlike the other gifts – like the ability to curse people and make magical potions to play with your enemies – the ghost gift was difficult to bear. I was fairly certain Bay would rather surrender it than keep it. That wasn't in the cards for her, though.

"Did you actually see this man or was it a dream?" I asked.

Bay realized what I was asking right away. "It was a dream," she said. "He was chasing me through the house. Instead of pink socks, though, he didn't have feet and he was bleeding from the ankles."

"Oh, gross," Clove said, wrinkling her nose. "Thanks so much for telling me that. Now I'm going to have nightmares."

"I won't," Thistle said. "I'm far scarier than any guy without feet."

Sadly, I figured she was probably right. "Girls, there was no body in the woods," I said. I saw no point in letting them freak themselves out when there was no reason – or benefit for me – and I hoped I'd be able to calm them since I had a favor to ask. "The time between when you found him and we made it back to that spot was less than ten minutes. Where did he go?"

"Maybe someone killed him and dragged his body away," Clove suggested.

"There were no drag marks, and you need to stop watching horror movies with your cousins because they always make you see things that aren't there," I chided.

"Maybe he died and came back as a zombie," Thistle said. "I saw that on a movie the other day. All of these people were in a farmhouse and zombies were going after them. They died first, and then got up and started walking."

"Zombies aren't real," I said. "You need to stop watching so much television, too."

"I saw that movie, and I didn't understand why they didn't run," Bay interjected. "The zombies were really slow. They were like Aunt Tillie on mornings before she has her coffee."

"Don't make me add you to my list," I warned, extending a finger and making her giggle. "There was no body in the woods. I don't know what you think you saw, but it wasn't a body."

"It was," Thistle said, stubbornly crossing her arms over her chest. "We know what we saw. You can't convince us otherwise."

"Fine. It was a zombie." I held up my hands to signify defeat. "If we're lucky he'll head to Margaret's house and we won't have to worry about him. She's so old and gristly it will take him years to gnaw through all of her skin and bones."

"You're so gross," Clove said, making a face.

"Not that we're not glad to see you, because we are, but why are you up here?" Bay asked. In some ways she's the smartest of the trio.

"I'm not happy to see you," Thistle said. "I am curious about why you're here, though." In other ways she's smartest of the group.

"I'm totally happy to see you and don't care why you're here," Clove added. She'll never be the smartest of the group, but she has her own special blend of mayhem that's going to be intriguing to watch as she grows older.

"I have a favor to ask of you," I said, choosing my words carefully. "I figure you owe me after tattling to your mothers last night."

"What do you want?" Bay asked, suspicious.

"She wants us to bake her cookies," Thistle said. "She couldn't con our mothers into doing it and now she has no one to ask but us."

Okay, she has control of the collective brain today. That much is obvious. "I'll pay you," I offered.

"How much?" Clove asked.

"Five dollars."

"Fifty and you have a deal," Thistle countered.

"Fifty?" What a bunch of money-hungry jerks. They almost make me proud. "I'm not giving you fifty bucks for cookies. There's no way."

"Then we're not baking you cookies," Thistle said.

"Hold up," Bay said, putting her hand on Thistle's arm. Her blue eyes were keen when they locked with mine. "I have a solution that helps everyone, and it doesn't involve money."

"I'm all ears," I said.

"We'll bake your cookies if you help us figure out who died in the woods," Bay suggested.

I opened my mouth to argue about whether or not they really saw a body and then snapped it shut. I was convinced no one died in the woods. I was equally convinced it couldn't hurt to pretend to investigate a fake death with them.

"Fine," I said, extending my hand. "You have a deal."

"We want hot chocolate while we're investigating, too," Thistle said, staying Bay's hand before she could seal the deal. "We might want some doughnuts, too."

"Don't push your luck," I warned.

"Fine, hot chocolate is enough."

I shook three small hands and exchanged multiple big smiles as visions of Margaret's face when she realized I stole the blue ribbon from her danced through my head. My reverie lasted only a few moments, though, because Bay's pragmatism dragged me back to solid ground.

"How are we going to bake without our mothers knowing?" she asked.

"You leave your mothers to me," I said. "I have everything under control."

I was almost sure of it.

FIVE

"What are we doing?"

Thistle jerked her head away when I tried to secure the strap of the blue combat helmet under her chin. She was naturally suspicious where I was concerned. I don't blame her.

"We're going to town," I replied. "You have to wear your helmet. I made a promise to your mothers."

"Yes, but you lie all of the time," Thistle pointed out. "What makes this different?"

"I don't lie all of the time," I corrected. "I expound on certain facts that other people might not believe are facts. It's different."

Bay made a face. "Facts are supposed to be something everyone agrees on. That's how they end up in research books."

Now it was my turn to make a face. "You need to stop spending so much time with your nose in books because you're going to grow up to be boring if you're not careful," I chided. "Men like smart women, but they don't like boring women. Well, I guess that's not true. Some men like boring women. Those aren't the type of men you want to associate with, though. Wait … what was I saying again?"

"You were saying that Bay is boring and I'm funny and cute," Thistle replied.

"That's not what I was saying," I said, remembering where I was in the conversation. "As for facts being universal, that's not even remotely true. Facts are affected by individual perspective. No, I'm telling the truth. That's a real scientific fact. I'm good at science. I could be a scientist professionally."

Bay wrinkled her nose as she fastened the strap of her purple combat helmet under her chin. She never gave me issues about wearing the helmet. I think it's because she's smart enough to recognize her own mortality. She's a worrisome little thing sometimes. Kids her age shouldn't be fixated on death. Because she sees ghosts, though, I think her life is going to be filled with crud like that.

"That doesn't change the fact that you lie to other people all of the time, and I don't want to wear this helmet," Thistle said. "It makes me look stupid."

"You do that to yourself," I said. "Also, there's a difference between lying to other people and making a promise to your mothers. I swore I would keep you safe because they seem to love you. I personally don't get it. I mean … I would've left you in the woods for wolves to eat when you were little if I had my druthers, but I promised my nieces, and that means you're wearing that helmet."

"You don't have to wear a helmet," Clove pointed out. "Why?"

"Because her head is hard and only a rock could break it," Thistle answered for me. "I heard Mom saying that to Aunt Marnie last week."

"Your mother's mouth is absolutely huge," I said. "She's going to cry her eyes out when I bring up all of these fun tidbits she's been passing on to you girls while I've been too distracted to notice."

"Well, that might be fun, too," Thistle said as she stopped fidgeting with the helmet. She was apparently resigned to wearing it into town to start our investigation.

"Did you guys feed and water the dog?" I asked. The mutt they coveted beyond everything slept on a blanket in front of the fire most of the time when it was cold, but they were fairly diligent about taking care of the Christmas gift I secured for them a few years ago.

"Yes, Sugar had breakfast and went outside," Bay answered. "I think he's hoping Mom bakes again later today. Something always seems to fall on the kitchen floor when Sugar is around."

"Yes, well, your mother is a sap," I said, gesturing toward the truck. "Everyone needs to get in so we can get going. I have an idea about who you might've seen in the woods."

"You do?" Thistle appeared to be caught between excitement and doubt. She didn't fully trust me. She probably never would. Smart girl.

"I do," I confirmed. "We just have one quick stop to make before we hit town."

"Are you going to plow in Mrs. Little's driveway again?" Clove asked as she settled in the middle of the seat next to Thistle.

"That's a horrible thing to ask me," I said. "Do you think I'm purposely mean to people?"

Clove answered without hesitation. "Yes."

"Well, it's good that you recognize people for what they are," I said. "We are stopping by Mrs. Little's on our way to town."

"Yay!" Clove clapped her hands as I circled the truck and climbed into the driver's seat.

"Is everyone ready?" I asked. Three solemn heads nodded. "Great."

"Just one thing," Thistle said, locking gazes with me. "Have you ever thought that the snow would be even better at the end of the driveway if it was yellow?"

I tilted my head to the side as I considered the question. "I like the way your mind works. Yellow snow it is."

"Double yay!" Clove clapped again.

"That gets annoying sometimes," I informed her.

"My eyes leak when you say things like that."

"WHERE ARE WE?"

Bay's expressive blue eyes were cloudy as I led the girls along the sidewalk in a quiet Walkerville neighborhood. I was still riding high from the Yellow Snow Extravaganza (all of the girls got in on the fun) in front of Margaret's house. I had no idea when she would see it. I was really looking forward to the outcome, though.

"This is Maple Street," I informed her, making sure Clove and Thistle were right behind us before focusing on the small ranch house, which was located in the final plot of a dead-end street in one of the most rundown neighborhoods in the area. "I think this is where your dead guy lives."

"How do you know that?" Thistle asked. "This morning you didn't believe us that a dead body even existed."

"I still don't think anyone died," I said, opting for honesty. "I do think maybe you saw someone passed out, though. It didn't hit me until you mentioned the pink socks. I happen to know someone who wears pink socks."

"Who?"

I gestured toward the house. "Edgar Martin."

The name didn't spark any sort of recognition from the girls.

"Who is that?" Clove asked. "Do we know him?"

That was a good question. "Do you remember at the summer festival when that guy got really loud and told everyone aliens abducted him and that's why he was late mowing lawns so it would be unfair to fire him?"

"No."

"Oh, I guess that was a little late for you guys to be out," I said, rubbing my chin. "Do you remember at the lake this summer when that guy was floating on the water and they called the fire department to resuscitate him – I mean fill his lungs with oxygen as a gag – and he claimed aliens dropped him in the lake by accident?"

Bay knit her eyebrows. "I remember the fire truck but not a man."

"Okay." I tilted my head to the sky and racked my brain for something they would remember. I snapped my fingers when a good memory pushed its way to the forefront. "Do you remember at the pet parade before Halloween this year when a guy dressed like a unicorn and pretended to walk himself and tried to win the big prize?"

"Oh, him?" Thistle made a disgusted face. "Mom said he was drunker than you during a solstice celebration."

I couldn't hide my scowl. "Your mother and I are going to have a really long talk before this is all said and done. I had no idea she's so ... chatty."

"Aunt Twila never shuts up," Clove said. "I don't know why you think it's so weird."

"No one asked you," I shot back. "As for Edgar, yes. He's the one who pretended to be a unicorn, because he was drunk. He was drunk in all of those stories. That's why I think there's a good possibility you found him passed out and not dead in the woods."

Bay ran her tongue over her upper lip as she considered the possibility. "I still think he was dead," she said finally.

These kids are stubborn. "Well, did you see his ghost?"

"No."

"Don't you think you would've if he died alone and afraid in the woods?" I challenged.

"Not if he was drunk and passed out in the snow," Bay replied. "I saw a thing on the Discovery Channel about dying in the cold. It's just like going to sleep. Ghosts hang around because they're sad about dying. Maybe he wasn't sad about dying."

I hate it when the little imp has a point. "Let's just knock on the door and see if Edgar is home," I suggested. "That way you'll be able to see him and tell me if he's the body you saw."

"What if he doesn't answer?" Clove asked.

"We'll cross that road when we come to it."

"Okay, but I agree with Bay," Clove said, falling into step with me as we traipsed toward the front door. "I'm pretty sure he was dead."

"Did your eyes leak?"

"They wanted to."

I pursed my lips to keep from laughing and knocked on the door three times in quick succession when we reached the top of the porch. The girls watched expectantly as I leaned closer to listen for the telltale sounds of someone stirring inside. The house was still.

I knocked again and got the same result. Thistle grew more smug with every unanswered knock.

"I think he's dead," Bay said finally, crossing her arms over her chest. "I hate to say I told you so, but ... ."

"I wouldn't finish that sentence if I were you," I warned, extending a finger. "He's not dead. He's just … passed out. He's dead to the world, so to speak, but he's not really dead."

"You don't know that he's even inside," Thistle argued. "You can tell us that until your lips fall off from lying, but we know the truth. He's not in there. He's dead."

"You're letting your imaginations get away from you."

"No, we're not," Clove said. "You didn't see him in the snow. We did. We know he's dead."

"Oh, geez." I pinched the bridge of my nose to ward off an oncoming headache. "Will you girls believe me if I take you inside and show you Edgar is passed out?"

"How are you going to do that?" Bay asked, suspicious.

I pointed toward the large window at the front of the house. "We can go through there."

Clove's mouth dropped open. "That's breaking the law!"

"You weren't so bothered by that when we put yellow snow at the end of Margaret's driveway," I pointed out.

"Yes, but we can't get in trouble for that because we're too young to drive," Thistle said. "We can get in trouble for this. We know better than to break into someone's house."

"Mostly because we've gotten in trouble with the police before when you made us do it," Bay added.

"I didn't make you do anything," I countered. "You wanted to do it. You enjoyed it, in fact. It's not my fault we got caught. That was a fluke."

"I don't know." Clove rubbed her mitten-covered hands together. "What if we get caught?"

"We won't get caught." I was fifty percent sure that was true. "We'll go in through the window, I'll show you that Edgar is passed out inside and not dead, and then we'll go out through the front door. You can let go of this dead body crap, and we'll return home so you can bake my cookies."

"What if we go in there and he's not the guy we saw in the woods?" Bay asked.

"Then we'll keep looking."

"I don't know." Bay hopped from one foot to the other as her gazed bounced between Clove and Thistle. "What do you guys think?"

"I don't want to break the law," Clove answered.

"I don't care about breaking the law," Thistle said. "I just don't want to get caught."

"We won't get caught," I said. "Trust me."

"**YOU ARE** IN SO MUCH TROUBLE!"

Terry's face was full of fury as he crossed his arms over his chest and tapped his foot on Edgar's snow-covered front porch twenty minutes later. He caught us in the act as we tried to force Clove through the open window – and convince her to open the front door once she was inside. Apparently the neighbors saw us or some such crap. That's what Terry told us when he dragged us outside anyway.

"I was doing a public service," I said, forcing myself to remain calm. "The girls have been working themselves up because they're convinced they saw a dead body yesterday. I was simply trying to prove to them that they were wrong."

"And how did that end up with you breaking into a house?" Terry asked.

"Well, they mentioned they saw pink socks," I replied. "I saw Edgar wearing pink socks the day he dressed like a unicorn. I figured they didn't see a dead body but a dead drunk passed out in the snow. I wanted them to give up on the dead body business before it consumed them."

"Yes, that sounds very virtuous of you," Terry snapped sarcastically. "I don't believe you for a second, though."

"That's because you're a very suspicious person."

"Did it ever cross your mind that you should just knock?" Terry asked. "That's what a normal person would do."

"We did knock," Thistle said. "No one answered. That's how we knew this dude was dead."

"That's very callous, Thistle," Terry said. "You don't know anything of the sort. I'm not convinced you saw anything in the woods yesterday."

"Do you think we're liars?" Bay's lower lip jutted out. "I'm not a liar."

"Oh, sweetheart, I know you're not a liar," Terry said, melting in the face of childhood anguish. He rested his hand on her shoulder as he knelt next to her. "I think you saw something in the woods and thought it was one thing when it was really another."

"That's not what happened," Clove said. "We saw a body."

"No, you didn't," Terry said.

"If we didn't see a body, where is the crazy unicorn guy?" Thistle challenged. "He's not in there. We looked around before you caught us."

"You mean you looked around before I caught you doing something illegal," Terry corrected.

"My eyes are leaking." Clove pressed her fingers over her eyelids. "My heart hurts."

"Stop that right now," Terry ordered, wagging a finger in Clove's direction before turning his eyes to me. "Are you happy? You're turning them into criminals."

"I'm unhappy about being caught," I answered honestly. "The criminal stuff doesn't bother me. And, truth be told, I am slightly worried that they really did see Edgar out there. What if he's lit and took off in the woods? He could die. It's cold out, and we both know he doesn't monitor his drinking."

"I … ." Terry broke off as he rubbed the back of his neck. "I'll see if I can find out where he is to put everyone's mind at ease. That doesn't mean you guys are off the hook, though."

"Are you going to throw us in jail?" Clove asked, horrified. "I won't do well in jail. Aunt Tillie told me. I'll be the first one made to be a … what did you call it?"

"Prison wife," I answered, not missing a beat.

Terry scowled. "Don't tell her things like that," he snapped. "I cannot believe you brought them here. I just … what is the matter with you?"

I had two choices. I could tell him the truth and admit to bribing the girls for cookies or come up with a lie that made me look better. It wasn't a hard decision.

"Bay had nightmares last night, and she's pale," I said, pointing toward the blonde. She was Terry's favorite and he would fall all over himself if he thought she was legitimately upset. "She's going to make herself sick if she keeps at it. I was trying to make things easier for her."

"Are you sick?" Terry tilted Bay's chin so he could study her face. "You do have circles under your eyes. Maybe you shouldn't be running around in the cold."

Well, that worked like a charm.

"I'm okay," Bay said. "I know he's dead, though. I can feel it."

"Oh, yeah?" Terry asked, his eyes sympathetic. "What do you feel?"

"Cold."

"I think that's because you're outside," Terry said, scooping up Bay and glaring at me. "Come on, girls. I'll walk you back to the truck and buckle you in. Aunt Tillie is taking you home. There will be no more breaking the law today."

"But … we're not done," Thistle complained.

"Oh, you're done," Terry muttered.

I tapped Clove's head to get her attention as I marched behind her. "When we get to the truck, tell him your eyes are leaking because you love him so much," I ordered. "He won't be able to yell at us if you do that."

Clove's smile was serene. "I'm on it."

SIX

"It's snowing."

The ride home was mostly quiet, all four of us lost in thought. The girls were convinced Edgar was dead in the woods somewhere, and even though I didn't want to admit it I was beginning to wonder if they were right.

They were so quiet – which worked against the norm, let me tell you – that I almost forgot they were in the truck with me.

I shifted my eyes to Bay as she stared out the window. She'd always been entranced by snow. Don't get me wrong, she prefers warm weather in the summer, but she likes snow for Christmas. I kind of like it, too.

"It is," I agreed, smiling as the large flakes pelted down from the sky. "It looks as if it's going to be a big snow, too."

"We should plow on the way home," Thistle said. "That way we can check on the yellow snow."

I really do like the way that kid's mind works. "We can do that," I said. "In fact, why don't we head that way now?"

"I thought you wanted us to bake?" Clove challenged. "Wasn't that the whole point of today's trip?"

"Clove, the whole point of today's trip was to prove to you guys that you didn't find a dead body in the woods," I said. "I think I've done that."

"You have not," Thistle scoffed. "You're only saying that to make us think something that's not true. I know the way your mind works. You can't fool us."

I knew the way her mind worked, too, and she was right.

"She's not trying to fool us," Bay corrected. "She's trying to convince herself that she's right and we're wrong. She's worried we really did see something and that Edgar Martin is dead and she doesn't want to be responsible for finding his body."

How in the heck did she figure that out? The older they get, the shrewder they get. It's frightening. If they all put their heads together now they come close to outsmarting me. Don't ever tell them I said that, by the way. I'll deny it to my dying day.

"I don't think he's dead," I said. "I think he was passed out when you guys came across him. Then I think being in the cold woke him and he wandered off."

"You said there were no tracks leading away," Thistle pointed out.

I did say that. Crud. "Maybe he stepped in the tracks you already made," I suggested. Hey, that's actually a possibility. I warmed to my subject. "Maybe he woke up and saw the tracks and followed them out and we didn't notice because we got distracted."

Thistle snorted. "You'll say anything to make us believe you're right."

That was also true. I decided to change the subject before things got out of hand. "Who wants to plow?"

Clove and Bay immediately raised their hands while Thistle took a moment to think. I narrowed my eyes as I watched her. I had no idea what was going through that busy mind of hers, but whatever it was couldn't be good.

"Can we go by Lila's house and mess with her driveway?" Thistle asked finally.

Now that sounded like a plan. "Absolutely," I said, taking the girls by surprise as I did an immediate U-turn. "We'll hit her house first and then swing back around by Margaret's place before going home. Your mothers are supposed to be shopping this afternoon – don't worry, I asked to make sure – and that gives us a window to make cookies."

"Let's do it," Thistle said. "I think we should make the snow in front of Lila's house yellow, too."

"No, not yellow," Bay said, her face lighting up. "We should make that snow brown ... like poop."

I pressed my lips together to keep from laughing. They were young, so they couldn't think of truly evil things to do to their enemies yet, but they were getting there fast. "I couldn't be prouder of you girls if I birthed you myself."

The truck jolted as I got too close to the side of the road, and I cast a surprised look in that direction. "Huh. What was that?"

"You took out Mr. Dorchester's mailbox," Thistle replied, blasé. "It was that red one that looked like a barn."

"Oh, well, that was ugly anyway," I said. "He must've moved it."

"Yeah. I'm sure he did."

"IT SAYS HERE you need one stick of butter and a half cup of salt," I said, resting my chin on the counter as I sat on a stool and watched Clove and Bay work behind the counter. Thistle, much like me, had no interest in baking and sipped a cup of tea as she watched her cousins work. I decided to read the ingredients to them to hurry things along because our plowing excursion took longer than I initially planned. By the end of the trip we added two other enemies to the list because we were having so much fun. The brown snow really did look like a pile of poop, by the way. It was glorious.

"There's no way it says to use half a cup of salt," Bay argued, her forehead creasing into a tense vee. "That would make the cookies taste way too nasty."

How could she possibly know that? It's not as if she's a baker. "It says salt," I shot back. "I'm not blind. I know how to read."

Bay wasn't convinced and she snatched the cookbook from me so she could look at the recipe. "It says we need half a cup of sugar and one tablespoon of salt," she corrected. "Where are your glasses?"

Well, now she was just hitting below the belt. "I don't need glasses," I argued. "Glasses are for old people. I have perfect vision. I could be a sniper in the military if I wanted. Seriously, I could kill people for a living."

"I don't think anyone disagrees with that," Thistle said. "You wouldn't do it with a gun, though. You would do it with your fingers and mind."

She had a point. "I still think salty cookies are probably delicious," I said. "Put extra salt in."

"Do you want to win or do you want to be right?" Bay challenged, taking me by surprise. "In this case you can't do both."

And that right there is why I'm convinced she's the smartest in the group some days. She can read me like a children's book with only pictures. "Who says I can't be both?"

"Common sense and taste buds."

I made a face. "Fine. I want to win."

"You only want to win so you can torture Mrs. Little," Thistle said knowingly as she slurped her tea. "Why do you hate her so much?"

That was a story they were definitely too young to hear. It was such a bad story I didn't want to know it. Plus, in the end, I didn't come out looking like much of a role model. Don't get me wrong, I'm not keen on being a role model, but despite what everyone says, there are a few things in my past that cause me shame. My association with Margaret is one of them.

"She's a bad person," I answered after a beat. "It's not just that she does bad things. She has a bad heart, too."

"Unlike you," Bay mused. "You like to do naughty things, but Mom says you have a good heart. She says you have the best heart sometimes. She just wishes you weren't so naughty."

"I guess you get that from me, huh?" I teased, my eyes flashing. "I don't generally consider myself naughty. It's more that I'm … active … and I work faster than most people think. That makes me a genius of sorts."

Thistle giggled so hard I thought she was going to snort her tea through her nose.

"I was being truthful," I said.

"You're so funny," Thistle said. "I want to be just like you when I grow up ... only meaner."

I shot her an appraising look. "I think that's the nicest thing you ever said to me."

"Yeah? Well, don't get used to it," Thistle said. "I want a mean reputation like you."

I stilled, the admission catching me off guard. "Do you really think I have a mean reputation?"

Thistle nodded. "People are afraid of you. I want them to be afraid of me, too."

"I don't think you have much to worry about there," I said. "I heard the principal called your mother in at the end of the semester and told her that everyone in your class is frightened of you."

"They're easy, though," Thistle said. "All I have to do is threaten to knock them down and make them cry to get them to do what I want. I need to start scaring adults. That's what I'm really looking forward to doing."

For the first time I realized exactly how much she reminded me of myself. I make jokes about it sometimes because I find it amusing, but perhaps her mother is right. I would never admit it to my nieces, but Thistle was clearly getting close to crossing a line from which she might not be able to return.

"Listen, mouth," I said, choosing my words carefully. "I know you think it's all fun and games to terrorize people – and it does have its merits, I'm not going to lie – but you don't want to be so mean that you chase everyone away. It's good to have a few people in your corner no matter who you are."

Thistle didn't look convinced. "You don't have people in your corner."

I arched a challenging eyebrow. "Oh, really? What about your mothers? What about the three of you? What about Officer Terry?"

"But ... you fight with all of us," Thistle said.

"Fighting is not the same as scaring everyone away," I said. "Think about it, do you really want to go through life without the rest of us? If you continue down this path, you're going to scare everyone away. You might not care about those twerps in your school, but I'm guessing you would be pretty sad if you scared away Bay and Clove."

Thistle rubbed her cheek as she tilted her head and considered my words. "I don't want to scare everyone away," she said finally. "I also want to terrify people when I hate them and they're evil. Can I do both?"

I smiled. "It's a balancing act," I said. "Something tells me you're up to the challenge of balancing two worlds, though. Just … think about it."

"Okay, but I'm still going to be mean to you when I feel like it," Thistle hedged.

"I would expect nothing less."

"IN THE NAME of the Goddess … what in the hell happened here?"

I lost track of time hanging out with the girls in the kitchen and before I realized what was happening I found Winnie, Marnie and Twila staring at the trashed room with what can only be described as outright fury. They held shopping bags in their hands as they gaped at the flour-covered counters and greased cookie sheets. Bay and Clove were just as messy as the counters.

"It's not what you think," I said hurriedly, racking my brain for an acceptable excuse. "We were attacked by a … flour gnome and it was so out of control I had to vanquish it. We just got through fighting it. Yeah, that's it."

Winnie made a disgusted face as she dropped her grocery bags on the floor. "A flour gnome? Do you really expect me to believe that?"

Was that a trick question? "Um … you tell me."

"We know what you were doing," Marnie said, resting her bags on the dining room table as she wrinkled her nose and stared at the mess. "You conned them into making you cookies for the contest. I just … what were you thinking?"

"Well, I certainly didn't bribe them, if that's what you're asking," I said. Wait … should I have said that? Probably not. That's what happens when you add bourbon to your tea when no one is looking. This wouldn't end well.

"She bribed you?" Winnie's eyes widened as she locked gazes with Bay. "What did she give you?"

Bay looked caught. "Um … ."

"She told us she would help us find the dead body if we helped her make cookies," Thistle replied, moving down a stool when I lashed out to slap her arm. She expected the move. "We thought it was a fair trade."

"We?" Bay challenged. "You drank tea. You didn't help with anything."

"I was super … super … ." Thistle often grappled to find the right word to express what she was feeling.

"Supervising?" Twila suggested.

Thistle snapped her fingers. "Yeah, that's it. I was supervising. Someone had to make sure Clove and Bay didn't make a mistake."

"I'm pretty sure that was my job," I said dryly.

"Says the woman who thought we should use half a cup of salt," Bay grumbled.

"I heard that," I said.

"I wasn't whispering," Bay shot back.

"Okay, that's enough of that," Winnie said, grabbing Bay's arm and tugging her away from the counter. "You need to go upstairs and take a bath. Wash all of that flour off. Dinner will be ready in an hour, so make sure you're not late."

"But we're not done with the cookies," Bay said. She's something of a perfectionist, which I find fascinating. I never met a project I didn't want to abandon halfway through it. Bay is the complete opposite. "We still have to put them in the oven."

"I'll finish the cookies," Winnie said, her smile stretched and tight as she glanced at me.

"You need to go upstairs, too, Clove," Marnie said. "Make sure you put those dirty clothes in the hamper instead of leaving them on the floor. You might draw mice in there if you're not careful."

Thistle moved to hop off the stool and follow her cousins, but Twila stopped her before she could take more than a couple of steps. "Where are you going?"

"Upstairs to get cleaned up," Thistle replied.

"Oh, no," Twila said, shaking her head. "You're not dirty. Do you know what's dirty?"

"Aunt Tillie's mind?"

Twila pressed her lips together and shook her head.

"The kitchen is dirty," Marnie said. "The kitchen is filthy, in fact. You two need to clean up the mess you made so we can cook dinner."

I glanced over my shoulder. Who was the other half of the "two" she referenced? "Which two?"

"You and Thistle," Winnie replied. "This was your idea and you sat there and watched them make a mess. You need to clean it up."

Yeah, that really sounded nothing like me. "I'm good," I said blithely.

"You're not good," Winnie countered. "If you don't pick up this mess, you're not getting any dinner. Do you understand?"

"Yes, but … ."

Marnie shook her head to cut me off. "No buts."

"I'm not in the mood to clean," Thistle said. "I think Aunt Tillie should do it alone."

"We just had this discussion," I growled.

Thistle ignored me. "I'm small and tired. I need a nap."

"You need to clean if you want dinner," Twila corrected. "Don't you want dinner?"

Thistle shrugged. "It depends," she replied. "What are we having?"

"What does that have to do with anything?" Winnie challenged.

"If it's something I hate I'm going to choose the nap," Thistle replied, not missing a beat. "If it's something I like, I guess I'm going to clean. I won't like it, though."

Winnie made a disgusted face. "We're having chicken legs marinated in red wine, mashed potatoes and corn."

Thistle screwed up her face into a strange expression as she thought. "I think I'll take a nap."

"We're also having red velvet cake," Marnie added, causing Thistle's smug smile to slip. "I believe that's your favorite."

"It is my favorite," Thistle said. "Crap."

"Yes, crap," I agreed, reluctantly taking the towel Winnie handed in my direction. "I blame you for this, Thistle. You were supposed to be watching the clock."

"And I blame you," Thistle shot back. "You were supposed to be watching us."

"And I blame both of you," Winnie said. "I want this kitchen clean in twenty minutes. If it's not, you guys aren't going to get any cake."

Well, that was a low blow. "I'm not going to put up with much more of this lip," I warned. "You're going to be sorry if you continue to cross me."

"Me, too," Thistle intoned.

Winnie didn't look worried in the least. "Clean!"

Yeah, I've definitely been off my game when it comes to doling out punishments this week. I need to take a long look at my naughty list and start handling the biggest trouble spots. Unfortunately, I have to clean first. Blech.

I cast a curious look in Thistle's direction as she packed the baking ingredients to carry to the pantry. "I think my eyes might start leaking soon," I admitted.

"Join the club."

SEVEN

I found the girls leaving their bedroom the next morning. They were instantly alert upon seeing me in their part of the house two days in a row. Suspicion runs deep when you have Winchester blood flowing through your veins. You're born with it. You can't hide from it.

"Are you going to punish us for yesterday?" Clove asked, her brown eyes reflecting worry. "If so, you should know that what happened yesterday wasn't our fault. We did what we were supposed to do."

"We did," Bay said, bobbing her head.

"I didn't, but you didn't really think I was going to do it so it doesn't matter," Thistle said. She was strangely blasé for so early in the morning. Usually she's grumpy and you can't talk to her until she has some juice and food in her stomach. She gets that from me.

"No, I didn't really expect you to do anything and you definitely held up your end of the bargain," I said, following the girls down the hallway. "You did help clean the kitchen, though, so I guess that should count for something."

"The only reason I did that was because Mom wouldn't stop staring at me," Thistle admitted. "It was as if she knew I was just waiting for her to look away so I could escape. I hate that about her."

"Yes, that's a mom thing," I said. "My mother was the same way. I always thought I could put one over on her, but she managed to catch me every time."

"What was your mom like?" Bay asked. She looked legitimately curious. "We've heard stories, but never got to meet her. We've seen photos, though. You don't look like her."

"No, your grandmother looked like her," I said, my mind briefly drifting back to my childhood. I was genuinely fond of my sister Ginger and missed her a great deal. I saw some of her mannerisms reflected back at me when I looked at her daughters – Winnie, Marnie and Twila – but they had a lot of me in them, too. I wasn't sure which traits were stronger – or better, for that matter. "It's too bad you girls didn't get to meet your grandmother. You would've liked her."

I was surprisingly wistful this morning. My melancholy mood wasn't lost on the youngest Winchesters.

"Do you miss her?" Clove asked.

"I do."

"I wish I could've had a sister," Clove said. "I would've been a great older sister. I would've tortured my little sister only fifty percent of the time."

I smirked. "You have sisters," I countered. "What do you think Bay and Thistle are?"

"Cousins."

"Technically I guess you're right," I conceded. "You haven't been raised as cousins, though. You've been raised as sisters. It doesn't matter that you don't share the same mother and father. You share the same heart."

"That's kind of gross when you think about it," Clove said, descending the stairs. "If we all shared the same heart then we would be stuck together and that would give me nightmares."

"Would it make your eyes leak?" I teased.

"Definitely."

I found Marnie, Twila and Winnie standing behind the counter when we reached the kitchen. The usual morning cooking activities seemed to be underway – egg carton open on the counter, bread sitting next to the toaster, a slab of bacon in Marnie's hand as she stared at the stove – but without the normal bustle that accompanied the items. I pursed my lips when I saw the blank look on Winnie's face and feigned confusion. "What's going on?"

"Why don't I smell breakfast?" Thistle asked, alarmed. "Are your hands broken?"

"No," Twila answered hurriedly, reaching for the bread. "We're getting everything ready. We're just running late today."

"Really late," I said, shuffling toward the coffee pot on the counter and pouring myself a mug of steaming caffeinated goodness as I made a big show of staring at the empty frying pans and toaster. "Are you girls sick?"

"Oh, I hope not," Clove said. "If you all get sick, who will cook for us?"

"Not Aunt Tillie, that's for sure," Thistle intoned. "If you get sick, we're going to starve."

"And no one wants that," I said, biting the inside of my cheek as Winnie's puzzled expression turned to frustration. "Do you think you're getting the flu?"

"Of course not," Winnie said, snapping her head up and glaring at me. "We don't get sick. We take care of ourselves."

"We definitely take care of ourselves," Marnie agreed.

"Then why isn't breakfast ready?" I pressed, tugging a strand of Bay's hair behind her ear and smoothing it into place. The girls take care of their own morning hygiene but sometimes they gloss over their hair in the winter because they know they end up wearing hats. "Breakfast is always ready when we come down. I mean ... is something wrong?"

I knew I was in danger of overplaying my hand when Winnie narrowed her eyes and fixated on me. Her hand rested on the egg carton and I couldn't help but wonder if she planned on hurling one at me. I knew she wouldn't cook anything in the carton. I'd taken care of that. They couldn't cook today no matter how hard they tried. In fact, the harder they tried, the more likely it would become that the knowledge of how to cook – even the basics – would seep out of their brains.

"What did you do?" Winnie hissed, the reality of the situation finally sinking in.

"What makes you think I did anything?" I asked, pasting my best "I'm innocent and you can't attack me without proper proof" smile on my face.

"Because we can't seem to remember how to cook breakfast," Marnie answered. "Do you see those eggs? We know they're eggs. We even know we're supposed to cook them. We can't remember how, though. It's as if we've forgotten everything we know how to do."

"That is terrible," I clucked, sliding a sly look in Thistle's direction. Her eyes were fixed on her mother's face and she seemed to be in awe. "Did you fall and hit your head?"

"We didn't hit anything," Twila shot back. "We were absolutely fine last night. We made dinner and did the dishes. Everything was perfectly normal when we went to sleep."

"Then we woke up and things still seemed fine," Winnie said. "That lasted until we hit the kitchen. We pulled all of the food out of the refrigerator like normal and then ... well, then we got stuck."

"Oh, this is a total travesty," I said, swallowing the urge to giggle. I wouldn't truly be able to get under their skin if I didn't play it straight. "Do you think it was something you ate?"

"I'll bet it was the memory monster," Clove said. "I think he lives in our closet."

"The only thing living in your closet is the mess monster," Marnie snapped. "It wasn't something we ate. Aunt Tillie did this."

"Oh, now, that's a serious accusation," I said, studying my stubby fingernails. "Do you have any proof?"

"We know it was you," Winnie spat. "We're not stupid. You gathered the girls before coming down. That means you didn't want to risk running into us without backup. Do you think I'm stupid?"

"Now probably isn't the time to ask me that question," I replied. "I mean, with you forgetting how to cook eggs and all. Perhaps you should go to a doctor."

"You're in big trouble!" Winnie screeched, grabbing a spatula from the bin on the counter and brandishing it in my face. "You cursed us, didn't you? This all comes back to us refusing to make you cookies to pass off as your own at the baking contest. Admit it."

Gladly. "I warned you guys something bad was going to happen if you turned your back on your loving aunt," I said. "Think about it. I raised you. I loved you. I took care of you. I paid for everything. What did you give me in return? Grief. That's what."

"Oh, that's such a crock of crap," Marnie said. "We love and take care of you just as much as you love and take care of us. This is a reciprocal relationship. It's not all about you."

Yeah, sometimes I think they don't know me at all. What they do know they seem to twist to their own designs for some unknown reason. "I think this is probably a great lesson on karma," I said. "What do you think, girls?"

"I think I'm hungry," Bay said, rubbing her stomach.

"I think it's funny, but I'm with Bay," Thistle said. "What are we going to eat?"

"There!" Winnie waved the spatula in Thistle's direction. She appeared to be growing more and more deranged by the second. "Did you hear that? What are they going to eat? You can't let them starve, and we all know you're not going to cook for them."

"Oh, I'm definitely not going to cook for them," I said, hopping to my feet. "Girls, grab your helmets. We're going into town for breakfast."

The girls seemed surprised but didn't give me any lip as they hurried out of the room. Winnie was incredulous as she watched them go.

"What a bunch of traitors," she groused.

"Yes, they kind of follow whatever direction the wind takes them, don't they?" I flashed my most evil grin to get my nieces' attention. "I guess I'll see you later. I hope you find something to eat."

"This isn't going to work," Winnie called out. "I'm not going to fall for this. We're not going to let you blackmail us into doing what you want."

"I guess we'll see," I called back. "Something tells me you're lying to everyone ... including yourselves."

I TOOK the girls to the Gunderson Bakery for breakfast. I'd known the owner, Ginny, for years. We had something of a tumultuous past, but we weren't exactly unfriendly. She was also keyed in to all of the area gossip, so I hoped she'd be able to assuage my fears regarding Edgar.

"Well, this is a surprise," Ginny said, beaming at the girls as I herded them toward a table. "I don't often see you ladies out for breakfast."

"Our moms forgot how to cook and we're starving," Clove announced. "I think we might pass out from hunger."

"You poor dears!" Ginny never had children of her own and she fell for every fake tear and imaginary injury these three could muster. It drove me crazy. "What would you like?"

"I want doughnuts," Thistle said. "I want, like, ten of them."

"Ten, huh?" Ginny smiled. "Do you want chocolate and sprinkles on them?"

Thistle nodded happily, but I held up my hand to still Ginny before she could take Bay and Clove's orders. "Wait a second," I said. "You girls have to eat a regular breakfast."

"Ugh! You can't bring us to a bakery and not expect us to eat doughnuts," Thistle complained.

"Yeah, that's mean," Clove said. "It makes my eyes leak."

"Okay, that's funny when you do it to other people, but I find it annoying," I said, extending a finger in Clove's direction. "From now on you're forbidden to do that with me. Do you understand?"

"Now I know my eyes are leaking," Clove grumbled, crossing her arms over her chest.

"Your butt will be leaking if you're not careful."

"Gross," Thistle and Bay said in unison as Ginny shot me a dark look.

"What?" I asked Ginny, frustrated. "You try spending hours with these monsters and we'll see how you feel afterward."

"I would love to spend time with these little angels," Ginny cooed. "Look how cute they are."

"Wow. You girls have her snowed," I said, shaking my head. "Good job."

"We learned from the best," Bay said, grinning. "Can I have a breakfast sandwich?"

"That's a good idea," I said. "If you all eat a breakfast sandwich and one of those hash brown things you can have a doughnut when you're done."

"I only want the doughnut," Thistle said.

"And I only want you to shut up," I shot back.

"Fine," Thistle grumbled. "Can I have the bacon and egg bagel sandwich and a hash brown?"

Ginny smirked. "You certainly can. How about everyone else?"

"The same for me," Bay said as Clove nodded. "Can I have a tomato juice, too?"

"Tomato juice? I don't know any little ones who like tomato juice," Ginny said, giggling.

"She's a weird kid, but she does love her tomato juice," I said. "I'll have a sandwich, too. I'd like some coffee, though."

"What about you two?" Ginny asked Clove and Thistle. "What do you want to drink?"

"I want coffee," Thistle said. "I take it black with no sugar."

"They'll have orange juice," I corrected before slipping out of my coat and following Ginny to the counter. The grill was right there, so she could make the sandwiches and keep up on conversation at the same time. I kept one eye on the girls for a few minutes to make sure they were behaving, but when they seemed content to gossip about how funny their mothers acted this morning I left them to it and focused on Ginny. "Have you heard any good gossip lately?"

"You'll have to be more specific," Ginny said, placing the bacon on the griddle. "I've heard a lot of gossip. For example, I heard that Judy Bristow wants to get a boob job, and I heard that you've been plowing in the end of Margaret's driveway with yellow snow."

"We did brown snow for a bit yesterday, too."

Ginny smirked. "It's not as if she doesn't deserve it. Is that the kind of gossip you're talking about?"

I shook my head. "Have you heard anything about Edgar Martin?"

Ginny tilted her head to the side, confused. She seemed surprised by the question. "I haven't heard anything about him since the unicorn incident. I heard talk people were going to try to force him into rehab, but that never came to fruition."

"It never does," I said. "You can't force someone into rehab. They have to want to do it for themselves."

"Why are you asking about Edgar?"

"Well, um … ." I risked a glance over my shoulder, but the girls were still caught up with talking to each other rather than eavesdropping. "The day of the tree-lighting ceremony the girls swear they found a body in the woods."

"What were they doing in the woods?"

"Looking for yellow snow to put on Lila Stevens' head."

"Oh, I like them more and more as they get older," Ginny said, giggling. "What does that have to do with Edgar, though?"

"They say whoever it was had on pink socks."

"Ah, like the unicorn," Ginny said almost to herself. "Did you search the woods?"

"We did and we came up empty," I answered. "He's not there, but he doesn't seem to be anywhere else either. He's not at his house. I wrote it off at first because I thought they were exaggerating. I thought Edgar must've fallen down drunk. Now I'm starting to get worried."

"The problem with Edgar is that he takes off whenever he feels like it and it's impossible to know where he is for long stretches," Ginny said. "I'm sure he's okay."

"I hope he is, but I promised the girls I would help them," I said. "I always keep my word."

Ginny made a face. "Really?"

"Well, I keep it to them," I clarified. "I would really like to track down Edgar. If he's dead out there somewhere, well, let's just say it could be a rough winter for a body."

"That's definitely true," Ginny said. "I haven't seen Edgar, but now that you've brought up his name, I have heard a bit of gossip about him. I ignored it at first because it made no sense, but ... well ... it might be of interest to you."

"What?"

"Now, it came from Viola and she's not always reliable ... ."

"What?"

"I'm not a big fan of salacious gossip," Ginny added.

Oh, I was practically salivating now. "What?"

"Viola said Edgar has been seen around town three times with Margaret Little," Ginny offered. "She thought they were having an affair. I, of course, thought that was ridiculous. But if you can't find him, I think you should start looking there."

I moved my jaw as I considered the possibility. It didn't make sense and yet .... Margaret was there the day the girls claimed they found the body. Perhaps she saw Edgar when he was leaving and didn't tell anyone.

"I'll bet she killed him," I said, my mind working overtime.

Ginny was amused rather than aghast. "Why would she do that?"

"Because she's evil."

"Oh, well, as long as you have completely thorough reasoning for throwing that out there, I'm totally with you," Ginny said, handing me a mug of coffee. "What are you going to do?"

"Bring her down."

"And people say December in Walkerville is boring," Ginny teased. "Something tells me it's going to a holly jolly Christmas after all."

"Did you have to ruin things by reminding me of that song? It's like an earworm."

"I'll keep that in mind for next time," Ginny said dryly.

"You do that."

EIGHT

"Stop doing that."

Clove, a bag of potato chips resting on her lap as we sat in my parked truck across the street from Margaret Little's house, made a face. "I'm not doing anything."

"You're rattling that bag so loudly I can't help but think that something is going to explode," I countered. "It might be my temper, so I'd be very careful."

"I am not."

"You are, too."

"I am not."

"You are, too."

"Oh, will both of you give it a rest?" Thistle asked, shifting in her seat. She kept her helmet on even though she complained it itched. I think she worried I would take off in a mad rush to run Margaret over if the mood struck, and she wasn't taking any chances. "You're giving me a headache."

"Hey, I've had a headache since you three were born," I shot back. "Do you hear me complaining?"

"You complain all of the time," Thistle said. "Mom says that's just the way you talk to other people and that we should ignore it. She says you don't mean to be a complainer, but you can't help yourself because it's just noise to you."

I stilled. I was hearing a whole lot of Twila-isms these days. I had no idea she was that ballsy. "Next time your mother says that, tell her the only noise in the house is that incessant droning she does when she claims she's singing," I said. "How does that sound?"

"Like you're feeling mean," Clove said, stretching her arms over her head as she tried to get comfortable.

After Ginny told me about Margaret's ties to Edgar, I couldn't get the possibility of her offing him out of my head. I know it's a long shot, but I've always thought she was evil. Maybe she finally decided to embrace her inner hobgoblin and call to the evil corners of the land to do her bidding.

No, I'm not being dramatic. Hear me out.

Margaret has been jealous of me ever since we were kids. At first she thought I was somehow cheating when it came to footraces and tennis matches, but then she realized I really was magical and made it her mission to be just like me. I'm not making it up. She's jealous.

If she conducted enough research, she might've gotten to the point where she found that she could call to evil forces and ask them to do her bidding. The Winchesters call to the four white light corners of magic. Evil witches call to the four dark corners. Margaret would definitely be an evil witch if she embraced the craft.

She might've thought she could take someone like Edgar – a man known to make an ass of himself and drink until he was in a stupor at least five days a week – and sacrifice him to the blood winds to give herself power.

Huh? What do you think of that?

"What are you thinking?" Bay asked, her eyes narrow slits as suspicion washed over her features. "You went to a different place there for a second."

"I'm pretty sure it was an evil place," Thistle said. "Did you see that smile? It made me think of that movie we were watching the other day. What was the name of it?"

"*Friday the 13th*?"

"No, not that one."

"A Nightmare on Elm Street?"

"Not that one either."

"Good grief," I muttered. "Someone really does need to monitor your viewing habits."

"We like horror movies," Bay said. "They make us feel better about our lives."

"And why is that?"

"Because no matter how bloody and terrible a slasher movie killer is, he's still nicer than you," Thistle said, grinning.

"Keep it up, mouth."

"It!"

"It what?"

"No, that's the name of the movie," Thistle said. *"It.* There was a creepy clown and he had horrible fangs when he smiled. You reminded me of that clown just now. What were you thinking?"

"I was thinking that we'll be hailed as heroes if we find Edgar alive," I lied. "We might even get Margaret locked up to boot. That would be the best Christmas gift ever."

Thistle rolled her eyes. "You're all talk," she said. "You don't really want Mrs. Little to be arrested. You won't have anyone to torture if that happens. Who else are we going to drop yellow snow on?"

"Oh, there's plenty of people in this town who have ticked me off," I said. "I'm sure I can find someone."

"And yet it won't be as funny as messing with Mrs. Little," Thistle said. "You'll be bored. I bet she's not a murderer anyway. She's probably just … kissing him."

I arched an eyebrow. "Kissing him?"

"That's what old people do."

"They do more than that," I pointed out.

"Yes, but I'm only going to be ten soon so I'm not supposed to know about those things," Thistle said. "My mind doesn't go past kissing."

"That's a good thing," I said.

"Mine does," Clove said. "I can't wait to get a boyfriend. He's going to be handsome and smart, and he's going to give me flowers."

I rolled my eyes so hard I was convinced I was going to fall out of the truck. "None of those things are important," I said. "Well, it's important that he's smart. You don't want to date a dumb one. As for the rest, you only need to find someone with a good heart who will love you for who you are without trying to change you."

"Do you think Mrs. Little is doing that for Edgar?" Bay asked.

"No."

"Then we should probably help him," Thistle said.

"You've got that right," I said, pocketing my keys. "Come on, girls. It's time to save the day … and make Margaret Little pay."

"Wow. That was almost like poetry … like Dr. Seuss," Thistle drawled.

"You're on my list."

"LIFT YOUR FEET."

"I am lifting my feet."

"No, you're shuffling your feet, and that doesn't work in snow," I argued, grabbing Clove's waist so I could lift her over a particularly large snowdrift. "Good grief, girl. What have you been eating?"

"The same thing as you," Clove shot back, scorching me with a dark look when I dropped her on the other side of the drift. Margaret's house is surrounded by two or three rows of trees. It's supposed to give the illusion of privacy, but in reality all it does is give me something to hide behind when I'm trying to spy. Trust me. I know. I've done this before.

"Well, I think you've been eating double portions or something," I said, wiping my brow. It's too cold to be sweating, yet I could feel it dripping down my forehead. I'm too old for this much physical exertion. I'm still in my prime, mind you, but traipsing through a foot of snow with whiny little girls is not conducive to a relaxing cardiovascular workout. "You need to go on a diet."

"You can't say that to her," Bay said, grabbing on to a low-hanging branch and swinging herself around the base of the tree. The snow was shallower closer to the trunks and she figured out pretty quickly that it was easier to stick close to the trees than wade through the big drifts. Unfortunately Clove didn't realize that. I constantly had to fish her out of piles due to her height. "Mom says it's never okay to make fun of people for their weight or the way they look."

"Well, you're mother is a mouthy cow," I muttered.

"I heard that."

I sighed and brushed my hair from my face. "Your mother is right," I said finally. What? I don't want to teach them bad habits. Er, well, I don't want to teach them needlessly hurtful bad habits. There are plenty of bad habits for me to imprint on their impressionable minds that don't include being downright nasty for no reason. "It's never okay to make fun of someone's weight or looks."

"You called Mom a cow, though," Bay pointed out.

"I was talking about the fact that she won't stop mooing in my ear when I want to do something," I said. "She sounds like a cow. She doesn't look like a cow."

"I think she looks more like a chicken," Clove said, purposely hopping into a big drift and giggling as she tried to wade through it. Margaret's house was set a hundred and fifty feet back from the road, yet it felt as if I'd walked ten miles with these miniature monsters. "She puts her hands on her hips all of the time and jerks her head back and forth. Sometimes when she's yelling I think she sounds like she's clucking."

"That's a good one," Thistle said. "I think you should tell her … and do an imitation while you're at it."

"Don't do that if you want to stay on the nice list for Christmas," I warned. "Save that for New Year's Eve. They'll be drunk so they might forget it."

"Good idea."

Bay seemed lost in thought as she swung around to the next tree, her eyes trained on me.

"What?" I asked, annoyed. She has a way of looking into your soul that's downright unnerving.

"I know it's wrong to make fun of people because of the way they look, but can I still call Lila a horse face when she's mean to me?"

That kid is far too worried about what's right and wrong. She needs to focus on smiting her enemies without caring about what's fair on the battlefield. That will keep her young and happy for decades. "Yes, that's totally fine."

"But you just said … ."

"There are exceptions to every rule, Bay," I said, cutting her off. "This is one of those exceptions. Lila looks like a horse's behind and you can tell her that because she's evil. It's the same reason I can point out that Margaret looks like the butt of a chicken. It's not nice to go off on other people, but when it's your sworn enemy, it's totally fine."

"I don't think that's really the rule," Thistle said. She'd wised up and began following Bay not long after we waded into the woods.

"It's the rule if I say it's the rule," I said, grabbing the back of Clove's coat even as she moved to keep walking farther into the woods. "That's far enough, short stack. All we need to do is get a clear view into the house. The big bay window in the dining room is right there. We should be able to see most of the main floor from here."

"That doesn't really work from this far away," Bay pointed out. "It worked during the summer because you brought us after dark and we could sneak right up under the window to take those photographs you wanted."

"I still don't get that," Thistle added. "You say it's fine for you guys to dance naked, but when Mrs. Little does it you think it's a crime against humans. Er, a crime against humidity."

"A crime against humanity," I corrected. "I still haven't been proven wrong on that, by the way. You need to pay more attention to your English lessons and stop worrying so much about who I'm taking photos of. You mimic what everyone says so it sounds like you have a bigger vocabulary than you really do."

"And you need to stuff it," Thistle grumbled. If she thought she said that low enough for me not to hear, she was sorely mistaken. Of course, she might've purposely said it loud enough for me to hear, in which case I was mildly proud of her.

"All that matters is that we're good here," I said, making sure I was mostly covered by the large pine tree at the edge of the property as I dug in my purse. "I brought help."

"What kind of help?" Clove asked curiously.

"These." I pulled the binoculars I lifted from Winnie's bedroom this summer out of my purse and grinned. "Now we'll be able to see directly into her house. If Edgar is there, we'll see. If she's dismembering him in the tub to get rid of the evidence, we'll see that, too."

"Oh, gross," Bay complained, wrinkling her nose. "You don't think she's really doing that, do you? That will give Clove nightmares."

"Uh-uh," Clove argued, shaking her head. "I don't get nightmares like a baby. You do."

"Oh, really?" Thistle was completely annoyed with the situation. She wasn't generally known for being outdoorsy. "Do you remember when we watched *Jaws* and you were convinced there were sharks in the lake?"

"That was one time," Clove protested.

"How about when we watched *Poltergeist* and you wouldn't go in the closet for a month?" Bay challenged. "We had to put your clothes away, and it wasn't fair because you got out of chores in the bedroom while we had to do everything."

"Yeah, I think you answered your own question there," I said. "She wasn't afraid of the closet. She was lazy and didn't want to do chores. Keep up."

Realization washed over Bay's face. "Hey!"

"It's too late now," I told her, lifting the binoculars so I could stare into the house. The curtains were open, but it was hard to focus the stupid things and keep track of what I was looking at. The first thing that loomed into view was a ceramic snowman that looked more freaky than Frosty. "Ugh. I swear some people shouldn't be allowed to buy knickknacks."

"Says the woman who has a rooster dressed like a slutty girl in her bedroom," Bay deadpanned.

"He's not dressed like a slutty girl," I corrected. "He's dressed like a burlesque dancer. There's a difference."

Bay didn't look convinced. "Uh-huh."

"Oh, and for the record, that rooster is a priceless work of art," I added. "I bought him from a flea market and added the outfit myself. I've gotten hundreds of compliments on him. People think I'm a real artist. I could do it professionally and everything."

"Only if the world goes blind and people with taste are killed by some alien or something," Thistle said, smoothly evading my hand when I reached out to cuff her. "Now do your spying so we can get out of here. It's cold and I'm bored."

"If you shut your mouth and let me concentrate, that won't be a problem," I said, staring through the binoculars again.

The girls were quiet for exactly thirty seconds and then Bay ruined the calm. "Did you hear that?"

"All I hear is you three yapping," I snapped.

"No, listen," Bay ordered, pressing her finger to her lips.

I did as she asked but all I could hear was the four of us breathing. "What do you hear?"

"It sounds like a man is yelling inside or something," Bay said, pressing her eyes shut. "I … no, I definitely hear a man."

I narrowed my eyes as I stared into the house, but I couldn't see anything. After a few moments, though, I did hear the faint sound of someone else's voice as the back door of Margaret's house opened. I grabbed the girls to hide them behind the tree, clutching them to me so they didn't make an error and wander out where someone could see them. I couldn't risk peering in that direction because whoever opened the door would see us. The voice was definitely male, though. Edgar?

I waited until the door closed to speak again.

"Did anyone see who it was?"

"You made us hide behind the tree," Thistle said. "We couldn't look because you wouldn't let us."

She had a point. Still, I wasn't going to admit that. "So no one saw anything?"

"I only know it was a man," Bay said. "I didn't get to see him and couldn't understand what he was saying."

That made two of us. "Well, we have only one choice," I said, making up my mind on the spot. "We have to get closer to the house."

The girls groaned in unison. They were loud enough to hide the sound of approaching footsteps until it was too late to make a run for it, because a dark figure was upon us.

"You're under arrest."

Well, crud.

NINE

I recognized Terry's voice before I swiveled. I wasn't particularly frightened. I knew he wouldn't throw me in jail, no matter what he said. That didn't mean I was keen to have a showdown with law enforcement on my mortal enemy's property.

That sounded melodramatic, didn't it? Oh, who cares?

"Hello, Terry," I said, pasting a bright smile on my face as we locked gazes. He didn't look remotely happy. "What a beautiful day for a walk. Don't you think it's a beautiful day for a walk?"

The set of Terry's jaw was grim. "Really? Is that the story you're going to go with? It's twenty-eight degrees, and you've forced three children to go on a march through thick snow so you can spy on a woman who collects porcelain unicorns. Think of a better story."

I opened my mouth to answer, but Thistle did it for me.

"We weren't spying," she lied. "We were hunting for Christmas elves. Aunt Tillie thought it would be a fun way for us to spend the afternoon because we're so excited for Christmas."

That story would never work for an adult. Terry wasn't an idiot, so it didn't work coming from a child either.

"Don't lie, Thistle," Terry chided. "I don't like that."

"She's not lying," Clove said, jutting out her lower lip. "It's true.

Aunt Tillie said if we caught a Christmas elf we would get everything we wanted for Christmas. I want world peace and hundreds of gifts to give to kids who don't have anything. It's really a good thing."

And that was much more convincing, especially coming from a child with a face that belonged on an angel and who was half buried in snow.

Unfortunately for us, Terry wasn't falling for that either. "Come here." He wrapped his arms around Clove's waist and lifted her out of the snow. He brushed off the clinging white powder before fixing her with a serious look. "Are you cold?"

"Not nearly as cold as the kids who have nothing for Christmas," Clove replied solemnly.

"You're going to make some man very afraid in ten years," Terry said. "He's going to take one look at those big eyes and fall head over heels in love. Then he's going to realize you own him and have nightmares."

"Will they involve clowns in closets?" Clove asked.

"I don't know what that means." Terry turned his attention to Bay as she tried to hide beneath the barren branch of a maple tree. "How about you? Are you hoping to catch a Christmas elf to provide gifts for those less fortunate, too?"

Bay bit her lip and shook her head. Crap! She was going to be my undoing. I just know it.

"We honestly are on a mission of mercy," I said. "The fact that we ended up here is just an odd coincidence. I had no idea we were so close to Margaret's house."

"Quiet," Terry ordered, never moving his eyes from Bay's worried face. "What are you doing here, Bay?" It was if he knew she couldn't lie to him. That's why he focused on her. Quite frankly, that's akin to child abuse in my book.

"We were just taking a walk," Bay mumbled, averting her gaze. Sheesh. I taught her to lie better than that.

"Why were you walking?" Terry pressed.

"Because … ." Bay darted an unreadable look in my direction. She looked as if she was being tortured.

"Oh, leave her alone," I said, giving in. "Fine. You've got us. We weren't looking for a Christmas elf. Arrest us. Throw us in a cell. Make this the worst Christmas ever for three bad little girls."

Terry scowled. "I am convinced you're the Devil sometimes," he hissed, reaching for Bay to draw her out from beneath the tree. "Don't say things like that to them. You'll frighten them and make them afraid of police officers. Is that what you want?"

I shrugged. "We were having a great time until you showed up," I said. "If they're upset, I blame you."

"Whatever." Terry smoothed Bay's hair as he tilted up her chin so they could lock gazes. "What are you doing out here?"

"I just told you," I snapped.

"No, you said you weren't looking for a Christmas elf," Terry countered. "I already knew that. You didn't tell me what you were doing."

"We're looking for the dead body," Thistle said, sticking out her tongue and hopping away from me when I reached out to grab her. "Aunt Tillie took us to breakfast at the bakery this morning, and Mrs. Gunderson told her that there's a rumor about the dead man and Mrs. Little."

"She thinks Mrs. Little chopped him into little bits in the house because she's a bad witch," Clove added. "We're here to see if that's true."

Terry was flabbergasted. "Why would you possibly tell these girls that?"

"I didn't tell them that," I sniffed. "They figured it out on their own. They're quite bright."

"Yes, they're regular geniuses," Terry said. "You know you were seen casing the house from the road, right? Mrs. Little called the station and said that she was convinced someone was going to rob her."

I snorted. "She knows my truck. She only wanted to get us in trouble."

"And that's her right," Terry said. "This is her property. You have no business being on it. While we're at it, you have no business plowing in the end of her driveway either. If I ever catch you, I'm going to have to write a ticket."

"And you won't do well in prison either," Clove said, bending over to pack some snow. "I'm not the only one."

"Clove, you're not going to prison," Terry said. "What are you doing out here, Tillie? Do you really think that Mrs. Little killed Edgar Martin? Seriously? Do you think she chopped him up in little bits and put him in her cookies or something?"

Well, when he put it like that it sounded ridiculous. It made much more sense in my mind. There was no way I was going to admit that, though. I decided to change tactics. "I think that Margaret was with us the day the girls said they found the body," I said. "I think something was definitely in that clearing – and so do you. The girls are imaginative, but they don't make up things like finding bodies."

"Okay, I get that," Terry said, adjusting his tone. "I think they saw something, too. I initially assumed Edgar got drunk and passed out. I figured he woke up because it was cold and wandered away before we got there."

"But you haven't been able to find him either," I said. "You've been looking and he's not around. Admit it."

"I admit it," Terry said. "I looked because I didn't want the girls to obsess about this. I also figured you'd feed their imagination because that's what you do when you're bored. It's too cold for them to be running around on adventures with you.

"I mean … will you look at this child?" Terry gestured toward Clove. "She's covered in snow and freezing. She'll get pneumonia. Do you want that?"

"Of course not," I said. "We've only been out here twenty minutes. We would already be done if you hadn't distracted us. We were just about to get closer to the house so we could see the man inside and call it a day."

"Get closer? You can't just peek through the windows at someone else's house," Terry said. "I … wait. What man?"

"There's a man inside," Bay said. "We heard his voice. We think it might be Edgar."

Terry didn't want to be swayed, but the idea of solving this case – although it wasn't really a case – held a lot of appeal. He clearly wanted to enjoy Christmas instead of worrying about whether or not the girls were running around the countryside and spying on neighbors with me.

"Are you sure it was a man?" Terry asked, rubbing his chin.

I nodded. "It was definitely a man."

Terry licked his lips as he stared at the house. "Okay. Come on. We're ending this now."

I knew he would see things my way. I turned to wade through the snow, but Terry stilled when the girls remained rooted to their spots.

"What's wrong?" Terry asked.

"We're tired," Clove said. "I can't walk any longer. I think I might faint."

Terry growled as he bent over and picked up Clove with one arm. She weighed very little so it wasn't difficult for him to lift her. He slid a sidelong look in Bay's direction. "What about you?"

Bay shrugged. "I'm tired, too."

Terry made a disgusted sound as he scooped her up with his remaining arm. He looked resigned when he glanced at Thistle. "Are you tired, too?"

"You're out of arms," Thistle pointed out.

"I have a back."

Thistle smiled as she scurried behind Terry. I had to help her scramble up his back, but when he had all of the girls securely affixed to his frame he picked the shortest route toward Margaret's house. He walked so fast, in fact, I had to jog to keep up. I momentarily wished I had a camera because the sight of him walking with the three girls clinging to him was adorable. He was a better father to them than the ones they were born with. He just didn't realize it.

Terry didn't put the girls down until we were at Margaret's front door. He was careful as he lowered each one, and then he checked them to make sure everyone was safe and settled before knocking on the door.

I wasn't expecting that. I thought we would come up with a plan before we alerted Margaret to our presence. For example, I thought he could distract Margaret while I punched her in the face and ran inside to untie Edgar in the basement, where she was planning to sacrifice him to the dark gods in front of her altar. What? That could totally happen.

Margaret wasn't in the mood for idle chatter when she threw open the door. "Did you arrest her?"

"Not yet," Terry replied. "She says she was helping the girls find a Christmas elf and got turned around. I tend to believe her. It wasn't a purposeful excursion."

The lie slid easily off his tongue. I couldn't help but be surprised. I knew he wasn't doing it for me, though. He was doing it for the girls. He didn't want to upset them.

Margaret's penciled on eyebrow (she stopped growing real ones years ago) arched as she graced Terry with a sour look. "Really? Do you expect me to believe that? She was hunting for Christmas elves? They're not real."

"Yes, they are," Clove said solemnly. "They live at the North Pole with the house-trashing fairy and sock-eating gnome. That's not important, though. We want to see the dead guy."

Margaret balked at Clove's fortitude. "Excuse me, young lady, but I don't believe anyone was speaking to you," she said. "Youngsters should be taught to refrain from speaking unless spoken to. That's how I would've raised children if I'd been so blessed."

She was so full of crap I was afraid to touch her in case she exploded and turned the snow brown on her own. "You didn't have kids because no one could bear to see you without your clothes on," I shot back. "People are afraid your body is like Medusa's and they'll turn to stone if they see it."

"You take that back," Margaret hissed, extending a finger. "I don't have to put up with your nonsense. You're trespassing."

"She's not exactly trespassing," Terry clarified. "I asked them to come to the house with me so I could investigate the possible sighting of a missing person."

Margaret narrowed her eyes to dangerous slits. She looked like a coiled snake about to strike. "What missing person?"

"Edgar Martin," Terry replied. "We have reason to believe he may be in grave danger."

"Because you're going to sacrifice him to blood winds," I added under my breath.

Terry ignored me. "Edgar hasn't been to his home in several days, and we have multiple witnesses who say they believe he was injured and lying in the snow at some point," he said. He was a master at manipulating words when he wanted to force an issue. It was something to behold. "It has come to my attention that you've been seen with Edgar several times over the past few weeks, and you have a man inside your house today."

Margaret's mouth dropped open as incredulity washed over her pinched features. She really did look like a chicken's behind … and she was clearly about to drop an egg. It was probably rotten.

"Who told you I've been seeing Edgar?" Margaret asked, sliding a dark look in my direction. "Was it her?"

"I'm not at liberty to divulge my source, ma'am," Terry said. "I don't care about your personal life. I care about locating Mr. Martin and making sure he's okay. If he's here, I only want to see him and verify he doesn't need medical assistance."

"Do you really expect me to fall for that?" Margaret asked.

"I don't care what you fall for," Terry said. "If Edgar is here, though, I want to see him."

"Well, you can't enter without a search warrant, and I'm not granting you entrance to my home," Margaret spat. "As for the rest … well … I'm going to sue you for slander, Tillie. I'm going to bleed you dry."

"Oh, knock it off, Margaret." I was at my limit. "I'm tired and I want to go home. Is Edgar here or not? That's all we want to know. The girls are obsessed with making sure no one died in the woods. How can you deny them peace of mind like that?"

"Yes, it's our Christmas wish," Clove intoned. "It's all we want."

"Speak for yourself," Thistle said. "I want that castle, too."

Bay licked her lips as she studied Margaret. She was serious as she took a step forward. "Please?"

Terry rested his hand on her shoulder. "Just tell them, Mrs. Little," he prodded. "They're not asking for the world. They're asking for one bit of information so they can sleep at night."

"My heart hurts thinking about poor Mr. Martin being lost in the woods," Clove added, her brown eyes glassy.

I had to give the kid credit, she was a master manipulator. She was going to be something special when she got older.

"Fine," Margaret said, blowing out a sigh. "He's here. He's been here for the last few days. It's not what you think, though."

"So you're not cutting him up into little bits in your bathtub?" Thistle asked.

Margaret made a horrified face. "Who told you that?"

"It must've been the Christmas elf," I said evasively, averting my eyes.

"No, I'm not chopping him up," Margaret said. "The church has decided to provide sober buddies to Edgar to get him through the holidays. I've been volunteering my time."

"Oh." Crap. That might explain why people saw her with him on multiple occasions. She wasn't dating him. She was just policing him. She was good at telling other people what to do, so this was right up her alley.

"Yes, 'oh.'" Margaret was smug. "The holidays are a rough time, and he had a setback the other day. I saw him in the trees when I was leaving and took him home. I didn't know it was going to be such a big deal. I thought the girls would forget about it, and Edgar was embarrassed."

"He should've been more embarrassed about the unicorn thing," Thistle said.

"I agree with that," I said.

"So … he's really okay?" Bay looked hopeful.

"He's really okay," Margaret said, her expression softening. "He's here today and then is heading over to Viola's house tomorrow. Are you satisfied?"

Terry glanced at me. "Are you satisfied?"

Heck no, I wasn't satisfied. Margaret was actually doing something good for a change. The world was clearly coming to an end.

"We should probably be going," I said, motioning for the girls to follow me instead of answering Terry's question. "We have cookies to bake and elves to catch."

"And mothers to laugh at," Thistle added.

"That, too," I said.

Terry ran his tongue over his teeth as he regarded me. "So you'll be going straight home?"

"Absolutely. There won't be one detour. I promise."

"ALL SET, GIRLS?"

It took me five minutes to get the girls back to the truck and another five minutes to get their helmets and seatbelts secure. By the time the truck warmed up everyone was more than ready to go.

"I'm ready," Bay said. "Are you surprised Mrs. Little is being nice?"

I opted for honesty. "Yes."

"Do you like her better now?" Clove asked.

"No."

"Do you want to plow on the way home?" Thistle asked, hopeful.

"Absolutely."

I lowered the plow so it was close to the road and hit the gas pedal as I pulled away from the side of the road. I saw Terry watching us as he walked up the driveway, and his eyes widened and he waved his hands as the snow bank at the corner of the driveway grew closer. He was pretty expressive for a guy who only wanted to say goodbye.

The truck jerked as I hit something hard, small pieces of wood flying in every direction. I crashed forward but the seatbelt kept me from slamming into the steering wheel.

"What was that?" Clove asked, turning her head.

"Mrs. Little's mailbox," Thistle replied. "It went boom."

"That came out of nowhere," I muttered. This time it truly was an accident. "She must've moved it because she knew I would hit it and she wanted something to complain about."

"Yeah, that must be it," Thistle said dryly. "Come on. If we're lucky, we'll be able to fill Lila's driveway with yellow snow before Officer Terry catches up with us."

"That sounds like a plan."

TEN

Everyone was exhausted when we got back to the house. Terry caught up with us just as we were leaving Lila's street. He gave me a dirty look, but all of the girls waved and blew kisses so he merely shook his head and let us leave without flashing his lights or tossing about empty threats.

Christmas miracles take many forms, after all.

I found my nieces angrily slamming things around in the kitchen. The house usually boasted a variety of scrumptious scents this time of day, but all of them were absent thanks to my curse. Hmm. I might not have thought this one out completely.

"Where have you been all day?" Winnie asked, furious.

"I took the girls for breakfast and then on an elf hunt," I said, pouring myself a mug of coffee. "We found Edgar, by the way. He's not dead. He's drying out at Margaret's house."

"What?"

"I know. I was disappointed, too," I said. "I thought she chopped him up or something. I'm going to have to rethink all of my life decisions now that she's done a good thing and helped her fellow man."

"I just … ." Winnie pressed her lips together and shook her head. "Well, at least you didn't get arrested."

"Nope. Terry didn't want the girls to start crying, so he let us go."

Marnie's mouth dropped open. "Are you serious?"

"He didn't want my eyes to leak," Clove offered, hopping up on the stool next to me and folding her hands as she surveyed the kitchen. "We're hungry. What's for dinner?"

"You're going to get sandwiches at this rate," Winnie replied. "We still can't cook."

"And we have a beautiful prime rib roast for Christmas Eve dinner tomorrow," Twila added. "We need to put it in early and slow roast it. Do you have any idea how expensive that hunk of meat was? That's on top of the turkey we got for Christmas Day."

My mouth watered at the mention of prime rib. It's one of my favorites. That didn't mean I was ready to cede my superiority over my nieces ... although I was definitely wobbling. "Do you have anything you want to say to me?"

Winnie narrowed her eyes. She's bossy so she likes being in control. She knows when she's licked, though. "If we agree to make cookies for you, will you lift the spell?"

"Yes."

"That easy?" Winnie was understandably dubious. "Don't you want to add certain conditions to the agreement?"

"Like you always do," Twila muttered.

"Nope," I answered. "I'm in a particularly giving mood. It is Christmas, after all."

Winnie made a face as she exhaled heavily. "Fine. We'll make your cookies."

I sensed a trap. "You'll make me really good cookies," I clarified. "I don't want any crap. For instance, I don't want cookies with a half a cup of salt instead of sugar just because you're feeling vengeful. I'm not stupid."

Bay shot me an angry look but wisely kept her mouth shut.

"We'll make you good cookies," Winnie gritted out. "Technically we'll be making our own cookies for Christmas, so you can have some of them. We would never make bad cookies for ourselves."

She had a point. "I want chocolate and macadamia nuts."

"Fine."

"If you want to add a little magic to sway the judges, I wouldn't be opposed to that either," I added.

"We won't be doing that," Winnie said. "It's not really winning if you have magical help."

"I disagree, but as long as I win, I don't care," I said, climbing off the stool and motioning to the girls. "Come on, troublemakers," I said. "Let's look for the Christmas elf in the living room. I think there's supposed to be a good movie on this afternoon and your mothers are clearly going to be busy baking."

"You are ... incorrigible," Twila muttered.

"Yes, well, it keeps me young," I said, smirking. "Oh, and by the way, we're going to have a talk about all of these pearls of wisdom you keep dropping on the girls. I'm going to wait until the day after Christmas, though. I don't want anyone mistaking me for the Grinch."

Twila balked. "What pearls of wisdom?"

"Oh, I don't know," I replied. "Perhaps little things like me complaining because I like to complain and it's just the way I communicate need to be discussed."

Twila scorched Thistle with a murderous look. "Really? I'm sure I never said anything of the sort."

"Oh, don't be like that," Thistle said, her grin impish. "You're supposed to be setting a good example for me."

"Run now," Twila ordered, slapping her spatula against the counter. "I can only take so much."

"Now you know how I feel," I said, pushing open the swinging door between the kitchen and living room. "Make sure you get going on dinner soon. We've had a long day and we're starving."

"I'm so hungry my heart hurts," Clove said. "I'll probably die from the pain."

"You took it a step too far, Clove," I said, cringing when I saw the look on Marnie's face. "You need to learn that sometimes less is more. Trust me. That's one of the rules I live by."

"I'll think about it."

CHRISTMAS MORNING DAWNED BRIGHTLY and the girls woke me with excited squeals as they pounded down the stairs. I took my time getting into my robe, and by the time I hit the main floor Terry was already there with a mug of coffee in his hand and a smile on his face as he watched the girls divvy up presents.

"What are you doing here?" I asked accepting a mug of coffee from Marnie as she walked past. "I thought you were coming for dinner."

"I am," Terry replied. "Santa had a special gift for the girls that he couldn't fit on his sleigh, though, and I had to bring it with me."

I pursed my lips. He was a good man. He drove me crazy and I often wanted to curse him for questioning my integrity, but he loved the girls with his whole heart and gave everything he had freely to them.

"Well, that's nice," I said, turning my attention to the center of the living room. The girls weren't allowed to open gifts at the same time. They had to wait their turn, which drove them crazy and made Christmas more fun for the adults, who enjoyed torturing them. What? Is that just me? Oh, well. It's still fun. "Have you talked to Edgar?"

"I have," Terry confirmed, bobbing his head. "He's embarrassed by what happened. He says he fell off the wagon the day the girls found him. He's actually thankful they did, though, because he thinks he might've slept right through to his death if they didn't wake him.

"When they took off to get us, he managed to get to his feet," he continued. "He was confused because he couldn't remember how he got there – or even where he was – and he followed the girls' footprints out of the trees."

"Why didn't he say something to us when he saw us coming?"

"He said he thought that I might arrest him for public drunkenness," Terry explained. "I have threatened him a time or two, so it wasn't out of the realm of possibility. I would like to think I'd be giving because of the time of year, but it's far more likely I would've hauled him in rather than let him ruin the tree-lighting ceremony."

I wasn't sure I believed that. "You have a wonderful Christmas spirit, Terry," I said. "Don't ever doubt that. You saw what we did at Lila's house the other day and you didn't even write a ticket."

"I thought about it."

"But you didn't do it."

"Yes, well, I didn't want Clove's eyes to leak," Terry teased, poking Clove's side as she skirted around him. Sugar barked and panted as sniffed saw the mountain of gifts. He would enjoy tearing through the leftover wrapping paper.

"It's nice you're here to spend the day with us," I said, leaning back in my chair. "It wouldn't feel like a family day without you."

I could've been mistaken, but Terry's eyes appeared to mist as he nodded. "Thank you." He made room on his lap when Bay – still in her nightgown and slippers – hopped on his knee. Her hair was a mess and she looked barely awake but her eyes sparkled. "Hey, little missy. I see Santa brought you a ton of gifts. You must've been a good girl."

Bay shrugged. "Sometimes I think I'm good. Other times I think I'm not."

"You're good," Terry said. "You're always good."

"And twenty," Thistle said from her place on the floor. "Ha! I told you I would get the same amount of presents. I just counted. So much for the naughty list."

Terry pursed his lips as he shook his head. He looked annoyed. "She, on the other hand, straddles a very fine line."

Bay giggled. "No, she doesn't," she said. "She has a big mouth but a nice heart. She's like Aunt Tillie."

"I heard that," Thistle barked. "That's the meanest thing you've ever said to me."

Now it was my turn to make a face. "Not three days ago you told me you wanted to be just like me," I reminded her. "Why is it okay for you to say it but not Bay?"

"Because Bay means it in a bad way," Thistle answered. "I said I wanted to be feared like you. I didn't say I wanted to be like you."

"That's not how I remember it."

"That's because you're old."

"Hey!" Terry barked loud enough that Bay jolted on his lap. He tightened his arms around her in a reassuring manner as he stared down Thistle. "You need to apologize to your great-aunt. That was uncalled for."

Thistle's face drained of color as she swallowed hard. "I'm … sorry."

The apology wasn't exactly heartfelt, but the fact that she said it at all was surprising.

"You need to think about what you say before you open your mouth, Thistle," Terry said. "I know you think you're funny, and I'm pretty sure that's where a lot of your attitude stems from. You see your Aunt Tillie getting away with stuff and you think it's because people find her funny.

"That's partly true," he continued. "It's also true that she does good things for people. Did you know she took cookies to the children's hospital in Traverse City last week? Do you want to know how I know that? I saw her when I was there taking gifts from the department."

Thistle's mouth dropped open as her eyes widened. "You did that?"

I shifted on my chair, uncomfortable. "I might've stopped by."

"She did it because she's a good person who just happens to like making mischief," Terry said. "That's what you need to realize. You can't do only the mischief half of that equation. You have to do the good part, too."

Instead of laughing, Thistle looked intrigued. "Why didn't you tell us?"

"Because it was nobody's business," I said. "I go every year."

"You lead by example," Bay said, rubbing her cheek as she glanced at her mother. Her expression was far too thoughtful for a happy Christmas morning.

"I do lead by example," I agreed, reaching inside my robe and removing the blue ribbon from the baking contest. I hadn't let it out of my sight since winning it the previous day. Margaret was stupefied … and angry … and that made me happy. That probably wasn't leading by example, but I was beyond caring. "For example, do you know what this ribbon means?"

Thistle nodded. "It means you beat Mrs. Little and she cried," she said. "We were all there. We saw it."

"That's right," I said. "And why is that important?"

"Because there are exceptions to every rule," Bay answered. "You can't call people fat and ugly, but you can call someone a horse face and drop yellow snow in their yard if they're your mortal enemy."

"Exactly," I said, beaming.

Winnie scowled as she pointed toward the largest gift in the center of the room. It was the one Terry brought for them. I had a feeling I knew exactly what was under the wrapping paper. "Girls, I think Aunt Tillie is still waking up, so you might not want to listen to her this early in the morning," she said. "Instead of opening all of your individual gifts, why not open the big one Terry brought for you to share?"

"I didn't buy that," Terry said. "Santa brought it and ran out of room."

Bay shifted her eyes to him. "You're Santa sometimes. You're Santa this time. We already know that."

Terry opened his mouth to argue and then snapped it shut. "Open your gift. I think you're going to like it."

Bay did as he asked, pressing a kiss to his cheek before joining her cousins. They each grabbed a side of the wrapping paper and counted to three as they ripped it off. Their eyes widened and I could hear a multitude of gasps and squeals when they unveiled the fairy castle from the catalog.

"Oh, my," Winnie said, her hand flying to the spot over her heart. "But that was so expensive."

Terry shrugged. "Santa doesn't care about that."

"But … ."

"Leave him be," I ordered. "He can't argue on Santa's behalf."

Winnie's eyes filled with tears as she nodded. "Girls, what do you say to Terry for helping Santa?"

Bay, Clove and Thistle swiveled in unison. "Thank you for being our favorite Santa," they sang out in unison. "We love you."

Terry's cheeks colored as he shifted on the chair. "I … you're welcome."

"Now he leads by example," Thistle said, poking my knee. "What did you get us?"

"I spent the week with you," I reminded her. "We plowed. We spied. We made yellow and brown snow. We solved a case. We tortured Margaret. We cursed your mothers. We cooked. We watched Christmas movies. I bribed you. You blackmailed me. We ate a bunch of doughnuts, too. What more do you want?"

Thistle shrugged. "Just this." She took me by surprise when she gave me a hug. I didn't know what else to do, so I returned it. Thistle was all smiles as she pulled away. "I can lead by example, too."

"You certainly can."

"Oh, now my eyes are definitely going to leak," Clove said.

I couldn't help but smile. "Merry Christmas, you little monsters. Open your gifts."

It was a merry Christmas indeed. I didn't even want to deafen myself with Q-tips when the singing started.

That's a win to me.

42427146R00268

Made in the USA
Middletown, DE
15 April 2017